MW00711398

The Lonesome Cobbler

The Lonesome Cobbler

Anelio F. Conti

VANTAGE PRESS

New York

This is a work of fiction. Any similarity between the names and characters in this book and any real persons, living or dead, is purely coincidental.

Cover design by Polly McQuillen

FIRST EDITION

All rights reserved, including the right of reproduction in whole or in part in any form.

Copyright © 2005 by Anelio F. Conti

Published by Vantage Press, Inc.
419 Park Ave. South, New York, NY 10016

Manufactured in the United States of America
ISBN: 0-533-15086-8

Library of Congress Catalog Card No.: 2004098328

0 9 8 7 6 5 4 3 2 1

To my wife, Dora Irene,
our children,
grandchildren, family, and
friends whose affection and
inspiration I cherish.

"The Lord created the earth for everyone to live happily in it but, little by little, a handful of political swindlers and greedy bureaucrats have been screwing it."

—A *cafone* of Montelieto

"The lack of scholastic privileges is not life threatening, but that certainly stunts the spirit and will of the youth for undertaking noteworthy initiatives."

—The Cobbler of Montelieto

"When gentleness is virtue, but not impotence of a forced upon listening, it is always right. That gentleness can humiliate the haughtiness of others more than the flashing eloquence of anger and of contempt."

—Silvio Pellico

Preface

The multiplicity of names I have used in this story have nothing in common with the real people who became part of the actions. I have chosen the names, not from popular lists of names or other sources, but out of pure imagination. If by coincidence, in the course of telling the story, you find a name and/or surname to be similar, sorry, that was not done intentionally. On the other hand, the names of factions and the leaderships, trades and professions are real. The plot of the story focuses on and revolves all around the unmasking of their behavior.

My true intention for writing the story was not to contest the ideals of factions or individuals, to inflate the ego of those in power, or to defame the wealthy and humiliate the destitute. I never intended to gain notability for speaking of the fortunes or misfortunes of the others. My primary intention was simply that of writing a story of classic interest; to come as close to reality as possible and have readers believe; to leave readers the message that stereotyping groups of people is discriminatory and counterproductive; and finally to draw the lifelike humor and experiences from the actions. Not only the lifelike humor and experiences I wished to draw from the story, but also the adversities, the desperation, the toughness, resiliency and wisdom of a people labeled inferior, declassed and *cafoni.*

—Anelio F. Conti

Acknowledgments

Although I have not sought the help of others to bring to completion this story, I could not have proceeded without expressing my gratitude to those who have been indirectly involved.

First I want to thank my wife, Dora Irene, for being the great support. Then I wish to commend my typist, Janet Silvestri, for her reliability, and finally, but not least, I wish to convey to my friends, and to all those who have encouraged me, the message that their unbiased criticism and incitements motivated me to keep writing.

Introduction

The events I describe in this story changed my view of the world about me, and never stopped exciting my emotions throughout the early years of my life. As time moved on, I began to understand and to feel reasons for the causes that advanced those events and this, without doubt, aroused my interest in describing the outcome.

Events arousing curiosity and concern, in the minds of common folks, occurred in the town of Montelieto while Fascist Italy rocked herself in false pretense of grandeur. In Montelieto, from the renovation of an old building known as "Casa del Fascio" (House of Bundles, symbol of Italian Fascism), to commemorations of past military achievements, to inaugurations of newly appointed Party officials—everything developed into a grand showy parade. Shouts of war and invincibility grew louder with time and were purposely designed to promote Fascist propaganda.

My view of the world about me began to change in one dramatic episode that occurred in my teens. I was proudly watching a boisterous Fascist parade with my grandmother, from the balcony of her house, when we heard knocks at the side door. We rushed to answer, thinking a Fascist enforcer might have come to urge me to join the parade. Grandmother opened the door but we saw no Fascist enforcer. Instead, not entirely to our surprise, we saw a troop of barefoot children begging for alms.

"Please madam, give us something to eat," meekly went begging one of the kids. "We are hungry. A piece of stale corn bread, a potato or any leftover food you could spare, will be appreciated."

Grandmother went back inside and returned with a basket half full of eatables. She distributed the food to the children, shut the door again and, taking hold of my arm, dragged me unkindly to the corner of the room. "Kneel down," she ordered sternly. "Turn your face to the wall and recite ten Our Fathers and ten Acts of Contrition."

"What for?" I asked resentfully.

"For being cynical to those who ask for alms. You must never reproach those who are hungry. Pray," she admonished. "Pray, so the good Lord will move to compassion for the hungry kids of Montelieto and you."

I prayed, but praying made many mistakes. Then after turning less angry toward Grandmother, in the back of my mind could see two demonstrable facts come to counteract one another. In one flash I could see crowds of boisterous people root for war and in another, a troop of barefoot hungry kids begging for a piece of stale corn bread. The two opposing realities quickly cast my mind and soul into a big turmoil.

Montelieto was the imaginary name I gave a rural, obscure town in the region "Ciociaria" of central Italy. Ciociaria is a name applied to a region where people wore footwear derived from skins of animals. The name of the town was chosen for the story, solely to protect the real individuals from discredit and embarrassment. I was born

in Pastena, (Frosinone) a small town among many in Ciociaria, and grew up there with the rise of Fascism. I have
used my town as a model for Montelieto because both
shared certain comparable characteristics. The story derives from self-evident facts, although the truth has been
built up to a substantial extent. That was worked in to
project a more accurate and clearer understanding. However, the plan of action is still difficult to fathom in more
modern times.

Virtually all the inhabitants of Montelieto were born
peasants and died so. Mainly all of them wore footwear
made from raw hides of animals, same as their forefathers
and sons and daughters after them. Collectively they were
termed "Ciociari" for wearing that crude type of footwear.
Montelieto with its people represented the lowest peasantry.

Illiteracy, poverty and dependency to the rich landowners, remained the unalterable status quo for the peasants of Montelieto. Since time immemorial, they had
struggled to draw a meager living from the sun-scorched
mountain lands. They shared the crops with the rich landowners and with the parish pastor (administrator of the
lands of the Church), in a perennial cycle of servitude. In
scanty harvests they borrowed food supplies in advance,
from their masters, hoping to pay back in times of greater
abundance. But the borrowing cycle never ended! As if pre-
ordained from nature, borrowing, scanty harvests,
droughts followed by torrential rains, remained an irreversible calamity.

To aggravate the burdens of peasantry, sharecropping
and servitude, the *ciociari* of Montelieto were stigmatized

with the label *"cafoni."* *Cafoni* collectively expresses derision and contempt. It had been said that the label describes peasants without land of their own. But this belief is incorrect because *cafoni* could come from or be found in every rank of society. Literally, "cafone" (*sing. masc., or pl., f*) translates to: churlish, boor, blockhead, dunce, stupid, plowboy etc., but all those derogatory words combined skim only the top layer of the true meaning. The word—unequivocally—implies lowly, declassed individuals from any given occupation or profession. But in large measure the word spells peasants with pitchforks at shoulders.

Why are *cafoni* found everywhere? An old, witty tale demonstrates this. Based on a local anecdote, the label "cafone" originated way back in a renowned monarchy. The tale goes on to say that a famous King was questioned by one of his ministers, in regard to why in the legislative chamber, nobody addressed him with his due title of nobility. The minister grumbled that like the remainder of his colleagues (who addressed one another with their respective title of: Baron, Duke, Count, Cavalier, etc.), he too should be addressed with his title of nobility, instead of his first name.

The King never answered. But annoyed by the thought of the silliness of his minister, on the closing of the next legislative session, the King asked the grumbling minister to stand up. Then calling the attention of the assembly, he pointed to the standing minister and said: "From this moment on, I want each and every one of you to address that *ca-ca-ca-fo-ne (ca-pho-nay)*, Cav-Cav-Cavalier!"

The King had a bad speech impediment. With his stuttering, he ended up referring to his grumbling minister with the word *cafone.* That new word spread to each corner of the Kingdom like a wild fire. Meanwhile, whether the King meant to address his minister as Cavalier (or whatever he thought the word *cafone* meant), we will never know for sure. Neither will we know for sure that the tale is credible. However, whether the tale is credible or not, should make little or no difference. We have already learned a thing or two about labels. So, knowing also that *cafoni* could be found even in a King's court, let's go ahead and read the story and find out for ourselves what those in Montelieto are up to.

The Lonesome Cobbler

Chapter 1

Earning a daily living for a class of peasants inhabiting Montelieto (a town in central Italy), became a hard struggle by the start of the fourth decade of the twentieth century. Burdened with near total dependency on having to share their crops with the rich landowners, the impoverished majority of peasants, labeled *cafoni*, saw golden promises of betterment gradually vanish. They had hoped that, with the rise and glamorous establishment of a totalitarian system of government, their tough situation would improve but that, like everything else, turned out to be an unrealizable dream.

Instead of improvement, oppression began to be felt every day more severe. Sharecroppers, small and big landowners—every occupation of the working class was taxed heavily. Farm products were controlled by Fascist Party enforcers. Not much of anything could be sold, or bought, without the Fascist seal of approval. Cigarette lighters, flashlights, radios, bikes—everything was required to carry a seal of approval from the State. Transgressors were penalized with stiff fines. The harvests of the fields were supervised and controlled by Fascist representatives who, based on their immoderate estimations, confiscated all the farm products in excess of the needs of the families. As a result, the lowly peasants were even robbed of the seeds essential for sowing, forced to abandon hopes for raising cash, and deprived of being able to store up adequate amounts of food supplies for their own sustenance. The Fascist representatives' pretext was always the same. They claimed that all food items were needed by the State to support and strengthen the Black Shirts (Fascist special army). They believed that the Fascist special army would fight and die to free the country of dependency and exploitation from the Western capitalists. Meanwhile, the peasants felt cheated and repudiated.

Hardships continued to mount for the declassed peasant sharecroppers, more so than the rest of the population. They either got used to carrying the stiff yoke of the Party in power, or knew they would be cast aside and have to suffer the consequences. When rumors of wars and other catastrophes affecting the continent began to spread, none of the peasants saw danger forthcoming. They looked upon the rise and establishment of totalitarian systems as not worthy of their concern. Neither did they foresee catastrophes striking anywhere. If they saw a rise, they merely saw it in terms of having to borrow more in advance from their rich landlords. Of catastrophes they had less worries, since their lives had been one long catastrophe.

The Fascists believed that war was the only remedy for the evils affecting both the poor and the rich. They focused their efforts on rallying everyone to the supreme cause. Shouts of war, and invincibility, rang more loudly as time went by. The entire country must be geared for war! So rich and poor, strong and feeble must join together, to move forward, for undertaking the great challenge to which the motherland had called them.

Montelieto was an obscure town, awkward and least likely to be taken seriously as part of any national activity. It was known as the town of donkeys and declassed *cafoni*. If *cafoni* had been incited to join the ranks of the Fascists, this was done for purposes of solidarity. The town was cut off from paved roads, and estranged from all trends of influence and modernization. Only the fittest people, who owned a strong donkey, achieved sporadic trades of goods with the more modern towns of the region. Those who didn't own a strong donkey, would have to rely on transportation by heads and on shoulders.

Essential food items were difficult to obtain in the fake and fanciful era of Italian splendor. Salt, sugar, fuels and farming equipment were always in scarcity. New clothing and footwear were a luxury. Coffee—real coffee—was unknown to the peasants of Montelieto. A vast majority of them had never tasted coffee in their lifetime. Like many other imported items, coffee was just not in their vocabulary. People poked fun even at the mere mention and lack of availability of imported items constituting luxury.

It happened that a robust unlearned young man, who charred wood into charcoal to make a living, for the first time brought on donkey back a load of his product to sell it to a modern town. He sneaked through the Fascist controllers' checkpoints and succeeded in selling his charcoal. Upon his return, the adventurous young man told his young *cafoni* friends all the things he had heard and seen.

"You wouldn't believe what goes on in the world! Down there, they have invented a type of machine which, in a matter of seconds, squirts out a beverage that tastes better than anything I have ever tasted. They call it: Espresso-machine-cappuccino," he said.

"Espresso-machine-cappuccino? How much you think it costs?" One of his friends asked in wonderment.

"Don't know for sure, but suspect lots of money," answered the first. "Perhaps thousands and thousands of *lire*." The dialogue between the two friends ended, but the younger of the two became excited in thinking about the espresso-machine-cappuccino.

"Damn!" he said cussing in disgust. "My friend is becoming too emancipated. I cannot let this thing happen to him while I remain behind!"

Right away, he went to work. He swore to char as much wood into charcoal as his friend had done, evade the traps laid by the Fascist controllers and go down to the modern town to sell the charcoal. From there on he couldn't wait for the day to buy the espresso-machine-cappuccino and become emancipated, just like his friend. But one thing was wrong; he had gotten mixed up between the cost of the cappuccino and the cost of the espresso-machine-cappuccino.

Early one morning the charcoal, donkey, and donkey driver were ready. They departed for the modern big town, arriving before sunrise. The whole load of charcoal was sold, and the young man pocketed the profit. Then whistling his favorite tune, he happily rode through the town looking for the first coffee shop open for business. In front of one he stopped, fastened the halter of the donkey to a lamppost, entered the shop and ordered the espresso-machine-cappuccino. He had not even made himself comfortable when a teenaged waiter brought him a steaming cup of cappuccino, and the impatient donkey driver began to sip to his heart's delight.

"My friend was right," he said to himself while sipping. "This is excellent! No wonder why it costs lots of money." He sipped some more, finished, got up and walked to the cash register to pay. He took out his wallet, placed all the money he had earned selling charcoal upon the counter, and started to walk toward the exit door.

When the waiter saw a pile of money on the counter and the donkey driver walking out, he called aloud: "Eh! Mister! Mister donkey driver, wait! You forgot the change. With all this money we could brew buckets full of cappuccino."

The donkey driver returned but, as the waiter tried to explain the financial discrepancies, the driver took all the notes in his hands, tossed them on top of the counter again and continued: "Keep all of it and, with the extra, brew a big bucket of espresso-machine-cappuccino for my she-ass waiting outside." Ironically, the cost of the express cappuccino was merely twenty centesimi (cents).

At the nonsensical request of the donkey driver, the astonished young coffee shop waiter walked toward his senior co-worker and asked: "Have you ever heard of such an asininity before? Where do you think that idiot has been serving time until now?"

"Nowhere," answered the senior coffee shop waiter. "If he is wearing footwear made of hides of animals, he must be a *cafone* from the hilly town of Montelieto—the home of the donkeys, of the peasants and of declassed *cafoni* ciociari. Those people understand only the language of the donkeys. A large number of them eat, sleep, procreate and raise their children in the same stable as the donkeys! They co-habit with domestic animals and vice-versa."

"Oh my God!" exclaimed the junior waiter. "He is wearing footwear made of hides of animals. We absolutely do not want that person hanging around our coffee shop. Should we close up so he'll go away?"

"I think it would be unwise to close up shop. There are hundreds like him up there. When one of them shows up, many more other will follow. They are like pests, indestructible. People do not call them *cafoni* for nothing," warned the senior waiter.

"So what are we going to do?" asked the younger man.

"Nothing. For the time being I would say: We better keep on brewing the espresso-machine-cappuccino and fill up the big bucket for his she-ass."

This silly anecdote came to be known in the times of the invention of some type of espresso coffee machine. It probably didn't happen word for word as described but that story, for sure, got stuck to the peasants of that town. This certainly hammered down the last nail upon the coffin of bad reputation, for which Montelieto already had been known in the past. It was affixed to that town, time and again, as a mockery of the inhabitants while it raised high suspicions, about Montelieto being a desirable place to live in and whether its people made any sense. In truth, Montelieto was not a desirable place to live in.

Because people of that region were recognized throughout the country, for wearing footwear made of hides of animals, folks from other regions unfairly took them for dullards. That emperors, eloquent orators, theologians and leaders of every sort were born and raised in that region meant nothing to the outsiders. That this region had been the birth of great generals and soldiers, artists, Popes and Saints, was not taken into account. The peasants of that region were mistakenly thought to have inferior intelligence, and that caused them to be addressed with the worst pejorative slanders of the language. Montelieto and its people personified the lowest peasantry. In all aspects, the town and the people constituted the following characteristic: SUB-STANDARD.

To be born and to have lived in Montelieto was a handicap. Of course, to have lived a full life, humanely speaking, should never be a waste of time. But in certain situations, especially when cruel entanglements in life have denied one the privileges of betterment, to draw negative conclusions is not so terribly wrong. Examples of wishing (or not wishing) to be born could be traced amongst the inhabitants of Montelieto. Lamentations of someone's disapproval with life's worthiness were heard quite often. The blasphemy: "I wish we from Montelieto, were never born!" could be heard from those people on a daily basis, as life to them became more impossible to live. That was true because the town and its people were never touched by progress. The town and the people stood alone amongst remote, arid, mountains in utter secrecy. Through the millenniums, Montelieto had seen the births of wealthy and powerful empires. It had endured barbarian invasions and the accompanying plundering. It had seen foreign dominations and renaissances. It had seen the making of empires, kingdoms, feudalism, Church States and their dissolutions. Finally, it had seen the re-unification of a sovereign State, signs of progress, and finally a totalitarian system of government come to power.

Unfortunately, none of those historical events had been of good omen for the people and the town of Montelieto. Perhaps even before the elephants of Hannibal that had destroyed the crops of the fields on their way to Rome, the people of Montelieto had endured all kinds of calamities and found themselves worse off after each turn of events. It was said that the town was attacked many times in the past, and set on fire, but it always survived. Nothing burned in there except the rafters of the roofs. The houses were built of rocks and mortar materials. The last attack, beside those perpetrated by the brigands/outlaws, came at the hands of a French brigade that put the town on fire, but on their attempt to force the doors open from the outside, they were repulsed while inflicting heavy losses. Over fifty citizens from Montelieto perished in the struggle.

During pauses between the struggles of those unfortunate events, the population went on worrying about the acts of nature. To draw any kind of living from the scorched, hilly farmlands was a constant hassle even when the climate was favorable. When the climate was not favorable, the poor sharecroppers had terrible nightmares. Food scarcity became unbearable. Droughts, torrential rains, floods and disease came to add to the already impossible human existence.

The last degrading era came in the ninteenth century, prior to the re-unification of the sovereign State. It was remembered by the elderly, to be the cruelest era. In those days bands of brigands/outlaws (who made their living by looting), roamed the town and the countryside, terrorizing, kidnapping and killing the defenseless citizens. The outlaws, having made their headquarters in the steeper mountains, held scores of hostages captive under strict surveillance. When the demands of ransom could not be promptly met, the hostages were shot, thrown alive down steep cliffs or mutilated and sent back to their families. The lucky few whose families could afford the cost of the ransoms, were released after one ear had been severed. As result of these horrible brutalities, the harassed population of Montelieto lived the worst miserable depravations.

During nighttime, the population retreated within the defensive walls of the town shutting secure with heavy timbers of oak, the two entrance doors that led inside. They lived inside the defensive walls, to fend off and fight back all attempts to force the doors from the outside, same as the Trojans under siege. People and domestic animals shared the same habitation. That was the best and only alternative to repel attacks and to insure survival. Progress and education for many years to come, was not on the agenda or in the minds of the citizens of Montelieto. The population, and the town, seemed to have been stuck in one inescapable vise of setbacks, from which they must find a narrow way out if they wished to survive. But there was no way out! That was their portion in life. Among many defaming stereotypes, they were known to be flesh born to suffer and, because of that, were cursed to continue to wither away, hopelessly, into nothingness.

Chapter 2

Years went by before silver linings began to appear on the murky horizon of Montelieto. After Garibaldi had proved successful in shaping the re-unification of the country under one monarchy, years of serenity followed. The two giant doors, only public access to the town, were kept open permanently and later disassembled. But the years of serenity were of short duration. The monarchy would not let peace reign for long. It shortly took the aggressive route to fight wars in East Africa against the Rases, with the dying Ottoman Empire, and finally joined World War I and then World War II.

Thousands of years had gone by, but nothing seemed to influence the tides of progress for the people of Montelieto. The political leadership went bragging to want to build an empire, but what they were building was new roads in Libya and East Africa. Nothing ever occurred to those braggart leaders to make them see that Montelieto, just south of the capital, badly needed the schools and roads being built elsewhere. The *cafoni* believed that, perhaps, the town was founded in misery and that in misery they would undoubtedly perish together.

The only positive asset Montelieto had remaining was its people. They were born into adversity and accustomed to hard work in order to earn a living whichever way adversity came. *Cafoni* ciociari they were and declassed peasants—but tough as nails and hardened by poverty. By and large, poverty was perpetuated from father to sons and grandsons. Ninety percent of them shared the crops of the fields with the big landowners, and with the Archdiocese. (The parish pastor collected the share of crops belonging to the Archdiocese). Poverty for the sharecroppers was simply an inherited patrimony.

Until the first quarter of the twentieth century, there were no public schools in Montelieto worthy of mention. At best, there had been some private schools where pupils were taught by local nobles, but that consisted only of the second elementary. That type of school, however, was a great privilege for the few youngsters whose parents could afford the tuition payments due the elite teachers.

Most of the peasants of Montelieto were virtually the same as slaves. Not slaves in the true sense of the word, but nonetheless slaves to their landowner masters for economic situations. The greater number of those peasants addressed their masters in a slavish obedience, referring to them as "Mister Lord" or "Mistress Lord." Many times those illiterate peasants, on occasional encounters with the rich landowners, showed respect for them by bowing low and touching the front brim of the hat.

With the inception of the totalitarian system, during the period between the two World Wars, the party in power succeeded in establishing, and to rule mandatory, an elementary education. It became obligatory to have the youngsters attend school all the way up to the fifth elementary.

The Fascist officials who shaped the destiny of Montelieto proved to be instrumental in providing and opening
two or three hovels in town, which they called school rooms.
Within these precincts, classes began being taught. However, at the start, attendance was only scattered. Illiteracy
ran rampant and was a long way off from being completely
wiped out.

Children had to travel on foot from the valley and hills,
in clement or inclement weather, to attend school. In rainy
weather, the frail children who made the valiant effort to
show up, arrived at their classrooms soaking wet and must
have remained so the entire school day.

The classrooms of the schools were dilapidated. The
clay tiles covering the floors shifted every time someone
walked upon them. Clouds of dust rose up to the ceiling
when the students entered a classroom in large groups.
There was no indoor plumbing within the school building
or the classrooms. No lavatory of any type existed inside
the school. When the young students needed to take care
of their personal needs, they had been instructed to raise
their hands high above their heads. The teachers then, at
their discretion, would permit the students to go outside.
At times, it was impossible for the young children to hold
until the teachers decided whom to let go first.

The main trouble was that not even on the outside
could the children find a private corner suitable to relieve
themselves. Because of this problem, they used whatever
corner they found convenient at the moment. Those children waited for pedestrians to clear the streets so they
could go against the walls of the nearest building. But as
it was not always possible to wait for pedestrians to clear
the streets, or stop them from coming or going, the young

children urinated and defecated right in the open nearby the walls of public buildings and even the local church. In an era of so-called "grandeur," that was one deplorable situation.

Meanwhile inside the classrooms, the teachers spoke of an imminent aggrandizement for the young generation. They spoke of "duty to the motherland," which everybody was bound to maintain dear to the hearts for promoting civilization and upholding the sacred rights of the land, and to march in pursuit of the old glories. "That," the teachers claimed, "was being commended to posterity as their destiny."

Baloney aggrandizement, the older students thought. *We would call ourselves lucky if we could have a good slice of white bread for dinner, let alone aggrandizement.*

In the classroom, a group of students tried their best to achieve. Others stayed in the background, outside of all curriculums, became assigned to benches in the rear of the classrooms, and were only rarely paid attention to by the teachers. When students failed to make the grades expected of them, inevitably they were sent back near the rear walls of the classroom. That section was openly referred to as the "stable of gathering jackasses."

Meantime, all the students were being injected with doses of patriotism on a daily basis from the eloquent teachers, who claimed that Fascism would be the salvation of mankind. Fascism, they preached, was not to be taken with indifference, nor was it a niche where cowards would want to take refuge in. According to the same blockhead teachers, times were ripe for the present generation to engage in war—to fight, and conquer, and propagate amongst the arrogant western democracies, the mastery of their heritage.

The greater part of the students felt that these speeches were given purposely for instilling in them the principles of Fascism. But that meant very little. The students came from impoverished families and were highly skeptical of any type of indoctrination unless they saw, or felt, tangible advantages forthcoming. Only the students whose families had strong connections with the Party believed the nonsense of the boastful instructors.

Both groups of students, though, got along fairly well. Although those coming from poor families were repeatedly sneered at by the rich, no major fights developed after the day's classes. Most of them were aware that simply being born in Montelieto could turn a person *cafone.*

There were several wealthy families in Montelieto. Those were not of highly aristocratic stock but, nevertheless, Lords. The families of Lords, with the church, owned the bulk of the fertile farmlands of the town and of its villages. How those entities had become owners was anybody's guess. Had the better farmlands been attained with the deceits of the feudal era? Or the papacies? Perhaps both?

To the average citizen of Montelieto it was immaterial how those entities had attained the wealth. The peasant sharecroppers had shared the fruits of their labor with the rich for ages, and nothing seemed to alter the status quo. Mountain dwellers too lived in the worst economic conditions. They grazed their cattle upon the sun-baked hillsides and farmed strips of mountain land not worth the seeds to be sowed on it. In mediocre harvest times the yield of grains produced on those mountain lands would not even equal the amount of seeds sowed early on.

Many healthy bodies went seeking work in the marshlands of the Roman plains under reclamation, but often were sent back home to Montelieto. They were penalized by the Fascist enforcers for not having the proper papers required for obtaining work anywhere outside of the town's own boundaries. The craftsmen of Montelieto were the same breed of *cafoni*. Not immune to poverty, hunger and misery. Cobblers, tinsmiths, barbers and all classifications of skilled trades, struggled against hard times just as much as the sharecroppers. To earn even a meager living was difficult and a big hassle for all.

Some improvements were achieved by a number of immigrants, around the closing of the nineteenth century and the beginning of the twentieth century. The immigrants ventured to foreign shores, with hopes of coming out of the sharecropper dependency. Many were successful in earning funds enough to afford a few acres of their own but, by and large, none really did completely escape from poverty. Those who had not succeeded stayed put in whatever unpleasant situation they found themselves, in a foreign land, and never came back.

For the able-bodied, the ones who had never adventured seeking work abroad, life remained stagnant. There wasn't much they could do. The only means of providing sufficient food for their families was to seek additional strips of lands, at sharecrop from local Lords, and drudge day and night to make ends meet.

Chapter 3

By early autumn, before the rains turned torrential, the peasant sharecroppers from the town of Montelieto were well on their way to bringing the harvesting of the crops to a close. From hay to fruits, grain to vegetables, the reaping season progressed every day closer to completion. Having anticipated the heavy rains and devastating flash floods, the sharecroppers speeded up their laborious operations so as to bring under control all the chores of the fields.

Those were major and significant days for the share-croppers of Montelieto—days in which all the bushels of crops harvested must be enumerated, and the final partition with the landlords accomplished. Only after this would the anxious sharecroppers learn whether the supplies of food due them were adequate for the needs of the family, and whether the fruits of their labor were to be duly rewarded.

But it seemed the rewards, like the crops, were not legitimate rights of the poor *cafoni* sharecroppers. Everything harvested from the fields had to be divided, in equal parts, with the affluent landlords. On one hand a great many of the sharecroppers felt their work was not the ideal occupation from which to derive a good living; but on the

16

other hand, the remainder of the populace concluded that to derive a good living from any occupation in the town of Montelieto, had never been an ideal situation. All of them recognized that the occupation of sharing the crops seldom brought deserving rewards, and that the rewards were seldom commensurate to the efforts involved. To everyone's knowledge the situation of making any kind of living sharing the crops, had remained certain and irrevocable throughout the centuries.

One thing which every *cafone* sharecropper could be sure of was that their servitude to the landlords remained unchangeable, and that the torrential rains indeed continued to occur. Shortly, many of them would see the sowed fields on the rolling hills being washed out overnight from the heavy rains, and by daylight they would see the fields in the low lands being devastated from the flash floods. Often they succeeded in sowing the least damaged fields again, but would soon see the same cataclysm recur. From here the exasperated *cafoni* sharecroppers would slacken their efforts and quickly abandoned hopes of raising adequate amounts of grain that would sustain them for the winter. Consequently they resigned themselves to destiny and patiently waited to resume the planting of the affected fields in better weather, by using different types of seeds that developed and matured earlier than grains.

Until late winter, when work in the fields could be resumed, the peasant sharecroppers did trivial chores around their hovels in the old town. Periodically they went out to the mountains to gather wood and haul it home on donkey back, in order to keep the fire going and the children warm. In the long evenings the male population experienced periods of boredom and anxiety. Usually, after having gulped down their regular supper of boiled potatoes with horse beans, they walked the streets of the villages in search of pastime.

After dusk swarms of youngsters, together with middle-aged males, crammed themselves inside the three taverns in town. They split in rival teams, and avidly drank wine, challenging one another in stubborn contests of card games and of "morra" (finger guessing game), to determine who was bound to foot the cost of the consumptions incurred. Violent fist fights erupted in the process. Invariably the wine was of inferior quality. It had a sour taste but evidently its effect was strong enough to make heads spin. When in the following evenings the tavern keepers denied their rowdy clients additional credit, the thirsty taverngoers then looked for alternatives. They would gather, instead, inside the shops around the town and the villages discussing problems and telling old folk tales until closing time.

Taverns, crafts shops and a shoemaker shop kept open until late hours, were invariably filled with groups of rowdy townspeople. Their preferred gathering place was the shoemaker shop at one corner of the town Church Square. Inside that shoe shop, by consent of the old cobbler who operated it, the rowdy *cafoni* gathered and were at liberty to speak their minds on any issue. Until their argumentations would arouse the suspicions of the Fascist guards or if the discussions didn't end up in shouting matches and fist-fights, they would be welcome.

That kind of arrangement was the perfect occupation to overcome the doldrums of the long evenings. During the early part of the evening, everything proceeded smoothly. The peasants who couldn't afford the cost of staying in the taverns entertained themselves in friendly discussions; they laughed, smoked cheap tobacco or listened to their host telling old tales. The old cobbler loved that set-up. He felt entertained by his fellow countrymen, and tacitly sympathized with them, putting himself in their shoes. Their worries became the old cobbler's worries. But when the discussions heated up and the old cobbler reached the limit of his tolerance, exasperated by the futility of restraining the quarrelsome *cafoni*, he would expel everybody from his shop, and lock the entrance door behind them.

The shoemaker's shop, inside which the peasant *cafoni* of Montelieto loved to congregate, was operated by an old cobbler named Pompeo Gazzaladra. He rented the shop, with the upper flat, from one of the rich landlords of the town, a man with whom he had kept an unending feud running. The two rivals never seemed able to agree, or reach a fair compromise that would settle the repetitive requests for rent increases on the part of the landlord. Pompeo Gazzaladra maintained that the requests for rent increases, were ridiculous when he had to scrape for pennies. The landlord, on the other hand, insisted that each year the government increased taxes more than last. The old cobbler always drew parallels of his economic situation to that of the poor *cafoni* sharecroppers.

Everyone around Montelieto knew Pompeo Gazzaladra was poor, but all also knew that he was a renowned master of the trade. He was admired by all for being friendly, straightforward, soft spoken and witty. Over the times those assets had earned him respect from his peers, and the honorary title of "Don." He was no closer to nobility than the rest of the peasant *cafoni*, but to everyone he had become known as "Don Pompeo."

On the opposite of the peasant *cafoni*, Don Pompeo was somewhat educated. He could read and write (on a certain level), and be an efficient communicator—to the extent of being thought knowledgeable by his fellow countrymen. The old shoemaker's father, Don Gerolamo Gazzaladra, a renowned cobbler himself, had been bestowed the same respectable title in his days, and had been successful in affording his only son, Pompeo, the second elementary education.

Evidently the believed academic background of Don Pompeo was not the only asset he possessed. Aside from being witty, he was shrewd—an old fox of a shoemaker, with tons of experience. At times, by quoting the headlines of borrowed newspapers and interpreting the subjects, in his shop the credulous listeners were frequently open-mouthed in astonishment.

Don Pompeo Gazzaladra loved Montelieto and its people deeply, but for the poor and discouraged, there was a special place in his heart. He could readily recall the events that had brought him and his people so much misery, which he felt had dragged them down to live under shameful conditions. As he sewed stitches upon stitches during the days, he often talked to himself, concluding in his mind that wars, illiteracy and greedy rich landowners had been the three major evils to obstruct the progress of Montelieto and its people.

The majority of the citizens of Montelieto were poor and illiterate peasant *cafoni*, sharing the crops with the landlords. Year after year they borrowed food products from the landlords, hoping to repay in better harvests. But that never happened. Don Pompeo was greatly saddened seeing generation after generation of young men wither away in nothingness, wasting their lives in poverty or perishing in wars. In his solitude Don Pompeo prayed. He entrusted all the youngsters to the Saints of Montelieto. After long days of prayers, discouraged and feeling there were no hopes or miracles forthcoming, he would often experience periods of conflicting emotions. While working in his shop alone, the thought of being helpless to change anything irritated him. He would then hit the working bench hard with his hammer, shut the door of the shop and go for a walk flanking the old defensive walls of town. The urgency of quitting work and going for a walk usually occurred to Don Pompeo in the late afternoon when the Church Square became deserted, and his boredom and nervousness became intolerable.

During those solitary strolls around the old walls of the town, Don Pompeo thought about the problems facing the people of Montelieto. He spoke so intensely to himself that passersby would rush to ask if something was wrong, and if he needed help. His answers were always reassuring. "Nothing is wrong with me," he would say. "I am fine. I wish this much could be said for my brethren of Montelieto." When at times he met with the old tailor and the sacristan (who also walked the same route from opposite directions), they sat down and spent the remainder of the late afternoon chatting.

The old tailor, an unusual type of fellow, was used to passing his best time in company of the two friends. He felt that they respected him for what he was, and did not ridicule or poke fun at him implying he didn't like girls.

The antithesis of the tailor, the sacristan was more open. But ever since the parish pastor had entrusted him with the non-clerical chores of the church, he refrained from speaking against the wrongs done to his fellow countrymen by religious and civil authorities.

Outspoken Don Pompeo was the least timid. Obligated to no one, his self-imposed duty was to side with the poor and the mistreated sharecroppers, and to defend everyone from the trickeries of the rich, civil and religious leaders by teaching his people inspired citizenship.

Chapter 4

Amid the setbacks and misfortunes that Don Pompeo observed befalling his beloved Montelieto, the most distressing was to see the political transition of the motherland. Replacing the monarchy, a totalitarian system came to power, led by an arrogant leader. Every time that leader addressed the masses with patriotic speeches, the tune was one of aggression. This leader foolishly believed that war was a mandate to the present generation, dictated by destiny. Don Pompeo was skeptical of that rhetoric. When he became frustrated listening to the same nonsense, behind the scenes he called the new leader crazy. Days and months would go by but nothing ever changed. The shouts of war reverberated every day more loudly and more threatening from Rome.

Late one afternoon, while listening to the public radio broadcast of seven P.M., Don Pompeo was downcast. That same evening he advised his friends to be wary, of "That man," he said, "That man whose picture is on the posters all over the walls of the Church Square, one of these days will get all of us killed! Worse than that, we will still be hungry. None of us can hope to eat good, white, bread two days in a row while that man is alive!

Don Pompeo then put his index finger vertically across his lips meaning silence. Again he drew index and thumb, from one side of his mouth to the other, like closing a zipper on his lips thus hinting to total silence. With that signal everyone understood what he meant, and all nodded approvingly by swearing strict secrecy.

A swarm of young kids suddenly passed by the shop of Don Pompeo, chanting slogans of war. "War! War! War! We want war! We want war!"

"Yeah," said Don Pompeo with a sneer. "They want war, and they must scream loudly, because those who gave them food coupons expect good propaganda. That fanatic postmaster and the fool of a Vice Mayor (Deputy Mayor) must have acted again on order of the Prefect. No doubts the Prefect has sent them additional food coupons. Those have been passed on to the kids for shouting slogans of war. We could eat that bastard of a Prefect alive, but run the danger of being locked up in the slammer if we dare open our mouths. You know that the Fascist guards are at his service?"

Meantime a tall kid, followed by several others, stopped in front of the shop of Don Pompeo. In his hands the kid held a cross with a crucifix affixed upon it. A hand written sign at the tip of the cross, in big misspelled letters read: "The capitalists have nailed me on this cross."

"Poor kids," Don Pompeo observed sensibly. "To wish to fight wars and to wish to acquire a stronger jackass is their only aspiration." He then sewed a few more stitches upon an emaciated vamp of a shoe, drove a couple of nails on the heel of it in anger and said: "What a big shame! The youth of Montelieto acclaim war? Were they ever told that wars have caused our poor town shameful illiteracy and humiliating poverty? Of course they were told! Virgin Mary!" he said pleadingly. "What sins have these children of yours committed? Has not this town of ours suffered enough?"

At this point Francisco Palla, called Cicco, a sort of midget and sharecropper of Signor Luigi, energized by the kids' chants of war, suddenly entered the shop of Don Pompeo. He walked near him and asked: "Don Pompé, wouldn't it be a good idea if we followed the example of the younger generation? If we had to fight a couple of wars against the West, and win, wouldn't we bail the country out of the sanctions? The people of Montelieto are starting to feel the stings of shortages and of hunger. Damn, we must attack!" Cicco said with persistence.

Hearing the nonsense of Cicco Palla, Don Pompeo stopped working. He looked at Cicco and laughed. Shook his head in disbelief and said: "Cicco Palla, son, you must have rocks in your head instead of brains. You have been told before that the very reasons we are not able to solve the problems of scarcities, hunger, unemployment and illiteracy are exactly because we have been fighting foolish wars. Who do you think will foot the cost of war and the consequences that will follow? Please understand that the poor people—not the high leadership—will have to bear the brunt of fighting wars whether we win or not, big fool of Francisco Palla."

Don Pompeo had never before addressed one of his countrymen as a fool, but this time he was irked to the limit and spoke angrily. Following Don Pompeo's rebuke, and for having been the object of low opinion of his fellow countrymen, Cicco Palla felt not embarrassed in the least.

("*Cafoni,*" had said Don Pompeo once, "do not know nor feel embarrassment.")

In the meantime, Cicco waited his turn for taking a couple of puffs from the cigarette that had been passed around to several smokers and agreed with Don Pompeo on the idea not to fight wars. He began to head for the exit door. "Sorry, I must go," he said. "My she-ass is about to give birth to a little donkey and she might need me."

"Damned," swore Gerardo Cipollone. "That blockhead of Cicco Palla worries about his she-ass more than he does for his wife. At least tonight he will stand as mid-wife."

"Right," agreed Mingo Pezzafina. "Last year while his wife was in labor with their second child, he was in the tavern of Marianna Pipanera getting drunk."

"Yeah," others inside the shop affirmed. "Cicco Palla is a super *cafone*, a loafer, and an ill-bred husband of the worst kind!"

Don Pompeo listened quietly for some time, then all of a sudden intervened and said: "Eh, guys! Let's not pick on Cicco behind his back. Wait at least until he comes back so he can defend himself. No *cafone* should poke fun at another," he said. "Besides, if Cicco is not a deserving husband, it should not be our concern. His wife will handle him in that department. A bigger problem is that another jackass is about to be born in Montelieto when there are already too many."

"Very true, we do have too many jackasses," someone among the *cafoni* said. By now though, the lantern above the working bench of Don Pompeo was fumigating the room. He arose from his bench stool, adjusted the wick, poured more petroleum in the lantern and said: "This will last for a few more hours until we close up. Today, I wish to inform you, the census in Montelieto has become final. Officially, there are 1,928 souls in our town—but not, of course, that everyone got counted. The provincial government is now able to report to Rome the number of people to be included in an eventual mobilization. Of the 1,928 souls, the males amount to 888, and the remaining 1,040 are females. The male population is decreasing rapidly. This census tells us that something awful is happening to our lovable town. Damned," cussed Don Pompeo. "If they have to fight couple of more wars, the kind Cicco Palla wishes to fight, we will be totally decimated!"

"This is not good news," said Cosimo LaBorgia. "But for those of us who are still alive it is not so bad. We males could end up getting one and a quarter of women each."

"You dirty rat," snapped back Camillo Feliciano, "You are always figuring how to screw somebody else's wife. You have the audacity to call others horny? Better you watch out for your own affairs because, one of these days, somebody will surely be screwing after your wife."

"Perfect said," added Ludovico Peluso. "But if both of you and your kind succumb and go to hell, we could end up getting two women each. The question Don Pompeo raises is simply why there are more women than men, that's all."

"That is easy to answer Ludovì," said Don Pompeo, trying to break the silly exchange of ideas and accusations among the three. "One major reason is that on the list of names over the stone of the monument of the fallen soldiers, there is not one single name of a woman. Moreover," he added matter-of-factly, "Pasqualina Pizzuta breeds females in batches like pancakes."

"Yeah," affirmed Guglielmo Sparacelli. "And also tell them, Don Pompé, that her first husband, Annibale Filippone, has been in South America for over ten years without sending his wife a penny. We should declare him missing in action."

"You sound like a bunch of fools, excluding Don Pompeo," finally spoke out Luigi Durezza. "What was Pasqualina to do, starve to death?"

"Good grief," exclaimed Don Pompeo. "You have found the perfect subject to lead you to exchanges of fists, and then only God knows to what else! Pretty soon is time to close up shop and you guys are still trying to discover who really was the horny one to father those girls of Pasqualina Pizzuta? Good night! Out, all of you!" said Don Pompeo. "Out! before you get on each other's throat."

Chapter 5

The early origins of Montelieto were not totally understood. The reason why, and by whom the town had been founded, were beyond anyone's imagination. At first look, the old town seemed not to have been founded at all. Instead it gave the impression it had been hurled, and embedded, on top of the hill by a jest of nature. That could be concluded by looking at Montelieto or by walking through its network of narrow, rocky streets which ultimately led into a larger street that, by winding up and down, ended in the Church Square.

One interesting characteristic of Montelieto was its location above the hill. The location must have been chosen, studied and deemed defensible by settlers who sought safety behind the barrier of the town's walls. But not one official word in regard to the city's origin or foundation, could be found in the annals of the City Hall of Montelieto. By giving ear to the local legend, the town had probably been there forever, even before Rome. But nobody knew for sure.

Perhaps the first settlers of Montelieto were shepherds. They could have been a small group of a religious society that had escaped the pagan persecutions, and had settled in those remote hills of the region Ciociaria. Several districts of the town are still recognized with the names of the Apostles of Jesus, and the remains of old chapels stand as testimony to the first settlers of the town professing Christian beliefs. Life in Montelieto continued to go on same as it had begun. No one entertained in the mind higher objectives.

There were no paved roads connecting Montelieto to larger towns of the region. Commerce, which consisted of the exchange of farm products, was achieved by carrying the merchandises on human shoulders or donkey back. The neighborhoods in the old parts of town were infested with fleas, mosquitoes, flies, and other nuisance in warmer months. There was no running water inside the town, and no sewer system that worked. Water supplies inside the defensive walls were always scarce. Those who could afford the cost, had cisterns built beneath their houses. They filled the cisterns by diverting into them the rain from the rooftops. Not everyone owned a cistern, and no rain ever came when it was most needed. The unluckier townspeople borrowed a bucket of water here and there, from generous neighbors.

Human excrement, accumulated into chamber pots during the nighttime, was dropped in the space between the walls of adjacent buildings, from where that trickled down a trench covered with slabs of stones. This was the only drainage. Rarely was the sewage drained from the trenches to the outside of the defensive walls of the town. Heavy rains washed out some of the slime.

The transportation of farm crops, firewood, and forage for the domestic animals, was usually done on donkey back. The ultimate power was that of a pair of oxen, which only the well-to-do owned. There were no trucks or any type of machine owned by the town until World War II. Just prior to that, the people of the general store had acquired a small truck. Also, around the same time, the post office had purchased an old type of van that replaced a horse drawn cart. That was used to pick up the mail at the railroad station of the nearest city. A priest from a wealthy family owned the only car in town. It was called the Topolino (tiny mouse).

Of all the citizens of Montelieto, only a handful lived a life conformable to human standards. The majority lived in close quarters with domestic beasts, sleeping eating and procreating in the same barns with the animals.

Having said plenty about the deplorable conditions of Montelieto, another truth must be mentioned. Among all imperfections, there was nothing deficient in the intelligence of the people, as opposed to the lack of which they had been accused. They were shrewd, indefatigable people, who had been choked to death with archaic rules devised by wicked systems from past generations. Unbelievable was the fact that in a region boasting the cradle of civilization, such abhorrent pockets of incivility and poverty were allowed to exist. The aphorism: "Cradle of civilization" had no connection with reality. Who cared about aphorisms? The truth was that even in modern times Montelieto was excluded from progress. To emigrate abroad seemed to be the only way out. Emigration within the State was prohibited, but it would have not solved anything even if it weren't.

Highways, schools with farming innovations, were being built in East and North Africa by the initiative of leaders who aspired to the acquisition of new empires. Their lack of discernment made them unable to realize that colonization of disadvantaged nations was out. To promote the good of others, they did not have to go to Africa. There was plenty of disadvantage right there, in Ciociaria!

To have named Montelieto with such a gentle, happy, name seemed foolish to a vast majority of the inhabitants. "Merry Mount" was not quite appropriate. If that town should have been named at all, many felt, a name befitting it should have been: "The mount of unhappy *cafoni*, declassed sharecroppers and donkeys." Nearly every *cafone* owned a donkey. That was the cheapest and easiest to obtain a domestic quadruped. A donkey was not at all pretentious. It ate anything—and nothing was just as nourishing. Like its owners, the donkeys were flesh born to sacrifice. As Montelieto ranked amongst the towns and villages, the donkeys ranked amongst animals—both *cafoni*.

The poor donkeys were used for every type of physical labor, unsparingly. By looking close at their physical appearance, it would not be difficult to know how compassionate or well off, economically, their owners might be. There was never a dull moment for the donkeys. Besides the hard tasks they performed on a daily basis, they were even used to provide entertainment. On feast days youngsters from the villages and from Montelieto, mounted the donkeys to race down the valley on dirt roads. The feast became an occasion of pastime because the donkeys would not engage in a competitive race. They ran disorganized and stubbornly refused to go forward. Many overpowered the rider and returned braying to the starting point.

During the winter months, the donkeys were only fed with straw, which was the most abundant forage but the least nutritious. That, no doubt, reflected on the aspect of the poor beasts. When spring came, shearing time also came. A few elders provided the shearing service for a pittance. They would set up shop in a secluded sunny place by the defensive walls of the town, and wait for the peasants to bring their donkeys for the "haircut." Swarms of young kids followed and looked at the operation of shearing, curious to find out whose donkey turned more rebellious. Not much entertainment existed there for the young or old. Every type of pastime must have been derived from the things that occurred in the natural way. The number one pastime of the young kids, was to observe the copulation of dogs. The other pastime was to see the she-asses taken to stud. Every type of farm animal breeding became a pastime. Kids pitched cocks against those of the neighbors, and became excited to the point of fighting each other.

The kind of toys young kids cherished consisted of the amount of buttons they kept in their pockets, and feathers of cock-pheasants attached on their hats. Quite often they ran into troubles with the town's postmaster, for chasing his cock-pheasants, and plucking away feathers off the birds' tails. The kids even gambled—not with money but with buttons and multicolor feathers. Those less astute in the technique, and the feeble, were stripped of all the buttons on the shirts and trousers. The postmaster lived hating the kids vehemently, and was pained to see his pheasants semi-deplumed.

The scarcity of toys for the kids, though, was not a matter that troubled the elders. There were many more scarcities that made the elders go on hands and knees. Especially Don Pompeo. His sensibility toward the needs of the young generation, and his inability to be able to change things for the better, troubled him immensely. He

had hoped to see improvements in the area of education,
ever since an early age, but was time and again deceived.
"The lack of schools and opportunities to learn is not life-
threatening," Don Pompeo used to say. "That just bars the
way, stunting the spirit and will of our youth, for undertaking noteworthy initiatives."

So whether the situation concerned the well being of
the young or old generation, Don Pompeo condemned it.
He ached for all of them. While he worked in the lonely
hours of the day, Don Pompeo often felt downhearted. He
anxiously anticipated the evening when, with open arms,
he waited for the company of his *cafoni* friends. Meantime
he opened and reopened the borrowed newspaper, but re-
folded it, annoyed to read the same news as of yesterday.

"Boasting and more boasting. Parades after parades,"
he would say. Then as he heard his neighbor sing patriotic
songs from her balcony, he felt his nerves wrench. His blood
boiled when she intoned the song he hated most. She always sang: *"Duce! Duce! Chi non saprà morir?"* (Oh my
leader! Oh my leader! Who wouldn't die for thee?) At that
Don Pompeo would answer enraged: "True, true, pumpkin
head, sing him to come to this town of ours and I will show
both of you Montelieto dying."

In the evening Don Pompeo regained his good frame
of mind again. Everybody felt he was the best host and
entertainer to have lived in Montelieto. In days of good
mood, Don Pompeo searched the town to find barefoot kids
to hire. He already employed several to broom the floor of
the shop. Always chose the feeble and shabby clothed. Paid
them two or three centesimi (cents) even before they
started work, and then sent them home. There was not
enough work for everyone. He had no money. Whatever he

had was kept in his pockets to donate at the right moment to those in dire need. Many times he talked to himself. One day pretending to speak to the kids he uttered the following words:

"Listen kids, tomorrow if we are lucky enough to collect the cost of repairing the shoes of the lazy taxman, Don Pompeo will buy two, maybe three, hot chestnuts each. Hear me, Federico?" (Federico was one of his preferred but most destitute of the town.) "Oh, Federico, Federico! What other cataclysm must we endure, before the decaying situation of Montelieto turns for the better? Let's hope the situation will improve, lest we all perish. Lord, what else can I do to help the poor kids, and especially Federico, who has a limping impediment? Go, go," he said in his soliloquy, pretending Federico was present. "Go to your mother Angelina and tell her, poor lady, that she doesn't owe me a single penny toward the cost of the special shoe I made for you. Where is she going to raise two *liras* for the cost? Tell her that I, Don Pompeo, will erase her name from the debt list of my shop. Tell her we are even and not to worry because when you outgrow those shoes, we will make another pair for the same price. Thanks for listening, Federico. The harsh truth is that we are together navigating in a rough sea, and on a ship already taking water. You understand what I mean, don't you, Federico? The sinking ship of the poor and the declassed *cafoni*?" Don Pompeo said wiping tears from his eyes as he fell silent.

Chapter 6

By the start of the fourth decade in the twentieth century, the Fascist leadership had no goals remaining on its agenda. From every corner of the nation, the citizens had successfully been indoctrinated and had joined the final cause of the motherland. The diffusion of the Fascist doctrine was completed.

Although the citizens of Montelieto were among the last to join the aimless files of the Fascists, this was no longer an issue. After the Fascists had finished administering their brand of medicine (castor oil), to people in general and to resisting personalities in particular, not much of any news was to be heard from Montelieto.

In the years preceding Italy's bellicose intention abroad, unexpected changes began to occur. The first indication of changes came by new directives from Rome. The provincial governor the Prefect, who commanded exclusive jurisdiction over Montelieto, was empowered to release funds for renovating places of public access. Montelieto was allocated funds earmarked to restore one old building, section of streets leading to it, sections of the Church Square, and the cost of the work for replacing the floor tiles of two elementary school classrooms. The proposal of the project aroused hopes for the many unemployed of Montelieto. Whether the project was aimed to promote Fascist propaganda or was real, nobody cared. People rushed to obtain working permits from the City Hall, and to officially enroll in the Party.

The renovation of the old building was undertaken first. In time the building was washed, painted, given a satisfactory face-lift and made ready to be named "Casa del Fascio" (house of the bundle) symbol of Italian Fascism. From there on, the old building turned out to be known as one of the most important buildings of Montelieto.

After the destiny of Montelieto was sealed with the destiny of the motherland, the project remaining to be undertaken in order to expand and diffuse Fascist doctrine, was aggression over the neighbors. That was called war. Shouts of war reverberated across the land, and Montelieto was not to be left behind. But the young peasants declassed as *cafoni* lacked proper training. If they were to join the Black Shirts (Party faithful) and fight, they must take war training, in order to be considered worthy soldiers.

With utmost expediency, same as that employed to renovate the old building into the house of Fasces, the Prefect acted resolutely. Since he had previously rejected all requests to open a state-run pharmacy for the town of Montelieto, he acted on impulse. Without further hesitations, the Prefect delegated one of his Fascist subordinate officers (a pharmacist by profession), to head the House of Fasces of Montelieto and its pharmacy. The henchman pharmacist, loyal follower of the Prefect, accepted the assignment without hesitation. He was proud of the promotion granted him by the Prefect and couldn't wait for each day to begin so he could exercise his opportunity to run the new Fascist branch of Montelieto.

Meantime, Party affiliates, City Hall administrators, and teachers with school children prepared and waited to welcome the pharmacist. They applauded his arrival with great enthusiasm, more than had anything before been seen in Montelieto. They applauded, chanted and shouted repeatedly: "Evviva Il Duce! Evviva Il Duce!" (Long live our Chief!) After brief words of acceptance and appreciation, the pharmacist walked to the House of Fasces accompanied by two militiamen. Then, still swollen with pride, he walked to his living quarter facing the Church Square. To that day, Montelieto had not experienced a bigger ostentation for any reason, not close by far to the inauguration of the Fascist *Podestà* (mayor).

As the grand chief reorganized and decorated the House of Fasces with Party paraphernalia such as flags, banners, radio broadcasts and pictures of Il Duce, all donated by the Prefect, he opened the pharmacy at his own choosing. Although he was a pharmacist by profession, he felt no duty or pleasure in practicing the requisites of the trade. He claimed to lack adequate supplies of anything, and closed his pharmacy regardless of the necessity of remaining open. After his afternoon siesta, he was seen lying down upon the deck chair on the balcony of his apartment, reading and smoking cigars until the evening news was broadcast from Rome. Then he proudly went to open the House of Fasces to fulfill the requirements assigned to him by the Prefect, and hoping someone from the countryside came to enroll.

This egocentric and flamboyant character began to flaunt his Fascist grand uniform up and down the Church

Square, taking military steps cockily. His demeanor became so inflated that the young *cafoni* of Montelieto began to behave circumspectly. They thought the pharmacist might actually even sleep in his grand uniform.

The exhibitionist pharmacist wore knee-high trousers, fashioned a la Zouave (military uniform), tucked below the knees inside his tall black boots. He also wrapped a tricolor sash around his protruding belly, and wore a black shirt and tie. On his head he sported a beret with a tuft of black silk threads attached at one side. When he marched in his grand uniform, the silk threads of the beret dangled back and forth at the rhythm of his strides. Also when he marched wearing the grand uniform, and held the Fascist *manganello* (club) twirling from one hand to the other, the young *cafoni* took him for a buffoon sent from Rome to Montelieto to entertain. He showily hoisted the national tricolor (flag) and Fascist banners, high above the public radio audible from the balcony of House of Fasces. The radio was invariably tuned high, by his henchman, any time the loud clamor of the masses could be heard from the capital.

For national holidays and newsworthy events, for every insignificant occasion, the pharmacist called assemblage after assemblage of Party faithful. After giving short, enthusiastic speeches, he would proudly lead the cortege of believers toward the monument to the fallen soldiers, singing patriotic hymns of war. The cortege, largely composed of World War I widows, old disabled veterans and loafers of the town, returned to the House of Fasces where they would be allowed to break ranks amid screams of: "Evviva Il Duce!" Not one *cafone* wearing footwear made of animal skins was ever invited to participate in a marching, singing cortege. They were believed to have no class.

If the *cafoni* wished to pay homage to the fallen soldiers, they must do that on their own initiative. Main reason why *cafoni* were never invited was not because they didn't consider the fallen soldiers worthy of acclaim, but because their shabby appearance would dishonor the haughty pharmacist who had figured, in his mind, the *cafoni* were really inferior. With that non-acceptance the pharmacist sent unspoken messages hinting that the fallen soldiers were all his kinfolks. For his information, the fallen soldiers of Montelieto wore the same footwear as their forefathers, sons and daughters. Then at one point they were given shoes and a uniform and sent to die in it for upholding the interests of capricious leaders—the likes of the pharmacist.

But in spite of the non-acceptances, the *cafoni* followed their conscience. Time after time, as the donkey drivers *cafoni* passed by the monument to the fallen soldiers, they stopped and paid homage to their relatives while their donkeys occasionally broke into loud brays.

The peasants of Montelieto, though, paid no special attention to their standing and the rank they occupied in society. They were aware that they had no standing in society, and didn't care—so long they felt comfortable within themselves and were not imposed upon by the stupid pharmacist. To no one's surprise, the peasants were also aware that people with no class could be found in every walk of life. Individuals of low self-esteem could even be found among the higher classes. *Cafoni* could be leaders who always defended a wrong cause, a teacher who himself needed to be taught lessons, physicians who had a hard time healing patients, priests who couldn't learn Latin and, lastly, a Fascist pharmacist who hated the poor sharecroppers.

The young were robbed of one day a week, Saturday, which the pharmacist had declared as: "Sabato Fascista" (Fascist Saturday). Every Saturday thereafter, the youngsters in town were obliged to report to the pharmacist, at the House of Fasces, to undertake drills and trainings of military significance. From the young age of the first elementary, to that of compulsory draft in the army forces, the youngsters were obliged to report to the pharmacist. No excuses were tolerated. Regardless of the youngsters' family economic situation, they were pressed to report in their best attire. Footwear of hides of animals was not allowed. But only a few kids owned shoes for special occasions. The remainder borrowed any size shoe from others, in order to comply with the rules. Upon arrival at the House of Fasces, the kids were checked by the henchmen of the pharmacist and chosen on condition of cleanliness. Those disqualified for their shabby appearance were promptly brought to the attention of the pharmacist. At that point the pharmacist would angrily lecture the youngsters and many times slapped, kicked and sent them back home. Protests and complaints from the families of the mistreated kids were prohibited. The ultimate purpose of the Fascist Chief was to tame the young *cafoni* and their families, to teach and indoctrinate them with the same Fascist principles, as himself and the Prefect.

By this time, every indication pointed to the pharmacist commanding the Fascist branch of Montelieto, to have become a tyrant and the citizens the victims. But neither the Grand Chief in Rome, the Prefect or this new tyrant of

Montelieto, had an inkling of how stubborn and resilient *cafoni* might be. Those lowly people of Montelieto could absorb all kinds of abuse and repudiation but would still maintain their heads high as *cafoni numero uno* do. No outsiders, and no Party leaders, could have altered the life-style of the peasant *cafoni* so as to turn it for the worse; there was simply no worse lifestyle. So the people of Montelieto began to shrug off the tactics of the much-hated pharmacist and swore to get even when the opportunity came around.

Chapter 7

It was true that Montelieto needed a leader, but it needed a leader who was not a ruffian of the Party like the pharmacist commander of the Fascist branch. It needed one who was in touch with prevailing human conditions. Certainly the townspeople needed not the type of leader whose aims were to satisfy the ideology of the Fascist leadership, or one who was being used for inflation of the ego of his superiors and himself. The people of that town had not much more to give. Their energy was spent in working the fields of the well-to-do landowners with no hope of escaping deprivation.

How could the youngsters of Montelieto be indoctrinated and prodded to aspire in the dreams of the pharmacist, when they lacked the main resources essential to free them from poverty? The elders, in reference to the situation regarding the scope of the Fascist Chief, used to say: "Blood is difficult to draw from a beet, even if the beet is also red." That is: When people are regarded as scum of the earth, do not ever expect them to do good deeds.

The type of leader Montelieto wished to be led by lived in town, but he kept himself at a distance, and could not be reached or persuaded to lead. He came from a highly respected family of that town. He was educated, wealthy, generous and sensitive to the needs of his fellow countrymen. This charismatic fellow countryman was in the clergy—not a foreseeable candidate aspiring to lead or become supporter of the Party in power. Reverend Orazio Palestrina was a priest by profession, but a true humanitarian and communist of ideology. Any day he and the pharmacist were expected to challenge each other to a fencing duel in the town Church Square. Ebullient as one can be, Reverend Palestrina had been known to lash out at his political rival with his fists, but the blows were warded off by the henchman of the pharmacist who saved his chief from embarrassment.

The priest's interest, aside from his secret involvement with the Communist Party, was to administer his family farmlands, ride his convertible car Topolino (tiny mouse) have fun and womanize.

Reverend Palestrina's habits, though, were not a matter of concern for the peasant *cafoni*. They knew by instinct, that a mandate from nature to the rich, was exactly one to have fun and live it up, same as sharing the crops was a mandate from nature sent to them to live in poverty. They had no reason to condemn or criticize how the priest led his personal life. Was he perhaps the first influential "devout" personality to court beautiful women? It was enough of a blessing that Reverend Palestrina cared about and was compassionate to his sharecroppers, that he understood their hardships and that he saw to it that even sharecroppers were entitled to a break once in awhile. He kept a list of names of the ones most needing work. He hired them to perform jobs on the parts of the plantation he wished to operate on his own terms. When he wasn't ready to employ all, he gave supplies of food to those left behind, charging them no interest. On the next opportunity he rotated the list of names to save work for those last left behind. Reverend Palestrina was seen more as Saint than a womanizer.

On the other hand, when it came to exercising authority on all matters concerning the daily activities in Montelieto, the pharmacist enjoyed great advantages over everybody, including the priest. He was backed by the Party and considered infallible, and not one soul would dare contest his motives as long as he continued doing the will of the Prefect. To the pharmacist, the priest was not a subject of concern. The priest was just thought to be an agnostic rich, deviated-religious-do-nothing, not in touch with reality. "A humanitarian, perhaps," the pharmacist used to say of Reverend Palestrina, "but not a patriot nor a Fascist, never! He doesn't have what it takes."

This assessment of the pharmacist suited Reverend Palestrina well. He wanted to be recognized as humanitarian rather than patriotic. Most importantly, he wanted not to be recognized for having Communist tendencies because he understood the risks it would entail. The Fascist Party leadership would not hesitate to have him destroyed. He could live happily knowing that everybody, including the pharmacist, took him for humanitarian.

Letting this situation prevail, Reverend Palestrina was not in danger of being exposed for his principles. Like everybody else he could hate the pharmacist and challenge him to a fight, not on grounds of being a Fascist, but on grounds of not being humanitarian. So the priest could hate and occasionally slug the pharmacist on the mouth without raising suspicions and thus, everyone was free to hate. Nobody cared, though, whether the showy pharmacist lived or died.

The pharmacist had no friends in Montelieto. His only acquaintance, one he called friend, was the Vice Mayor (Deputy Mayor) of the town. This man also was hated by the citizens for his overbearing cockiness and lack of consideration for the needy *cafoni*. The two detested petty tyrants used to walk side by side, up and down the Church Square, intimately talking of politics and war. At other times, the pharmacist and the Deputy Mayor were joined by another subject who shared the same Party doctrine. He was the postmaster of Montelieto. If the latter was not seen as mean a tyrant as the first two, he was nonetheless hated for befriending the others.

This happy trio, aside from sharing a common bond in the Fascist doctrine, shared another interest that motivated them to socialize. They each owned a specialty of the same grapevines. The pharmacist and the Deputy Mayor, accompanied by the postmaster, were used to strolling about sunset to the outskirts of the town, where the latter owned a vineyard. On their way, to and fro, the threesome engaged in friendly and lengthy conversations concerning the grapevines.

They would each make comments on how to improve the vineyard, the quality of table and wine grapes, and also what incentives better attracted the sharecroppers to increase production. Although their ideas of producing more and getting better quality of grapes had been on their agenda for some time, neither of the three had any knowledge of agricultural techniques. The Deputy Mayor and pharmacist were not close neighbors, but both owned the same kind of grapevine growing from their courtyard upward to the balcony of their apartments.

The pharmacist's grapevine had a remarkable shape and vitality that was the envy of passersby. The grapevine was greatly productive and exceptionally vigorous; it embellished the whole appearance of the balcony in the shape of a very beautiful pergola. Passersby looked at that with great wonder.

But when it came to harvest the grapes, all the nice things said about the grapevines meant very little. The pharmacist and the Deputy Mayor both came from out of town and had been learning, little by little, about the habits of the citizens of Montelieto. Their occupation required good skills for writing and reading, which was an occupation commonly not understood among the people of that town. But of grapevines they knew nothing.

It happened that within the first experiences of their new hobby, the pharmacist and the Deputy Mayor thought they must be living in the wrong town. With the first signs of the grapes turning purple, they began to have nightmares. The problems of the pharmacist became more complicated than those of the Deputy Mayor.

Long before the tyrants had come to live and work in Montelieto the little unruffled *cafoni* had, year after year, figured out that the grapes upon the balcony of those two out of town tyrants, belonged somewhat to them and the owner of the apartments. By the first year when the pharmacist had taken possession of the grapevines, things had begun to change. He wanted to have the grapes all for himself. But the grapevines, although shooting upward from the courtyard, had plenty of roots sucking beneath the Church Square, and that belonged to the public.

Bitter altercations began to erupt between the little *cafoni* scoundrels and the pharmacist. He kept threatening to have them locked up in jail unaware that this was exactly what the little *cafoni* wanted. At least the Deputy Mayor had to assume the responsibility of feeding them once they landed in the city slammer. But the exasperated pharmacist was determined not to be taken by the scoundrel *cafoni* of Montelieto, therefore, he began to get tough. His tactics were to shame the *cafoni* of Montelieto as much as he could. "Stupid donkey drivers," he called them. "Uneducated, dumb breed who like your forefathers are subhumans not worthy to be classified with any rank of civilized society."

The *cafoni* responded that they were all those things because of bureaucrats like him. The pharmacist went so far as to be seen pacing the balcony, with his hunting gun at shoulder. But all the bickering and scary tactics got him nowhere.

The little *cafoni* attacked the grapes when the pharmacist went to work at the pharmacy. By climbing the grapevines, downspouts and gutters, or going from rooftop to rooftop, the little *cafoni* got to the balcony and the grapes. One day, upon his return home from work, when the pharmacist learned that his property had been trespassed yet again, he burst into fits of rage. He became frustrated to the point of seeking help from the Deputy Mayor and the postmaster.

The same evening, as they took their regular stroll, they came up with "the barbed wire idea," which both acquaintances of the pharmacist advised him to put into effect if he cared to keep his sanity and his grapes. The pharmacist acted swiftly. By early morning he hired a fence-installing outfit to perform the barbed wire job. He instructed the workers to wrap up around the vines, down-spouts and balcony whatever amount of barbed wire was needed. At the accomplishment of this task the pharmacist was overjoyed. He felt totally secure. The same evening he bragged to his two acquaintances that not even an ant could have climbed the balcony to get to his grapes, and that the stupid *cafoni* could no longer pose a threat.

Apparently, the new method implemented by the phar-macist, in order to protect his grapes from the little *cafoni*, pleased him very much. In the early part of the evening as he, the Deputy Mayor, and the postmaster returned from their usual stroll, they were seen on the balcony of the pharmacist, inspecting the efficiency of the barbed wires and laughing uproariously. The pharmacist bragged to his acquaintances that Montelieto had not seen yet how deter-mined he could become when enforcing the rules.

But among the three, the postmaster was doubtful of the protection devised by his friend for preserving the grapes. Although he had given his tacit approval, and had contributed to the idea of the barbed wire, he felt that the type of protection implemented by the rude pharmacist, was an exaggeration valid only to bolster his pride.

The postmaster was not quite sure how the barbed wire action would be interpreted by the citizens. They could have been offended, thinking that the barbed wires were an act of war between them and the pharmacist. There were not only the little *cafoni* to worry about, but the bigger ones as well. Things could become ugly at any moment, same as the postmaster had seen years ago when the *ca-foni*, having had enough from Father Ponzio, had ousted him from the church and town while he tried to celebrate the mass.

I cannot imagine the same thing happening with the pharmacist, thought the postmaster. *Ousting the pharmacist is a totally different matter.* A very grave matter! With the ousting of Father Ponzio, to save the *cafoni* from being incarcerated, the Archbishop of Gaeta and the prayers of the Pope helped. *With the eviction of the pharmacist from the House of Fasces, we could be wiped out by the Party legions from Rome,* he thought within himself.

As the postmaster then wished his two acquaintances good night, he descended the stairs of the pharmacist's apartment in a hurry, and quickly crossed the Church Square to get home hoping that the *cafoni* of Montelieto would not hold a grudge even against him.

That same night, fate struck the grapes of the pharmacist. While he dozed on the deck chair upon the balcony of his apartment with the shotgun across his lap, someone was snatching grapes off the pergola above him. And when he felt a bunch of grapes drop on his face, he woke up with a start and, aiming the shotgun at the noise, let go two consecutive shots.

Believing he had hit the perpetrators, at the sound of a loud thump below he said: "How do you like that, stupid clown? You damned thief, I have got you this time!" He retired then to his room, and happily went to sleep.

Chapter 8

Time went by. Another grape season had arrived in Montelieto, and the Fascist tyrant had wasted another year without proving his toughness to the Prefect or to the *cafoni*. On the first anniversary of the raid on his grapes, the thick smoke inside the shop of Don Pompeo could be cut with a knife. Not only the smoke emanating from the cheap brand of tobacco could be cut, but even that which emanated from the heat of the *cafonis'* rage. The word that the pharmacist was reinforcing his apartment with additional barbed wire had spread like wild fire. To add fuel to the fire now came Guglielmo Sparacelli furiously accusing the pharmacist of oppression and abuses to his young son.

Sparacelli entered the shop of Don Pompeo totally enraged. He stood by Don Pompeo's working bench and said: "Listen everybody! Last Saturday, that turnip head of a pharmacist slapped my son Giovannino on the face! Because my kid showed up at the war drills wearing animal hide footwear, that no good son of a bitch took liberty toward Giovannino. He is the worst arrogant tyrant to land in Montelieto ever since Father Ponzio! Did you know what he told me when I complained? He said that if I had a complaint, to place it in the office of the provincial governor of the chief town of Frosinone."

"Bullshit, Sparacé," said Mariano Albarosa, spitting outside after having remembered to open the door only one time out of three spittings. "You should not waste your time placing a complaint to his boss. Chances are that he will tell you to go to place your complaint to Palazzo Venezia in Rome."

"What in hell are you talking about stupid Mariano," said Gerardo Cipollone, the strongman *cafone* from the district of Pozzo dell' Oro. "We should get to him right now and chase that damned tyrant out of town, like we did with the priest, Father Ponzio."

"I disagree," shouted loudly Peluso, who was not able to prevent his rage from exploding against the infamous pharmacist. "I have a better idea," he said. "We should muzzle the leech with the harness of my donkey, and tie him up to the oak tree until he eats the bridles and the bark. I swear he has this treatment coming."

"Wait a minute," finally spoke Don Pompeo saying, "You are not going to do any of those things, understand? Be patient and the day will come when even Fascism cannot protect him and he will feel the same embarrassment as he makes us feel. Stay put, I advise, and act as good citizens as you can be, because only then we will find the ways to protest his abuses. What we must concentrate on, is to help Guglielmo to restrain his rage even if this is against our principles. Although he should have known better than to let his kid go shabby, we still wish to help Guglielmo—even though he had been forewarned not to let his son go to the drills of war in shabby garb. We do this for Giovannino," said Don Pompeo. "Thanks to God I don't have any children of my own," he mumbled in an undertone.

"Hush, hush," whispered Albarosa who was still standing by the door. "It sounds as if someone wearing heavy spiked boots is approaching."

"Can't be him," said Gerardo Cipollone. "He wouldn't dare walk by here at this hour of the night. I think he is too chicken to be digging his own grave."

"Sure," affirmed Cipollone's brother. "But he is inclined to send out his henchmen spying. The sacristan has told me that the faces of new henchmen have been seen walking in company of the pharmacist. Yesterday two henchmen, in grand uniform, were sent to the borders of Montelieto and the railroad, to confiscate the farm products not allowed to be sold outside. They returned leading a donkey loaded with two or three panniers half full of eggs, salami and other foodstuffs. Who do you think gave them authority to confiscate our stuff? Barabba, the sacristan, told me he has heard that the leaders across the land are plotting to confiscate all the excess farm products, in order to fill the government food granaries."

"Food granaries . . . filled with excessive farm products?" laughed the other Cipollone. "They sure need their heads examined. Of excessive products we should not be concerned in the least."

"Right, actually what we have of excessive in farm products is debts and moldy straws. I'll say let them come right ahead and confiscate," challenged Guglielmo Sparacelli.

Meantime while some continued discussing the rumors started from the sacristan, others talked about the activities of the pharmacist and of his new ideas to preserve his grapes.

"The only excessive farm products they might find in abundance here, will be more hate for him," said Camillo Feliciano.

Then from near the parapet of the cistern of Don Pompeo an imitation of a cat was heard. Not only imitation, but really the *meow, meow,* and *spits-spits* of two angry cats.

"What the hell is that?" Cipollone said with curiosity.

"That must be the kid of Gennaro Pennamoscia," replied Albarosa. "Were you not here last year when he told us how he pilfered the grapes of the pharmacist? And the reasons why he did?"

"No," said Cipollone, "but I would like to know all about it."

"Okay," answered Albarosa. "Let's sit down back there so I can explain."

No sooner had these two made themselves comfortable, than Peluso and Feliciano joined them. But when Cipollone told them to butt out both stayed back because, figuring Albarosa was abiding by the rules laid down in the shoemaker shop, he could be telling Cipollone something that he had been left behind.

"Gennarino," Albarosa began to say, "is the younger son of Gennaro Pennamoscia. He lives with his father, out in the country, adjacent to Saint Andrea forest. Once in a while he comes to Montelieto to do errands for his daddy. Lately he has come in town to take part in the drills of war requested by the Party. The pharmacist, though, has refused to let him participate with the other teens his age. That makes Gennarino mad as hell. The pharmacist told him that he was too dirty to join the others. Gennarino's older brother's occupation is charcoal maker, so you can have an idea how soiled both of them might look. All the wood they need for charring, they steal in the nighttime, from the state forest. Not so much Gennarino—but his brother who is strong as an ox, and so mean that the Fascist forest inspectors do not want anything to do with him. Just to give you an example," continued Albarosa, "one time he saved the donkey of his friend and neighbor from sinking in a mud hole. He fetched the donkey out of the hole and carried it to the barn of the friend upon his own shoulders."

"I knew that," said Cipollone. "But was it he who pilfered the grapes of the pharmacist?"

"Well, yes and no."

"What do you mean yes and no?" Cipollone said, losing his patience.

"Yes he did, and no he didn't, but let me tell you what these two brothers are able to do. Gennarino and his brother, Filomeno Pennamoscia, can see in the night better than cats do. Filomeno, whose name derives from that of his mother Filomena, bless her soul, is known as the wildcat of Saint Andrea district. And Gennarino, whose name derives from that of his father, is known as the tomcat. Together they are no more than a couple of fearful baboons. I tell you that if the pharmacist does not come up with a better idea than the one of the shot gun and barbed wire, he will not taste his grapes again."

Cipollone who was by now quite annoyed by the slow poke Albarosa, got up and said: "Damned be Mariano Albarosa! If you do not hurry up I am going to kick your fat butts. You think I have all night to listen to you?"

"Okay, okay," replied Mariano. "I will speed up. Gennarino," he said, "was helped by Filomeno to get on the roof of the building, by climbing the downspouts of the gutter of Don Pompeo. Then he tiptoed to the roof and dragged himself right on the balcony and the grapes. When he heard the pharmacist snoring on the deck chair of the balcony, he began to snap off as many bunches of grapes as he could. He had stuffed the inside of his shirt to become as bulky as a mattress. On the next trip back, after he had deposited the grapes with his brother, Gennarino accidentally dropped a bunch of grapes on the face of the pharmacist," said Albarosa with excitement. "Then the pharmacist jumped up from the chair and, looking up, said: "Scat, scat, scat, go away damned cat!" Gennarino then answered with his perfect *meow, meow, spit, spit, spit,* at which the dumb pharmacist grabbed the shot gun and blasted two consecutive shots at the pergola. With the shots Gennarino meowed as if he were hit—and simultaneously dropped the biggest bunch of grapes into the garden below. At that fake thump the pharmacist believing he had hit something, said with a sense of relief: "Yeah, miserable animal. I have got you this time, wild thief!"

"The pharmacist then returned happily to sleep inside and Gennarino finished by cleaning up all the remaining grapes," Albarosa said with delight.

"Good job, Gennarino boy. That dumbbell of a pharmacist thought cats eat grapes!" Cipollone was laughing amusedly.

"In the morning," continued Albarosa, "the pharmacist almost went crazy. He got hold of the Fascist guards and asked everybody for an explanation, but no one came up with a close finding. He nearly had a heart attack."

"Well," said Cipollone, "I am beginning to believe that if he didn't have a heart attack last year, he could have one this year. I see Gennarino in town and have a strong suspicion that he is waiting for Montelieto to go to sleep, and for his brother, Filomeno, to hit town. By tomorrow who knows—we could see the pharmacist gone insane for real, and the Fascist branch of Montelieto in need of a new leader."

In the midst of all the confusion and thick smoke Don Pompeo kept his cool. With two or three strikes of his hammer on top of the wooden bench, he could have stopped everyone from being noisy, but he enjoyed the topics of the conversations and let everybody speak their mind. Besides he had finished sewing the soles of a pair of shoes, and that was what he planned to do for the evening. Pretty soon he must have closed the shop but was not really in a big hurry. In his mind he had been examining everything that was said and done, and what actions his friends might resort to in the days to come.

Don Pompeo had learned many things this evening. He had learned of the good friendship his peasant friends had for one another, the hate, the threats and accusations toward the pharmacist, and many other things happening in Montelieto. Then more soberly he realized that the solution the pharmacist had adopted, in order to protect his grapes, was not going to be the remedy to the problems he faced in Montelieto.

While on one hand he has attained temporary peace of mind, Don Pompeo thought, *on the other hand he has exacerbated, further, the disputes between him and the young* cafoni. *The animosity toward one another is of bigger dimensions than that which the problems of the grapes might have created. It is just reciprocal hate. Beginning with the grapes the problems have escalated to bigger dimensions each day. Ever since the pharmacist has landed here in Montelieto, he has totally alienated the citizens of this town with his arrogance and dumb pride.*

"Who is the scum of the earth here?" Don Pompeo asked himself. "We are the sons, daughters and grandsons of those who contributed to the greatness of Rome. They were the very first to join the Roman legions on their march southward, and now look around—look around Montelieto! Through no fault of ours, we have become the victims of foolish Caesars, unwise kings and dictators and badly administered government policies. That's what we are," Don Pompeo continued to say. "We are the ones who have no material possession, no education, no schools, no land we can call our own—and that fool of a pharmacist makes us relive every bit of our misfortune at every encounter! I am old and have been waiting my whole life to see the trend take a better turn, and although I believe change will come, there are no indications it will come unless drastic measures are taken first."

At this point, unexpectedly, Luigi Durezza and Cosimo LaBorgia came suddenly barging inside the shoemaker shop. Damiano Grifone was outside, still mounting his jackass. They had been hoeing the olive trees of the priest, Reverend Orazio Palestrina, but were late because after having received their pay, they stopped at Marianna's tavern without going home at all, until all the money was gone.

Grifone dismounted his jackass and, getting up from a hard fall, he staggered into the shoemaker's shop.

"Good, good evening, Don Pompé!" he was able to mumble before he dropped his body upon a pile of scrap. "I look, look and look all day for Luigi and Cosimo but I can't find them."

"Ah, ah!" said Don Pompeo. "These guys have been together until now and can't find each other? This is the right atmosphere for trouble. They obviously are too tipsy to make any sense, so we better call it quits for tonight."

In the meantime, Durezza and LaBorgia had already began to make trouble. LaBorgia had confronted Peluso scolding the guy for having slandered him the previous night, and having made insinuating remarks about he and Pasqualina Pizzuta. Durezza slugged Feliciano for the same reason and a brawl was in the making.

Don Pompeo, who saw troubles coming, acted quickly and with the help of the brothers Cipollone began to throw everybody out of his shop. "Enough is enough," he hollered loudly. Then grabbing first one battler and then the other by the arm he patiently said: "Let's go. Let's go to see your families—and may God help all of you."

Chapter 9

Finally Don Pompeo was left alone in the shop filled with smoke and although his heart seemed to have followed the noisy friends, he began to feel relaxed at last. But with the solitude, excitement set in again. Every time Don Pompeo felt excitement or had inbibed more than a couple glasses of wine he talked to himself at length. His soliloquies lifted him up from solitude and boredom, whether he was in his apartment or working in the shop in absence of his peers.

He was amazing in his soliloquies as he rehearsed the plight of his fellow *cafoni* sharecroppers and the wrongs done to them by the Lords and the Fascist henchmen. Even more amazing was to hear Don Pompeo make pledges of support for the underprivileged and the destitute of Montelieto. That night, same as many others, he happily renewed his commitment to all.

After some time spent in the shop talking alone to himself Don Pompeo went directly upstairs and opened the window which looked down on the Church Square below. He took fast glances outside, up and down the square, and saw that the tobacco shop and the barbershop, too, had closed. If it had been not for a small group of people arguing in the far corner beneath a street lamp, the Church Square would have been entirely empty. Don Pompeo took another look at the people arguing and, without being surprised, recognized that they were the ones he had ousted from his shop just a while ago.

"By golly!" he observed to himself. "It seems that the later it gets the more argumentative those guys become! If they keep on, they could wind up in the slammer. The Fascist guards will not put up with that foolishness much longer."

At that point Don Pompeo rested his elbows on the window-sill and, out of curiosity, turned his attention to the squabble going on at the Church Square. But when he could not overhear the sources of their argumentations clearly, he moved back inside saying: "Whatever they have to settle is not too important. More likely those friends of mine are still hollering and accusing one another to determine who was the horniest fool to have fathered the girls of Pasqualina Pizzuta.

"My good Lord!" Don Pompeo uttered while assuming a more dignified deportment. "Thanks for letting me see the urgency to close up the shop, and for giving me the strength to oust out those guys and come upstairs. But what I have said, Lord, does not mean that I am less fond of my friends. I ousted them from the shop because it was getting late, and also because of their continued arguments on a subject which implicated every one of them. Please, Lord, enlighten them if it is your will. I do understand that to enlighten us *cafoni* from Montelieto, is not possible by the work of human doing. That is the reason our hopes rest on your intervention, most high Supreme Being."

Don Pompeo then walked slowly to the corner of the room where a pulley hung beneath the ceiling. He began to pull the short end of a chain that ran through the pulley down to the floor below, into a cistern inside the shoe shop. As he pulled up the chain, he whistled his favorite tune in the tempo of the strokes given by his hands and arms. All of sudden a crate dripping water appeared on the other end of the chain within reach.

Don Pompeo stopped whistling at that point and, by extending one arm fetched a bottle from the crate. Then he slacked his grip on the chain to let the crate sink down the cistern again. Subsequently he made himself comfortable, and began to take short sips from the bottle without even bothering to reach for a glass.

"Pretty good stuff!" Don Pompeo said savoring the wine with gusto. "A little warm, though," he grumbled. "That cistern down there seems not to cool things like it used to do. I suspect it is getting dry," he said talking to himself. "Oh well," he then said after having taken a third or fourth sip from the bottle. "We will not run the danger of dying from thirst. Our good Lord will see to it that the cisterns of Montelieto are refilled with a bountiful rain."

After having grumbled more in regard to the quality of the wine and the exact temperature his cistern ought to maintain, Don Pompeo got up, grabbed a rag, and began to shoo away some mosquitoes that had been buzzing around him. Then we walked by the window and closed it while still cussing at the mosquitoes that would not go away.

"It's all my fault," he said. "I should have known better than to leave the damned window open for this long! As it looks right now, in this room I will either suffocate from sultriness, or be eaten alive by these blood-sucking mosquitoes. Tonight will surely be a very long night!"

In exasperation Don Pompeo retired to his room and, as he had done on other bad nights, quickly leaped into bed to cover himself beneath the sheets. His head had begun to spin quite a bit and his face felt hot and burning. "Good," he said once he felt safe from the stings of the mosquitoes. "This is the only efficient way to fend off the attack of those damned pests."

Beneath the sheets Don Pompeo thought that if it had not been for the arguing of his rowdy friends, who might possibly be locked up by now, plus the nuisance of the mosquitoes, this could have been a peaceful night. As if it were the work of a magic hand, calmness had begun to descend upon the sleepy town of Montelieto and its equally sleepy people.

Even Don Pompeo's neighbor, Elvira Schiappino, had stopped bickering with her husband. She could have beaten up Arturo for coming home late again or, worse than that, she could have punished him by talking the poor guy into making love to her—but both fell asleep. Not one whisper could be heard from the other two tenants of the same building. The retired Italo-American couple minded their own business, and their neighbor—the pharmacist—must have fallen asleep upon the deck chair above the balcony.

Don Pompeo felt a little tipsy, but he was not a drunkard by any means. He never drank so much that he staggered or made no sense. Yes, he liked wine but only to the limits of feeling in good spirits. This night though, in the privacy of his home, he got carried away and abused the bottle quite a bit more than usual. He did so to put at ease the constant anxieties; for Don Pompeo it didn't take much drinking wine to detest the Fascist leader of the branch of Montelieto. The mere thought of him made his blood boil.

Don Pompeo was a strong believer in the philosophy and wisdom of the Casa Savoia (House of Savoy, the monarchy) but lately, since the arrival of the Fascist leader to Montelieto, he was not so sure anymore. In his half asleep, half awake state, still somewhat agitated for having to eject his beloved friends from his shop, he continued talking to himself.

"Can one imagine what is happening in the world? And most importantly what is happening to our country? What has become of the monarchy my father fought for, and was so proud to be reunited with? Ah! Garibaldi, Garibaldi, our hero! Oh, how much blood your Red Shirts have shed for us! How much short-lived has been your sacrifice and your valor! You gave moribund Italy to the Casa Savoia to be restored to long life, and now Casa Savoia gives it to Il Duce to let her die? Damned," Don Pompeo cussed continuing to address his hero.

"Why, Garibaldi?" he kept saying. "Why must we be the eternal sharecroppers, peasants and *cafoni*? Why must we be the pawns of the Fascist pharmacist? Why? Why Garibaldi? Ah! Tyrant pharmacist," cried Don Pompeo exhausted.

On the opposite of many noisy nights, when Elvira never seemed to stop singing, this should have been an ideal night to rest and recuperate from loss of sleep, but Don Pompeo was too excited to do so. He had been struggling beneath the sheets for quite some time, and just as he reached the point of relaxation, another fixed idea suddenly would pop up in his mind. But his strange state of agitation could not be caused totally by the nuisance of the mosquitoes because Don Pompeo had been battling those bloodsucking insects during summer in Montelieto, for all his life.

Without any doubt the mental agitation that caused his sleeplessness, had started yesterday morning. He had become agitated when he saw all those additional barbed wires being attached to the balcony and on the downspouts of the building where he lived. Add to that the malevolence of his friends' sputterings last night, from one against the other in his shoe shop, and the result was a very nervous Don Pompeo.

Don Pompeo was also worried about the conflict that had started in East Africa. In his half asleep, half awake state of mind, he saw and heard Il Duce pledging that he would bestow upon the king the crown of Emperor. Then all of a sudden he recalled the battle of Aduwa, at the closing of the Ninteenth Century. At the mere thought of this he jumped up from under the cover of the sheets and exclaimed aloud: "My God! *Aduwa?*"

The remembrances of Aduwa had given him ugly nightmares many times during his life, but when he realized that he was still in bed in his own room, he said: "Thanks Lord, thanks for giving me the opportunity to escape!" Don Pompeo had recounted the episode of the battle of Aduwa in his shop time and again, and all had heard what took place in the closing years of the nineteenth century. He was twenty-one when he served in the special corps and was sent to Eritrea to fight.

At the beginning it went good as expected. Don Pompeo was even given the honor of first cobbler of the regiment but, as the war intensified, the young General commander of the expedition army, was unexpectedly drown into a big battle. The Italians, engaged fully by a superior force of Ethiopians, fought but were eventually overrun at the famous battle of Aduwa. Don Pompeo's regiment was totally wiped out, and only a handful of soldiers managed to escape to safety at the port of Asmara.

Now Don Pompeo, only half awake but more soberly, remarked: "Gosh, did we get our asses kicked by the Ethiopians! We were plainly at fault. Our King had no right to send us there to expel those people from their own land, beat them up and tell them how to live. Nonsense," he said now fully awake. "Those people had lived there from the beginning and we should have not intruded in their homes and lives on the pretext that we would liberate them. Liberate them from what?" he added with irritation.

"And now we wish to liberate them again? Ah! Crackbrained kings, crazy leadership," he said sneeringly. "When will you learn that we, here in Montelieto, are the ones in need of liberation?"

Don Pompeo got out of bed, walked to the kitchen, took a drink of water, and while drinking he heard the clock from the church belfry striking. "Darn!" he said. "Only two A.M.? I must get back to bed for a few more hours."

As he entered the room he heard a noise coming from the roof above him.

"What can that be?" he asked himself. "It for sure is not the wind," he said. "Could there be cats on that roof?"

He tried to listen by opening the window a little but couldn't hear a leaf moving. After returning to his room, just a short while later, he heard the same noise again. This time it sounded as if someone was walking on the roof, going back in the same direction he had come from. Every so often the noise was repeated. *Someone was definitely walking, going across the roof at a slow pace!* The noise moved back and forth from above Don Pompeo's roof toward the apartment of the pharmacist. All of a sudden a thought flashed in Don Pompeo's mind.

"Ah! Ah!" he said whispering as if afraid to disturb someone. "Wasn't Mariano Albarosa speaking to Cipollone about what Gennarino Pennamoscia is able to do? Gosh, I should have figured this out last night. That kid has been the object of ridicule and abuse from the pharmacist and his henchmen for too long. There is nothing wrong with the kid. He, same as many in Montelieto, is poor and uneducated but the pharmacist cannot understand that Gennarino is not the one to be blamed. I have a very strong impression that Gennarino feels lots of resentment toward the Fascist pharmacist. I know he will get even some time. And when his older brother hit town like Cipollone was hinting to me last evening, that pea-brain pharmacist can kiss his grapes goodbye!

"In the morning," said Don Pompeo taking cover again beneath the sheets, "we shall find out what's going on over this roof of mine. For the time being let's wish the tomcat and wildcat of Pennamoscias will finish up their job and not be disturbed by anybody."

Once back under the sheets, Don Pompeo was not able to close an eye. He could clearly imagine what the morning would bring but continued debating with himself about what his involvement should be in that situation. "When the pharmacist finds out what I strongly believe will happen," he said while catnapping, "he will surely raise hell in the Church Square. Without any doubt, there will be a war between him and the young *cafoni*. If the theft of the grapes has already occurred, I had better stay away and not have the kids believe I am there rallying them against the pharmacist," said Don Pompeo.

Chapter 10

That sunny beautiful morning turned out to be laden with tension for the citizens of Montelieto—especially for those living nearby the Church Square. Just as Gerardo Cipollone had predicted last night inside the shoe shop of Don Pompeo, when he said that the pharmacist could go crazy by sunrise, it was happening for real.

When the pharmacist got up he walked to the window where he usually went to stretch his arms and legs, but looking outside on the terrace of the balcony he saw something that made him suspicious. On the terrace several leaves and small shoots from the vine of his pergola, were strewn around. Tormented by mistrust toward the *cafoni* of Montelieto and still wearing his pajamas, the pharmacist opened the balcony and lo and behold, saw his pergola being systematically stripped of grapes, bunch by bunch.

At this sign that he had been cheated of his grapes by the *cafoni* kids, the pharmacist broke into a hasty craziness. He walked back and forth with both hands holding the sides of his head, and moaning desperately: "My grapes! My grapes! They have stolen my grapes again! I'll lock them up. I'll shoot them. I'll kill all those bastard *cafoni*!"

When the townspeople heard the pharmacist rave, they began gathering in the Church Square. First came Caterina Panzona and her daughter Assuntina, both tavern keepers. Then came Arturo Schiappino the blacksmith, followed by Barabba the sacristan. After those two came the town crier, Vittorio Settimo, the casket maker Romualdo, and Carlotta Gioconda the cleaning lady. Then all together arrived Donato Rotunno, one of the ragmen, Elvira the blacksmith's wife and Davide Persichella, the knife sharpener, with a flock of little barefoot *cafoni* pulling his working bench on wheels. When Elvira discovered her husband Arturo talking intimately with Caterina Panzona in a solitary corner of the Church Square, she burst into a fury. She began to call Caterina names and vice-versa—until both women started to pull each other's hair.

"You are a whore!" Elvira was shouting to Caterina.

"You are a whore, fat and a bitch!" shouted Caterina in return.

But then Elvira fell and Caterina landed on top of her. Elvira, who was twice the size of Caterina, wrestled her rival under and yelled: "You skinny bitch, if you don't stop that love affair with my husband, I am going to crush you into crumbs! And you, horned beast," she said yelling at her husband, "I shall teach you a good lesson tonight."

While the two women kept pulling hair and shoving each other around, Assuntina joined the melee on the side of her mother. Marianna Pipanera, who was Caterina's bitter business rival, joined in the fray, too, taking sides with Elvira. Soon a genuine free-for-all developed.

Vittorio Settimo, the town crier, seeing that the Church Square was filling with passersby, walked to the corner of Via Arella and availing of the opportunity to deliver his early morning announcement, began to yell in his sing-song style. "Citizens of Montelieto! This morning . . . Rodolfo the merchant . . . from the seaport of Gaeta . . . has arrived . . . with two barrels . . . of fresh herrings . . . some herrings . . . are still alive." Vittorio took a breath of air then continued to finish up the first announcement. He said: "If anyone . . . wishes to eat . . . fresh herrings . . . must go quickly . . . to open space of Via Napoli, and Saint Niccoló . . . where Rodolfo . . . is waiting . . . for you . . . with the herrings."

Almost nobody heard Vittorio singing his announcement, for his yelling became muffled from the noises of the uproar. And while he went on to further sing-song political announcements, three riders on donkey back emerged from behind the church, to come trotting down the Church Square. Luigi Durezza, Damiano Grifone with Cosimo LaBorgia advanced through the square holding with one hand the farm tools upon their shoulders, and with the other hand the rope of the halter of the donkeys. The first held a rake balanced on his shoulder, the second held a long-handled hoe and Cosimo LaBorgia held a pitchfork carried in the same manner. The three had started to go to finish up hoeing the olive orchard of Reverend Palestrina, but upon hearing that the pharmacist was going insane, they rode by to investigate. As the three joined the commotion, still holding their farm implements at shoulder, they created a scene of pre-battle formation.

The pharmacist was nowhere in sight. He had locked himself in the house and nobody could imagine what was the matter until a little *cafoni* pointed to the pergola. The last to appear on the scene were Mariano Albarosa and

Gerardo Cipollone. Mariano was headed to Peluso's barn to take his she-ass at stud with Peluso's donkey, but when the she-ass sensed other male donkeys nearby, she got loose and trotted braying for the Church Square to join LaBorgia's donkey. Gerardo, wishing to have his donkey's shoe replaced by the blacksmith Arturo, found the shop closed and rode into town to do other errands.

Inside the balcony stood a nervous pharmacist. He peeped through the window of the balcony by lifting the bottom corner of the drapes, and as the crowd increased in number, he gave long sighs as he imagined the worst. "These *cafoni* are a bunch of fools," he whispered to himself for fear of being heard. "This is a rebellion against the State that must be squelched. But who is going to do that? Not me, that's for sure," he said. Then he peeped out again, and seeing three people riding the donkeys still holding the long sticks of their farm equipment, the pharmacist uttered: "Damned *cafoni*, even the cavalry? It begins to shape up like the Battle of Waterloo, but I must admit that I am not as bold as the Duke of Wellington."

Before the pharmacist got himself dressed he went downstairs and by way of the back door, he sneaked out to cross the alley in order to get inside the post office. As he tiptoed to the post office, he was spotted by Don Pompeo who just then happened to open up the window for the first time since last night.

"Look there," said Don Pompeo. "Where in hell is that fool going half naked? I do not see anyone chasing after him and he is already scared to death. Well, all I can say is: He must be plotting some tricks with that other screwball of a postmaster."

Don Pompeo went down to the shop, opened the door and looked at the crowd. He knew exactly what was going on but figured that nothing drastic was going to happen. *These friends of mine are just curious. They are capable of resorting to ugly actions, but not this time.* Then thinking about the deadly raids the Party guards were authorized to enforce, said: "God forbid! That's what makes me worried. Regarding the pharmacist? Damned," cussed Don Pompeo. "What perverted and misapplied authority! The Prefect would have seen better results if he had given Cicco Palla that much power. No way, not Cicco Palla," he said. "Poor Cicco would tremble at the sight of two mice fighting. What I mean," said Don Pompeo correcting himself, "is that much authority should have been used and put to work by the boldest *cafoni*. *Cafoni* like the brothers Pennamoscias, the Cipollonis, even of the Pelusos or Elvira Schiappino, if the Prefect wished to enforce his rules on the citizens of Montelieto. Those four are the most strong-willed creatures molded by nature, the most fit to lead and most courageous, not the types of Cicco Palla and the Fascist pharmacist."

Then Don Pompeo closed the door and took a fast look at the list of things he must do. There was nothing that couldn't wait. He was not in the habit of beginning work early, except for emergencies. But since he was downstairs, he thought to spend some time reorganizing. Besides, the little *cafone* kid was about to come over and clean the floor. So, by staying he could have spared the trouble to come downstairs again.

While Don Pompeo worked, he reminisced about the sad situation that Montelieto and its people had to endure through the years. It seemed that every time a feeble ray of hope appeared on the horizon of Montelieto, a cloud of uncertainty would cover the sky again.

"And now even the arrogance of the pharmacist we must endure," he said. "We, in this forgotten town of ours, are always reminded of our inefficiencies and of our lack of skill and grace, but no one ever cares to do anything about it. If someone keeps reminding a sick person of how sick he or she looks and acts, can we call that good therapy? We, and Montelieto, are the sick—the most sick economically, the most sick educationally and the moribund morally," Don Pompeo said talking to himself. "You who claim to be educated, to have authority and smartness, don't waste your time reminding us that we are poor shoemakers and *cafoni* sharecroppers, for we have been aware of that fact since birth."

The little *cafone* kid, Federico, knocked at the door and called: "Don Pompé! Don Pompé! Will you open up?"

"Wait a minute," answered Don Pompeo. "Do not be so impatient."

"Don Pompé," said the kid, entering, "I hope you don't blame us for having created that disorder in the Church Square. The pharmacist has blamed us young *cafoni* but we didn't have anything to do with his grapes. There are so many barbed wires attached around his apartment that, even if we wanted to steal his grapes, we couldn't climb over the balcony."

"Okay, okay," said Don Pompeo. "You just tell me the truth and I'll believe you."

"Sure, I will," said the little *cafoni*. "Don Pompé, honest, we didn't steal the grapes of the pharmacist. Giustino, Niccoló and me, we tried, but were not able to. Look how many bruises I have on my legs. You ought to see Giustino and Niccoló, they got wounds all over their body."

"I believe you," said Don Pompeo. "Now if you wish not to broom the floor because you suffered so many bruises, that's okay with me. I still will pay you the two cents, maybe three, just for being honest with me."

"I am fine," said the kid. "Please let me do my job."

While the little *cafone* cleaned the floor he kept talking to Don Pompeo informing him on everything that had taken place outside. He told Don Pompeo that the grapes of the pharmacist were totally gone, and that Elvira Schiappino had put three or four women out of action. Federico said that everybody was shoving everybody around, blaming each other's son, but that none of the kids had any part in that. Elvira almost killed Caterina and Marianna Pipanera, but the latter was fighting on her side. "I think Elvira beat them up because they pick her husband's pockets or something. She said they gyp Arturo out of everything he owns."

"Well, well," said Don Pompeo. "Whatever those madams gyp out Arturo of is not our business. We will just pray that nobody gets hurt, understand?"

Shortly, as the disorder in the Church Square began to break down, several adults were seen leaving, each resuming their customary errand. Only the young *cafoni* stayed behind, roaming the square. Meantime the pharmacist, who had taken refuge inside the post office, unaware that the disorder had been subsiding, urged his friend the postmaster to wire a telegram to the Prefect of the chief town of Frosinone. He wanted to inform his superior of the dangers forthcoming with the rebellion going on in Montelieto. The telegram read:

Excellency . . . rebellion at the House of Fasces of Montelieto . . . dispatch reinforcement with urgency . . . two squads
of militia *manganello* (with clubs) desirable . . . stop.
                    Evviva Il Duce! (Hail to the Chief!)
                    Fascist branch of Montelieto.

When the Prefect received the telegram his first impulse was to disregard the pharmacist's request, but then
he felt an obligation to respond, just in case what he read
was true. The Prefect had been aware that the pharmacist
could blow out of proportion, any situation that required
little diplomacy, since that was exactly the reason why the
pharmacist had been assigned to the Fascist branch of
Montelieto. The Prefect felt that by assigning him to the
forgotten town, the pharmacist could no longer be of embarrassment to the Party. (The understanding of the high
leadership in Frosinone was: "Who would pay any attention to the boastful character in Montelieto?")

But whatever way the Prefect put it, he felt the responsibility for his subordinate officers' everyday involvement
with the masses. So, still skeptical of the rabble rioting in
Montelieto, he gave an order to the Commander of the Fascist militia to wire back an answer. The pharmacist read
it, while quivering:

"Attention   leadership   Montelieto . . . request   granted
. . . two squads militia manganello . . . dispatched on trucks
. . . with expediency . . . stop.
                    Evviva Il Duce!
                    Commander militia, Provincial Headquarters."

When the pharmacist heard the postmaster unscram-
ble those words, he felt energized. He rushed back to his
apartment doing the Passo Romano (a military goose-step)

and still wearing slippers and pajamas. On his way upstairs, he was jubilant. He repeated to himself: "Finally!
Finally! I will have the satisfaction of placing all those
sons-of-bitches of *cafoni* under arrest! I swear to send them
to scrub the stairs of every House of Fasces in the province
of Frosinone, until they then are clean enough to want to
eat upon!"

He then looked outside and discovered that many older
cafoni had departed. Gone were even the three cavalry subjects. But this didn't matter to the pharmacist so long as
the young *cafoni* remained. With the latter he had maintained the painful grudge. "Forget about those old goats,"
he said. "They were schooled in nothingness by the past
generation. Then they all became ignorant and seasoned
cafoni, more difficult to be taught a lesson in obedience
and Fascism."

The lunatic pharmacist, Fascist Chief of Montelieto,
had sworn to his superiors that upon arrival to the new
assignment, he would aggressively begin to discipline the
young *cafoni* of that town, teaching them tough lessons in
civility, obedience and Fascism. Sure, the Party leadership
would not hold him back. They felt those three prerequi-
sites to be essential items for the future aggrandizement
of the country and of its Party.

But the youths of Montelieto were far from answering
those requests. They were far from giving impetus to any
movement, nor were they proud of their country, especially
if they were led to join the cause headed by a jerk of a
leader. The young *cafoni* felt that the ideals of the pharmacist were crazy and misleading. No *cafone* could be expected
to follow in the footsteps of a leader at the strokes of the
whip. The youngsters of Montelieto were not acting uncivil

through any faults of their own. They had been emotionally thwarted for too long by archaic laws, perpetual neglect and from the predations of greedy bureaucrats. They needed work, education and honest leadership.

"The lack of scholastic privileges is not life threatening, but without doubts it dwarfs the will and spirit of the youth for undertaking noteworthy initiatives," Don Pompeo had said often. And to the pharmacist he had once cursed so: "Your arrogance and misapplied authority, one of these days will turn fatal to you, to your superiors and to everybody else involved!"

The pharmacist scoffed at Don Pompeo, and began to address him "senile old shoemaker."

In Montelieto it rarely happened, but every time a heavy truck took the uphill road to get on the Church Square, the glass of the windows rattled quite hard. For many houses, this was not a problem because sections of the window glass had either been replaced with cardboard or pieces of stockade of cane or of bamboo.

When the pharmacist heard the glass of the balcony begin to rattle, he stuck his ears out to determine where the trucks were coming from. He heard the loud rumbling of the trucks and smiled, then he closed the window and sighed with great relief. If the provincial commander had really dispatched the two trucks with the militiamen, as he had promised to do with his telegram, the exasperated pharmacist could have started feeling vindicated.

"I must get ready to go meet with my colleagues," he said happily as he began to put on his grand uniform. What he didn't know was that the *cafoni* had heard the rumbling of the trucks too. At the first sign trucks were coming, a troop of *cafoni* ran quickly through shortcuts to meet the trucks at the curve of the steepest uphill. From there they were hoping to hitch a ride back to the Church Square and have fun.

As the trucks came almost to a standstill at the curve, the young *cafoni* lined up and gave the Fascist salute; then they ran to hang on to whatever part of the rear gates or sides of the trucks that was convenient.

"Let them be!" ordered an officer as the militiamen attempted to push back the young *cafoni*. "By listening to the leader of this branch of Montelieto, these youngsters could very well be the provokers of the rebellion. Let's give all of them the ride back; before they get out of sight we can arrest them."

About a dozen or more of young *cafoni* rode with the militiamen cheeringly on the trucks arriving at the Church Square. As they descended, the young *cafoni* buzzed around the trucks admiring the tires, lights, or climbing to take a peep into the cabin. At this very moment the pharmacist appeared on the scene coming down the Church Square doing his impressive walk of Passo Romano. From a short distance he stopped and shouted: "Evviva Il Duce!"

"Evviva Il Duce!" replied the Captain of the militia with a tone of greater authority. "And may I ask you, Lieutenant, where is the rebellion taking place?"

"Well," uttered the pharmacist looking around at the nearly deserted Church Square, "the provokers of the rebellion are those punks who are looking at the tires of our trucks. If we are not careful they are liable to steal them!"

"Steal them?" said the Captain, unimpressed. "And what do you think they will attach the tires to, the hoofs of their donkeys? In any case," said the Captain, turning to his sergeant major, "arrest them all."

The young *cafoni* were at once put under arrest. They were grouped in a military arrangement of three abreast, and led quickly to the meeting room of the House of Fasces for further interrogation.

"Who is the oldest, and the leader, among you?" asked the Captain looking at the young *cafoni*, some of whom were wearing the footwear of animal hides. Others were barefoot.

"It is me, the oldest, my Duce (my supreme leader)," answered a very thin boy.

"Eh, kid," adverted the Captain. "Don't be so quick. I am not your Duce. I am only a Captain for now. Tell me, what is your name young fellow?"

"My name is Federico Favetta, Signor Capitano, but everybody calls me 'Favetta,' (small horse bean). The pharmacist calls me *cafone*. I am the only one employed. I broom the shoe shop of Don Pompeo Gazzaladra, every morning for only two or four cents. When Don Pompeo doesn't have money, I still broom the shop and don't expect anything."

"Very nice of you," said the Captain, forced to interrupt as the kid seemed not to want to stop talking. "Now if you can speak for all your friends, I must ask you some important questions."

"*Ma si che va bene con noi, Signor Capitano.* (But sure it is okay with us, Captain sir.) *Allora incomincia a sparare* (Now start to shoot questions)," replied Federico.

Look at that brazen face, the pharmacist thought as he took a glance at Federico and then at the closed holster of the Captain's pistol. *Stupid feather-brain of cafone, if I were*

*the Captain I wouldn't hesitate one second before letting
you feel the barrel of that gun on your throat.*

"Very good," said the Captain to Federico. "I want to
know exactly what happened this morning. You must tell
the truth, because if you are found lying, all of you will be
severely punished. Favetta, did you and your friends really
ignite the rebellion in the Church Square?"

"No, Signor Capitano."

"Remember, Favetta, I want the truth," said the Captain, sternly.

"Okay, Captain sir, we did not start any trouble at
all, honest!"

"So, who started the rebellion then?"

"Him," said Favetta, pointing to the pharmacist.

The Captain looked abruptly toward the pharmacist
and saw him quickly assuming a position of attention without uttering a word. Then he turned to Federico and asked
with severity: "I must know everything from you, immediately, because we have other commitments on our agenda
to be solved. I want you to be honest, quick and specific."

"Captain," Federico started hastily, "I was sleeping in
the barn, with the donkey of my father, when I heard noises
coming from the corner of the Church Square where the
pharmacist lives. I ran quickly and when I found out where
the noise was coming from, he seemed to have gone crazy.
He walked back and forth upon his balcony with both
hands holding his head. Then I knew he was crazy. All of
a sudden Elvira Schiappino came down but when she saw
Arturo talking very close to Caterina Panzona, she began
to scream like this: 'Whore and swine, you are the biggest
bitch of Montelieto.' When Marianna Pipanera arrived
with Assuntina, all of them began to fight. Elvira's breast

fell out of her shirt and she screamed at everyone because those women had slept with her husband. She said they cheated him of all the money he makes shoeing the donkeys of Montelieto. Then Durezza, Grifone and LaBorgia came riding their donkeys. After, the she-ass of Albarosa that was in heat, came trotting and braying until she made friends with LaBorgia's donkey. And Gerardo Cipollone was shaking his head on top of his donkey. But when he saw all the barbed wires on the balcony of the pharmacist he said: 'Damned, it is unbelievable! You tell me that even with all those barbed wires they plucked away clean the pergola of the pharmacist?' "

"Wait a minute," said the Captain, interrupting. "Federico, you mean to tell me that the pharmacist has barricaded his apartment with barbed wires? What was the reason? I want to know the exact motive."

"Signor Capitano, the pharmacist has fortified his apartment, balcony, gutters and downspouts because he is afraid we will steal the grapes from his pergola over the balcony. Until last year we had stolen some, when we were hungry, but this year he has wrapped all that barbed wire every place and we can't climb to the balcony any more. We have tried but couldn't, and he always has fits of anger and calls us stupid *cafoni*. Honest, Captain, if you don't believe me, ask Giustino and Niccoló. That's why we hate the pharmacist."

"I do, I do believe you," said the Captain. Then turning to the pharmacist said: "Lieutenant! Wait for me in your office, I have something to tell you."

Before the Captain went to see the pharmacist he asked the group of *cafoni* to stand up and listen. He said that if they truly believed Federico had spoken the truth, the young fellow deserved a nice round of applause. The young *cafoni*, within hearing distance of the pharmacist, did exactly so. They, with the participation of the Captain, stood up and applauded shouting loudly, "Favetta! Favetta! Favetta! Hail to Favetta!"

When the Captain entered the office of the pharmacist he saw a man bent on vindictiveness. He was livid with rage! The poor embarrassed pharmacist had plenty of reasons to feel angry. After all, he had tried to have his enemies arrested, and now he had seen the about-face of the Captain even to the extent of applauding them. This was more than he could bear. Humiliated in the town of the *cafoni*? Oh no. He would rather die instead.

But at any rate, the Captain of the militiamen from the chief town was not a fool, but instead he was the epitome of common sense and Fascism. Those traits he had shown by sparing the pharmacist from being humiliated directly in front of the *cafoni*. When he approached the pharmacist again, the Captain said: "You, my dear Lieutenant, act always in haste. For this time I will not report your foolishness to the provincial commander—but from now on, I advise you to think more with your head than with your stomach. Be an asset to our cause, not a detriment. Know that these youngsters are the very ones who will make our motherland great. They will be the future Fascists who will destroy the arrogant democracies, understand? And by the way, your grapes could have been despoiled by wildcats or raccoons with other wild nocturnal animals, isn't that so? Furthermore, we must always set a good example if we wish to be followed by the masses. See it?

"Now, for punishment you will receive no commendations from me whatsoever. Still I will be fair to you. I will not report negative details of your conduct to our Prefect nor will I give him ideas for your demotion. I think he has already punished you enough—that is, by assigning you to take command of this branch of Montelieto."

At this point the Captain, with a grave look on his face, made the pharmacist repeat three times: "Long live our Duce," and energetically exited the office leaving him in attention position. The Captain then entered the meeting room where he had left the young *cafoni* with the sergeant major, and called on Federico Favetta saying: "Federico! I am very proud of you and your friends. My good wish for all is that you remain strong and honest as you were today, that you become responsible for your actions, and that you be courageous and brave because very soon our motherland will be calling on you."

The Captain then saluted them with the most rigid Fascist salute simultaneously shouting: "Evviva Il Duce!" At that the young *cafoni* shouted back: "Evviva Il Duce! Evviva our Captain! Evviva the *cafoni* of Montelieto!"

To the sergeant major the Captain said: "Ready the militia to depart!" Then he rushed downstairs, and left amid the happy cheers of the young *cafoni* who chased after the trucks down the outskirts of Montelieto.

Chapter 11

The noisy commotion in the Church Square of Montelieto had occurred by strange coincidences. From early on in the morning, the day had been filled with outbursts of anger and confrontations, accusations and reproaches all caused because of the Fascist pharmacist. When people met in the town, going back and forth on their errands, they found in common the same subject to gossip about—that is—the pharmacist, the theft of his grapes and the national militia.

But nobody could determine firsthand, when and how the theft had occurred, and why the national militia had been called to intervene for a matter of such a minor importance.

There had been less fuss raised in Montelieto on other occasions when incidents of major seriousness had occurred. No significant show of strength, on the part of the state police, was made when the parish pastor was ousted out from the church and sent back to his archbishopric. And much less ado was seen when an emigrant of Montelieto came back home unannounced, from the United States of America, and in only one night had done away with five people. Some of the victims were either those who had cuckolded him, or were conspirators who had paved the way for the love affairs his wife had been indulging in.

No comparisons or parallels could be drawn between the three incidents, but the pharmacist feared that the rebellion for ousting the parish pastor had close similarities to the incident of the grapes. He had formulated in his mind a very wrong impression about the *cafoni*. He believed the *cafoni* of Montelieto could have expelled him from the town if he had not been quick in asking his superiors for reinforcement. For the whole day and evening the pharmacist was not to be seen anywhere. He remained in complete isolation in his apartment for days and weeks to come.

In the same building the old cobbler, Don Pompeo Gazzaladra also spent the day in idleness. He peeped out once in a while, but had no worries that something of major gravity could have resulted from the early morning hubbub. Those kinds of uproars had happened quite frequently, and were mostly triggered by the same nonsense.

Caterina Panzona, with Elvira Schiappino and Marianna Pipanera, had perpetuated their feud ever since anybody could remember. They would start a love-making affair with each other's boyfriend or husband, on the spur of moment, and then accuse one another of being promiscuous whores. And as for what concerned the three look-alike lancers of cavalrymen impersonated by Durezza, Grifone and LaBorgia, that came as no surprise to the people of Montelieto. They had started going to hoe Reverend Palestrina's olive orchard, but were stopped by the commotion and thought to be revolutionaries from the cucumber head of the pharmacist. Those things were all regular occurrences same as the sun rising every day. Hardly a day went by, in that old town, that farmers carrying farm equipment on their shoulders didn't parade across the Church Square, or the braying donkeys were not running across from everywhere with their owners chasing after them.

By mid-afternoon things had quieted down in the Church Square. People went as usual, doing their errands without blaming the youngsters for the tumult that had. occurred in the morning. Meantime Barabba, the sacristan, called on Don Pompeo to ask whether he would enjoy strolling outside the old defensive walls of town, just to look at the valley and enjoy the late afternoon breeze.

"Why not?" Don Pompeo promptly said. "I have not much to do anyway. I will open up the shoe shop later in the evening."

The two friends walked along slowly while chatting until they reached the boulder on the outskirts of town where they were accustomed to rest. They continued the conversation concerning a variety of subjects, but mostly touching upon their difficulties and those of their fellow-countrymen at making a living. While they enjoyed the late afternoon breeze, they looked at the valley below and tried to recognize and identify the respective sharecroppers working the fields of their Lords.

"That must be Albarosa," said Don Pompeo doubtfully.

"And those people over there must be the Pelusos," said Barabba. "They work like horses but never are able to keep their heads above water, that is—they never seem to get out of debt."

"I understand," said Don Pompeo. "They will get out of debt when they end splitting up fifty-fifty with their Lords. As it looks now, the only thing they do not split with their Lords is the sweat. Eh! Eh! Look over there," pointed out Don Pompeo. "Someone is riding into town."

"I see," answered Barabba. "That must be Reverend Palestrina riding his mule. He bought the mule for one of his most influential sharecroppers and uses it at his own disposition. This morning I saw Sardone, the sharecropper, attach the baskets to the saddle of the mule and Reverend Palestrina mounting on. He told me that the hoeing trio had promised him to wrap up the job at his olive orchard, and that he wished to check on what they were up to. I know he always brings wine with goodies to eat, to celebrate when the job has been performed properly. He cannot get to the orchard on his Topolino, you know? The pathway to it is not made for cars."

"I know, I know all that. Now, why do you think those three thick-brained dolts jump at the opportunity to hoe Reverend Palestrina's orchard?" Don Pompeo asked.

"The reason they jump at the opportunity, is that Durezza, Grifone and LaBorgia are treated well," answered Barabba. "Reverend Palestrina drinks and tells jokes with them, and when they get a little high on the spirits, they all start to swear together. Then Reverend Palestrina asks them to kneel and to confess right beneath the olive trees. He has forbidden them to call him 'Father.' One time I heard Reverend Palestrina say to them: 'You sons of bitches, do not ever call me Father. I am not your Father. By now I should know so darned well who my children are!' The Reverend challenges them to contests of strength and ability to hoe the hardest, and he stays until he feels entertained, then he rides back to town. I wish I knew how to hoe because those opportunities to eat white bread, salami and cheese, and then get high on good wine, would not be so bad. Damned," said Barabba. "All I am is a poor sacristan, barely capable to work with candles around the altar."

"Sure, I see," said Don Pompeo. "But if you knew how to hoe, then you could be subjected to confess to Reverend Palestrina."

"Yes, it happened once. Not anymore though! We had a long misunderstanding that time. Although this was not the case with me he usually tells confessants that, for penitence of their sins, they should spend a couple of hours in the tavern of Marianna Pipanera or Caterina Panzona, and bring them to bed. This is exactly what happened last year to Durezza, Grifone and LaBorgia at Easter. They were sent to the same tavern to do penitence, but they found three or four hotheads from the country district of Cavatelle. The latter, too, were given penitence, after a couple hours of which, bottles, glasses, and chairs started to fly out of the window. I believe the cost of the damage, caused by the penitents, was covered and settled by Reverend Palestrina. Mine is a total different story. He and I had to dispose of the portable confessional we had been using because we couldn't hear each other from inside that."

"You threw away the portable confessional, into the scrap pile?" Don Pompeo said with surprise.

"Yeah!" Barabba replied. "But there is more to it than I can say. I will tell you all some other time."

"Father Palestrina, Reverend Palestrina, Monsignor Palestrina—he has so many titles. Ah! Palestrina, Palestrina!" Don Pompeo uttered with a tone of incredulity. "The Communist priest! Oh pardon, Barabba—I should have said: The Communist, Capitalist, Atheist, and Humanitarian priest. How can he be a Communist when he owns so much?" marveled Don Pompeo. "A true Communist should turn all his/her assets over to the State. I think that would hurt the pocket quite a bit. We," said Don Pompeo, "me, you and the remainder of the *cafoni* of Montelieto, could turn all our assets over to the State and still lose nothing. But to become a communist? I am not so eager."

"I agree," said Barabba. "But Reverend Palestrina is still a generous priest. He has never turned away one little beggar or *cafone* who knocks at his door to ask for alms."

"Absolutely," observed Don Pompeo. "He is a very good-hearted priest. A quality many rich of that kind do not have. Extravagant priest? Well, we pardon him. It could be worse, you know? We could be dealing with a rich tyrant."

"Not so loud, Don Pompé," advised Barabba. "He is almost within hearing range. He could suspect that we are talking about him."

"Oh, don't worry," said Don Pompeo. "He will not fire you. If he does, you still have Father Alfonso to work with."

"Yes, but . . . "

Barabba did not finish the sentence, as Reverend Palestrina arrived on the scene all of a sudden.

"Good afternoon, loafers," said Reverend Palestrina from a short distance, cutting Barabba cold with the "but" on his tongue. "The Fascist militia must have chased you guys out of town. I do not blame them one bit for thinking of you two revolutionaries."

"Good afternoon to you too," responded the two in unison and Don Pompeo adding quickly: "We might be revolutionaries alright, but never Communists, Reverend."

"Never Communists, uh?" Reverend Palestrina reproved. "You have become quite cockish since your monarchists have entered into marriage with the Fascists! With all respect to the House of Savoia, how many times must we tell you, the day the Fascists will finish up screwing the monarchists, we'll even have you join our files? My dear cobbler you ought to know this marriage cannot produce anything else than Communist humanitarians."

"Yeah," replied Don Pompeo. "That would make you very happy, wouldn't it, Reverend? You know that yes, humanitarians do exist, but for sure they are not bred by Fascists or Communists. Most likely they are bred by monarchists."

Reverend Palestrina who never took those kinds of jabs seriously, came near and dismounting his mule asked: "Do you mind if I sit on the boulder with you guys?"

"Not at all," replied Don Pompeo. "But only if you sit on the far side, near your deputy, Barabba. I do not care to stay near when you start throwing punches madly."

The Reverend had been informed by the hoeing trio on what had taken place in the Church Square at sunrise and had figured to rub it in a little to his two political rivals.

Barabba remained completely silent but moved closer to Don Pompeo letting Reverend Palestrina accommodate. The sacristan was a pillar of strength in his belief, and could never be swayed an inch by the political rhetoric of others because, as the exact opposite of the priest, he was a very devoted Christian.

Don Pompeo, on the other hand, was slightly confused in regard to politics. He had been a deep-rooted monarchist since birth, but when the King of the House of Savoia allowed a totalitarian figure to come to power, Don Pompeo began to have some reservations. Don Pompeo referred to the King as "that half pint," because the King had lowered the height of prospective inductees to his own. "And that is not quite enough," maintained Don Pompeo. "What in hell does he want to accomplish, create an army of Cicco Palla size?"

As Reverend Palestrina made himself comfortable on the boulder near Barabba, Don Pompeo asked: "How is the hoeing of your olive orchard progressing, Reverend? Are those guys going to wrap it up by evening?"

"I think it is coming along great. My trusted hired hands have promised they will close the job after sundown. I do not doubt them one bit because they have also sworn to finish up the flasks of wine after closing. But just in case, for your information, my dear Don Pompeo, I will go to check on the work tomorrow."

The sun was sinking deeper behind the mountains when Sardone came to get the mule. Barabba who didn't have a chance to put a word in the conversation, thought to walk back to ring the bell announcing the time for the novena. Sardone received the okay to drive his mule in the stable and the priest, with Don Pompeo, were left by themselves. Then Reverend Palestrina turned to Don Pompeo and asked: "I have heard that this morning your neighbor, the pharmacist, was seen to have gone almost crazy. Is it true? Also I have heard that you didn't dare show your face on the outside of your niche of the apartment. Were you afraid to be arrested, or something? You should have let me beat the nonsense out of the pharmacist's head last year, when he put down the *cafoni* in public, remember? You allied with the pharmacist! If you hadn't intervened, by now we wouldn't have so many problems."

"Alright, alright," said Don Pompeo annoyed. "You really wish me to answer all of your questions?"

"Sure I want you to answer—if you have an answer."

"Fine," said Don Pompeo. "Your political foe has not gone insane at all. He was insane the day he accepted the offer to lead the Fascist branch of Montelieto. Me not showing my face on the outside during the uproar was to spare our townspeople from further embarrassment. The militiamen might have figured I was there to rally the crowd and they could have made arrests for uprising. I was not afraid of anything else. I intervened between you two opposite Party hardliners, because you—your family name to be exact—is the only honorable asset remaining to Montelieto. In this town of donkeys and *cafoni*, we have at least one educated citizen who sides with the poor . . . but . . . "

"Goodness gracious!" Reverend Palestrina exclaimed, interrupting. "Don Pompeo, I must admit you have flattered me with those compliments!"

"Yeah, but you are never around when we need you. You are either at the orchard, taking a nap, or in and out of town chasing after someone. This should un-flatter you, I think, Reverend."

"It surely does," said Reverend Palestrina raising his voice. "The orchard thing and naps I don't mind, but the chasing after someone out of town and especially in town I resent. Those are rumors spread by the fanatic Christians, just because I am not a believer and, most of all because they are a bunch of fools."

"Reverend," Don Pompeo said firmly. "There might not be good Christians in Montelieto, but there are no fools, none. There are only peasants, sharecroppers, and *cafoni*, but no fools. And you do not have to confess anything to me. I am only a poor shoemaker, not an Archbishop. I want you to know I have been a loyal friend of your family for many years, and would be honored if that friendship continued uninterrupted with you."

"But sure you are a friend and one of the most trusted by my parents with my uncle Napoleone. That same respect, undoubtedly, will continue mutual. Then, insofar as the chasing in town is concerned, I must say that Valentina the seamstress, does come to visit occasionally, but only for the purpose of having me try on a couple of shirts which I order as the need arises, that's all."

"Couple of shirts, uh?" Don Pompeo said calmly. "I understand that, Reverend. One shirt of pink fabric's name is 'Isabella,' and the other of blue flannel is named 'Gianpaolo.' "

"Damned!" Reverend Palestrina swore aloud. "You mean to tell me that all this gossip goes around in Montelieto? How in hell could they know? Must be that frog-legged Dorotea, my housekeeper, who had spread such a rumor. I shall fire her ass immediately when I get back home."

"Cool down, cool down, Reverend. You must not do such a thing. Your hastiness will certainly make it worse," said Don Pompeo, soberly. "We must be careful not to extinguish a hot fire with a hotter fire. Aren't you aware that the *cafoni* of this town, whether they are your sharecroppers or not, all love and respect you? At this point in time it is not Dorotea who is your stumbling block. What gives you so little clout is your farfetched ideology.

"Tell me, if you can, what has Communism got to offer? I do not believe Communism is synonymous with humanitarianism. To be good we do not have to acclaim Communism, you know? For being such it just takes brotherhood, compassion and generosity. We must never retreat from pouring out those virtues. I also wish to ask you to please reject that agnosticism embedded in your mind and embrace fine religious traits. Shed that tunic of yours, if you find it to be burdensome. Enter competition with the pharmacist and lead the Fascist branch of Montelieto back to a saintly monarchy."

"You must be kidding, my dear Don Pompeo," replied Reverend Palestrina. "You have already been told that Fascism with monarchy are in a loving matrimony. One compliments the other in injustice and together they make life miserable for the citizens. Furthermore, I must repeat to you that only when they'll finish screwing each other, and their marriage is dissolved, will there be hope that some good will emerge in Montelieto. They are the same, my old monarchist friend—one body, one soul. I shall never turn crazy enough to wear the same uniform as the pharmacist! That gives me skin disease just by the mention of it. Me? Fascist, or a monarchist? And oppress humanity? Never!"

"Fine, it is your prerogative. No one is imposing it on you," said Don Pompeo.

"Glad we understand each other," said Reverend Palestrina.

By this time Barabba had already begun ringing the bells announcing the novena when Don Pompeo said: "We must go, Reverend."

"We sure must," said Reverend Palestrina. "It is getting to be late and we must go. Also I want to remind you that whatever we have said shall remain buried here beneath this boulder, and my apology for having called the people of Montelieto a bunch of fools. We ought to know what these people really are, don't you think?"

"Right, beneath this boulder here," replied Don Pompeo. "Now I wish you a very good evening, Reverend. And by the way," he whispered to the priest with a clear under-tone, "from now on, be careful not to order too many more shirts."

Then, smiling, each wished the other good evening and both headed for their respective homes.

Chapter 12

Reverend Palestrina arrived home more agitated than usual. His demeanor aroused doubts of tension even in the mind of Dorotea who, very seldom, had seen her Lord showing quite a noticeable nervous strain. In all humbleness Dorotea asked: "Father Palestrina, is there something bothering you? It is not the hoeing hired hands, is it? Is there something that I can do, Father?"

"No, not at all, I am fine," answered Reverend Palestrina. "But if you do not mind, you could make a bowl of that good vegetable soup—you know how to make so well. I am as hungry as a starving wolf. For the time being I will be resting on the loggia. Please let me know when the soup is done."

Reverend Palestrina went directly on the loggia and lay down upon his preferred cot, at an angle where he could observe a larger section of the horizon. As he rested and looked out in the space of the sky, many thoughts flashed through his mind. He closed and opened his eyes but the image of Don Pompeo stayed fixed in his mind. "How could that old shoemaker know so much?" said the priest in wonderment. "Is he the only person to know what I am about? Where has he learned of Isabella and Gianpaolo? Should I really fire that frog-legged Dorotea?" he said somewhat upset. At that point he got up from the cot and went to lean upon the parapet of the loggia still thinking.

"That Don Pompeo," he said. "What a character! He must be the most eloquent and amazing shoemaker of them all. Damned! If he knew Latin he could be a priest himself, perhaps Archbishop—maybe even Pope? But," said Reverend Palestrina, regaining some of his serenity, "Don Pompeo is not a blabbermouth. He is a shoemaking philosopher full of good wisdom and, for me, short of really embracing the Party of the Fascist pharmacist, it would be better to take heed of his philosophy."

Reverend Palestrina meantime had been noticing that the sky was, amazingly, filling with bright stars. He began to count the brightest stars but couldn't reach too far. Suddenly some falling stars flashed criss-crossing the sky until he was unable to count further. He there upon chose a more propitious spot and began to count again where the skyline sank between the peaks of mountains, but the same flashes of falling stars would make him lose concentration once more.

When he heard Dorotea calling, "Father Palestrina?" he answered, "Coming!" Then turning to look at the sky with unabated fascination, he exclaimed loudly, "Majestic Montelieto sky! You are so beautiful! I know that I am an unbeliever, but tonight I feel as if some kind of diabolus must be dwelling up there."

The reasons why Reverend Palestrina was not a believer were not well-known to the people of Montelieto. Neither was there any clear evidence that he had become a Communist. Only Don Pompeo, and perhaps Barabba, had a strong notion their priest could be both Communist and unbeliever. However the shoemaker, who had been in touch with the Palestrina clan longer than anyone else, and also the sacristan, under no circumstance would talk, make loose comments in public, or even whisper a word in the negative against the family.

Don Pompeo had known Reverend Palestrina ever since he was a small child and had seen him grow to an extraordinarily intelligent young man. But as Reverend Palestrina approached his mid-teens, he developed a tendency to get into trouble. His parents had to rush many times to their son's rescue. The young man was more inclined to intermingle with the kids of his family sharecroppers than with the rich in his circle, and this worried his parents to some extent. Fearing the young man would follow in the steps of his bachelor uncle, who frequently became involved with young women and then dropped them, the Palestrinas sent their son away to school. However, even in school, the young student continued getting into trouble. Year after year his parents went again to the rescue and donated large sums of money to the seminary, hoping their irresponsible son could be helped to rehabilitate. As time passed Reverend Palestrina excelled in his studies, got himself in more trouble, hated his hypocritical superiors and ridiculed the effeminate professors until he, too, was ordained to the priesthood by mistake.

When Reverend Palestrina was assigned as parochial vicar of the parish of Montelieto, thanks to his family's influence, he found the pastor Father Ponzio aligned with the Fascist sympathizers of the town. The young priest, instead of being sociable with the boastful group, thought that all the civil and religious figures were tyrants and lunatics of the Party in power. Father Ponzio was eventually expelled from the church by an angry mob of peasants, and Reverend Palestrina remained carrying on with his early assignment and helping the newly appointed pastor, old Father Alfonso, whenever he was in the mood to do so.

Father Alfonso, on the other hand, was a saintly pastor and a good Christian who minded the affairs of the parish, without regard to influential political parties and their power. And for what concerned his associate Reverend Palestrina, Father Alfonso cared very little whether he helped with the work of the church or not.

When the Fascist pharmacist, amid great exultation, was installed as the leader of the Fascist Party (Montelieto branch) Reverend Palestrina found the celebration unbearable. He knew precisely what was entailed. He was pained to think that, in a short time, the peasant sharecroppers of his town would be driven on the road to oppression.

Dorotea's vegetable soup was still steaming upon the dining room table when Reverend Palestrina sat down to eat his supper.

"This is good," Reverend Palestrina said, as he gulped down the first spoonfuls. "It is excellent! I should not have threatened Dorotea like I did a while ago in front of Don Pompeo, when I said I would fire her ass. I think she really deserves praise for her mastery around the kitchen."

Dorotea asked Reverend Palestrina if he were still hungry, saying she would be glad to get a refill for him. "There is more in the kettle," she said. "Don't be bashful."

"Certainly I would like a refill," answered Reverend Palestrina. "If you keep on making this good soup who could resist it? Then I am not the bashful type, you know? Besides, if I happen to gain weight I will always have you to blame." Dorotea said thanks, smiled at her master and walked back to the kitchen.

Reverend Palestrina took a long look at Dorotea and thought how advanced she had gotten in her years. He had never paid much attention to her before, and had always assumed she was there to look after him, as had his mother. Dorotea appeared to be struggling with a lack of mobility but yet she was the same old sweet lady, innocently disposed to please her Lords. She had been the servant of the household Palestrina even before the Reverend was born, and to fire her as Reverend Palestrina had threatened, would have been a big mistake. Dorotea never married and had dedicated her life to help and see to it that her services satisfied her masters to their highest expectations. The elder Palestrinas felt that Dorotea's honesty, respect, attachment and duties for the family had been impeccable.

Without doubt, Reverend Palestrina, too, was aware of Dorotea's fine qualities. He had only threatened to fire her as a defensive measure, when Don Pompeo had put pressure on him in regard to his love affair with Valentina. If there was anybody at fault it was he. He had caused the problems—not Dorotea. He had been a womanizer ever since his pre-seminary days. It was even rumored that he had impregnated a much older nun in his early days at the seminary, but nobody ever found out the end result of the relationship. And no townspeople of Reverend Palestrina could figure out how he got through his seminary studies without getting in more trouble. He was good looking, impulsive and reckless; and when he was ordained the same townspeople couldn't figure out why he even wanted to be a priest. Everybody, though, had a very strong premonition that Reverend Palestrina would never make the pastorate of the church of Montelieto. The townspeople would be better off if he had left the clerical life to someone else, and had pursued the tradition of his elders who had been known to be the most compassionate to the sharecroppers. They would have rather called the priest "Don Orazio Palestrina" than "Father" to which he was terribly opposed.

By and large, Reverend Palestrina was not a bad person at all. He was the only heir to the most fertile farmlands of Montelieto, and after his parents died he had totally lessened the interest for the church to take control of his inheritance. None of his sharecroppers cared whether or not he had love affairs so long as he continued to be fair to them and was able to alleviate some of their anxieties at times of need.

Reverend Palestrina's feelings for the people of Montelieto were reciprocal. Except when the problem of the women was not the prime factor, he felt for the people of his town and was as responsive as Don Pompeo to them. If he did not touch everyone with his political philosophy, for sure he had touched many for his generosity.

After Reverend Palestrina had finished his second bowl of soup, he went back on the loggia to smoke a cigar before he retired to his study to read. He paced the loggia for a while puffing at his cigar then stopped and again leaned with his chest on the parapet, and thought in silence. *That old Don Pompeo,* he thought. *He told me to be careful not to order so many shirts in the future. That's not funny. That old fox of a monarchist knows everything that happens in this town! Not that he is a blabbermouth, of course, or that he is checking on me. He learns everything from his friends but oftentimes he sends a signal to promote*

*in them good behavior. I hope Barabba has not informed
him of the incident of the confessional and what took place
between me, him and his wife.*

But what Reverend Palestrina wished wouldn't happen, had already happened. Sigismondo Barabba, the sacristan with his younger wife, on occasion helped Dorotea to prepare baskets of food and to fill flasks of wine to be taken by Reverend Palestrina to feed the hired workers who were hoeing or harvesting his olive orchard. The Barabbas frequented the mansion of Reverend Palestrina at any time they were called to perform odd jobs and were always welcomed. This type of help was asked from the Barabbas above that which they gave around and in the church, every time Reverend Palestrina officiated the rites of the Eucharist.

For Easter season, when everybody from Montelieto went to confession, Barabba took charge of the need of the parish and saw to it that everything worked right. He cleaned up, moved the statues to their proper niches, and added portable confessionals so as not to have crowds form in front of the permanent confessional. The week preceeding Easter, two or three missionaries were sent to help Father Alfonso to see to it that together, with the help of Reverend Palestrina, everyone got confessed. Barabba, who was also a good Christian, went to confession every Easter and this time, as usual, proceeded to go to confession kneeling down in front of a portable confessional, unaware of who the confessor was inside.

Sigismondo Barabba knelt down while the confessor recited a short prayer. Then the confessor pulled open part of the grate and said: "Make the sign of the cross." After that he quickly asked: "What sins do you recall having committed?"

"None," answered Barabba, truthfully, after having recognized Reverend Palestrina's voice.

"What do you mean none?" insisted the confessor who had also recognized Sigismondo Barabba. "Why have you come to confess then, liar?" Reverend Palestrina opened the grate wider and asked: "Don't you remember that you stole my vintage bottle from the cellar, and the jar of olive oil, and the vessel of flour?"

"I cannot hear a word you are saying, Father," said Barabba.

"Damn you, Barabba! How many times must I tell you not to refer to me as 'Father?' " Then Reverend Palestrina opened the grate of the confessional all the way and asked: "Can you hear me now?"

"Uh!" replied Sigismondo, placing his hand behind his ear, alluding to producing better hearing.

"Damned," cussed Reverend Palestrina again. "There must be some sort of echo inside here. Let me come out there, Barabba old man, and you come to talk from the inside so we can find the problem."

"That's a good idea!" hollered Barabba.

While Reverend Palestrina knelt in front of the confessional, Barabba accommodated himself inside. Then opening part of the grate he said: "Make the sign of the cross."

Reverend Palestrina obliged.

Barabba asked again: "What sins have you committed?"

"What do you mean sins, I do not sin. I am the confessor, remember?"

"Liar," said Barabba opening the grate all the way. "Don't you remember when you went down into the cellar with my wife and I waited, waited, and waited but you never came up?"

"Uh!" said Reverend Palestrina, putting his hand behind his ear just as Barabba had done before. "I cannot hear a damned word you are saying. My advice to you is hurry to come out and help me dump this damned portable confessional on the scrap pile. It must be defective."

"I can't understand myself," said Reverend Palestrina still leaning with his chest on the parapet of the loggia. "I should have never become a priest. What good is it to be an atheist priest? And what joy is it to be a priest only to please one's old relatives? They thought by being ordained a priest I would quickly become a canonized Saint. Now they are all gone and I am left here to keep the vows. I will never make it and I don't intend to. I won't hide for long behind this collar of respectability and be a hypocrite. True goodness comes from compassionate hearts rather than from religious hypocrites. Titles of honor such as Holy, Monsignor, most Reverend and Father are a bunch of nonsense! Those titles are just a maneuver intended to make the poor, the fearful and the hopeless pay for the atonement of their sins with cash. Who is the sinner here? Still, I would want it to be understood that I am not obstinately opposed to religion or clergy. I can freely testify that there are priests, who are respectful of the laity and are God-fearing Saints. Then, on the other hand, there is a small group of sexual perverts and screwballs who deceive their followers and defame their profession. I can honestly say that I am neither of the two. And that I do not take advantage of others, especially the poor, nor deny women are not my weakness."

Reverend Palestrina moved from the parapet of the loggia and paced some more. He wanted to retire in the library but felt no urge to read anything. Then he threw himself upon the cot again and thought. *If I have my way,* he figured, *it won't be long before I'll be able to hug Isabella publicly, and Gianpaolo and Valentina. Hug the offspring of a sharecropper?* he questioned himself. *Who in hell cares whose offspring they are? They are part mine and for sure some day I will see to it they don't make the same mistakes that I have made.*

Reverend Palestrina meditated for a long while and dozed briefly upon his cot. Then he awakened and searched for a blanket to cover himself, but there was none. So at the point when the breeze from the north was getting colder, he got up and shivering said: "I had better retire to the inside, before my *cullions* will freeze."

Chapter 13

Don Pompeo arrived at his home at the same time Reverend Palestrina arrived at his, but was not nearly as excited or hungry. He was feeling good for having spoken his mind to his friend, but he was not going to have the grand luxury of resting on a cot, or upon the loggia of a mansion, like that of the priest. Or the privilege of having a housekeeper to look after him and the right to ask her to prepare a bowl of hot soup. He rested, instead, on his worn-out couch to gaze around the poorly lit room, thinking.

Suddenly the radio above the balcony of the House of the Fasces began to make loud cracking noises, and Don Pompeo guessed that the zealous henchmen of the pharmacist had turned the radio on. At this point the clock of the church belfry struck the hour of nine P.M., and Don Pompeo quickly pulled out his watch to double check its accuracy.

It is time for me to get downstairs and open the shop, he thought. *There might be some old war widows coming over to pick up their shoes.*

He went downstairs and opened the door facing the Church Square and saw the first groups of people coming out of the church. The novena had ended. But people didn't stop by as he had foreseen. They rushed past Don Pompeo's shop instead, to gather again beneath the balcony of the House of the Fasces, where the radio was already broadcasting a special news journal.

With the first loud shouts of "hurrah!" Don Pompeo didn't think of anything. He just frowned in silence but, at the next round of hurrahs, he peeped out of the door and said: "They must have learned of something that I don't know. Must be good news. Bah! Either way we'll adjust to it," he said returning to his working bench. "We shall find out later what is going on."

Don Pompeo had just sat down on the stool by the bench when Mariano Albarosa entered the shop looking quite happy. "Good evening, Don Pompé," he said greeting the old shoemaker. "It seems that you are becoming increasingly disinterested about learning what is happening in town."

"What do you mean disinterested?" replied Don Pompeo.

"I mean that this morning, with all the uproar going on, you were not to be seen by anybody, and same thing this evening. I came to make sure everything is okay with you. Don't you care to know that the war in Africa is going in our favor? Tonight, the news report has said that the Black Shirts have occupied Addis Ababa, the capital of the nation we are fighting. You ought to hear the screams on the radio coming from Palazzo Venezia, it sounds as if we are invincible!"

"Alright, alright," replied Don Pompeo unimpressed. "You are telling me that our troops have occupied Addis Ababa, the capital of Ethiopia? And those loud screams of approval resound from the square of Palazzo Venezia in Rome? Big deal! I must tell you, Albarosa, that they ought to be ashamed to celebrate over other people's misfortune and defeat. We, as good Christians, shouldn't find joy in somebody else's sorrow, you hear me?"

While Don Pompeo was talking to Albarosa, other *cafoni* entered the shop but most of them scoffed at the news of victory. "Montelieto itself should be occupied!" someone said loudly. Everybody knew, by instinct, that every national achievement would be followed by more taxes, and more farm products would be demanded from the government at low cost to refill the State-operated food granaries.

"The best news of all," said Don Pompeo, "is that the war will end soon and that there will be no more casualties on either side. I hope that the Negus will be able to negotiate favorable peace terms, so his people won't feel the stings of the defeat until they can rebuild their lives. Unfortunately, the ones who have perished cannot rebuild anything. They paid for the cost of the spoils of victory, and of defeat, with their lives. Lucky break for Montelieto this time," sighed Don Pompeo. "We have sacrificed only three thus far: the two volunteers from the mountain district we have lost and, of course, the son of the doctor as everybody already knows. Three young men is a big price to pay for any town small or big. And I would like to know whether this was necessary. Was it?" he shouted loudly.

"No," answered the *cafoni* inside the shop. "Damned no! Never are wars necessary."

"Alright," said Don Pompeo. "I am happy that you agree with me."

But he had not even finished the sentence when Cicco Palla entered the shop panting. Cicco went directly to Don Pompeo and whispered in his ear with anxiety: "Don

Pompé," he said, "we are in trouble. I believe Durezza, Grifone and LaBorgia have been killed."

"Killed? Do I hear you right? Killed?" repeated Don Pompeo in disbelief.

"Yes," replied Cicco Palla. "Three people are lying face down in a pool of blood, upon the large slate of stone near Valle dei Biffi. I recognized their three donkeys grazing on the field of the priest."

"You recognized the donkeys but not the people lying on the slate of stone? This is a serious matter," admonished Don Pompeo. "I hope this is not another of your scary experiences when you must travel in the dark of the night. Tell me exactly what you saw, because we must notify the *Carabinieri* (State Police) and then the families concerned."

"Sure," said Cicco Palla, shivering with fear. "I was late coming home from the farm of Signor Luigi because my donkeys had run astray. Every time I caught up with them they began to run farther into the valley. After about two hours they trotted in the field by the barn of Umberto Sardone, where he entrapped them with his rope."

"Never mind Sardone and his rope, what did you exactly find out about the three killings? I must know."

"When I passed by, after taking the shortcut near Valle dei Biffi, I saw the three bodies lying face down in dark ponds of blood."

"How could you know if the dark ponds were blood? Did you dismount your donkey, to take a good look at the faces and investigate?"

"No, the moon was shining right on them, but I did not see their faces. Neither did I dismount my donkey to investigate. I was quite scared. But I saw their donkeys eat all the oats of the priest!"

Gerardo Cipollone entered the shop all of a sudden and said: "Hello, Don Pompeo and guests. Full house tonight, uh, Don Pompé?"

"Yes," answered Cicco Palla quickly. "Full house except for the blessed souls of Durezza, Grifone and LaBorgia. They have been killed by someone upon the stone slate near the Valle dei Biffi."

"What?" Cipollone said. "What do you mean blessed souls and killed, dumb fool? I just came from that short cut and Durezza, Grifone with LaBorgia are not dead at all. I shook them up hard but couldn't hold them up straight. They fell again one on top of the other. LaBorgia fell on top of Grifone and regurgitated on his chest. "Pass it around!" Grifone grumbled, at which Durezza answered: "Hell no, I don't want another sip of it."

"They are as drunk as skunks but in no danger of dying soon. They are tough as nails. I turned them face up and now the moon will take care of the rest. It is shining right on their faces," said Cipollone.

"My good Lord!" Don Pompeo exclaimed looking up at the ceiling. "What a great relief! Cicco? Cicco Palla, boy?" Don Pompeo called. "Where are you? Come near because Don Pompeo wishes to talk to you."

Cicco Palla was nowhere to be seen in the shop. While Cipollone was explaining the incident of the three drunkards, Cicco had slipped out of the shop like a little mouse, without attention having been paid by anybody.

"Thanks, Gerardo," then said Don Pompeo. "Thanks for turning our friends face up. They could have drowned in their own regurgitation you know? Evidently Reverend

Palestrina must have brought bigger jugs of wine, for them to drink."

"He must have," said Cipollone, "I have seen these men loaded before, including myself, but never loaded like to-night. I wonder whether they were able to dismount their donkeys or the donkeys made them dismount. In any case, they are okay and that's all that matters. This won't be the last time they will be getting drunk, I am more than sure of that. Tomorrow we will know what happened. But this is not too important. To know or not to know changes nothing."

"Right, Cipollone boy," said someone from amongst the *cafoni*. "We have many more subjects to talk about. There is the question of the grapes of the pharmacist, and of the Captain with his Black Shirts. I wonder why they were summoned, and why they arrived in Montelieto with that much urgency."

"You may not be wondering for too long, Peluso," said Don Pompeo. "From this day on there will be more than one subject to talk about. That is—the grapes of the phar-macist, his superiors, the Party, and all the *cafoni* kids of Montelieto. The pharmacist, according to the testimony of the Favetta kid, has been warned sternly. The Captain of the Fascist Black Shirts must be a very fine officer, but the Party . . . the Party . . . well, of the Party I will give you my impartial opinion. The Party's fundamental principles are to re-institute a sense of order and direction in every rank of our society. We can see the past accomplishments of the Party stand for good example of its objective. One of its most remarkable accomplishments is that of draining the marshes of the Roman plains," said proudly Don Pompeo.

"You guys should know that since creation and up to this day, no Caesars or Emperors or Kings, have succeeded in reclaiming so large a wasteland as our Duce has. This highly complicated project will shortly be completed, and the total of five cities will spring up where malaria and mosquitoes once abounded. Littoria, Sabaudia and Pontinia have been already settled, so will be Aprilia and Pomezia in the foreseeable future."

Don Pompeo pounded harder with his hammer upon the shoe he worked on, every time he mentioned the name of one of the cities sprung or about to be sprung in the drained marshes. But Albarosa who was listening carefully, told Don Pompeo that the *cafoni* of Montelieto could not perceive that highly publicized undertaking to be a part of the solution to their problems.

"We were *cafoni* with the marshes, and we remain *cafoni* without the marshes," said Albarosa. "I have begged, pleaded, argued to secure employment, perhaps ten times in the last several years, but was as many times denied work. And when Reverend Palestrina sent my application asking for an eventual settlement in the newborn cities, Rome wouldn't even answer."

"Yeah!" Peluso concurred. "I had the same experience. I went there in person, to seek work at the employment office of the city of Littoria, but was refused any type of work. They, the bureaucrats, told me that I couldn't speak properly and advised me to seek work in the employment office of my chief town if I cared not to get arrested. Another cafone from our area told me that they have settled the three new cities with people, all from the northernmost regions, people who couldn't even speak Italian. We, the southern *cafoni*, always get our ass kicked from Rome. Do you think that is fair?" Peluso cried.

"It is not fair," said Don Pompeo, "and I do understand you very well, Peluso. It is unfortunate that those partialities must be irremediably prevalent in our government. Perhaps some day we will be able to have effective representation for our citizens, and then the difficult situation of us *cafoni* will be solved—maybe even by the end of next millennium," said Don Pompeo jokingly. "Then insofar as the people being settled are concerned, I think they were not much better off than we are. The mountainous regions have high illiteracy, just as high as ours, and the reason they have been favored is perhaps because they have been more prone to follow the Party's doctrine. We *cafoni* are shunned from everybody," said Don Pompeo.

"The point that I wanted to make, when I spoke on the merits of draining the marshes, is that only Il Duce has prevailed in such bold undertakings. Now merit must be given to he who merit deserves! What I said before is not the whole accomplishment. There is more. Our Duce rebuilt one of the most modern train stations of Europe in our capital, and made every train run on time. The Party supporters and the well-to-do say times couldn't be better. They say crimes are non-existent, thieves are locked up, the mafia has been literally wiped out, and what more can we expect from a leader?"

"White bread, work and peace!" screamed Cipollone.

"Wait your turn, Cipolló," said Don Pompeo. "Now when all those things I have mentioned touch the existence of everyone here, our lives will be improved, then I will tell you a miracle has happened to the Party and to Montelieto. Your turn to talk is up, Cipolló."

"Good, but I want to know what was that made you change your mind and praise Il Duce so much. It appears to me you have taken lessons from the Fascist pharmacist. Are you changing your mind for real and don't want us to know?" Cipollone said.

"I resent that, Cipolló. Sounds like you are accusing me of being a Fascist! Be careful what you say dear Cipollone, because you could offend people here. Just understand that this shoemaker is not, and will not be what you think. I am a monarchist since birth, and I will tell you that all the projects accomplished by Il Duce, were financed by our King. The King disburses our money, our Duce gets all the honors, and we starve. In return the King is crowned Emperor, pays exorbitant toll to access the colonies, our Duce hollers, and we starve again. Understand, Cipollone boy? We starve even in the accomplishments."

"I understand that, but I would like to know the day when even a small accomplishment will touch here us in Montelieto," said Cipollone.

"Never," replied Don Pompeo. "Never if our Duce is let loose, by the King, to fight more wars. These two peg-tops believe other nations must pay for their mistakes. Why must other nations pay for the foolishness of our peg-top leaders, puzzles me. Our Duce has been developing a brotherly relationship with his colleague from up north, but he fails to understand the dangers involved in that step. He ought to be told: Whom do you think you are fooling with? Do you think you are fooling with that half-pint of a King of ours?"

Chapter 14

Weeks and months went by, seasons changed and more destructive floods occurred—but the livelihood of the people of Montelieto remained the same. If anything had changed it had changed for the worse. What had not changed was the hospitality of Don Pompeo, who continued to allow the frustrated citizens of Montelieto to congregate in his shop. This privilege too, though, was soon going to be taken away. Don Pompeo's shoemaker shop would no longer be that cheerful forum where poor, ordinary citizens mingled to give vent to their uneasiness, and could criticize or approve whatever had been taking place in that forgotten town.

By this time, the Italian Black Shirts' victory in East Africa had given more impetus and more credibility to the Fascist Party and its followers. The leadership and masses of the faithful strongly believed Italy had proven unstoppable. In their beliefs, the Western neighbors must have conceded Italy the rights of navigation to and fro in the new colonies overseas, or face ugly confrontations. Those irrational requests of rights over the jurisdiction of the neighbors brought everyone involved big headaches. Amid

diplomatic negotiations, threats and promises of reconcilia-
tion on either side, no results were achieved. At every
round of high-level negotiations, Italy became more un-
yielding and belligerent ready to drift away, steadily, in
the thrall of the neighbors from north of the Alps.

As these new developments took place, the activities
of citizens in public places began to be watched. The pharmacist, commander of the Fascist branch of Montelieto,
was given authorization to assign watchdogs to investigate
and report to him, any activity suspect of plot against the
Party. So barber shops, saloons and tobacco shops, under
no circumstance could allow people to congregate on their
premises, without permission from the pharmacist. The
shoemaker shop of Don Pompeo, too, was classified in the
same category as the others. Later on the shop was spared
from the strict scrutiny of the watchdogs, by Don Pompeo
allowing them to attach propaganda posters in front, inside, and all over the shop, at the wish of their Chief.

From there on, Don Pompeo continued to let his friends
congregate in his shop on the understanding that they
would not act boisterously, split in groups, and would visit
only on alternate evenings. Even so, when the argumentations became heated and led to accusing the Party of ha-
rassment, it was agreed that someone from inside the shop
must mount guard and signal the others when the pharmacist watchdogs were approaching the vicinity.

"If I am not mistaken the victory achieved by the Black
Shirts is the forerunner of bigger conflicts," said Don Pompeo. "The elite army has crowned the King with fresh lau-
rels and aspires to reap more of those in bigger
conflicts—precisely the types of conflicts we do not want
any part of. A re-unification of our country was achieved

by the King of Savoy and Garibaldi over a half century ago. Now, I tell you, no bastards have the right to screw it up! Sure, we must defend our soil with all our strength, but we shall never be instigators nor shall we follow those who want to subjugate other people overseas. If we are to go overseas we must go there seeking work! We must learn new trades and look for opportunities to improve our lot. Opportunities to afford education for our children, and chances to shake loose from our necks the stiff yoke of sharing the crops which is choking to death the people of Montelieto."

"Bravo! Bravo, Don Pompeo," a young voice shouted from among the crowd. "Evviva, Don Pompeo!"

"Evviva, Don Pompeo!" All the others hollered. "We don't need the barren lands of the deserts overseas. We need roads and schools right here in Montelieto, and we need work and peace. To hell with the boastful Emperor!"

"Fine, fine. I do not want you to create a riot. Calm down and let's hope that whatever course of actions our leaders take won't be fatal. Let's pray the good Lord will stop the hate building up, and will allow peace to reign in this world."

"That's true, Don Pompé," said Mariano Albarosa. "We really should go, and should let our youngsters go overseas seeking opportunities to improve our lot, but to raise money to afford the sea-fare would be as difficult as draining 'Mare Nostrum' with a nutshell."

"Nutshell, eh? Never make it, Albarosa. And since we are on the subject, I would like to know where you have learned that there is a 'Mare Nostrum.' "

"From Romualdo the casket maker when he gets drunk," said Albarosa. "He knows quite a bit about geography."

"If we do not listen to Don Pompeo," intervened Guglielmo Sparacelli saying, "we may never go anywhere but we will die hungry."

"Right," agreed Carlo Spaventa. "If we cannot raise money for the sea-fare, I suggest we die first, so our souls can go overseas via air mail."

"You guys make no sense," said Alfonso Suzzera. "You either follow the advice of Don Pompeo or die poor. Quit making excuses and let's go overseas even if we must swim over 'Mare Nostrum.' "

While a couple of others entered the discussion on whether it was affordable and/or prudent to go somewhere, a soldier who had recently been drafted in the army as a cavalryman, suddenly entered the shop of Don Pompeo.

"Good evening," said the soldier, greeting Don Pompeo. "Don't you ever get tired of sewing stitches on those shoes, and of listening to the nonsense of these slackers?"

"I sure do get tired of sewing stitches."

"We have heard you, Fedele Tranquillo," said Suzzera. "You have inherited the good breeding of your grandfather's jackass. Without any doubt in my mind, you are as big a *cafone* as the day you were recruited. I cannot understand why they don't lock you up in Gaeta (military prison), so you won't be an embarrassment to the citizens of our country."

"Of course I do get tired," spoke quickly Don Pompeo, trying to get in between the two before a fist fight broke out. "But I am too old to join in the army, and very much used to listening to the cries of these friends of yours. Fedele Tranquillo, may I ask what devil has brought you back home so soon? Have you, by any chance, been awarded a sharp-shooter furlough of some sort?"

"Oh no," said the soldier while giving a few strokes of brush on one of his boots. "I have not been assigned a firearm yet."

"What on earth could have happened to you then?"

"Nothing. I just won a bet from the Captain," said Fedele Tranquillo with indifference.

"Won a bet? What kind of bet are you talking about?" asked Don Pompeo.

"Well, it all happened while the Captain was delivering a speech and I couldn't stop yawning. He came over and ordered me to stand at attention and asked me why I was so sleepy. I answered him that I was not sleepy, but was so hungry that I could have eaten a horse."

"Oh no—that I won't let you do," said the Captain. "No soldiers of mine," he said firmly, "will spread the rumor they are eating horses in this Cavalry outfit of ours. We are training for war, you know? Come here, we shall take care of your appetite," said the Captain.

"He took me by the arm to the kitchen of the camp," said Fedele, "and gave orders to the chief sergeant to cook *pasta e fagioli* (pasta and beans). When the *pasta e fagioli* was done, the Captain made me sit near a stockpot full and said: 'Fedele Tranquillo, eat to your heart's delight. I will send you on four days furlough if you can eat four mess-tin full of *pasta e fagioli.*'

" 'Fine,' I answered," said Fedele, "but what if I eat more than four, Captain, sir?"

"Well," he said, "that's unlikely to happen, but I will add one day of furlough for every mess-tin full of *pasta e fagioli* you eat above four. Fair enough?"

"Of course it is fair, Captain," Fedele said. "But at six mess-tins he stopped me, took the stock-pot away and cussed me out saying 'Damned are you, Fedele. You must be really bottomless. I do not want to be responsible for you to spend the rest of your army stretch on furlough'."

"Now I have six days of furlough," said Fedele Tranquillo, happily beating with both hands on his belly as if it were a drum.

At this point everybody in the shop marveled at the audacity of Fedele to challenge his Captain, but all believed him capable of taking the Captain on that deal. Then Emanuele Quinto rose from sitting on a squashed-up cardboard box and doltishly said: "Fedele gives me the impression he is super bottomless. The most I could eat of *pasta e fagioli* was only five-and-a-half mess-tins full."

"Baloney," said someone. "Emanuele wants to make us believe he is not as bottomless. We know better."

"This is exactly what I have been saying all along. We were born *cafoni* and will die so,"said Don Pompeo. "They do not call us *cafoni* for nothing! Every time we are given a chance to show a little good breeding, we act stupidly. We, from this town, have acquired the reputation of Ciociari *cafoni* for thinking that to practice good breeding is a waste of time. Ciociari is not a slander invented just to defame us, because that is an inherent trait. But *cafoni* is contempt. One imbecility after another has earned us the label *cafoni* which will be hard to erase," he said throwing the shoe he was working on upon the scrap pile in disgust.

"To oust the parish pastor from the church, was another of your big mistakes," continued Don Pompeo. "That
didn't improve our image on the State level. Because you
acted uncivil inside the church and Father Ponzio attempted to have you thrown out, that was no reason to oust
him and disarm the two *Carabinieri*. Who do you think
was at fault?"

"Father Ponzio," said Sparacelli aloud. "We didn't expel him from the church because we wished to continue to
act uncivil, but for bigger reasons. He was a staunch Fascist and had kept threatening us with excommunication if
we didn't repay at fifty percent higher, the loan of grains
we borrowed from the church granary last year. He kept
telling us that God needed grains to feed the poor, and the
soldiers, who will have to go to war and who are hungry.
What did he think we were, overfed?"

"And that is not even the whole story of why we kicked
Father Ponzio out of the Church," said Peluso. "There was
much more to it than he cares to know. Just to mention
one, don't you guys remember what he told Sisto Panduro?
When the poor boy went to pay up the cost of dispensation
of marriage for wanting to marry his second cousin? Father
Ponzio told Panduro that, if he really wished to marry his
second cousin, it would cost him up to two or more big
capons."

"I don't exactly recall the details. Did the Panduro boy
pay up the cost of the dispensation of marriage or not? I
know he is living, quite happily, with his wife," said Don
Pompeo.

"No, he didn't pay up. Panduro couldn't afford two capons. He brought the priest only one, which he had borrowed from his neighbor, but that was not enough to cover
the cost—according to Father Ponzio."

"What happened then?" asked someone.

"Nothing. Father Ponzio's insistence unnerved the boy, to the limit of his patience, that had him answer the priest so: 'To hell with you Father Ponzio! I do not believe it costs that much for someone to marry their second cousin. I could only afford one capon. Besides, for your information, we are now living together and she believes she is already pregnant.' "

"Damn!" Peluso yelled aloud. "The Panduro kid, by getting his second cousin pregnant, really showed the priest how to reduce the cost of dispensation of marriage!"

"I wonder, though, what ever happened to that capon. Did Sisto boy take it back?" asked Cicco with concern.

"Dear Cicco, if you would really like to know, the capon went back and was banished from the Church, together with Panduro. When he took it back to his neighbor's hen coop, the capon felt so cockily as to want to start cock-a-doo-dle-doo like this: 'To hell with you Father Ponzio! To hell with you!' " Damiano answered Cicco, wittily, amid loud laughter.

"You see, Cicco, my boy, what power a bureaucratic pastor can muster up?" Don Pompeo said amusedly. "A priest with Father Ponzio's skills and selfishness, can even make capons cock-a-doo-dle-doo same as roosters, and parishioners blaspheme him madly."

"I totally agree with you, Don Pompé! Damn! It seems to me we are being taken even by those who have been schooled to teach us how to save our soul," said Sparacelli

"Nobody will be able to help you save your soul, big fool Guglielmo. It doesn't matter how hard up you are because, you and only you are the one responsible for your soul. Certainly not someone as greedy and starving as that pastor," a wise guy was heard saying from among the crowd.

"That's true," Albarosa affirmed. "Now that we have a saint pastor there are no more problems between us and the church."

"Right," agreed Spaventa. "Our new pastor Father Alfonso, is not as eager. He must be a *cafone* among priests like we are *cafoni* among people. Barabba, the sacristan, knows more Latin than Father Alfonso. But he is a smart enough priest to understand we do not have much to give, so he saves his breath."

"Yeah," said Don Pompeo with doubt. "You can justify the rude actions in any way you want. But I tell you if it were not for the Bishop and the Pope's intervention, who begged the Fascists for your clemency, Father Ponzio would have had you dragged to the front lines by the neck."

From here on, things had begun to take a different direction. What had worried the sharecroppers in the past was no longer a major concern. New problems began to appear on the horizon. And the problems were not those of seeking work, and looking for opportunities to eat white bread two days in a row—but those of wanting to eat any color bread and stay alive. There had been reports that inferior people across the continent were losing their identity, assets, and place in the society. They were being plundered of their properties and forced out of their homes and businesses. If the rumors were proved to be true, the *cafoni* of Montelieto must be on the alert. They could be in line to lose their identity. Not so much that they ever held a place in the society, but because they, too, were seen as inferior, declassed citizens and creeping things to be sacrificed for the honor of the Party.

Damn, was that ever frightening! People, human beings hated for no reasons, plundered and marked for oblit-
eration? The mere thought of it obfuscated the mind of Don
Pompeo and his peers. Still the rumors persisted! People
were saying that, in one night, declassed individuals
around the continent had been beaten and brutalized. They
called the night: *Notte dei vetri frantumati.* (Night of the
shattered window panes.)

When the confused *cafoni* asked Don Pompeo whether
the rumors carried any truth, he didn't know what to say.
He told them that he felt Montelieto with its *cafoni*, held
every record in disrepute. "Now, though," he told them one
time, "we have new partakers for inferiority, and for disrepute, who have been unjustly accused fomenters of the
world disputes and of the conflicts."

"Yeah, but I don't understand. If those people are labeled inferior and declassed, like we are, how could they
create problems and conflicts in the world? That makes no
sense to me," said Albarosa in puzzlement.

"I believe you are hard of hearing, Albarosa," said La-
Borgia wishing to make a point. "We, both groups, are seen
as easy prey, taken for fools and be beaten upon, that's all!"

"LaBorgia," called Don Pompeo. "I am proud of you.
For a change and by mistake, you have come up with a hell
of an answer!"

Those incredible events tormented the mind of Don
Pompeo immensely. He felt long jolts of cold run down his
spine only to think what might become of the *cafoni*. In the
secrecy of his thoughts he asked himself: "Are we really
inferior and declassed citizens? Of course we are, Lord, but
that is not our fault."

The next afternoon, the town crier Vittorio Settimo, summoned by the pharmacist and postmaster, was seen running toward the post office with great urgency. The sacristan, Barabba, promptly went to alert Don Pompeo, who hurried out of his shop to find out what was going on.

"Must be a matter of major consequence," said Don Pompeo to the sacristan. "Let's wait and see what Vittorio is up to." While they sat talking on the stairs by the entrance of the church, they saw Vittorio coming straight toward them.

"Good afternoon," said the town crier with great excitement.

"Good afternoon to you too, Vittorio. May we ask what's going on around here?"

"Nothing," said Vittorio. "I will say only that the news is not so good."

"What do you mean not so good. Have they shot someone in Rome?" asked Don Pompeo.

"God forbid! It's much worse than that."

"Worse than that? You mean they have shot both of them? Vittorio, you ought to know we are your trusted friends, and we deserve to be told, right now what your announcement is all about," said Don Pompeo.

"Alright, alright, if you guys insist. According to the wishes of the pharmacist, I will make the announcement tonight when the people gather beneath the balcony of the House of Fasces to listen to the eight o'clock news broadcast. The Prefect has sent a telegram to the postmaster, which tells the pharmacist to pump up the spirit of the *cafoni* with a highly important message of national interest."

"National interest? What can that be—another tax increase for us bachelors who do not produce more poor kids?"

"No, it's not that, no tax increase. They know by now we can't even spare air. I think Italy has severed relations with the neighbors to the West and formed a pact stronger than steel with the neighbors to the North. They say this pact will never break. It is based on trust and great friendship and Italy must celebrate the occasion."

"This is nonsense. The pact will lead us to disaster! And the leadership wants us to celebrate?" Don Pompeo questioned.

Meantime Don Pompeo was encouraged by some initiatives taken by the pharmacist at the advantage of the citizens of Montelieto. Even if the initiatives were taken for propaganda purposes, the old shoemaker didn't mind. The Fascist pharmacist gave authorization to school officials to open and use a large room in the House of Fasces for teaching the illiterate. When Don Pompeo saw young kids with books under their arms, he took his hat off in a sign of respect and thanked God.

"One of these boys, someday, will be able to tell about the sacrifices, the servitude and the true reasons why the peasants of Montelieto have endured those terrible privations and been labeled inferior, declassed and *cafoni*," said Don Pompeo.

Still Don Pompeo felt loneliness and remorse. He felt remorse for the time he put down his *cafoni* after having gulped a liter of special vintage in company of Reverend Palestrina. He recalled the time when in the euphoria of the red spirit, he had translated a proverb from the Bible shown to him from the sacristan. The proverb said: "It would be less difficult to lead a camel through the eye of a needle than for a rich man enter the gate of Heaven." But he had placed his own altered meaning on the saying: "It would be less difficult to let a donkey go through the eye of my needle than to teach a *cafone* from Montelieto good decorum."

Don Pompeo, though, knew in his heart that the derogatory remark was not meant to defame his *cafoni*. He was sure they knew he hated to see them suffer. He felt they must have appreciated his efforts when he came to their defense the day they acted uncivil in front of the Archbishop at the Sacrament of Confirmation of their kids. He had begged the Most Reverend, on behalf of the *cafoni* saying: "Please Father, pardon them for they do not know what they are saying."

And the Archbishop smiling answered: "I pardon them, but they might be told not to blaspheme inside the church, and that they are a bunch of fools." Then almost choking with emotion Don Pompeo said: "Please, *cafoni* of Montelieto, forgive me."

Don Pompeo was not senile. He was of course getting older and weaker, but more concerned for what would become of his people. He poked the remaining lit charcoal against the clay pot on the brazier, and thought to call it quits after drinking the last hot cup of dry figs beverage. As he went to lock the door, he saw someone leaning against the other side of the glass. Don Pompeo recognized the casket maker barely able to stand up.

"Come in, Romualdo," said Don Pompeo, holding him by the arm. "Come in so you could weather the storm of spirits going on inside you!"

Romualdo barged in and, dragging Don Pompeo with him, fell sprawling on top of cut up cardboard boxes. He

stuttered a few incomprehensible words and began to re-
gurgitate. But Don Pompeo, who had seen that before, was
not surprised. He packed the last pieces of lit charcoal
closer to the pot, and went over to prevent Romualdo from
suffocating by sinking his head inside the pile of cardboard boxes.

Then, looking at his friend with fatherly patience, he
said: "My boy Romualdo, I see you are at it again. I have
a hunch that tonight the ceramic crucifix on the wall above
your bed, will be flying out of the window one more time.
How many times must your poor mother Maria Maddalena,
go searching in the street below for the broken pieces of
ceramics so they can be glued together again? You know
she is desperately poor and cannot afford to buy you a
brand new crucifix, every time you get drunk? Ah! Romualdo, Romualdo! Why must you expect the crucifix to answer your requests when you are so drunk? You should
know better than throw all the effigies of the Saints out of
the window just because they won't talk to you. Here, sip
some juice of dried figs," said Don Pompeo holding the cup
to Romualdo's lips.

Romualdo sipped some juice but dropped his head
upon the pile of cardboard boxes again. After some time he
raised his head and told Don Pompeo not to worry about
him because he felt the Saints were all at his side.

"I am sure they are," replied Don Pompeo. "But I pray
you keep them fastened on the wall where they belong, if
you wish to have everyone on your side."

"I will try to do that, Don Pompé. Now I must go, because Mother will be looking for me all over town."

"Good boy, Romualdo, go! But please stay away from that cheap wine of Marianna Pipanera—for your own sanity and that of your poor mother Maria Maddalena."

"I will promise to do that, Don Pompé. Do not worry, we will be alright," said Romualdo as he staggered to the door.

Then, turning the doorknob open, Romualdo said: "Thanks, Don Pompeo. Thanks for helping me sober up. Do not worry about what concerns my Saints, because they all know who I am. Right now they have their hands full, but we must put our trust in them. You must feel assured that, someday, they will be moved to compassion and perform a miracle or two for you and me and my mother—and everybody from this accursed town of Montelieto!"

"I am sure they will, Romualdo," said Don Pompeo. "I am sure they will."

Chapter 15

Before hopping in bed, Don Pompeo knelt down to recite the evening prayer and invoke Heaven's blessings on himself, and all the citizens of Montelieto. He also made a special request to Heaven on behalf of Maria Maddalena by praying that she be granted sanity and courage for dealing with a nutty kid like her son Romualdo.

"A kid approaching the age of thirty?" he said, talking to himself. "Oh well," he said, "that's exactly what he is in the eyes of his mother . . . a big kid."

Don Pompeo lay awake in bed during the first part of the night, in a state of grave anxiety. He wondered what could have caused his unusual restlessness; was it Romualdo's drunkenness of last evening, or news of the formation of the pact of steel and the plundering of inferior people. What could have had such a profound effect on his frame of mind? But after further consideration, he realized that the establishment of the great pact had perturbed his mind and soul.

Still tossing and tossing in bed, he thought of Maria Maddalena. He recalled how cute she used to be in the times of their youth. He recalled her perfect legs, her proportionate and firm bosom, and of how capriciously she would rush to flirt with the boys of town and of the villages.

"Unfortunately," Don Pompeo soberly contemplated, "from those innocent flirtations, she went to heavy petting; from heavy petting to love affairs, and then she conceived and bred Romualdo without her ever landing a husband. I know," he said, "how difficult it must have been for a washerwoman of the town to raise a child on her own, seeing him grow to manhood, as an underemployed drunkard. Yeah," he said, "I have always figured that the trade of casket maker must only be profitable in times of high mortality. Only then could a casket maker enjoy full employment! But as to what concerns me, and all of us elderly, I wish Romualdo would remain unemployed for some time to come. Not of course that we wish him more hardships, but for the fact we are not ready to fold up for providing him work. He will be fortunate if the much talked about forthcoming mobilization will include his class. I believe it will because Romualdo is the right age whether he acts it or not."

But Don Pompeo found it hard to remove from his mind the thought of Maria Maddalena. He recalled when he too had a little fling going on with Maria Maddalena, and how quickly she would drop him and be attracted to the next suitor.

"Damned how fiery she was," he said to himself. "There cannot be any connection of kinship between me and Romualdo. We, the Gazzaladras, have cobbler genes in our blood, and nothing in common with the casket makers. Then for what concerns Maria Maddalena, I must say that she was a very beautiful girl. Look at her now, though. Her legs have taken the shape of those of a frog, her firm bosom is hanging flat around her stomach, and her once cherry red lips are even sporting a nice mustache!

Damned old age," he continued in his frustration, not quite resigned to the thought of it. "Beauty and youth vanish like a thief in the night. On the other hand, ugliness and bad habits linger on with us to the end!"

Don Pompeo recalled many other episodes of his youth with Maria Maddalena, but felt a sudden drowsiness and fell asleep. For the remainder of the night he slept lightly until he was awakened, for good, by the chime of the clock striking the hours from the bell tower of the church.

"Already five?" he queried, stretching his arms. "This is the time for me to get on my feet. Besides," he added, "pretty soon I must pass the water." He got up, searched for the chamber pot beneath the bed, pulled it out, and started to urinate.

"Hell," he cussed after having given it some effort. "It seems to me that I am beginning to piss like a bird!"

Don Pompeo laughed amusedly at his own joke, but in doing so he coughed repeatedly as he attempted to get into his clothes. Finally dressed, he walked by the front window, raised the blind and down the Church Square saw Father Alfonso pacing back and forth impatiently, holding a book beneath his arm-pit.

"Given his age the old priest looks pretty good! Father Alfonso already up?" Don Pompeo said but not totally surprised. "He must be getting ready to officiate at the early morning mass. Or he might have been locked out again from his own church, by the cleaning lady Carlotta. She must be giving the last strokes of mop on the main aisle."

Father Alfonso was not at all locked out. He was in the habit of taking quick walks each morning, up to the time when Carlotta had wrapped up the chores of cleaning. Until the group of elderly women, and the two deaf sisters had arrived to attend the early mass, Father Alfonso kept walking. On the opposite of his assistant pastor, Reverend Palestrina, Father Alfonso was an early riser. He preferred to officiate at the early mass that the widows of World War I requested for the remembrances of the souls of their departed husbands.

In those days the widows were a greatly respected group among the *cafoni* of that town and Father Alfonso held them in good repute. The widows had been granted small pensions for the loss of their husbands or sons in World War I, and Father Alfonso relied on the generous and prompt oblations they gave him to cover the cost of the liturgy service. That generosity allowed Father Alfonso to raise some quick cash and also to afford him an occasional cigar with a bottle of wine.

That particular morning Don Pompeo, too, had the urge to attend the early mass. Not so much that he was in the habit of attending early masses, but for the fact that he wished to forget the mental strain of last night, and start the day with a different viewpoint on things. He entered the church and tiptoed toward the altar to take a seat, two or three pews behind the two deaf sisters and the group of widows. Across the aisle, four or five older folks were kneeling down and coughing repeatedly while holding rosaries in their hands. The remainder of the pews were either sparsely occupied or empty.

"A very cozy and peaceful atmosphere," observed Don Pompeo. That was the type of mass Don Pompeo enjoyed best. No loud singing, no wild-about-music organist, the perfect type of mass in which every worshipper could maintain concentration, focused on the gospel and the religious rites.

After the communion, as Father Alfonso blessed the congregation and spoke the last words of the liturgy saying: "The mass has now ended, go in peace to obey and serve the Lord," Don Pompeo was the first to head for the exit door, and to walk onto the Church Square. As he came out he was greeted by several passersby, including one of the rag pickers and the town crier who, holding in his hand a large brown sheet of paper scrawled with red ink, walked slowly rehearsing some of the lines and talking to himself.

"Good morning, gentlemen! What good news have you this morning for Montelieto?" Don Pompeo asked looking toward the town crier.

"Much, much news. Just relax and listen a minute so you can judge it for yourself," answered the town crier.

The town crier then walked to the corner of Via 24 Maggio and Via Piave, just around the corner from Don Pompeo Gazzaladra's shoemaker shop. He unfolded the sheet of brown paper, and began to sing-song his announcement. "Attention! Citizens of Montelieto, attention! This morning . . . the high . . . leadership . . . from Rome . . . has declared . . . a mobilization. All able-bodied citizens must be ready . . . to defend . . . our soil . . . from . . . an attack . . . of the enemy

"In the near future . . . the classes . . . from 1912 . . . to 1918 . . . must report . . . for training. The official recall notice . . . will follow . . . by mail . . . some time . . . in the days to come. On this occasion . . . the Secretary . . . of the Party . . . exhorts . . . each . . . and every person . . . to stay united . . . for . . . the common cause." The announcement closéd then with a rousing "Hail to our Duce! Hail to our King! And long live Italy!" After that, with a stronger tone of voice, in his own words Vittorio screamed: "Evviva Il Duce!"

The news that had been telegraphed from the capital to the smaller communities of the country was required to be passed on to the citizens in whichever way the city leadership saw fit. Montelieto chose to have Vittorio, the town crier, travel through the streets and inform the citizens of the great news, at the cost of a few pittances of corn meal or horse beans, given to him in the form of food stamps.

After the national news had been spread, Vittorio restarted telling the local news on behalf of the merchants wishing to sell things. With his sing-song style, he advertised all the items marked on his list, informing the population on the availability of whatever product was in store, the prices, quality, and conditions for obtaining the items. In exchange for this valuable service, Vittorio would be repaid with all sorts of scrap food. From the general store he was rewarded with the scrap pasta (spaghetti, etc.) left in boxes and half chewed by mice. From the chicken men he got the feet and neck of the chickens, and from the tavern keeper he got some spoiled wine already turned to vinegar.

But the poor town crier didn't mind the small amount or inferior quality of his rewards and was happy to be doing any job at all. Although he was chiefly at the disposition of the City Hall of Montelieto he was free to do whatever odd job came along, including making announcements in the street of Montelieto on behalf of the merchants.

Indeed, he felt somewhat privileged in comparison to many of the other destitute in town. His best friends ragmen Diodato Bello with Donato Rotunno, and the knife sharpener Davide Persichella, had much worse luck than he. That is not to mention Pasquale Lottagreca who repaired ceramics dinner plates and bowls. Those friends of Vittorio, with several others, ate even contaminated food not fit for human consumption. That included dead hens, pigs and hoofed animals butchered at the point of dying from disease.

That morning, as Vittorio finished announcing the local news, he approached Don Pompeo and winked an eye at him without saying a word. He hoped to receive Don Pompeo's commendation on how efficiently he had delivered the announcement.

Don Pompeo quickly understood. He winked back at Vittorio and said: "Very impressive the deliverance of your announcement, Vittorio—but very shocking the news. Ah! you deranged leader in Rome," he said shifting his interest from Vittorio. "You couldn't lead a flock of ducks to roost. You don't have a vague idea what this recall entails, Rome! I tell you what it entails. It will be a horrible shock and misfortune for me and for every citizen. Your mistake will deprive me of the friendship of, at least, thirty-five of my closest friends in Montelieto. And the worst shock of all is that your mistake will lead you to bigger mistakes, until I will end up being, a lonesome cobbler indeed."

Then turning again to Vitterio, Don Pompeo said: "For the time being we can't undo anything, Vittorio. Let's just be of support to our friends and their dear ones. You, Vittorio, have done a super job by not breaking down at the bad news. I hope you collect abundantly for your good work. I have noticed a long list of merchants on your order of announcements, wanting you to advertise their stuff. That is good. It will provide work for you, at least for today."

"Yes, work is fine but what I will collect I don't know. Certainly it won't be as abundant as you imagine. You must know better than anyone else that the richer they are, the more crumbs they will offer. But that doesn't matter much at this point so long we, me and Annamaria, can avert starvation. Poor wife of mine," lamented Vittorio. "She is a Saint among women! She has raised seven kids on almost nothing. I still cannot comprehend the reasons why she stuck with me, a poor town crier?"

"Well, well, now hear me," said Don Pompeo encouragingly. "Do me a favor, Vittorio. Please do not disesteem yourself this low. It is not fair. I fully believe that Annamaria stuck with you because she is a good woman, and because she loves you. And I do know, too, that you are a good, caring husband. The problem is that nowadays we have grown old, and because of these damned wars, our deserved rights to a pension are hardly ever talked about. Only the first World War widows seem to be making it alright in these bad times."

"True," said Vittorio. "I should have perished same as those friends of ours. If I had perished, Annamaria would have been assigned the pension and be able to live a life with much less privations. At one point I prayed I would perish, but to no avail. Soldiers died left and right of me every day, but I seemed to escape all the worst situations—just by a stroke of luck."

"That is totally nonsense," said Don Pompeo refusing to approve Vittorio's preposterous reasoning. "Even to wish to die for Annamaria is nonsense. You, my dear friend Vittorio Settimo, must be reminded once again that you are from this town of Montelieto and that is the main reason why you were spared, nothing else—understand? This way you can suffer poverty the same as everybody else."

Then, as they both had a hearty laugh, they wished each other a good day and left the Church Square going their separate ways. Vittorio Settimo headed straight for the populated farming districts to deliver the national news, and Don Pompeo headed home and to his shop.

Don Pompeo walked slowly the already semi-deserted Church Square, went by the post office where his friend, the mailman Ottaviano worked, borrowed a two-day-old newspaper from him and headed home. He read the newspaper for quite a while but, as he got upstairs to his apartment, he felt terribly weary.

Perhaps the ordeal of Romualdo of last night, the early morning service of Father Alfonso with the yelling of the town crier who announced the mobilization, had left him confounded. He must have rested and eaten some lunch even before thinking of opening shop. A few hundred grams of fettuccine, and a small glass of wine could have reinvigorated him. Then a little siesta, and hopefully go to work downstairs later in the afternoon.

"Much, much better," Don Pompeo uttered, satisfied as he wrapped the last few fettuccine around his fork. "Now," he said, "we shall relax a little and then we will decide when to go to work." He lay down on his worn-out couch and began to doze, but was abruptly disturbed from his sleep by the loud voice of his neighbor Elvira, who was singing at the top of her lungs, the popular song "Faccetta Nera (Little Black Face)."

"Damned old bitch, Elvira," cussed Don Pompeo with irritation. "She seems to always know the time when I wish to rest up. Oh, her poor husband Arturo! What an unfortunate blacksmith. He has to put up with that fat bitch until she buries him! For Arturo's sake let's hope she won't bury him alive. I am quite sure that last night, while I took care of Romualdo, he must have had a close call," said Don Pompeo. "When I saw him, early this morning, he didn't know which angle to turn his face to, in order to conceal the biggest shiner I have ever seen. Damned, that was for sure a 'faccetta nera'," marveled Don Pompeo. "And Arturo still wished to cover up for Elvira? He lied to me when he said that he had accidentally fallen down and bumped himself on the doorknob. Arturo, that big fool! He thinks I buy those excuses. How could someone six feet tall fall down and bump his face on a doorknob? Perhaps the spirits made him see the door flat on the pavement," laughed Don Pompeo. "I know that doors are hinged vertically and chances are that Elvira snapped the door off the hinges to hit him, or he could have bumped into her fists. Of course Arturo deserves to be taught a little lesson now and then but gee! Not every other night! It seems the more Elvira tries to keep him out of the tavern of Caterina, the more he seems determined to go there and get drunk."

Don Pompeo shook his head in disbelief, got up, looked out of the window to ascertain whether Arturo was at work and said, "No, I do not think Arturo has something going with Caterina. She is way too old for him, although she still has flashes for romance. Wolves do not change habits—they only change fur. I think the purposes of Arturo, though, patronizing Caterina's tavern on an every evening basis, must be purely those of staying away from his domineering wife as much as he can, getting stoned and have some peace of mind while in that state. That is, until Elvira catches up with him."

Meanwhile Elvira continued singing "Faccetta Nera," in spite of her husband. Perhaps she wished to remind him of the big shiner he took last night. Or she wanted to remind him to stay away from Caterina, if he wished not to have the other eye taken care of once he misbehaved.

"Waste of time, Elvira," muttered Don Pompeo to himself. "Arturo has this thing of getting high in the company of Romualdo, and you will never stop him short of chaining him to a lamppost. Truly, I must say that if I were him I would join the toughest of the army outfits without giving it a second thought, and never ask for a furlough!"

Don Pompeo's view of Elvira and Arturo's bickering was not merely a view for engaging in speculations, to be nosy or to have the desire to interfere with their lifestyle. The whole thing and the comments made by Don Pompeo were triggered by Elvira's continuing to sing when he wanted to relax. Don Pompeo, no gossip he, would never spread to others his neighbor's marital incompatibilities, although this was no a secret to the eyes of that community. What went on inside the town of Montelieto was everybody's business. Don Pompeo loved his neighbors same as every other fellow countryman of his but, in his mind, he wished they would act more civilized as opposed to putting up embarrassing shows of *cafoni*. Neither would he have the courage to knock at the partition wall, to send Elvira the signal to stop singing. She was terribly strong, big-mouthed and so devoid of common sense that he wanted nothing to do with her. "To hell with Elvira," he said. "Let her sing her heart out. I better go downstairs and do some work if I wish to distract my mind and avoid the danger of becoming compromised."

Chapter 16

Elvira's loud singing of patriotic songs had become quite a nuisance for Don Pompeo, but there was not much he could do to change that. She, with her husband, had signed in and pledged allegiance to the Party since some time back, and no outside influence could sway their thinking. If it were not for Arturo's frequent visits to the taverns of Caterina Panzona or Marianna Pipanera, those two subjects got along pretty well. Domineering Elvira talked Arturo into agreeing to many decisions she made and to follow her patriotic impulses. Elvira was also stupid, cunning, and vindictive to an excess.

The pharmacist looked upon Elvira's allegiance to the Party as the ultimate duty and offering to the motherland. He was proud of the fact that a few others had followed in Elvira's steps. But they were no more than a handful of supporters, and the reasons for such a small enrollment were not because they wanted to uphold the Fascist principles, but felt they could benefit from increased economic purpose. The so-called Commander in Chief, (the pharmacist), had the authority to dispense food coupons allotted by the Prefect in order to bolster Fascist propaganda, and with those enticements, he courted the uninformed citizens, hoping they would join the Fascist ranks. None of those adherents, though, were motivated by Party loyalty. Their short flare-ups of loyalty survived only as long as the food supplies lasted. Then they would begin to scream again and threaten to leave, as the worried pharmacist reunited them under his wings with promises of more food coupons.

Don Pompeo was well aware of what was going on. He understood the reasons why some people of Montelieto had joined the Party and why Elvira sang so loudly. She pretended to impress the pharmacist with her patriotic songs, hoped to inflate his ego and leave him the message she was getting on the nerves of the old Italo-American couple. This irritated Don Pompeo. The old Italo-American couple had no enemies. They minded their own business; and more so than other couples who could afford to be generous, they were considerably more open-handed with the poor and hungry kids of the town. Don Pompeo was frequently forced to defend himself from the accusations of the pharmacist, who was against any type of sociability, and accused Don Pompeo with the Italo-Americans of plotting against the Fascist Party.

"They should have stayed put in their adopted land," Don Pompeo used to say of the Italo-Americans. "They feared hardship in America and look what they got into! They got into a situation where the word peace has become a madness."

But all those nuisances and displeasures were not life threatening and did not really torment the mind of Don Pompeo. What worried him most of all, were the steps of major importance taken recklessly by Rome. The first hasty step was the Alliance. The "do-nothing" attitude in regard to the annexation of small neighboring states, and the plundering of inferior people's assets was the other. Now—mobilization? Those were more than nuisances to be concerned about. In due time those decisions taken with haste by the leadership, gave motion to instability while reinforcing in the minds of the partners, the belief that Italy would fight any type of warfare breaking out in the globe.

Finally the conflict broke. In time, Italy was suckered into it and Don Pompeo experienced ugly nightmares. In view of all those occurrences Don Pompeo made remarks more emphatically than before. He said to his friends: "When Italy opens the package of the great Alliance, she will find in it the ticket to our destruction."

The first person to enter Don Pompeo Gazzaladra's shop that evening was Cicco Palla. In entering Cicco spoke to the old cobbler reverently as if he were greeting some higher nobility.

"My special regards to you too," answered Don Pompeo. "I haven't seen you much, lately. I thought perhaps you were offended the night when you imagined that the hoeing trio of Reverend Palestrina been killed. When I rebuked you for wanting to declare war, you went home because your she-ass was about to deliver the little one. The night you imagined the killings nobody was to deliver anything, but you were nowhere to be found. Were you perhaps worried Cipollone might beat you? If something was said here that could have offended you, please accept my apology. We all make mistakes at one time or another. Then in regard to the declaration of war, I want you to know that our warmonger leaders will plunge us into a war, whether we want or not. And let's hope that Damiano Grifone, Luigi Durezza and Cosimo LaBorgia will not get killed for real."

"Oh! God forbid that," said Cicco Palla. "I know, we are getting closer to a war. The hoeing trio is saying that Reverend Palestrina has been speaking of war every day. One nation, far, far away, has already been attacked. Damiano told me Reverend Palestrina wants to give them a good confession before they go to fight, just in case something bad happens. No, Don Pompeo, I do not feel offended at all. Neither do I feel embarrassment for the things said to me when I suggested declaring war. Of Cipollone I was little scared, but I was not embarrassed. He, with LaBorgia, is insinuating that I am less than a half pint. They say my kids are taller than me when they are sitting down. According to them my children are beautiful, but don't have one iota of my looks. That makes me mad. They all go repeating Damiano's words when he found out that I was getting married."

"What had Damiano said?"

"He said: 'Are you getting married for real? Hurry up Cicco, so we can have children.' "

"Yeah, but he didn't mean that in the real sense," said Don Pompeo.

"I do not care to know the sense. All I can tell you, is that my children were born in my house, and that is what counts the most."

"Sure, Cicco, sure."

"Besides, you yourself Don Pompé, tell us that thoroughbred *cafoni* do not get offended nor understand embarrassment."

"Right, I am happy we have reached an understanding. Once more we have established that *cafoni* are born without the gene that causes embarrassment. Now let's put this subject to rest and talk of other important matters."

"Yeah, it would be much better."

"Fine, so tell me how your little donkey is doing. Is he growing as you had expected?"

"He is doing alright, thanks. If he keeps growing so fast, in a year or so I will train him for some light work."

"Of course he will, Cicco. You have a great skill when it comes to raising strong jackasses. But is Signor Luigi willing to let you keep him? Isn't he thinking to sell the jackass?" asked Don Pompeo.

"Oh no. Signor Luigi will let me keep the young donkey because he says that on the farm, the more jackasses the better."

"Damned hypocrite, that Signor Luigi! He never changes," blurted out Don Pompeo. "He is the eternal exploiter of his poor sharecroppers, always orchestrating newer methods for demanding more from his dependents." Don Pompeo could not see eye to eye with Signor Luigi. The big landowner was not the popular type among tradesmen or sharecroppers. Although in public Signor Luigi spoke well of his dependents, in private he was in the habit of making strict, and even stricter demands upon them.

What a tyrant, that Signor Luigi, thought Don Pompeo. He then attempted to warn Cicco Palla about Signor Luigi's ploy, but all of sudden Spaventa entered the shop. After Feliciano and Suzzera came Albarosa, followed closely by Guglielmo Sparacelli. The five new guests had not even made themselves comfortable when the hoeing trio of Reverend Palestrina stopped by. While Durezza and LaBorgia entered the shop to greet Don Pompeo, Grifone was heard cussing at his she-ass who kept coming back to the door of the shop as if she, too, wished to join the group inside.

"I cannot let you go in," Grifone was heard saying to his she-ass in a not so polite way. "Don Pompeo does not have time to entertain donkeys, you hear?"

"Ah! Damiano, Damiano, selfish boy! Let the animal come in. One more should not make that much of a difference. Your donkey may feel lonesome in that dark barn of yours and perhaps wishes to socialize," said Don Pompeo.

"What do you mean lonesome, dark, barn? If it's good enough for my wife and me, why not she? Who does she think she is, the she-ass of Father Alfonso?"

"I guess you have made your point Damiano. We do not want to go against your wishes. I am curious though, why Reverend Palestrina has kept you guys working so late. He must have had an important job that needed to be accomplished quickly."

"Yeah, he sure did. This is our seventh week we are working on the same job, and will not finish until next Friday," said LaBorgia. "Friday, weather permitting, and masons showing up, we will close early and then celebrate as usual."

"The masons? What hell is Reverend Palestrina building in the olive grove, a brothel?"

"Sort of," answered Durezza. "He tells us that it is a shelter. An anti-war shelter or something like that."

"That is not an anti-war shelter," said LaBorgia. "Reverend Palestrina said it is an anti-bomb shelter, dummy!"

"Okay, okay, let's not start again this evening. Let's not attack each other with offensive words, but just enjoy each other's company. God only knows this could be the last evening we gather here. Don't you guys know that a mobilization has been called? I recall the three of you were born at the start of World War I, and now you are of age to fight if a war breaks. It is just a matter of time. Our participation in it comes with the same package of the great Alliance. Your parents fought in World War I to make the world better, and now it seems you must fight again to make it better once more. In between the wars we have starved and entrusted the monarchy to Il Duce. Now only God knows how many wars we must fight before the world really does become better. I was past my prime age in 1914 and didn't taste that war, unlike many of our fellow countrymen from Montelieto. Understand though, that I had already had my ass kicked from the Africans at Aduwa in 1896, and was lucky to escape and grow past the age of mobilization in 1914. Still it is hard to understand the motives why Reverend Palestrina is so enthusiastically building an anti-bomb shelter over the foothill, when the fight is in Northern Europe. But then, what Reverend Palestrina does is not really an issue. He might have in mind things we do not know. The most important thing is that he employs our own people, and that is what counts."

Of course Don Pompeo wouldn't express his suspicions in front of his friends regarding the intentions Reverend Palestrina entertained for building any type of structure in the olive orchard. Don Pompeo knew that even before the seminary days, young Orazio Palestrina had placed his interests with the orchard where he sought to join youngsters of his age. He knew also that young Orazio was determined, that someday, he would expand and make permanently comfortable, and more useful, the large and rough chalet his grandparents had built such a long time ago. The true intentions of Reverend Palestrina were to build a mountain chalet where he could travel to and fro on mule's back, and spend some time away from the daily routine of the mansion, Church, and town. Perhaps he could spend the nights there to enjoy the fresh air of the hills, look at the beautiful night sky, and even bring with him the company he liked best—women. Because the war had begun and the Fascist pharmacist was gearing for it, as a subterfuge Reverend Palestrina made his hoeing trio believe he had built a bomb shelter.

The old shoemaker had figured out pretty close what was going on. But the personal affairs of the priest should not be anybody's business. If it fulfilled his ambitions doing the things he wished to do, why not? He had plenty of money and could spend it as he wished. So if Reverend Palestrina spent his own money to make himself comfortable, and meantime provide some temporary work for the unemployed of Montelieto, Don Pompeo sent him his blessings. Yet on the vigil of the first mobilization, things could turn out not as anticipated. Reverend Palestrina could have to do without the help of the hoeing trio and—even worse—without excuses to avoid mobilization himself. He was the right age and ran the danger of being called to serve his country as chaplain in the armed forces.

"God forbid! Reverend Palestrina called up in this mobilization? Yet we ought to keep in mind that the leadership wants to have the cannons blessed, before taking them to the front," said Don Pompeo. "What hypocrisy! Bless the guns so they'll have accuracy to kill more people? Unfortunately, this has been a practice of the past, to have highly respected religious leaders bless the cannons at the start of wars. This is a bad omen for the Reverend."

"If all those things happen, and Reverend Palestrina will have to manage his olive orchard without the help of the hoeing trio, I with some young kids could give him a hand. And if he is called to bless the cannons he could be assigned to the same artillery outfit where Cipollone served his compulsory army stretch. He could find himself blessing Cipollone too," said Cicco Palla.

"Yeah, Cipollone was discharged from the heavy artillery unit just couple of years ago," said Albarosa.

"What if I, too, am called in a future mobilization in the cavalry regiment, like has been Fedele," said Cicco Palla looking straight at Don Pompeo.

"No chance," laughed Damiano aloud before Don Pompeo could answer. "You will never grow to the size of our King for another hundred years. You should be also reminded that our King is not very tall. And don't you ever believe that Reverend Palestrina will come carrying a stepladder, so you could mount a horse."

"It will not work, Damiano, joker," said Luigi Durezza almost choking from the smoke of the cigar he had been sharing with LaBorgia. "You come up with that nonsense thinking we will laugh and give up the cigar. This was given to us from Reverend Palestrina to share, remember?"

"I am happy you guys find humor even in the face of critical situations. Whether Reverend Palestrina blesses Cipollone's guns or Cicco's ladder is not what we wish to happen. The important thing is that religious leaders from the other side are not called to bless their armies, because then we could have a hell of war on our hands. And Cicco, you shouldn't get offended about what these guys are saying. I am sure they like you just as much as I do. You will have my friendly hospitality here, in this shop of mine, at any time you feel lonely. Come and I'll be your friend. Together we will wish and pray that these jokers come back home safely, from wherever they may go."

While Don Pompeo spoke, Cicco Palla squirmed out of the shop without turning back or wishing anybody the usual goodnight. Instead he slammed the door forcefully to leave behind the message that he had again been a subject of ridicule, just because of his size. When Don Pompeo heard the door closing, he looked up and said: "Cicco wiggled out again, eh? I feel for him. When someone has to resign himself to the idea that he cannot serve because of his size, it is discouraging. You guys ought to be more understanding and less sneering. Cicco should stand up and defend himself, though, and not run away. On the other hand, perhaps Cicco should thank the Lord he was created a half pint! He will certainly not be going to the front! And if the able-bodied should all perish in the war, he and that pot-bellied pharmacist could be the ones to re-populate Montelieto. But God save us from that! We do not wish this town of ours to be re-populated from those two."

Then in his own words Don Pompeo said, "We better leave this re-populating issue to Reverend Palestrina."

At Don Pompeo's humorous observation all the *cafoni* laughed aloud and collectively shouted: "Yeah! Let the Reverend re-populate Montelieto." Then all together they screamed: "Evviva Reverend Orazio Palestrina, our nutty priest!"

Chapter 17

To no one's surprise the proximity of a mobilization leading to an impending conflict, had inflated the ego of the tyrant pharmacist to an unbearable degree. His self-importance and faked authority became manifest in his daily actions, more so than ever before.

While conducting the youth of Montelieto in the required war drills, the pharmacist's arrogant behavior, of course, reflected that of the high leadership of Fascist Italy. In those perilous days all the youngsters who participated in the drills of war in town found themselves handled rudely and menacingly as if they were traitors. Those who had difficulties in complying with the one-sided demands of the pharmacist, or those who attended the drills of war in shabby garb, were slapped and mistreated by the pharmacist's henchmen. They were admonished, sent back home, and challenged to produce their donkey-driver parents' protest.

Meantime as the ego of the pharmacist inflated, with the news of mobilization and war, so did the rage of the parents whose youngsters were abused. When that rage had reached the breaking point in the following evenings, the deceived parents assembled inside the shop of Don

Pompeo to discuss ways of organizing a revolt. Having lost their patience, they were intensely determined to kick the arrogant pharmacist out of town. The opportunity to get even (which Don Pompeo had predicted), did not seem certain of appearing.

"I am beginning to believe that we will never be able to get even. Let's get him while we are still alive," said Cipollone, losing his patience.

"Okay, okay," said Don Pompeo. "You have been told many times that I share your feelings wholeheartedly. However, I will repeat, I am not going to encourage you to get even and let you possibly turn the situation for the worse! In my judgment, a revolt against that imbecile will cause terrifying consequences for our people. Please sober up! Understand that I, too, will suffer the injustices with you, until the end of time."

The parents of the abused kids of Montelieto did not have to wait long for their retaliation to come around. Even though in the blink of an eye they could have smashed inside the House of Fasces, thrown out the petty tyrant and his paraphernalia, and sent him crying to his boss, the Prefect—that would not have been quite advisable. Taking the law in one's own hands and mounting a disorderly protest against the Party in power could have been extremely risky in those wicked times.

Don Pompeo frequently tried to dissuade the angry parents from taking such hasty and impulsive action. Even though the indignities and injustices of the pharmacist pained Don Pompeo deeply, still he cautioned the parents not to act on impulse. To oust out the pharmacist from the House of Fasces would not serve the interest of one single child of Montelieto.

We must find a better way to deal with that potbelly of a pharmacist, Don Pompeo thought. "I know there are many options to be considered," he said to his friends, "and I believe that among those options, some would be more sensible. We could assemble beneath the balcony of the City Hall and show the *Podestá* (mayor) our frustration in dealing with the pharmacist and his drills of war. It would also be helpful, if we appealed to the moderate Fascists in town, to intercede with the mayor, and exhort the pharmacist to be more considerate of the kids who live in poverty. I will volunteer to supply some of those kids with more decent footwear, at very low cost. Also, to intercede on our behalf could be the Baroness, the doctor, and the parish pastor."

"They could," Albarosa said interrupting, "but I doubt those bureaucrats will side with us."

"Nobody will side with us," said Peluso. "The only person who sides with us *cafoni*, and expects nothing in return, is Don Pompeo. His advice is truly sincere."

"We are all aware of that," said Durezza. "I still want to ask Don Pompeo, though, how effective any of those options he mentioned could turn out to be."

"Glad you have asked, Durezza. The most effective remedy is one I failed to mention. First could be that I, myself, go to kick the pharmacist out of the House of Fasces, and chase him away from Montelieto. The second efficient option could be that we entrust the task to Reverend Orazio Palestrina. He, for sure, would beat the nonsense out the head of the pharmacist, with his fists."

"Yeah! That's the right option," yelled the *cafoni*. "Let's go with the second."

"I understand your feelings of revenge, but we can't ask Reverend Palestrina, a man of the cloth, to use his fists in our behalf—not yet. That would put him in danger of being arrested. He is the only respectable figure remaining in Montelieto who is not Fascist oriented. My advice to you is to keep the Reverend out of this. We will consider none of the options, for the time being, understand?"

Don Pompeo was not so gullible as to believe something good would result from pursuing the measures he had suggested. Neither the influential personalities nor the moderate Fascists gave a hoot for the drills of war, or for the poor youth of Montelieto. They all courted the Party leaders anyway. What Don Pompeo had in mind was to distract his friends from making reactionary moves and thus cause even more problems. So, to put his friends at ease, Don Pompeo told them that together, they would follow new strategies. To the parents of the abused kids, he suggested to keep them home, but to send word to the pharmacist that the kids would be ready to attend the drills of war, as soon as the shoemaker Don Pompeo supplied them with the proper footwear. "That will put the responsibility squarely on my shoulders," said Don Pompeo. "I will deal with that bull-head of a pharmacist, by myself! Of course I would prefer not to have anything to do with that damned tyrant; honestly, I'd rather spend my time talking about the funny tales that have occurred here in our town than to talk about all the difficulties that screwball creates for us."

"That is a very good idea, Don Pompé," said Cipollone.

"Of course it is a good idea," agreed Pezzafina. "Don Pompeo never comes up with a bad one."

"Yeah! Why don't you guys hush, so Don Pompeo could start telling us some good tales?" said someone. "Don Pompé, start with the one about the sacristan you did not finish telling when Barabba entered the shop," the same one said.

"Yeah, let's hear that one, Don Pompé. By this hour Barabba is already in bed."

"Fine," agreed Don Pompeo. "After that you will clear away from here, and go straight home without looking for trouble, understand?"

"We do, we do understand, Don Pompé."

"Well, then I must tell you that a long time ago, a poor sacristan hired by a priest on permanent basis, a man who lived on the handouts from the pastor of the parish of Montelieto, Father Eusebio, suddenly became envious of his employer and benefactor. For the entire period of his service to the priest, the sacristan Candeloro Acceso had seen his boss invite to the Presbytery, for dinner, the conductor of the band and two soloists who played music in town on the feast days. The sacristan, with his wife whose job was housekeeper of the Presbytery, served the dinner for the pastor and guests. Candeloro knew next to nothing about classical music but, even so, he had become fascinated by it and the maestro.

"That made him go begging Father Eusebio to let him invite the musicians for dinner, at least once in his lifetime." Father Eusebio agreed.

"Candeloro had acquired all the fine traits for serving special dinners. When the pastor, Father Eusebio, during dinner saw that the bottle of wine ran empty, and wished to impress his guests, he would ask the sacristan to please go to the cellar to refill the bottle with fresh wine.

"Candeloro, having been instructed in advance what to say, at that point would turn to the priest and ask: 'Father, from what barrel number shall I draw the wine this time?' "

"At that Father Eusebio, after contemplating theatrically for a second or two, would say: 'Well . . . this time, Candeloro, draw the wine from barrel number five instead of barrel number two.'

"The pastor had zero barrels of wine down in the cellar but, nonetheless, wished to impress his guests with his bounty. Candeloro had the same number of barrels as had the priest, and not much of a wine cellar and even less of a house. But he and his wife went scraping for pennies to buy some food and two or three bottles of wine kept downstairs for a special occasion.

"On the next feast day, the musicians came for dinner at Candeloro's house. When Candeloro saw the bottle of wine run empty, he turned to his wife and said: 'Dear, would you mind to go refill the bottle with fresh wine from the cellar?'

"On her way downstairs his wife turned to him and asked: 'From what barrel number should I draw the wine this time, my love?' Candeloro, then pretending to memorize the barrel numbers, and wanting to impress his guests as much as Father Eusebio was used to do, said: 'This time, dear, draw the wine from barrel number six of the fifth row northwest end of the cellar, instead of number two in the fourth row.' "

"Damn!" Cicco Palla swore amid laughter. "The barrels of wine of the sacristan are really hard to figure out!"

"Right, my boy, who knows how many barrels he had," said Don Pompeo pretending to have no idea. "Who knows how many!"

Finally all the *cafoni* left the shop of the shoemaker and went home. They went out laughing at the trickeries Father Eusebio and the sacristan had fabricated, as a ruse to appear well-to-do. Some even laughed at Cicco Palla himself for being unable to count how many barrels of wine Candeloro had stored in the cellar.

The old cobbler then retired upstairs, and felt happy to have restrained his unpredictable friends with a tale. "If that is what takes to distract them from being unruly, I know many more of those. Still, I understand their frustration; I feel it myself. Harsh duties have been imposed upon us for too long, and we feel we have no rights whatsoever. That is our sad story," said Don Pompeo.

On the following afternoon Don Pompeo had a good chat with Reverend Palestrina. He informed his clerical friend of the discipline the pharmacist had lately been imposing on the youngsters in town. "The Fascist chief has a deadly obsession with the drills of war and with the kids. He wishes to conduct the drills, militia style; he demands instant obedience, steady attendance and perfect tidiness. When the kids come short of those requisites, that ruffian—whose example they are commanded to follow—abuses them! I hope he will change his attitude and leave the poor kids and their parents in peace," said Don Pompeo with concern.

"I don't believe he will ever change. Those types of arrogant Party hard-liners are selected from the pits of vileness. You see? The Party has control over every aspect of our life. I wish I could be of help," said Reverend Palestrina.

"Of course we know you would help, Reverend. But I am beginning to feel we got stuck for good, not only with the Party, but even with the pharmacist and with the Prefect."

"The Prefect? Yeah! That could open up a window of opportunities. I could politely mention to him the problems of the poor sharecroppers of Montelieto. He is an inveterate Fascist, but I believe he is basically a decent and truly patriotic citizen. We were buddies, and debated on many subjects during our first years of school. Then he began to repudiate the teachings of the seminary, and eventually joined the *Camice Nere* (Black Shirts). Years later he was promoted and then became a powerful figure in the Party. I will send a note to remind him that the youth of Montelieto can't be a model to the Party unless their situation is given an objective look. Without any doubt in my mind, the Prefect still remembers me. I will let you know in what way he replies," said Reverend Palestrina.

"Thanks, Reverend. I didn't mean to inconvenience you."

"No inconvenience at all, dear Don Pompeo. You will be more than welcome. Have a wonderful evening."

The old shoemaker returned home hoping for the best, with a feeling that Reverend Palestrina took to heart the many difficulties facing Montelieto. *He sincerely wishes to be of help,* thought Don Pompeo.

On his way home Don Pompeo talked to himself. He figured out, in his mind, how great a leader the priest could be, if his line of work were reversed. "What a great leader could Reverend turn out to be. What a super leader! But, to be honest, the question remains: What in hell can he do to save us from that swellhead of a pharmacist, or from illiteracy? I believe not much at all, at the present," Don Pompeo went mumbling to himself all the way back home.

Chapter 18

The State-controlled radio broadcasts, transmitted from the capital to the nation in the evening, began to sound more assertive and alarming than ever. By praising the power and invincibility of the future "partners in the common cause," the war bulletins stirred up the emotion and the patriotism of the crowds to a higher degree. The time for pacifism was up; there were not going to be any more high-level talks. No more annexations of smaller states, no more efforts of diplomacy. Only war. From there on, all future conquests would have to be won by aggression and by test of battle.

Several nations in Europe were mired in an ugly and crazy mix up of political differences and denials of pacts. Each nation accused the others of wrongdoing. War against one another was every day becoming more real and unavoidable.

In view of what was occurring, Don Pompeo felt crushed with disappointment and distrust. Although he had envisioned problems on the horizon, he had kept his hopes high for his country. Perhaps the monarchy, if it had played its cards smartly, could have maintained both its neutrality and the empire. He also hoped that leaders of strong convictions, whose nations had been feuding over old grudges, would have used keen foresight for prolonging or avoiding confrontation. But none of those things materialized. Three or four years down the road of the empire a terrible conflict was in the making. The likelihood that his beloved *cafoni* could be heading for further hardships made him tremble.

On the other hand, the rumors of war gave more impetus to the Fascist pharmacist for achieving his dreams. He became more defiant and sarcastic. As he commanded repetitive, rigid drills of war to the group of trainee *cafoni*, in his heart, he entertained dreams of violent conflicts that would involve all the youth of Montelieto. When he observed the Italo-American pensioner listening to the radio broadcast with Don Pompeo the Fascist tyrant said: "You little American bastard, I swear to have your pension cut in no time! You will have to pay the price for having declined to join our Fascist Party. I want to see you eat potato peelings and than we will send both of you to Washington to make your complaints," he said loud and clear so the bystanders could take notice.

Don Pompeo had no illusions that a mobilization would not occur, and that Europe was not in a political mess. Neither had he any illusions that the anti-bomb shelter, recently completed by Reverend Palestrina, could save lives. He laughed at the idea of a shelter and said: "That shelter Orazio has built in the olive orchard, is situated near three kilometers all the way uphill from Montelieto. And how can that nutty priest save anyone in case of an attack? How quickly could he get there on mule's back if an emergency arises? Has he got in mind to fly in his next project? Even if a full-scale war breaks out, nobody even knows where Montelieto is. Well, I must tell the Reverend he better learn how to pray to the Lord with good faith so the good Lord will have heed for us all."

That same afternoon Don Pompeo's siesta was cut short by several loud knocks at his front door.

"Damned will be you, Elvira!" he swore. "Can't you ever act a little bit civilized in this neighborhood of ours? If you must get back the boots of the pharmacist, the hours open for business are posted on the door of my shop. Could it sometime enter your pumpkin head not to be so loud and disturbing to those around you?"

While Don Pompeo continued cursing the person knocking at his door, more hard knocks made the door rattle. "What are you trying to do, pull unset the door-knocker and the door off its hinges?" he said while opening in disgust.

Instead of Elvira knocking at the door, to Don Pompeo's surprise he saw Sigismondo, the sacristan, quite shaken up.

"What is troubling you, Sigismondo?" Don Pompeo asked. "Why this early? It is still too hot for taking a stroll—don't you know that my dear friend?"

"Of course I know it is too hot, but I have come here not to ask you to go for a stroll! This is an emergency. I wanted to be the first to inform you that earlier this afternoon, I saw the mailman Ottaviano speaking with the pharmacist. He then left in a hurry with a bunch of yellow papers in his hands. He looked upset and when I asked what was going on, he said that the mobilization notices had arrived and he had been urged by the pharmacist to deliver the notices to the people in the farming districts. He told me that the remaining notices, those addressed to the young men here in town, will be dispensed this evening at the time of the radio broadcast. I am worried because the names of my boys, Antonio and Pietro, could be on the list."

"Sorry to hear the bad news, Sigismondo. Nobody can do anything about that. It is unfortunate that our youngsters have to pay for the mistakes of our leadership, so early in their lives. Let's hope this mobilization will be the last and that it is called only for retraining purposes. We want our kids to come back home safe and sound."

"I know you are concerned and sincere, Don Pompé. And I do understand that neither we nor the kids whose names are on the notifications list have any choice."

"Right. We will learn this evening who will be recalled. Let's hope it won't be the whole six classes they have been projecting to recall to arms for sometime."

"Yeah, let's hope so. I must go now my friend. See you later in the evening, goodbye."

After they said goodbye, Don Pompeo locked the door and returned inside. He was not in the mood to rest up anymore. The news of the mobilization had already interrupted his siesta and he was upset. He put on his working clothes, instead, and went down to open the shop. On that afternoon, he could feel tension in the air. People walked nervously back and forth from the Church Square and Don Pompeo (in his thoughts), called on those whose sons might be on the list of names of the recall. "Hope it is not for your boy, Maria Rosa. Not your boys Vittorio. Damn, I hope there is not one name of those boys I have known in Montelieto, and instead might catch only the colleagues of the Fascist pharmacist."

The word that the call to arms had arrived at Montelieto spread quickly. Before Ottaviano returned from the farming districts, people were already gathering beneath the balcony of the House of Fasces. Male and female, young and old, were gathering but nobody seemed to be interested in listening to the war bulletins. They waited worriedly to hear Ottaviano call out the names on the notification cards. A short while later, Ottaviano was seen going upstairs to the House of Fasces with a stack of papers in hand, a step or two in front of the pharmacist. He stepped out on the balcony and, with a loud voice, began reading from a piece of paper handed to him by the pharmacist.

"Fellow citizens of Montelieto," he read. "This evening we have news of major interest to share with you. Our dear fatherland is in danger of being attacked from a rude and shameless enemy. We, the fit and able-bodied of Montelieto, on this day are called upon to defend the honor and sacred soil of our forefathers. With great pride and spirit of sacrifice, we must answer this call and pledge to defend our beloved fatherland with all the strength of our will."

After having read more lines of old rhetoric, Ottaviano gave the speech sheet back to the pharmacist, saluted him and shouted: "Long live Italy! Long Live Il Duce!"

To that call for hurrahs, only a few replied with: "Long live Italy!" One single, feeble voice called out: "Long live Il Duce," but that was whistled sneeringly from several among the crowd below.

Then Ottaviano spoke again and said that, based on the instructions of the pharmacist, everyone must remain calm. "Those people whose names are called," he said, "are invited to come upstairs, receive their papers and descend the ramp on the other end of the portico."

By that time, there was not one single soul inside the shoe shop of Don Pompeo that would be company for him. He felt alone and abandoned, and his nerves wrenched with the first shouts of: "Long live Il Duce!" coming from the House of Fasces. He also spoke to himself and said: "I understand Ottaviano's shoutings. He must shout as loud as he can if he cares to keep his job. I know, though, that deep down he doesn't mean what he says. On the other hand, that bastard pharmacist, ruffian to the Prefect, cannot open his mouth without shouting hurrahs to Il Duce."

Then, annoyed at staying alone, and anxious to learn the names of his younger friends about to be called, Don Pompeo went outside, walked a short distance flanking the building, and stopped to rest against the cornerstones facing the Church Square, where a big crowd awaited the news. Don Pompeo looked out and at the other corner of the same building saw his neighbor, the Italo-American pensioner, standing alone.

"Let's go see the old American," said Don Pompeo to himself, starting to walk. "He must be worried about the things happening this evening. I cannot understand the reasons why he has stayed here for so long before returning to America. He was injured while serving in the United States cavalry, assigned a small pension and I am sure that little something went a long way here in Montelieto. Who can tell, though, what's going to happen to that? His claims to have returned here to weather the storm of economic hard times in America make little sense to me. Perhaps he imagined a bed of roses here. Bed of roses? Poor fool. Look what he got into! For the remaining days of his life he has to be humiliated by that no good son of a bitch of a pharmacist, Santuccio Santamiddia, the tyrant of troubled Montelieto. That leech does not deserve to be addressed with such a nice Christian name. That is exactly the reason he is known as stupid sloth and a pimp . . .

"Good evening, Domenic! Are you enjoying the show?" said Don Pompeo coming closer and whispering to the Italo-American in a friendly manner.

"Not as much as I would like to. It is not so pleasing to learn these youngsters will soon be going to war. Shoot and get shot? Virgin Mary!" Domenic said in reflecting aloud.

"Yeah, I share the same feelings," said Don Pompeo.

Meanwhile, from the balcony of the House of Fasces the mailman, Ottaviano, spoke again. He said that all veterans whose names he was about to call must report to the same outfit they served last in the same city, within three days' time. He also said that he would begin calling the names in alphabetical order, and that all bystanders must remain quiet. "First the surnames will be called. Second, the first names, and third the date of birth and the paternity." That, Ottaviano pointed out, would be done for precaution to avoid misunderstanding and a mix-up of identity. He said that, in Montelieto, many men carried the same name as well as surnames that usually raised doubts of the person's true identity. The mailman then proceeded by unfolding a sheet of paper and began to call out the first names on the list.

He called:

"Albarosa Antonio, di Mariano" (of Mariano), "class of 1915."

"Amabella Romualdo, class of 1916, paternity un-
known."
"Barabba Pietro, di Sigismondo, class of 1914."
"Cipollone Gerardo, di Antonio, class of 1914."
"Cipollone Gerardo, fú Antonio, class of 1914." ("Di"
denotes living father, "fú" deceased father.)

Then Ottaviano called: "Durezza Luigi, class of 1916,
paternity unknown." And so on up to the last letters of the
alphabet. As the ones called walked upstairs, the Fascist
pharmacist promptly handed each their respective papers,
assumed a position of attention and at the top of his lungs
screamed: "Long live Il Duce! Long Live Italy!"

By this time Francisco Palla, who had been searching
for Don Pompeo in the crowd, came nearby and greeted
both him and Domenic with a good evening. He turned
then to Don Pompeo and said: "Thanks to God, they have
finally caught Cipollone Gerardo, fú Antonio. I was afraid
they would only call Cipollone Gerardo, di Antonio. What
a relief!"

"Yeah! But that doesn't mean you will be immune from
the wrath of many others. In order for you to be safe from
the sneers and threats of beatings, they have to mobilize
the entire population of Montelieto—women, children
and all."

"I know that, Don Pompé, but for the time being it is
a relief for me not to worry about Cipollone and the rest of
the hoeing trio of Reverend Palestrina. As for what concerns the others, who knows what will happen? I might be
called myself," answered Francisco Palla.

Meantime the mailman Ottaviano proceeded calling
more names, going up to the letter P. He called: "Palanca

Francisco, di Romeo." At the first syllables of "Palanca," Palla stood high on the tip of his toes. When the mailman called: "Palandra Francisco (no paternity)," Francisco Palla stood higher yet when hearing the first sound of Pa-landra, but Don Pompeo told him not to get excited with the sound of the first syllables of the names. "You could never be among those who are being called to arms. Not even by a remote chance," Don Pompeo stressed.

"You can never be sure, Don Pompé. When Ottaviano called 'Pa-lan-dra Francisco no paternity,' I almost fainted! I came very close to answer the call to arms. 'Pa-lan-dra Francisco, and no paternity,' sounded the same as if it was me. For a minute I thought they had forgotten I am 4–F," Francisco Palla said.

"Okay, okay, I understand you, *testa di cocuzza*, (pumpkin head) and that's one reason I care about you a trifle more than the rest of the *cafoni*. Now let's stay quiet and listen to Ottaviano," said Don Pompeo.

Ottaviano finished calling the names going as far was the "V" and "Z." He had some difficulty pronouncing the last name of Vizzacchiero but then said loudly: "Finally we are at the last name of the 28 men recalled."

After a brief pause he called: "From the class of 1914, Zuccone Primo, no paternity." Then he spoke to the crowd, saying: "The pharmacist now wishes you to enjoy the bulletin of war. Enjoy the evening and good luck to all of you."

Not very many remained behind to listen to the bulletin of war. Neither would they enjoy the rest of the evening. They all went home to families, and all were wished good luck. Domenic, quite shaken from the thought of an immediate conflict, wished Don Pompeo and Cicco goodnight.

Walking slowly back to the shop, Don Pompeo talked with indignation to Cicco in regard to the mobilization and its impact on the people of Montelieto. Cicco reminded Don Pompeo that if they recalled all those people, that could hurt even Reverend Palestrina. According to him, the Reverend could lose the privilege of hiring the hoeing trio at his convenience. Then Cicco said that in view of all the things happening lately, he could enjoy some advantages. He said that when all those veterans were gone, he could have a better chance to be asked to work for the Deputy Mayor at least couple a days per week, sweeping and picking up the donkey dung in the streets of Montelieto.

"Certainly," answered Don Pompeo. "Reverend Palestrina, though, is not going to get hurt. It is Durezza, Grifone and LaBorgia who are in danger to get hurt for real. Then as to what concerns you, my dear Cicco, yes, I must say that in the worst of situations, there will always be something or someone who escapes the wrath of misfortune. Sure, I agree. You will have better chances to pick up the dung of the donkeys of Montelieto."

"I don't know whether I am lucky or not. Between the hours I spend working the piece of land of Signor Luigi, the cleaning of the streets, and the grooming of the horse of the Deputy Mayor, there isn't much more time left for me to do anything else."

"Oh, yeah! We could say you are a very busy guy, Cicco. On the other hand you are a very lucky man, compared to all those poor boys who have been called to arms."

"About the recalls to arms, I wish to ask if you have noticed something that I have noticed."

"Don't know, but what was the thing that attracted your attention, and not mine, Cicco?"

"While Ottaviano was calling the names of our friends, I heard there were lots of S.O.B.s among them, in Montelieto. I am not the only one who has 'unknown paternity,' you know?"

"Who ever said you're the only one? I have known all the time there are many S.O.B. and many, many *cafoni* in our town!"

"Glad to be understood. Goodnight Don Pompé," Cicco Palla said elatedly.

"Goodnight, my boy," answered the shoemaker adding: "And let's hope that this recall to arms, or the so-called mobilization, is meant only for retraining purposes."

Chapter 19

The departure of his friends from the shores of Montelieto to the front was one of the bitterest pills for Don Pompeo to swallow. Several of those recalled back to arms began to leave the following morning. A few more departed in the next two days, all depending on the distance and time allowed for them to report to their old outfits. Don Pompeo's shop remained open the whole day and whole night, so to indicate easy access to those friends who wished to come to say goodbye. Above his working bench, on the wall, easily visible from the entrance, the old cobbler had hung a piece of cardboard upon which he had written with white chalk: "FAREWELL, MY BOYS! PLEASE COME BACK HOME SAFE."

But not too many could read that long phrase.

Early on in the morning, Don Pompeo would be seen standing near the postal van, waiting to wish a thoughtful farewell to those who were leaving.

Those were long days of painful agony in the life of Don Pompeo. After the first shock of seeing his dear friends leave the shores of Montelieto, there wasn't much news that would impress him. Not even the swift and ruthless invasion of an unprepared nation, by a superior power, had a more powerful effect on his frame of mind. He had reached the conclusion that logic, goodness of heart and respect for one's neighbors, were virtues vanishing from the human society. So he resigned himself to the idea that if such evils, coupled with effectiveness in battle, were to be implemented to subjugate more nations, it would not be long before that superior power took control of the entire continent.

In the following days Don Pompeo regrouped his thoughts and decided to go back to work, which would help him to forget. But the likelihood that a superior army was bent on taking control of the continent troubled him immensely.

More troublesome for him was the fact that the leaders of Italy could be easily attracted by the results of the lightning attack and, thus, rush itself to the onslaught. If that were to be the case, the six classes comprising the first mobilization would never be sufficient. The occupation of Albania-Montenegro in the early spring had been carried out with selected battalions of Fascist troops and special army groups, but that had been brief and virtually a campaign without casualties. That conquest had been engineered and achieved only to make news, and to have Il Duce, with the King, look good in the eyes of the presumed "partners." To wage war on the Western neighbors though, as appeared to be forthcoming—that would be an involvement of enormous proportions which could easily backfire.

In view of the fact that in his opinion the occupation of Albania was executed to impress the presumed partners, Don Pompeo spoke up to the *cafoni*, saying: "Hell, if our Duce wished to impress his counterpart, he would be better off waging war on the town of the Republic of San Marino. There he could have at least a fifty-fifty chance of success."

At this point in time though, neither criticism or ridicule would be effective. The reality was that the country was embarking on a voyage of no return and there was nothing anybody could do to stop it. To keep his sanity Don Pompeo could not go on and on speculating, and remain untroubled by the events occurring on the national level. The kingdom that he had been fond of, nowadays had fallen into a position of inferiority to an autocratic government; the great Fascist Chief in Rome couldn't be swayed away from his dreams of grandeur—not even after wiser advisers told him that to wage war on the West, even jointly with the invincible "partners," could turn fatal. The words spoken by the old cobbler of Montelieto which said to his friends: "One day that man, that man whose picture on the posters attests to arrogance, will get all of us killed," could only verify a prophecy.

Time went by slowly. Spring was blossoming amid cries of greatness and calls for war. Don Pompeo had resumed his work with the same ambition but missed the company of his dear *cafoni*. Slowly, a younger group of teens began to frequent the shoe shop and this gave Don Pompeo a reawakening of the senses. Those young kids attended the elementary school on a regular basis and never failed to greet Don Pompeo when passing by. Other older teens who came from the farming districts, attended night classes taught by Father Alfonso and Reverend Palestrina in their respective houses. The old cobbler felt delighted to see that illiteracy was perhaps on the downgrade even in the times of great uncertainty.

On a late spring morning of 1940, Don Pompeo heard a loud outburst of voices explode in the Church Square below. As the bells from the belfry began to ring in a festive beat, he thought: *This is nothing new. The inevitable has occurred.*

He looked out and saw school children, teachers with every Fascist sympathizer, gathering beneath the balcony of the House of Fasces. The pharmacist dressed in his grand uniform, along with his henchmen, were seen giving instructions to the crowd on how to proceed on the march to the monument of the fallen soldiers. After the crowd of people was lined up into a cortege, they started marching toward the monument, singing. The Church Square became suddenly empty. While the bells from the belfry continued ringing, Don Pompeo went down to open the shop as usual. There, on the outside, in front of his door, stood the town crier Vittorio Settimo.

"Good morning, Vittorio," said Don Pompeo.

"Good morning to you too."

"Going to work with all that tension in the air?"

"No, I am not. With that loud din of the bells, people won't be able to hear my announcements. Sigismondo with his young kid, are ringing those bells like mad. You know the reasons for all that noise, don't you?"

"I sure do."

"The war was declared last night. I hope it won't be as long and cruel as the big war. For the sake of those boys who must go to fight, I pray it will be over soon."

"Let's hope so, Vittorio. The whole situation saddens me beyond belief. I, too, will pray for the sake of the boys of Montelieto. For the time being I wish you good work and a good day."

"Thanks. I will start delivering my announcements as soon as the cortege returns from the monument, and the bells will then quiet down. Good day to you, too, Don Pompé."

Don Pompeo spent the day in great distress. He wished to focus his thoughts and energy on the job, in order to work and forget, but that was hard to do. He worked and worked but felt the same profound anguish. When loneliness seemed to become intolerable, to his great surprise he received an unexpected visit. The door of his shoe shop opened and a polite Madam entered, greeting him warmly. "Good evening, Don Pompeo," she said.

"Good evening, Dorotea. This is a nice surprise. May I ask what has brought you to these neighborhoods at this hour? Are you perhaps, running errands for Reverend Palestrina and stopped by?"

"Yeah, you could say errands. To come to see you is certainly one errand!"

"How did you two saintly people handle the news of the declaration of war? Were you shaken?"

"I was, but Father Palestrina took it with calm. He had already anticipated that would happen for quite some time. Father Palestrina wanted me to come over to ask whether you had time to come to see him this evening. He said that after you have wrapped up your rush orders, he wishes you to visit with him and talk for a while."

"Of course I will. There is nothing more important on my list of chores than for me to visit with the Reverend. I shall come by at the time he dismisses the class."

"Fine, we shall see you around nine this evening. Father Palestrina will be happy to see you."

Dorotea left but Don Pompeo didn't have the wildest idea why he was so urgently needed by Reverend Palestrina. Sure, there had been emergencies in the past, when he was needed to service the family footwear, but never on the spur of the moment. So he finished the work started before Dorotea's visit, and ran upstairs to change into something clean.

While changing he wondered what Reverend Palestrina wished to chat about. *Perhaps he wants to tell me how the Christian nations are treating one another? I know he will remind me they are like fishes in the sea. The big fishes swallow the small. Yeah, but that is not exactly what is happening here. More likely he will tell me that bigger nations want to subdue both the smaller and the bigger. Could, perhaps, Reverend be looking for a dispatch-bearer? One who arranges a duel to death between him and the pharmacist? That could never happen! I couldn't imagine even a chicken accepting the challenge of Reverend Palestrina!* Don Pompeo mused. *No way, Reverend, believe me no way!*

At nine P.M. sharp Don Pompeo was at the door of Reverend Palestrina's mansion. Dorotea, who was showing the young student out, told Don Pompeo to proceed into the den. "Father Palestrina will happy to be with you in few minutes, Don Pompeo," she said.

"Fine, I'll be waiting."

While waiting Don Pompeo thought about Dorotea. "How lucky that woman is to have been working for the Palestrinas," he said. "She still reflects that young innocence, as when she and I were in our mid teens. Dorotea could have been my lady but she chose to be a maid to the rich instead. I know she made the best choice. Now she is the only person who has the privilege to address Reverend Palestrina as 'Father'."

"Happy to see you, Don Pompeo," said Reverend Palestrina.

"Happy to see you, too, Reverend."

"I must say that with all those shouts of: 'Long live our Duce' of late, I have never heard a word of praise from you. No hurrahs for your King, either. Have you, perhaps, given up on him? If you have, you are in the right place. I have saved an application for you to join us humanitarians."

"Ah! Reverend Communist! You seem to want to rub it in, a little, every time. To join you one has to be insane."

"Hush, hush," admonished the priest. "There is still a young man in the classroom within hearing distance. One of my best students is finishing up solving a very sophisticated problem. We do not wish to disturb him by having to listen to our political silliness. Some day this kid will be someone if he maintains the same interest in learning. Come, I want you to meet this young man so you will know first hand, that not everything will be lost for Montelieto. Many among this younger generation will rise above the pits of ignorance and illiteracy. I promise you this much," said Reverend Palestrina. "But that will happen when your two pig-headed leaders abdicate, or when the present system is overthrown, my dear Don Pompeo.

"Titus, meet Don Pompeo, the most renowned cobbler of our province in Ciociaria," said Reverend Palestrina.

"Pleased to meet you, Don Pompeo. I have heard many good things about you. You are not only a renowned cobbler but a cobbler with a big heart. My grandfather believes you ought to be mayor of Montelieto, because you are the only genuine and honorable first citizen. And Reverend Palestrina ought to be the Prefect (governor) of the province of Frosinone. Sorry I must hurry. By now my grandfather will be waiting at the outskirts of town, with the horses, to give me a lift back home. I am glad to have met you Don Pompeo and will be looking forward to meeting you again. I wish you and Reverend Palestrina a great evening. Goodbye."

"My good Lord!" Don Pompeo said turning to the Reverend. "Where has this chap come from?"

"You know, he is from the *Del Pio* (of the pious) clan. I suspect his young father will be next in line to be recalled to arms. Two of his uncles have already been recalled. They are a family of great integrity. We have farmlands that border each other's but, according to my father and uncle recollections, there has never been a dispute about border interference that couldn't be settled amicably. They are very respectful of the rights of others. However, don't ever step on theirs!"

"Oh, I know the brothers Giovanni and Antonio Del Pio."

"Right, but let's get comfortable and leave the Del Pios be. I have not asked you to visit with me to talk about the Del Pio clan. There are other matters I wish to talk over with you, and I am serious this time."

"Are you really? Okay I'll be listening. Are you by any chance, rejecting the clergy, Reverend?"

"No, not yet. The things I wish to talk about are much more important. For an opening, we must say that I will maintain the position of my profession unaltered. I am contemplating no immediate change for the time being. As you are well aware, we are going through complicated times. The possibility that conflicts could spread alongside our borders is now reality. If this keeps up, it will be difficult to hide. The next mobilization, without any doubt, will include my class. I know chaplains don't shoot people. Yet I believe they are required to go where casualties happen. Not many, more than you, know I am the right age. Once I have gone away, it won't be easy for me to maintain control over my olive orchard, my houses, farmlands and the sharecroppers.

"My dear shoemaker, I want to tell you life is not so easy for priests either. Particularly for priests of my character—a well-to-do priest, a spoiled priest, unbeliever and a . . . "

"A father, Reverend," quipped Don Pompeo.

"Exactly! You took the words off my mouth—a father without responsibility. I want very much to be responsible but I can't continue paying support and alimony for the kids and their mother openly. And it is not always possible to have Valentina coming over with the excuses of taking measurements for sewing my new clothes. This will be my chance to give her some cash for the support of the children. She mentioned that she had run into some debt with you for having charged the cost of new shoes on your list of unpaid items. Please let me settle that debt. Also, I want to see to it that you take care of her future footwear needs and those of the children. Let me know the cost of the work so I can reimburse you."

"I believe you would reimburse me, Reverend, but there is no need to do that. Valentina is not merely beautiful, she is a good and responsible mother who can take care of her own house expenses. She worries about paying me, more than I worry about collecting. She doesn't deserve a libertine father like you, for her children, Reverend! Why don't you shed that black robe of yours and marry her, for your own good. What are you waiting for?"

"I am not waiting for anything. The commotion of declaration of war of this morning still rings loud in my ears. The parade, those loud bells! Damn, it was almost enough to go crazy. These are hard times. We are opening conflicts already on three fronts. On the western Alps there is not much going on, but in East and North Africa we have committed many, many soldiers. If I am not wrong, the six classes of the first mobilization, with the special army and the classes of conscripts will not be sufficient. Another mobilization that will include many more classes is imminent. There have been rumors that another conflict will break soon, in the Balkans any day. How many damned fronts can they open? We are already involved with more than we can handle.

"And although we are not expected to do so badly in the first hours, I wouldn't keep my hopes high. Without doubt there will be military reverses, and more soldiers and war armaments will be needed. Hell, if all this is going to materialize, the only ones able to walk in Montelieto will be women! In light of all this, I believe will not be shedding my tunic in the foreseeable future. Valentina, with the children, will be really worse off if I must go to war. I want to tell you, Don Pompé, that I should have married her long time ago, even before I became a priest."

"I agree and am happy that you, at least, begin to understand that even a rich priest has responsibilities. You must realize that to be a Casanova and a priest at the same time is dangerous. That carries with it unpleasant consequences. Now, Reverend—pay those consequences! Quit giving me excuses of this and that, just pay up. Pay up the total support of your children and Valentina, do you hear? But in retrospect, thinking about the loving committal your dear parents had in guiding you to the right path, and raising you to become a responsible human being, what advice could I give you that would undo your past extravagances? I care very much for you, Reverend. Since you were born I felt an attachment to you as if you were my son. But if you had been lucky enough to be my son, I guarantee you that at this time you wouldn't have so many problems. You could have been known as Don Orazio Gazzaladra, the second and then first, after me, cobbler of Montelieto, he who saw to the needs of Valentina and his children. Reverend, I believe I have spoken loud and clear. Now is about time to retire, for both of us," said Don Pompeo.

"But the evening is still young, Don Pompé. I wish you could stay a little bit longer. There are other things I wish to talk to you about. I want you to know that the wheat threshing business we introduced as a benefit to the farmers of Montelieto is not progressing the way I wished it would. I am not speaking in terms of profit and loss, but the overall situation of being associated with it. The group of local tradesmen who adventured with me and provided the wheat-threshing service for the farmers, has changed philosphy. They have become hardliner Fascists, pawns of that imbecile of Santamiddia. Together with the controllers of farm products, appointed by the pharmacist, they are making life miserable for the farmers and me. They do not have the interest of the farmers at heart, as was intended originally. They look only after their own interest. They have become a bunch of cheaters. Whenever misunderstandings arise, and these need to be ironed out by honest negotiations, they accuse me of being a dissenter and send word to the Prefect that I hamper their way to good progress."

"Pull out quickly," advised Don Pompeo. "Pull out, before those leeches implicate you for some imagined wrongdoing. You are dealing with gangsters! Pull out, my son, pull out. You must know, Reverend, I want you to understand that for Montelieto and its *cafoni*, there couldn't be a greater injustice than having you accused by the Fascist Party as a dissenter. They could destroy you in the blink of an eye! Cool down. Quit contesting the pharmacist. He is a nobody, but he has power. Please do not let us down. With the turmoil happening in the world, we need you more than ever. As we have managed to change your image from Communist to that of humanitarian, let's do the same with this last. Do not align yourself with any faction for the time being. Wait. Make believe you are supporter of the Fascist cause, even if unwillingly, so that you can alleviate the problems they might create. You do not—and *must* not have to go defending the rights of the peasant *cafoni* at this point in time. Break away from the mechanic and his wheat-threshing surrogates, as quickly as you see that to be feasible."

"Yeah, I will pull out from that association of gangsters. Who could stand to see that picture of Il Duce staring at me every time I look at those machines? They have attached the picture just above the chute, where the bushels of grain are counted. My decision is made. Sardone, my sharecropper, asked me to let him in the business, if I could find the opportunity. So now I have found it! I will sell my share of interest to Sardone and Sons. I guess I should say

giving it to them for considerations of future reimburse-
ments, more than to say selling. But I don't regret my decision. He has agreed to see to it that the service to the
farmers will continue, and has assured me that he with his
sons will not be pushed around. I believe him. He is tough,"
said the Reverend.

"You have to understand, dear Don Pompeo, that I am
not acting selfishly. Neither am I running scared. I am
renouncing everything in order to gain peace of mind. For
the purchase and implementation of the business of wheat
threshing, I have lost more than I have gained. All I did
was to make a genuine effort to benefit the farmer-share-
croppers. The new machines were the first agricultural innovations ever made for the people of Montelieto.
Remember how back-breaking a task it was to beat out the
grain from the husks of wheat, using conventional
methods?"

"Of course I remember. I also know the sharecroppers
have a special place in their hearts for you, Reverend. They
know you are the first rich landowner who cares for the
meek. No one finds or hold you culpable for being a plea-
sure-seeking priest. To them you are the 'Extravagant
Priest' but still the admirable Reverend Palestrina. You
have helped in many ways, but there is nothing you can
do now. They are sent to war and, perhaps, will not come
back. However, another generation of sharecroppers will
be born and the cycle of despair will remain. When will this
cycle of servility end, Reverend? Tell me, will it ever end?"

"Yes, I do believe it will end, dear Don Pompeo."

"What makes you believe it will end?"

"The war. The defeat. Defeat will be favorable for us. It will destroy this bad system, and there are no worse, I promise."

"If that happens, will you promise to build a high school on behalf of the youngsters of Montelieto? Even in my absence?"

"Yes, old cobbler, that is the first item on my agenda. I promise."

Chapter 20

The innovation Reverend Palestrina had been instrumental in implementing years ago, was seen as a great improvement by the peasant/sharecroppers of Montelieto. It had reanimated the will and hopes of both the young and the older generation. For the priest also, the bold initiative implied great achievement. To have been able to organize and to form a cooperative of peasant *cafoni*, and lead them to undertake a feat that demanded mechanical skills, was an achievement in itself. Reverend Palestrina never regretted his decision. He had promoted the idea of acquiring the wheat-threshing machines, not so much to turn the business to his advantage, but to introduce new agricultural improvements to the forgotten people of his forgotten town. Not one single rich and prestigious master of Montelieto before him, had dared sponsor any type of innovation that would benefit the sharecroppers. The rich and prestigious wished only to perpetuate the status quo and leave their dependents ignorant.

But in trying to raise adequate sums of funds, though, for the purchase of the wheat-threshing machines, the priest met with great difficulties. That became a stumbling block. The members of the newly formed association showed good will, but all lacked the means to raise cash to afford the required share of the cost. Determined to fulfill his original plan, Reverend Palestrina volunteered to sponsor the purchase of the wheat-threshing equipment with his own money. He offered to pay in advance more than one third of the cost; the association in turn pledged to repay their portion of the debt to Reverend Palestrina, in the form of bushels of grain earned from the service provided to the farmers. To that effect the deal was ratified. The peasants began to esteem the priest, not so much for his profession of devoted churchman, which he lacked, but more for his spirit and the astuteness of a devoted entrepreneur.

With the arrival of the threshing machines, a new era had blossomed. Troops of youngsters chased after the machines from wheat field to wheat field, fascinated by the loud noises raised from the diesel engine. Curious folks spent time admiring the machines at work.

The wheat-threshing campaign took from seven to nine weeks to complete. From the start, the association employed several poor youngsters from the town of Montelieto, as helping hands. Reverend Palestrina had usually recommended that those in charge should hire the teens that needed work the most, and his requests were usually honored. The association employed six, seven or more teenagers to help with the numerous chores concerning the functions of the machines. One boy was assigned to cover the needs of the diesel engine. His primary task was to haul tanks of petroleum, on donkey back, from the general store in town. He took the empty tanks back and returned with them filled.

Two other boys were assigned to feeding the oxen that dragged the machines to the wheat fields. The machines were not self-propelled; they were mounted upon sturdy chassis with heavy steel wheels, and very difficult to move from one field to another. The association also employed a water boy in charge of any need for water, and yet another boy whose assignment required good strength and dexterity. The latter was known as the "bellows boy." His main task was to operate the bellows for firing the coal at the heading of the diesel engine. The engine could only be ignited after the heat, in the chamber of ignition, reached the right degree.

All of the teenagers worked exclusively for the head mechanic who, jointly with his assistant, supervised the entire operation. When the work of threshing was completed on a wheat field, the machines were dragged to another field, where the coal at the heading of the engine had to be reheated to allow ignition. The head mechanic, with the help of his assistant, used to ignite the gigantic engine by applying the strength of their arms on the heavy spokes of the flying wheel. They jerked the wheel with powerful thrusts, back and forth, to make the wheel rotate until the engine ignited. Whatever involved the functions of the machines, that chore required the utmost physical strength.

However, people did not object to the machine's demands. The new technology of threshing the wheat by mechanical expedients was seen as a God-sent relief, as opposed to the conventionally primitive methods they had used in the past. The new ways of handling the threshing energized everyone, including the Reverend.

For a number of years the innovation worked as it was originally intended. To have the pleasure of enjoying the new wheat-threshing service was a grand privilege for the peasant/sharecroppers of Montelieto. The first agricultural improvement had stunned the community. Seven and one-half percent charge, payable to the association was quite high, but yet manageable. By availing of the wheat-threshing service, the farmers saved valuable time and energy to be applied to other critical chores of the fields. Not a day would they let go by without giving praise to their priest!

But good things never lasted for the harassed *cafoni* of Montelieto. With the arrival of the Fascist pharmacist, Chief of the House of Fasces, unpleasant things began to change—for the worse. The great Chief set out on to commandeer people's lives and their livelihood. He had not been appointed at his new post merely to sign up sympathizers to the Party and run the pharmacy—but also to take control of the goods produced from the farming community. The great Chief had authority to control (in a manner of speaking), even the air the peasant *cafoni* breathed.

Commencing with the Ethiopian war adventure, Italy had been imposed stiff sanctions by the non-belligerent nations. That motivated the Fascist Party to promote propaganda that pressed everybody to produce more. To restock the depleting food supplies, the Party ruled it mandatory for the farmers to report to the local authorities the total amount of the harvests—voluntarily. When that brought no results, the Party authorized the local authorities to enforce the rules by appointing Fascist controllers of the harvests. These new rules were welcomed by the pharmacist. To enforce them he appointed several loafers from the slums of town as henchmen, to the position of controllers of farm products.

That left the sharecroppers betrayed. With the new rules, they had acquired yet another participant to the take of their products. First, as mandated from nature, they owed the landowners half of the harvest, secondly they owed seven and one-half percent of their share to the threshing association, and lastly, the portion remaining for their family use, was presumptuously confiscated by the Party controllers of farm products.

With the start of the conflict, the livelihood and lives of the farming community began to be examined ever more strictly and impudently. That kind of scrutiny, though, was not limited exclusively to the *cafoni* sharecroppers. It extended over all levels of non-Fascist citizenry. Rich landowners were burdened with heavier taxes; professionals, including the clergy, were pressed to preach the Party's ideology. Tradespeople began to see depleted the means of support for lack of necessary material. Scarcities were widespread. Food stuff all types of fuel, clothing, and leather products with other items were rationed. Everyone began to experience the biting pinches of insufficiency.

The old cobbler, too, felt the stings of scarcity. If the war dragged on, he foresaw that his own suffering from poverty and hunger would not be too far off. The only alternative available to him for continuing to keep his shop open, was to replace the leather products that were in high demand. To be able to repair and build any type of footwear, Don Pompeo began to use inferior material including cardboard, wood and pieces of automobile tires discarded from the army forces.

In the evenings, the frustrated shoemaker talked to his few remaining peers, and tried to encourage them to become more supportive of one another in the face of adversity.

"Il Duce," Don Pompeo said to them, "has promised to lead us to victory, only with his beautifully chosen rhetoric. But we know better. For too damn long we have lived on beautiful rhetoric, and only many crumbs of the essential things in life. Now we are facing the stark reality, my friends. Our leader will soon learn what the tough army he claims to lead to victory, is made of," he said, distrustfully.

Then, turning more serene Don Pompeo said: "We have two kinds of armies, you know. On one hand we have a very well dressed army, and well paid Black Shirts totally loyal to Il Duce. And on the other hand we have an army of shabbily clad and badly equipped soldiers alienated from the King, and loyal to neither of the two. The latter have been bamboozled by the former with the promises of victory, and goaded to spill *en masse* inside the Egyptian frontiers. Let's hope they will find their way back alive."

At that point Don Pompeo stopped working, raised his head to look to his friends and, before wishing them goodnight, he quoted a cynical proverb of his own creation that depicted, the position of the two leaders and the country: *Il Duce propone, Il Duce dispone, mentre Il Re dorme e Italia piange.* (The Duce proposes, the Duce disposes, while the King sleeps and Italy weeps.)

Chapter 21

The sad scenario of shortages and uncertainties increased in severity for the entire duration of the conflict. That was a reality that neither Don Pompeo, Reverend Palestrina, the association of wheat-threshers and sharecroppers-*cafoni* could reverse. Events of major consequences permeated the gloomy scenario of Montelieto. By the summer of 1940, the first major warring enemy Northwest, had been put out of action from the famous Axis partner. The army in Cyrenaica, still unopposed, had realized a move inside Egypt. In East Africa events were also favorable and the Navy with the Aviation, were claiming good results at sea and the bombing of Malta.

But none of those favorable events were of good omen for the sharecroppers of Montelieto. There had been talks of a larger mobilization coming soon and the wheat-threshing task was upon them, at the same time that a shortage of reliable farmhands was being felt. Regardless of what was occurring in the world though, the farmers-sharecroppers felt the same urgency to go ahead with the important task of threshing their crops. Stereotype label of *cafoni* aside, they were determined to complete the chores vital to them for meeting the family's needs before anything else.

For the current season, things seemed promising on the fields and everyone looked forward to a bountiful harvest.

By late summer the association of wheat-threshers had been successful in providing service to almost the entire farming community. There remained one last wheat field to service before the threshing campaign could be called closed. That particular wheat field was the last to be serviced but one of the largest and most profitable insofar as the threshing outfit was concerned. They would gain bountiful profit since their machines would be engaged the whole day on the job, without the time consuming stops and starts of regrouping from small to smaller fields.

The owner of that special wheat field was not a sharecropper and he was not bound to share his crops with anyone, except to pay the cost of the service and dupe the Fascist controllers of farm products as he had done in the previous years. Everything pointed to a very special day. The farmer, who was well-to-do, would treat everyone involved in the work with an abundant and special meal and wine when the task was accomplished, providing everything turned out okay.

The threshing machines had been dragged upon that last wheat field and were ready to engage in the work. With an incredible dexterity, the head mechanic and his assistant intersected their arms to get an even grip on the sturdy spokes of the flying wheel of the diesel engine. That wheel, counterbalanced to the main pulley that regulated the transfer of energy to the threshing machine, served as the medium for igniting the engine. The two giant mechanics positioned themselves with their feet on the ground to a suitable angle, and gripped their hands firmly on the grease spokes of the flying wheel. On the count of *one, two, three,* they simultaneously applied the strength of their arms on the spokes to sway the wheel back and forth, with vigorous thrusts of rotation. However, the engine was not ready to ignite at the first attempts. It only puffed rings of black smoke up in the air and released a sticky drizzle of petroleum from the exhaust pipe on its roof. That was all. The drizzle of petroleum blackened the immediate foreground. Meantime all further efforts of the mechanics to ignite the engine turned more strenuous and unsuccessful.

After several more attempts, the exasperated mechanics slackened their effort. They drew back to catch their breath and reapplied the same procedure—but still to no avail. The damned internal combustion engine simply refused to start. Profuse perspiration trickled down from the face and nose of the head mechanic. He wiped his sweat with a burlap sack, tossed it on the ground and with both feet stepped on it enraged. Finally he turned to give a dirty look toward the engine, extended one arm and, with his index finger outstretched, made a quick circle in the air. His message was readily understood. It became clear to the boy operating the bellows that the coal at the head of the engine, had to be heated to the degree required. At the circling in the air of the finger of the mechanic, the young boy released his grip on the handle of the bellows, spat on the palm of his hand, and with a renewed determination continued to spin even faster. He knew from experience that the coal had to be hotter.

Spin, spin, spin, the impatient mechanic motioned, again rotating his index finger in the air. Of course, the young boy knew that, but his arms were getting numb from the shoulder down. Although he was used to doing hard work under the scorching sun, still he was of tender age.

Like his co-worker, he had to support himself by doing odd jobs. He had been abandoned by his parents since infancy. His father had immigrated to Argentina and was never heard since; his mother had been whoring around with the drunkards in the slums of town, and had given birth to some other kids out of wedlock. For the young boy there was no other way. He had to earn one meal per day to survive.

But the family situations of the *cafoni* boys, their problems and poverty, were not issues that the mechanic took to heart. There were more than a handful of teens who lived the same indigence and the mechanic could not hold interest in their welfare or bad luck. He just kept an ear open to listen to the grating sound of the vanes, which the young boy let rotate by spinning the handle of the bellows. The anxious mechanic could tell, even from a distance, how efficiently the young boy was doing his job. Every time the cracking noises of the vanes diminished, the mechanic sent signals to the boy by motioning him to spin faster. After several interruptions caused by the boy, who kept changing hands on the grip, the intolerant mechanic walked closer to the boy, smacked him hard on the face and shoved him away, enraged. With the hard shove the young boy went stumbling forward to fall down several feet away.

"That will teach you to maintain interest on the job!" said the mechanic referring to the hard smack. Then he tucked up the sleeves of his shirt higher on his arms, took hold of the handle of the bellows and began to spin it madly. He perspired profusely and cussed. After some time the coal began to reach the degree of heat required for the mechanic to re-attempt the procedure of ignition. "One, two, three, one two, three," the two strong men counted aloud, while jostling the huge flying wheel repeatedly. On the third try the engine ignited, puffing wildly. Its roaring thuds deafened those around it. At that point the two strong men drew back. In haste transferred the power from the engine and finally, to the astonishment of the bystanders, through a series of heavy leather belts the threshing machine was energized.

The belts transferring energy from the diesel engine to the threshing machine released a piercing sound as they gained velocity. When all the gears were activated, they raised clouds of brownish dust which covered the foregrounds. But not minding the noises or dust, everybody went to their assignment. The cheering farmers gathered the sheaves of wheat near the threshing machine and the work had begun. The machine gobbled down the sheaves of wheat with unbelievable voracity. When larger than normal bites were fed into it, the engine exerted to its highest degrees. Hour after hour the work of threshing the wheat proceeded satisfactorily. The straws were shredded to the desired size and baled neatly, while the grains were stored inside burlap sacks and stacked up in piles. Conversely to the old methods of threshing the wheat with conventional implements, the efficiency of the machines was stunning, an impressive agricultural improvement. With pencil and writing pad at hand, two Fascist harvest controllers took the count of the bushels of grain shelled.

But for the young boy whose face was smacked, there seemed to be no improvement in the whole rotten situation. His reddened cheek still gave the boy's face a burning sensation. Just thinking of "privileges" and "improvements" made him cry. How could people have power and at the same time be so heartless? A photo of Il Duce mounting a white horse attached to the side of the threshing machine seemed to be alive. The young boy wished Il Duce could dismount the horse and arrest the mean mechanic. Although the boy could not read and therefore was not able to make sense from the writing: "Noi vinceremo (We will win)," beneath the photo, he had figured that those words must allude to significant grandeur. He stood dejected and crushed, aside from the mechanic, holding one hand on his reddened cheek. No writing, no grandeur, and no Il Duce could help the boy. He felt he had been born in decadence and he entertained no hopes beyond that.

Thanks to the good Lord, though, the machines continued performing better than expected. If everything proceeded at that pace, the entire outfit would be busy until dark. The young boy took comfort in that thought. If the mechanic wished the young boy to operate the bellows that would have to be next season. This was the last remaining field of the wheat-threshing campaign and the owner, Giovanni Del Pio, wouldn't let his workers down. He, for sure, would see to it that everyone was fed and, no doubt, there would be wine served.

Beneath the fig tree, in the thickest shade, the head mechanic dozed on and off. In his sluggishness he could hear the loud and steady rhythmical thuds of the engine, while made him real drowsy. In his dream he wished to own a similar machine, but one that raised much less noises. He also saw in his imagination, a good amount of wheat belonging to the outfit as a percentage of their payment. Lastly, before waking up, he saw in his dream Giovanni Del Pio hassling intensely to hide as many bushels of grain as he could, from the attention of the stupid Fascist harvest controllers of the Party. In his drowsiness he smiled; but from time to time, the mechanic opened his eyes to give fast glances to the puffing engine, closed his eyes again and went back to rest his head upon the stack of burlap sacks under the fig tree.

It was late afternoon. Until this time the engine and threshing machine had performed to expectation. Although the engine had misfired a few beats within the last minutes, there were no reasons for alarm. The threshing machine still continued devouring the sheaves of wheat with increasing swiftness.

But as time progressed the misfiring of the engine was repeated with more frequency. At one point the mechanic jumped to his feet, walked near the engine, revved it up and returned untroubled beneath the shade. He had not even made himself comfortable when the engine began to thud wildly. It accelerated for some time, misfired, lost power, and then re-accelerated. The leather belts transferring energy to the threshing machine hissed and flapped against one another and to the pulley, creaked loudly—and suddenly stopped. The operation of wheat-threshing came abruptly to a halt.

In panic, the mechanic rushed to the engine. With the help of his assistant they checked all possible sources of interruption. They looked, touched, turned on every possible mechanism of mechanical failure but nothing they did helped. The more switches the mechanic tried to engage, the more his exasperation and limits of his patience. The mechanic turned to the owner of the wheat field and philosophically announced: "Signor Giovanni! I believe I have bad news for you. The engine has totally run out of petroleum. Even worse is the fact that we do not have any more in the tanks. This morning the pharmacist told Eugenio, the petroleum boy, that the Prefect has run short of petroleum, and has temporarily stopped shipments to the general stores of the region. Our chief town of Frosinone and the Prefect know we are completely out of petroleum. Sorry, Giovà. All I can say today is one hell of a bad day."

Giovanni felt quite shaken up at the news but in those hostile times, unpleasant news was a daily occurrence. Really bad news arrived unexpectedly from different sources, other than that of the mechanic and the petroleum. Even before the wheat-threshing work started, bad news was coming to Montelieto. They mourned the first casualty, one of their own who had perished on the frontline. And now another mobilization had been announced which, unlike the first mobilization called last year, was of much bigger proportion. The people of Montelieto were stunned to learn that the classes up to 1899 had received the call to arms notification. Something drastic was happening to the *cafoni* of Montelieto. From the chief town of Frosinone, the Prefect had stopped shipments of petroleum allocated for agricultural operations, but he never stopped sending out notices of mobilization. In fact he kept urging the pharmacist (the Fascist Chief of the House of Fasces of Montelieto), to take charge and see to it that the recall notifications were delivered as quickly as possible, so everyone could report on time.

The pharmacist was elated. Right way he authorized one of his henchmen to help the mailman, Ottaviano, deliver the recall notices and accomplish the assignment requested by the Prefect. Older soldiers departed from Montelieto every day and, as the pharmacist saw them leave, he envisioned in his mind a swift and irresistible victory. He also took pride knowing that his political rival and idealistic antagonist, the priest, Reverend Palestrina, too, had been served the recall to arms notification. The little scoundrels *cafoni* had seen and heard the prideful pharmacist talk intimately to the Deputy Mayor and tell him explicitly: "If the Prefect had left it up to me, I would recall all the priests and send them to the hottest frontline. Particularly that hot-head two-faced Palestrina who thinks he is too good to become a Fascist like us. His grandiose formula to eradicate poverty with humaneness does not stand logic. Poverty will be eradicated only at the time when capitalism is destroyed. We will win! Evviva Il Duce!"

Meanwhile Don Pompeo, the old cobbler of Montelieto, was living in emotional distress. He rarely spent the entire evening at work. He saw his beloved countrymen go to war and felt great pain. He dreaded each sunrise for fear the new day would bring yet more anxieties.

When the time came to go to wish goodbye to Reverend Palestrina, Don Pompeo was totally heartbroken. He arrived unannounced at the mansion of Palestrina and was led inside by Dorotea who, without delay, accompanied him to her Lord's study. The priest and Don Pompeo talked soberly the whole evening. This was not an occasion to throw jokes at one another as they had done in the past.

During the visit, Reverend Palestrina assured Don Pompeo he would come back home soon and safe, at which time he guaranteed that he would always act in fairness toward others and would assume responsibility for his actions and try to be useful in lightening whatever burdens he could alleviate for the people of their cherished Montelieto.

That resolve set well with Don Pompeo. Never before had he heard the Reverend speak with such sincerity. For brief moments he stood mute. Then, following a warm embrace, the old shoemaker regained his self-confidence and told the priest: "Reverend, I am proud you are a son of Montelieto. Now we must part. You go and practice what you were trained to do; bring comfort to those who need easement of pain, in the name of the Lord, and I promise to do the same for those who need to be comforted here. Meanwhile, son, I'll remain 'The Lonesome Cobbler' until all of you boys return home."

Chapter 22

"Out of petroleum?" Giovanni Del Pio complained loudly to the mechanic with dismay. "And how do you think we are going to complete the threshing of my wheat? You don't have the faintest idea what this involves! We will be made to bear unbelievable toil and privations if we are forced to return to using the old, conventional methods. This I find absolutely absurd. Do you realize what you're doing to me, my friend?"

"Oh, no—no conventional methods here," said the mechanic, trying to reassure Del Pio. "Don't you understand what Il Duce has been saying? We live in times full of glory, Giová. You should know, after we have beaten the nonsense out of Britain and her associates, like we have done to France, we will have access to all the petroleum we need. Meanwhile I will send a distress message to our Prefect and ask his highness to try to procure some petroleum. The rest we'll leave up to our Fascist brigades. It won't be too far off before those brigades, with our mechanized divisions and navy, will bust open the locks our enemies have placed on the Suez Canal, Gibraltar and the Dardanelli Straits. Once we have achieved that goal, we'll be in a position even to get to the oil wells of the Americans. Signor Giovanni, I wish you were realistic!"

"Oh my God!" Giovanni said within himself. "This man is talking like a fool. Getting to the oil wells of the Americans? He is absolutely cracking up. I am not even so sure that those key points he expects to be busted open really exist. He must have heard those rumors from Romualdo while getting drunk in the taverns of town. What I do know, beyond any doubts, is the fact that we have run out of petroleum and the prospect of getting it from the oil wells of the Americans is totally nonsense. This poor country of mine in the hands of the fools!" Giovanni said in an undertone for fear of being heard. If the mechanic had heard such negative remarks, he with his stool pigeons of the Party, would have forced Giovanni to drink a glass of castor oil. (Incidentally, that type of oil was still available.)

Giovanni Del Pio foresaw major trouble coming. He could not scream at those he presumed to be responsible because his protest could mean swallowing more castor oil. He recalled the nauseating taste, and the terrible bowel movements he suffered a few years ago when forced to drink a cup of it for being a resister to the Party. Besides, the Fascist "controllers of farm products" were still on his premises and he must be careful. They were mean creatures whom he hadn't yet had a chance to push into intoxication. He could not put into practice the wise strategies he had devised in the past, when handling the controllers of farm products. Giovanni had been successful, in many previous harvests, with the strategy of getting them so drunk that they were not able to see the machines and his grains. After they had lain down snoring, he had succeeded in hiding amongst the straw, all the bushels of grains subject to be confiscated. But this time, that damned petroleum guzzling engine had screwed up everything! What could unlucky Giovanni do in that situation? Not much.

Meanwhile, the mechanic advised the Fascist controllers to return home, saying there was no chance of getting any petroleum from the Prefect in the foreseeable future. Therefore it would be expedient for all concerned with the threshing machine outfit, to head back to town as soon as permissible. After having decided to leave the machines anchored on the field of Giovanni until the question of the petroleum was resolved, the mechanic turned to his crew and said: "Take down the canvas from the wagon and cover up the machines properly. The weather might change, and we do not want to get our equipment and machines soaked with rain. Now go, start loading up the wagon with the bushels of grain due to us, and let's get back to town."

The dependents of the mechanic executed the orders in a hurry, spurred the oxen to drag the wagon, and moved on the way to town. The mechanic ran fast to reach the moving wagon, got hold of the rear gate of it, hopped on and yelled to Giovanni del Pio so: "Signor Giovanni! Do not be troubled by the fact that we have not accomplished the job. You must understand Giová. Our Duce will not let his people down. Some day, he will get us all the petroleum we need, and much, much, more!"

That will never happen, Giovanni thought in disgust with the mechanic and his annoying rhetoric. He felt low contempt for him and for the vainglorious leaders who could not provide petroleum for the exasperated farmers. He then gave another glance at the huge heap of sheaves of wheat to be shelled, raised his eyes as if to implore heaven, looked once more at the moving wagon and disdainfully spat toward it.

For some time Giovanni felt depressed. He was the last farmer to be serviced, on the route of the threshing outfit, but the very first to have been denied for lack of petroleum. On one hand he still entertained hopes that the mechanic could be influential enough to obtain a few couple more oil drums but, on the other hand, he thought to rely on the braggart mechanic would be simply a waste of time. If the mechanized divisions were to make a run to the Suez Canal, as the mechanic had believed, would not those machines be in need of lots of petroleum? And if the tanks guzzled as much as the diesel engine of the mechanic, where were they going to get it? Besides, if there was a shortage of petroleum at home, Giovanni figured, how could the mechanized divisions ever dream of arriving in Suez?

Giovanni, though, could not be worrying about the problems Fascism had gotten his country into. All he cared about was to reap a bountiful harvest from his fields, and provide for the support of his grandchildren until his three sons returned home. Trouble was he could not handle the mounting chores of the farm on his own strength, and there were no available, dependable, farmhands to hire. So he relied more and more on the landless sharecroppers of the district to furnish the necessary help. But these, too, were as old as he. Whichever way he looked, simple solutions were unavailable.

Giovanni understood all that. He also understood that he should consider himself blessed for owning good strips of fertile lands of his own property. Until the Fascists decided against imposing more exorbitant taxes, and confiscating

the best part of his farm products at minimum costs, he
could stay above water. That would keep him away from
poverty even if he made no profit. He thanked the Lord to
have given him the opportunity to come out of dependency
on the landlords, by acquiring good farmlands with the
savings he had put aside abroad. Around the closing of the
last century, Giovanni had worked cutting timbers in the
western United States for a number of years. At this advanced age though, he was happy to have come out of poverty although he regretted his semi-illiteracy.

He also was grateful to the good Lord every day, for
keeping his sons safe. One of them had been drafted two
years ago, was trained and then sent with the first troops
on the occupation of Albania, but never came back home
on leave. Of the other two boys, one was recalled with the
first mobilization and sent to North Africa, the other was
deployed some time later, to the island of Rodi as artil-
leryman with an anti-aircraft unit.

On the evening of the wheat-threshing fiasco, with
great resolve Giovanni put his troubles to rest, at least
temporarily. He invited his friends and neighbors, and all
those who had helped thus far, to come to his farmhouse
to share a bite together. Although the work was only one-
third accomplished, he still wished to give his neighbors a
treat. Many came. All chose to eat outside, beneath the fig
tree, by latern light. They ate and discussed the problems
confronting them. Some cussed at the mechanic, and all
cussed at the Prefect and the Supreme Commander in
Chief. Still the ill will engendered by every discussion was
annoying to Giovanni. Nobody seemed to have a good thing
to say.

Tired of listening, Giovanni walked to the water well where he had stored the best wine for the "controllers of farm products," pulled on a rope and brought above ground a large kettle containing cool flasks of wine. The wine, meant for the purpose of completely inebriating the Fascist controllers of Giovanni's grains, was now available for everybody to drink. "To hell with those peg-top heads of controllers! My neighbors can savor the wine just as much," said Giovanni.

The flasks of wine were slowly passed around until all of it was gone. Then Giovanni's neighbors left happily after bidding him good night. Giovanni stayed behind for a little while, then took a lantern in his hands, walked around the premises and proceeded to lock up the gates. On his return, while walking by the threshing machine, he saw a human foot jutting out from beneath the canvas covering the machine. He went near to take a closer look, raised the canvas, and to his surprise discovered a person lying on the ground on a heap of straw.

"What in hell are you doing here, young fellow?" Giovanni asked in anger. "Don't you know better than trespass over somebody else's property? Get up you rascal, before I get you by the feet."

A very young figure of a person slowly arose. Once standing, the young man shook off pieces of straw from his worn shirt, apologized to Giovanni for the intrusion, and began to walk away.

"Wait a minute! You will not walk away without giving me an explanation. Were you hiding there to steal something once I retired?"

"No," said the young voice. "I just chose to spend the night in that cozy place to rest up. I wished that tomorrow

Benito, the mechanic, would bring the petroleum so I could earn my meal for spinning the bellows."

"By golly! You will certainly starve to death before the Prefect will send Benito the petroleum. Benito, Benito, he must be related to our Duce," said Giovanni with sarcasm.

"No, he is not. They say he has become the henchman of the pharmacist," said the young boy.

"Never mind who he is related to. We both know he is a leech. Come here! Come with me," said Giovanni.

They walked together to the fig tree, near where Giovanni had stored the leftover food inside large baskets.

"Eat all you need, or I'll have to feed it to my dogs before the food spoils. But this food is too good to give it to dogs, you know?"

The young boy ate with a great appetite, taking chunks of fresh baked bread and cheese with spiced olives in his mouth. At times he seemed to have difficulty chewing and swallowing as if worried the food would be taken away.

Giovanni looked at the boy and asked: "So you work for the association of wheat-threshing people eh?"

"Yes, but mostly I work for the mechanic."

"That big mouth, hot-tempered squealer," said Giovanni. "He treats people worse than some people treat wild beasts. He thinks he and the pharmacist own Montelieto!"

"I know. But I have to endure the abuses. There are no other means for me to earn an evening meal and, at my age, I am beginning to feel embarrassment when I have to go knocking door to door begging for alms."

"Damned will be this government," said Giovanni looking at the young boy. "They want to fight wars against people who are better equipped economically, so they could make them poor like us. Shame on them."

"Yeah, but I hope you don't think it is me who roots for war. Although I do at times, the purpose is only to get food coupons from the pharmacist."

"No, I don't think it is your fault. The fault lies right there, at the head of the State. In light of all this, I advise you that if you hope to stay alive by waiting for the mechanic to come here with the petroleum and then give you employment in exchange for food, you had better forget it. They could not care less for those who suffer. Listen," said Giovanni. "I wish to make a deal with you. If you think my proposal is fair, say yes or no. I am not rich but I have some food left. I pay my debts with farm products. If you do not mind the monotony of life on this farm, you could give me a hand here in exchange for abundant food, plus a few used clothes and footwear. What do you think of my proposal, young fellow?"

"That sounds great! But I must tell you I am not a farmer by trade."

"Don't you worry about that. You will learn a trade by looking at what I do."

"Thanks, Uncle Giová," said the young boy giving him a hard and friendly hug.

"Very good. Today could turn out to be my lucky day, after all. The barn is still open; go there and find the best berth for sleeping on. You will find the hayloft cozy until we make other arrangements. Rest well because tomorrow I will make loud noises about feeding the cattle before sunrise. Good night, my boy," said Giovanni.

"Good night," replied the elated guest.

The young boy went to sleep on the hayloft, inside the barn of Giovanni, with his heart bursting for joy. He had heard that the Del Pio clan were generous, good-hearted, and honest, hard-working people. The young boy thanked Jesus for having looked after him by opening Giovanni's heart. Now all that remained to be determined was his own worthiness. His sincerity toward Giovanni must have taken top priority. He felt he was born in misery and worth nothing his entire life, but from here on he knew he had been given the chance to prove to himself and to others differently. And just for that he was not about to screw it up.

Meantime the wagon carrying the people and grains of the wheat-threshing outfit, stopped in front of the general store where the bushels of grains were to be deposited. After the accountant of the Fascist Party consortium had figured out the price of the grains, and had subtracted the cost of the petroleum used, the remainder would go to the association of the wheat-threshing outfit. These were rewarded more than fairly. It was no secret that they worked to their own advantage and, of course, to that of the Party. They also promoted the system of ideas that set in motion the belief that the country must become self-sufficient in producing its own sustenance in all areas. No one, though, had ever figured out that the monumental task had fallen only upon the poor sharecroppers who could least afford it. All the farmers, including the well-to-do, had already been stripped of every incentive to produce.

Inside the tavern of Marianna Pipanera, across from the general store, the head mechanic and his association comrades were celebrating the end of the wheat-threshing campaign in good harmony. Being committed almost for the entire summer to hard work and suffocating heat had not been so appealing for anybody. The campaign, though, had brought the association many rewards, and this induced the head mechanic to celebrate in good spirit and with lots of spirits.

Still in the back of his mind, the mechanic could see the disappointment on Giovanni Del Pio's face, when he was left with his wheat field in total chaos. With a sudden change of heart, the mechanic dispatched one of the Fascist harvest controllers to send word to the pharmacist that, due to a shortage of petroleum, the job on the largest wheat field of Montelieto remained incomplete. In order for the association to gain a better profit, it would be greatly appreciated if he were to make a direct request to the Prefect for allotting Montelieto a couple of extra drums of petroleum.

Upon his return, the Fascist harvest controller explained the pharmacist's position on the matter. Under no circumstance would the pharmacist forward a request to the Prefect when he understood his Excellency to have run out of petroleum. For the Prefect to obtain additional petroleum, he must make a request for it from the Ministry of Energy (home office). That would be quite embarrassing for him to ask the Ministry of Energy for two drums of petroleum.

Meantime, while the wheat-threshing people celebrated, the pharmacist was not interested in what they were doing, nor did he care about the chaos Giovanni del Pio had gotten into. He was seen glued to the nearby radio upon the balcony of the House of Fasces, waiting to hear from the capital the latest bulletin of war. News of major importance seemed to be imminent. For the duration of the summer, until early autumn, high achievements had been reported on the battlefields. In North Africa, an avalanche of troops had crossed into Egypt. Special troops in East Africa were even now taking control of several key points. That evening Il Duce began to address the crowds in a menacing tone of voice. He threatened to go to war in the Balkans immediately if the states concerned didn't agree to his terms in three days time.

A handful of people were listening to the bulletin of war that evening. It was drizzling quite hard when the news broadcast began. Troops of young kids were seen hopping from one archway to another to avoid getting soaked. When the pharmacist learned that Il Duce was about to open another front, he screamed at the top of his lungs: "Evviva Il Duce!" There was no response from below in the Church Square. Then with greater enthusiasm he screamed again: "Evviva Il Duce!"

At that second hurrah one young voice was heard saying: "Alalá!" (a war cry). Not knowing whose voice had responded with a war cry, the pharmacist called on the young voice and said: "I am very proud of you, young man. Your great enthusiasm shall inspire the youth of Montelieto. You will be a good asset and hope for our great nation."

The young man was the semi-illiterate *cafone*, Federico Favetta.

Under an umbrella, beneath the balcony of the House of Fasces, two people were listening to the bulletin of war from the nearest corner. The pharmacist stretched his neck out and in the dusk recognized the pair. They were the Italo-American pensioner and Don Pompeo.

"That no good Yankee," said the pharmacist to himself. "How can one love his neighbor if he is an American? And you," he said pretending to address Don Pompeo (who could not hear him), "aren't you ashamed to be seen in the company of a Yankee? You old monarchist should realize that, with us Fascists, we form one body and one soul. Tell him that at the rate we are winning on the front line, it won't be long before he will be asking for mercy!"

The two elderly men walked to the shoemaker shop of Don Pompeo, shoulder to shoulder still shielding themselves from the rain and were shortly reached by the young kid Favetta.

"Don Pompeo," called the kid. "If you heard me respond to the pharmacist with: 'Alalá!,' I did so because I was told he had received food coupons from the Prefect. Tomorrow I will go and tell him it was I who answered with the war cry. For sure he will give me a coupon good for scrap pasta."

"Don't do that, Federico," warned Don Pompeo. "If you wish to please Don Pompeo, then every time they want you to respond with a war cry, at the Hail to the Chief, run away instead! Run and come to see me, if you are hungry. I will increase your pay of one cent for the service of brooming my shop, so you'll be able to buy your own scrap pasta. And to both of you I wish to say, my friends, that after having listened to the boisterous war bulletin of this evening, I feel the monarchy is dead. From this moment on, my party affiliation will be that of 'uomo qualunque' (the man in the street) and nothing else, you hear? Good night, friend."

For the remainder of the evening, Don Pompeo was upset. In his imagination he heard Federico respond to the pharmacist with provoking war cries and felt irritable toward him. During the night, though, in his mind he debated whether to reproach the kid was the thing he wished to do.

"Federico deserves a little scolding," Don Pompeo said at one point. Then after some soul-searching he came to the conclusion that he was blowing the situation out of proportion. "I believe am being unfair to Federico," he said to himself. "What can the poor kid do, starve? It should be plainly understood that nature has endowed us *cafoni* with astuteness and I must say that will compensate us in a small way for our lack of education. In my view, without that sharp natural instinct the poor *cafoni*/sharecroppers would be just as good as dead," Don Pompeo summed up.

Chapter 23

The pharmacist, with two of his henchmen, stayed awake resting on the balcony of the House of Fasces until the wee hours of the morning. They kept the radio tuned on the war bulletin, eagerly waiting for events of great importance to be announced. In their hearts they harbored the same wish—to hear the much talked about surrender of one of the last resisting Allies.

But that news never came about. And as for what concerned the news of the shortage of petroleum—nobody cared. From here on, the Fascist pharmacist, the Party harvest controllers, and the wheat-threshing outfit, seldom gave another thought to the problems they had gotten Giovanni into. The fiasco of the shortage for petroleum on Giovanni's threshing field troubled nobody. The wheat belonged to Giovanni so the problems were only his to solve.

On the other hand, Giovanni worried quite a bit. He spent the entire night half-awake, rehearsing in his imagination all the arduous chores of the farm, hoping for them to be worked out. He also thought of the young boy to whom he had offered work on the farm. Was the kid sleeping comfortably upon the hayloft? "Of course he is resting comfortably," said Giovanni with confidence. "At that young age, given the same situation I could have slept on a bed made of thistles. Poor boy! How terrible it must feel to know one is unwanted. That lousy mechanic and his gang never wanted to have to worry about the poor boy. Ah! Benito, Benito, you traitor! You think the boy is better off going around Montelieto begging for alms, don't you? But who cares what you and your kind believe? Here on the farm we'll go forward making our own rules—that is: hard work and lots of food."

Early on in the morning, before sunrise, Giovanni Del Pio was up. He paced from the farmhouse to the threshing field and barn, figuring where to start next. He scratched his head while walking and cursed the country leadership. The young boy, too, was up. He was in the habit of arising early in the morning, before the head mechanic came to awaken him with strong kicks. As he jumped up on his feet and saw Giovanni pacing back and forth, the young boy went near and said: "Good morning, Uncle Giová. I am ready to start work anytime you tell me what has to be done."

"Good morning to you too, young man. Never mind work. We have plenty of time for doing that. Right this moment, it is time for breakfast. First things come first you know? Come on, let's go get it," said Giovanni pointing to the farmhouse.

The boy followed Giovanni in great surprise. When he entered the house he stood in awe. A tempting aroma of freshly baked bread nearly made him faint. What in the world was happening to him, he couldn't understand. The mere word "breakfast" itself, sounded strange. He had seldom heard and never experienced that. Inside the kitchen, an aged Madam was intent on doing her domestic chores. She paced from the kitchen to the dining room table leaving upon it smoking plates of food.

"Make yourself comfortable," Giovanni told the young boy. "Let's eat some warm food that will give us strength to think straight and figure out what we ought to do next. I want you to eat with good appetite though, because Mrs. Del Pio will think she is one of the best cooks around."

"Oh you, Giovanni! It seems you always find humor in everything. Even in a critical situation you still are able to find something to laugh at. You know I have never claimed to be the best cook around," said Rosetta, giving her husband a sweet smile.

"Well, you are the best I have my dear, and the prettiest I know."

"Thanks, but whom do I have the pleasure to meet," said Rosetta, looking first at her husband then to the young boy.

"Peppe of Montelieto, sorry," said the young boy.

"Pleased to know you, Peppe."

"Same with me. They all call me Peppe although my name is Giuseppe. I guess they do not want to bother calling me by my real name. It doesn't make any difference, though, by which name they call me," said Peppe unconcerned.

"I am happy to have met you anyway. Giovanni has spoken to me in regard to your situation working with the association of the wheat-threshing people. But you must not worry for the time being. Serve yourself to the food you need. We are happy to help out."

"What do you mean, *we* help out, Rosetta? We ought to make it clear from here and say instead, we are happy the young man will stay on the farm to help *us* out," said Giovanni.

"Right. We are happy someone young as Peppe will help us out."

While chatting with the lady of the house, the two men had devoured their food. Giovanni got up from the chair, thanked his wife for the excellent breakfast and walked outside. He looked at the huge pile of sheaves of wheat to be yet threshed and wondered what was going to come of it. Peppe followed, went closer and waited for Giovanni to talk.

"You see?" said Giovanni with great concern. "We derive our whole livelihood from this wheat. The screwballs in our capital, though, have endangered that livelihood by acting irresponsibly. The government, the Prefect, the Fascist controllers and the mechanic, including the pharmacist, are a bunch of blood-suckers. They live off our sweat—and live quite comfortably. When we need them is when they disappear in the woods of bureaucracies. You know what I think, Peppe? To hell with them! I shall not droop in expectation of their petroleum, then die! In previous times we didn't have the luxury of the wheat threshing service but were able to handle that task without these kinds of heartaches. Damned Prefect, we have lots of bread right in front of our eyes and you let it go to waste for lack of petroleum? We will not wait for you to get it, even if we must extract the grains from the husks with our bare hands.

"Peppe, I want to let you know that in the barn, we have old implements which do not require petroleum to operate. Those have been catching dust ever since the threshing machines were introduced. Today I have the feeling we'll dig those unpredictable implements out, as these are unpredictable times, young man. Instead of moving forward with more modern innovations, on account of the damned shortage of fuel, we are shrinking back into the primitive age. If our soldiers find themselves in this same situation we are experiencing, how could they dream to win a mechanized war, as the leadership dreams to win? In this crazy set-up, don't you think we ought to beat out the grains of wheat from the husks with the sticks? Trouble is, I am more than seventy-two years old and my limbs are not as strong as they were. I am suffering from rheumatism as well. Come with me and I will show you what I mean about the sticks we once used to beat out the grains of wheat."

They entered the barn and Giovanni pointed out to Peppe a corner where those weird old implements hung. "Climb up, get a couple of those and toss them down. I will show you how they work."

Peppe climbed up, took the sticks as he was told and came down. "What are these things called?" he asked.

"Flails," said Giovanni swinging one in the air.

"Flails?"

"Yes, flails, a type of weapon used to fend off the enemy, I was told," said Giovanni. "The primitive warriors did not have tanks or petroleum and had to defend themselves with home made weapons. If those weapons were good enough to fend and beat up the enemy, why could they not beat the husks of wheat? It takes strength of one's arms and good determination to use them, that's all. Unfortunately, though, at my age I miss that strength. Still I could compensate that with determination and know-how."

"But I have lots of strength. I wish you would let me work with this," said Peppe swinging the other flail in the air.

"Of course, I'll let you use it, but first you must learn the ways it functions before using it."

The flail was, in fact, an old type of weapon. Nobody, though, could say when it was used to fight the enemy. Its modified replica was used until recently, as an efficient implement to thresh wheat and many other cereals. It was made with two sturdy poles (sticks) of unequal length. The longer, approximately six feet, was the main implement to which the shorter sticks (forty inches) joined their two extremities with strong, flexible strips of animal hides. The operator of the flail held, with both hands, the longer stick. By making the shorter stick swing in the air, he or she would let it acquire velocity and make it land upon the cereals with a great impact. An expert operator could maneuver the flail and make it land on the desired spot over the cereals, given an inch or two. To maneuver the flail a certain skill and dexterity was required, but by no means any degree of education. Depending on the amount of cereals to be threshed out, two, three, or more pairs of good workers could pulverize a thick layer of cereals in a given time. The workers, fronting each other at a measured distance, developed a rhythmical cadence of powerful shots to fall upon the cereals below at the timing of: *one-two, one-two,* and so on, repeated by each pair. Until newer methods came in use, the flail was the most efficient way to thresh cereals.

Giovanni Del Pio looked at Peppe and said: "The threshing task that must be accomplished requires hard work and determination. We have to have strong arms. There are no strong arms here that I know of; they are fighting wars. Sure, I could supervise the job but to get it accomplished is another question."

"I know exactly what you are looking for, Uncle Giová. There are strong, idle, youngsters in Montelieto who would jump at the opportunity to work in exchange for a decent evening meal. Some of them, just like me, are too young to volunteer for war but old enough to get sick and tired of going begging for a lousy potato and going to bed hungry. Everybody, except the rich and those who control the State granary, is having it rough. Foodstuff has been rationed for a long time."

"I am aware of that," said Giovanni. "Now if you believe you could help, go ahead, go. Go back to town and choose at least three of your buddies who can be trusted, and bring them here. But please do not do that openly. Invite them to the shoemaker shop of Don Pompeo and have him make the proposal in my name. Don Pompeo will advise each one to stay quiet for their own benefit. The old shoemaker, I am sure, is already aware of what is happening here on my farm. Alright, listen; you first must contact Don Pompeo, tell him I have sent you to him for help, and he will advise what to do next."

After dusk Peppe returned with three of his young friends who had been recommended by Don Pompeo. For Federico, Giustino and Niccoló, there was nothing they wouldn't do to please Don Pompeo.

Giovanni Del Pio was aware of that arrangement. So he met with the boys and cordially spoke to them about his intentions. Over dinner he discussed in detail the work that would involve them. "We do not want to do the work in daylight," he said. "The risk of being observed by the Fascist harvest controllers is not worth taking. They have the authority to impose a penalty for threshing the wheat without their seal of approval. But we will not reveal anything. We don't need their seal of approval. So we'll thresh the wheat in the nighttime when nobody will know our business. All the grains we are able to extract will be hidden in the straws, in the barns and the hay-stacks. We'll dump it into the wells if necessary, but we will not give it away to the henchmen of the Party for free. Tonight I am going to show you a few tips on how to do the work with ease. Tomorrow we'll rest—and, at dusk, we'll start and continue doing our work, come moonlight or dark."

In the morning Giovanni instructed the boys how to use the flail inside the barn. He paired them, gave each a flail and let them practice on bales of straws. Then he told them to stay put for the day and wait for some good food he was bringing from the house. By night the boys were ready. Giovanni paired himself with his brother Antonio who came to help out, and assigned Titus Del Pio, Antonio's grandson, to relieve the six flail operators.

In less than ten nights, the work was accomplished. Antonio congratulated his brother for having had the wisdom and courage to undertake such a critical farming project and complete it. Giovanni thanked him and the boys from the bottom of his heart and said soberly: "Brother, you have just found out where there is the will, there is the way."

When the three boys knew their work was finished, and began to get ready to return to Montelieto, Giovanni and Antonio asked them to wait. "I understand Peppe will remain here to help my brother," said Antonio. "Giovanni needs help on a daily basis. And so do I. Although the threshing of my cereals has been accomplished, there are still so many chores to work out on the farm. To be honest, I do not know how to handle all that by myself. I could hire the three of you right now."

"You will not do such a thing without consulting with me, Antonio! I wanted to hire the three other boys myself. But I tell you if two volunteer to work for you, I will hire the third to work with Peppe."

"That's fine with me. But we must first hear from them whether they agree or not," said Antonio.

"Of course we agree," the three boys answered by raising their hands up.

"Wait a minute, let's make this selection fair," said Giovanni. He took some pieces of straw in his hand and said: "Here I have three pieces of straw of unequal length. No one knows the length except me. This is a sort of toss of the coin. The two of you who pull from my closed hand the short straws, will go with my brother. The one who pulls up the longer straw, will remain here to help Peppe. Do you think it is fair enough?"

"Yes, fair," answered the boys.

"Alright, soon we'll know who goes and who stays. Good. Giustino and Niccoló, I wish to tell you that my brother is an interesting host. If he'll come short from being interesting, his grandson will remind him. Titus will show you around the farm and I can see how happy he will be to have you in his company."

"Uncle Giová," called Federico who had drawn the longer straw, "will you let me stay sleeping where Peppe sleeps?"

"I don't see why not. Especially so if you do not mind to sleep in the barn on the hayloft for a little while."

"Oh no! I don't mind it at all. I have been accustomed to sleeping in the barn with the jackass of my father. Now my father has gone to war and we don't have a donkey any more. Mother has sold it to make ends meet. I want you to let me go tell her and Don Pompeo what a good job I have! The least thing I want to do is to disappoint Don Pompeo by not being able to broom his shop. He pays me two centisimi and four if I do not holler the war cries to please the pharmacist when he screams: "Hail to the Chief," said Federico Favetta.

"We'll do all those things, Federico, I promise. If you want me to, I can come to talk to your mother and Don Pompeo. In the morning we will ride to Montelieto together and straighten everything out," said Giovanni.

Meantime the Fascist harvest controllers from Montelieto had not even the smallest clue about Giovanni Del Pio's resolve. They did not give a hoot about who lived or died in the farmland, so long as they continued digging into the farm products stored in the granary of the State—to which the pharmacist held the key. Olive oils, wines, grains, cheeses and all other sorts of farm products were stolen from the Fascist bureaucrats and never reached their original objective. But that was not a problem for Giovanni. His main worry remained that of how to deal with the mechanic. The threshing machines were still anchored on his field. Should that misbegotten derelict of a Prefect send the mechanic some petroleum, troubles could arise; the mechanic could come back wanting to finish the threshing work and thus learn of Giovanni's tricks.

"No chance," said Giovanni. "He with the controllers will spend the entire autumn getting drunk. If the devils bring the mechanic back here, I will bribe that jackass so much he will never forget."

The petroleum from the Prefect never arrived. The rainy season was almost upon them and Giovanni enjoyed an abundant surplus of grains, not accounted from anybody and hidden in the straws to be sold in the winter months at black market.

Thanks to Peppe, with the three other little *cafoni* from the ghetto of Montelieto, the initiative taken by Giovanni Del Pio turned out to be successful. After it seemed that the harvest would go to waste for that year, the turn around was more than welcome. The arrangement Giovanni made with the boys, which had been agreed upon at the time of his offer of employment, gave him more vitality to start the planting for the next season. He treated the boys fairly, as if they were his own and even better than his, at times, because he lived up to the rules and traditions of the clan Del Pio, which was: "Recall not the good you have done, but that which you have failed to do," a saintly virtue that was not at all widespread in those times. Perhaps it had never really been put into practice by those whose goodness could have alleviated the misery of the less fortunate. Aside from the clan Palestrina, in Montelieto only the shoemaker Don Pompeo Gazzaladra, practiced and believed in that saintly virtue.

The *cafoni* believed such a virtue didn't even exist. They had been accustomed to sharing the crops voluntarily and were recipients of unfairness at the hands of mean-spirited, greedy Lords all along, and much more lately at the hands of a wicked political system.

Giovanni introduced the boys to the work and lifestyle of the farm, assigning to each the chores he believed suited them best. Being the stronger of the two, Peppe was assigned to handle the needs of the plowing oxen and cows. Federico, who still had difficulty with his impediment, was assigned to handle lighter chores, that of doing errands around the farm which required the use of cart and mules. Both boys were happy. Giovanni, too, was happy. When he talked to Rosetta about the adjustments the boys were making, he appeared energized and proud to find them sincere in every way. He felt as if he were a great teacher of persuasion.

Madam Del Pio, though, appeared worried with every day that went by. She felt less enthusiastic about the progress her husband and the boys were achieving in performing the chores on the farm. Perhaps she missed her own boys who she had not heard from for so long. Giovanni could read her feelings so well, since he felt the same way.

"How could we pretend everything is well and not feel pain, darling?" Giovanni told his wife, saying he shared her feelings.

"Right, we cannot pretend we are happy considering the conflicts happening in the world," she said.

"Absolutely, but we cannot give up. The farm must be maintained to the best of our ability and it must be kept solvent for the good of our kids. They will return! God willing, they will come back home safe."

Giovanni's words of encouragement, and his positive attitude, lifted up Rosetta's spirits immensely. She appeared to have been suddenly relieved of mental stress. She looked at her husband passionately and said: "Yes, God willing they will return, because the good Lord won't deny a good father, a good husband, and a good neighbor, the pleasure of being rejoined with his children. The attention you give these boys, my dear, will certainly be rewarded. You are a good man," said Rosetta to her husband. "And I am also certain that you will be fair to the less fortunate, whatever it'll take. Sometimes I wonder what crushing need makes these boys want to stay here with us. Don't they miss their loved ones? When you introduced Peppe to me, he mumbled: 'Peppe of Montelieto, sorry.' Why? Doesn't he have a family name? Is he sorry to be part of Montelieto or to be Peppe?"

"Both," said Giovanni. "Montelieto is not the joyful mount which its name denotes. And Peppe is not such a happy kid. You must know he was born in the worst slum of Montelieto. Sure, Peppe does have a family, but a family that has tasted hunger and deprivation. Annibale Filippone, his father, immigrated to Argentina at the time Peppe was born and has never been heard from. His mother became whorish and beat her children during the times. Peppe is the product of a broken family and the victim of a system that blames its inefficiencies on others. He, like many kids of Montelieto, will grow old in nothingness if this system is allowed to continue inevitably on the path of war, says Don Pompeo. Peppe is extremely smart but like Federico, Giustino and Niccoló, will never have a fair chance in life, if forced to live in that adversity. There is nothing wrong with Montelieto or with its *cafoni*. The problems were imbedded there, from the start, at the hands of greedy Lords and inefficient leaderships. You never must believe, my dear, that people in this town do not go to bed hungry. I agree with the opinion of Don Pompeo Gazzaladra who has been saying: "This town of ours is poor but will become a haven of peace after the present system is dissolved, after the Fascist pharmacist is buried, and after its people are able to cast away the defaming stereotyped appellatives of sharecroppers, illiterate and declassed *cafoni.*"

"I agree with you and Don Pompeo, Giovanni, but to erase all the defaming appellatives laden on us, seems impossible. It is not just something one dislikes and throws away, you know? Labels affixed with rudeness are degrading."

"Right, but not impossible to erase. The slanders came with the same package of poverty and ignorance perpetuated by bad systems and we have spent part of our lifetime subjected to those bad systems. Ever since the wane of the Roman grandeur, each system has proven more corrupt than the other. Still, I believe Don Pompeo ways of thinking have validity. He says that no evil system can last forever. If good systems fall, evil ones must fall also. For example, he says that the Roman Empire fell because of corruption and for inefficient Duci (leaders). What it is that makes us believe we have an efficient Duce nowadays, and no corruption?"

Chapter 24

The first year of fighting was favorable for the Axis nations. Virtually from every corner of the continent, results of great significance had been achieved. Half a dozen of the belligerent States involved in the struggle had been knocked out of the contest with lightning-like humiliating defeats. In Africa too, the early confrontations had brought positive results. The invasion of Egypt was gaining momentum and further to the south east the most stubborn enemy of the bunch was driven from its strategic territory of Somalia. The resisting stubborn enemy, mauled in the first phase of the war, was believed to have had enough, and in a short time could be expected to capitulate.

By mid-autumn though, the stubborn ally believed to be beaten began to regroup. Although the newly opened front in the Balkans instilled some confidence, in Africa and in the Mediterranean, unexpected reversals began to be felt. Among the first surprises was the blow delivered to Il Duce one bleak November night. Enemy aircraft succeeded in attacking a renowned shipyard of continental Italy. Many of the most powerful battleships, cruisers and destroyers were torpedoed and sunk in the sneak attack. Constant air raid sirens pierced the pride of Il Duce and his followers. The attack became analagous to Il Duce's running out of petroleum—not only on the domestic front, but even on the battle front and shipyards.

The domestic situation, and above the dearth of fuels, began to be depleted of other vital items. Rations of foodstuff were cut dramatically on a daily basis, as were clothing, footwear and farming equipment. Those few not feeling the pinch of the shortage were the rich landowners and the Party bureaucrats who could quietly dip their hands into the State's granary. The remainder went scraping as best they could in order to procure any meager sustenance at high cost.

By this time Giovanni Del Pio had totally given up hopes of obtaining any petroleum. Not because he needed it for completing the current year threshing of the wheat, but for the future harvests as well. He felt no shortages of farm products and had no illusions of short-term recovery for the underprivileged. Giovanni and his brother Antonio had foreseen troubles coming their way and acted in anticipation by hiring the young boys from the ghetto of Montelieto. If the year 1940 was ending in the negative, how much better could the next year be? And the next, and next if the war dragged on?

Skeptical of Il Duce's promises of victory, the two brothers had assured themselves of reliable help, at least for the current season seeding of the crops, and the next harvest—hopefully until the young hired hands would be of age and liable to conscription. But that would take a minimum of three more years and by then the Del Pio boys should be back home. Three more years of war was just a pessimistic thought. Antonio and Giovanni's boys had been recalled with the first, and some with the second mobilization. Not much of any good news had been received by the two brothers since, except learning that their boys were fighting in North and East Africa. The two times Antonio and Giovanni had received any news from their boys the communications had spoken of "loyalty to the Commander in Chief (Il Duce), and of victory."

Knowing their boys, that kind of language was unbelievable. How could they have changed in such short time? They were well aware, though, that these were not times of freedom of speech. Letters from war zones, and the answers from home were being strictly censored. If any sort of news was to be exchanged with the soldiers by mail, both sides' correspondence must have spoken in favor of Il Duce and passed inspection.

Reverend Palestrina, too, wrote occasionally to his friends of Montelieto. Although he had succeeded coming home once on a business leave, he wrote to inform his most trusted sharecropper, Sardone, on the fine details of the estate. Reverend Palestrina had been assigned to the special army battalion of Granatieri, but his main duty was to bless the troops and guns departing for the front from the seaports. He even blessed Cipollone's artillery unit, then told the battalion commander he wished to see his countryman to wish him good luck. The Reverend met Cipollone, hugged him and told him to be careful because Montelieto and Don Pompeo needed him.

Reverend Palestrina wrote to Valentina, but in a tone that raised no suspicions. The scrutiny of their letters by the censors of the army and also by the Fascist henchmen of Montelieto, hopefully accomplished the concealment of their love affair. He also wrote to Don Pompeo, his beloved shoemaker. His letters were brief but highly praising of Il Duce. One time he wrote: "Il Duce of our great people, will deliver us to victory." It was evident that the letter had been opened, scrutinized and re-sealed. Yet in another letter Reverend Palestrina said that Il Duce possessed superior intellect and that he had been bestowed upon Italy as leader by destiny.

"How could this priest have changed his political orientation in such a brief period of time? It is pure mystery," argued Don Pompeo. "It seems impossible! Reverend Palestrina could not turn into that big of a fool overnight! The supporter of the human cause, stooping so low as to embrace Fascism? And preaching his philosophy to others? God forbid that," said Don Pompeo. Then, re-reading the words written by the Reverend he said: "Yeah! My good boy, if you keep on using your head like that, it means even you are taking precautions."

Reverend Palestrina was not a fool by any means. He took grave precautions in writing to the people he cared for the most. Upon his visits to Montelieto he had asked Don Pompeo to keep an eye to Valentina and the kids, in the eventuality things turned for the worse. And it was pretty certain things would turn for the worse, he confided to Don Pompeo. He also had informed Sardone and Dorotea to let Don Pompeo have access to indispensable foodstuff in his granary. The priest loved Valentina and the kids more than ever, and in his absence from Montelieto was concerned that they would go hungry. He had already made plans on how to resign from the clergy and rectify the wrongs he had done to Valentina and the kids, but the times were not opportune now. If he had disrobed at this point, given his age and schooling, he would be assigned to take command of the rugged unit to which he belonged, and sent away to critical areas on the front lines. Somehow, the Reverend must prevent that from happening, but he was not chicken. He had loved to take command of a company of soldiers and lead them to distinguish themselves in battle. But he didn't believe in wars. He was a philanthropist, rich land owner, unbeliever—but very much inclined to do good to those who were not blessed with wealth like him. If Reverend Palestrina had been a womanizer, that was because he had made no true commitments with anybody. The commitments he had made for being ordained to the priesthood were done in haste, all influenced by strict Christian parents who believed they had raised a son who was a Saint. Far from becoming Saint, though, Reverend Palestrina had now grown up. Valentina and her kids remained the love of his life.

The following year began adversely for Il Duce's plans. His special army was losing ground in East and North Africa. It appeared that the King was not going to be able to hold on to his crown of Emperor for much longer. But as the year progressed into the summer, to save face about the fiasco tasted on the southern fronts, Il Duce committed himself to send troops to the Eastern front. A strong army was selected mostly from the best of Mountain Corps, and sent off to Russia on a voyage of no return. The bold move caught several other insufficiently trained young *cafoni* from Montelieto who never made it back. Despite the shameful defeats delivered to his objectives in Egypt and elsewhere, the bold move saved face for Il Duce in front of his colleague behind the Alps who had dared to fight Russian Communism. In light of that foolish venture, Reverend Palestrina quickly postponed his plans to disrobe the mantle of priesthood, opting to remain at his relatively safe post and reconsider the matter of disrobing later on, in a more promising situation. So Reverend was not about to take hasty action. He continued blessing the ammunition, the guns, and the soldiers going to the front line to kill—and every day felt himself to be more of a religious hypocrite. He wrote again to Don Pompeo and in one of the brief letters told him that the collapse of the Allies was not too far off. But again the envelope had been tampered with.

Meanwhile Don Pompeo spent the working hours of the evening in boring solitude, and many nights in sleep-lessness. He scoffed at the news of the collapse of the Allies and as he disposed of the letter in his waste basket com-mented so: "Not too far off, eh? My dear priest, better you say and make believe lies if you care to come back safely. You could say whatever the censors of mail want to hear, and you can be sure I do not believe you. For me it is im-portant to know you are okay, Reverend."

Don Pompeo felt terribly saddened to see both younger and older *cafoni* recruits, depart for the front to defend the honor of Il Duce—and die. He was pained to see Mariano Albarosa devastated upon learning that his youngest son Giovannino had been sent overseas. Gennarino Pennamos-cia, too, had departed for the front line. The two kids un-justly abused by the Fascist pharmacist chief for being unpresentable at the drills of war, were given shoes and sent to die. "They would never put their lives on the line to defend the honor of the pharmacist," said Don Pompeo.

Late news of fatalities occurring on the front lines had already begun to arrive in Montelieto. Young boys had per-ished at sea on their way to Libya, boys Don Pompeo had known since birth. He had seen them fight desperate poverty while growing to manhood and then, so early in life they were no more. What an infamy to die without having had a chance! Oh, how many times he had shared their sacrifices and sorrow! Don Pompeo attended the services in the Church, together with the desolate parents of the perished boys, as Father Alfonso blessed their souls in absence of the bodies.

The grieving old shoemaker, Don Pompeo, had pinned a black strip of cloth upon the sleeve of his shirt, and kept it permanently attached as a gesture of mourning and of respect for all fallen soldiers and their families. On the other hand, the Fascist Chief of the Montelieto branch appeared to celebrate and to equate the promotion of propaganda with the news of fatalities. The ego-inflated Chief dressed up in grand uniform on the morning Father Alfonso was to bless the souls of the dead soldiers, but looked as ridiculous and hateful as ever. He participated in the short services, arriving early with a small cortege of old veterans, widows of World War I, a group of his henchmen, and some of the Fascist controllers of farm products.

The two deaf sisters also attended the blessing services. They kneeled down for the entire service praying devotedly. Looking at the arrogant pharmacist, dressed in grand-uniform, Don Pompeo felt only low contempt for him, as well as an almost irresistible impulse to get hold of the tricolor sash wrapped around the waist of the haughty man and wrap it up around his neck instead, to choke him once and for all.

Meanwhile, when it appeared that the fall and winter fighting had ended with disastrous defeats for Il Duce, by spring an air of optimism began to be felt. Although the

Empire in East Africa had been totally lost, in North Africa and Russia, a joint Axis force took the offensive once again. After a series of seesaw battles, the joint Axis proved victorious on all fronts. The route to the Suez Canal, to the Caucasus Mountains and Moscow, appeared now wide open. The Party supporters in Montelieto—the pharmacist and his cohorts—all predicted the conflict would be ending any day now, in favor of the Axis. The joint effort of the Axis Army, and their march toward victory, seemed now just unstoppable.

The euphoria of the hard-line Fascists spread quickly over every rank of the Party. They believed there was no powerful enemy apt at impeding the Axis Army drive to Russia's oil fields, the Ural Mountains, and perhaps Siberia.

But for the bereaved parents of the young *cafoni*, there was nothing to be cheerful about, and no strategic, oil-rich regions on earth worthy of the sacrifice of their kids. They knew so well that their young men had been sent away on a mission only to satisfy the ego of the Commander in Chief, and make him appear important in the eyes of his associate. Even if riches were to be won, that still meant nothing to the helpless parents. Neither they, nor their boys, could ever dream of sharing in the spoils of victories, until the end of time.

Meanwhile, Don Pompeo's heart pained for all. Same as always, he piously began to entrust to the Saints the sanity of the parents and the return of their young sons, safely back home to Montelieto, from wherever they might be.

Chapter 25

Unaware there might be more bleak days to come, the sons
and daughters of Montelieto saw the year 1942 record the
highest sacrifices. For the third consecutive year, the elder
sharecroppers were faced with mounting chores on the
farms and all other sorts of shortages. Important tasks
were having to be postponed for lack of farmhands, and
often parts of the harvests went totally to waste. This contributed to the hardship. At home and abroad on the front
line, the *cafoni* of Montelieto had not much more to give.

That year, however, marked the very height of the Axis
conquests and ever stronger the promise of ultimate victory. Emotions ran high within the ranks of the Fascists
of Montelieto. The flamboyant pharmacist, Chief of the
House of Fasces of the forgotten town, lived those days in
one indisputable presence of power and of importance. He
dressed in his grand uniform whether commanding the
drills of war to the troubled youth of town, or lying down
snoring on the deck chair over his balcony. For even the
most insignificant pretext, he made sure the poor *cafoni*
respected his authority. The thinking of the citizenry was
thus put into confusion. If the auspicious predictions of

victory meant more escalating oppression at the hands of the overweening pharmacist, they wanted no part of that.

By summer and early autumn, that year of high conquests also marked the beginning of the end to power of a superior army. The news of military achievements became unreliable. After much bombast, even the state-run radio broadcasts began to be less audible. The broadcasters had very little to say, and audio interferences regularly disrupted the news programs on daily basis. Listening to the duplicity of reporters, though, the loud radio broadcast interferences were simply nothing more than weather-related incidents. That wasn't true. The people believed that those interferences had been jammed in from some sort of enemy radio frequencies, and consequently they lost interest.

Don Pompeo, too, had lost interest. Even with the flood of Fascist posters attached to the walls outside and inside his shoe shop, Don Pompeo had lost the immunity given him by the Fascist Chief for staying open late. The pharmacist had arbitrarily cut the evening hours for the cobbler to conduct business. He claimed that the curfew of the brownout did not apply anymore, and that the blackout order declared by Rome must be enforced. The same strict rule was applied to the order that no more than two persons could congregate, at one time. As a result of that, the old cobbler lost freedom to even entertain his *cafoni* friends. But brownout or blackout, there were hardly any regular and able *cafone* to entertain. They had all been recruited or recalled to arms.

The elderly seemed to have been disappearing too. Davide Persichella, the knife sharpener, and the town crier Vittorio Settimo, were rarely seen anymore. Neither was the ragman, Diodato Bello. This latter had no more to collect. His merchandise was very much needed but nothing was discarded by the townspeople anymore. So Diodato had changed his line of work and went cutting thickets in the woods to sell whenever he could. His new work left the ragman no time to visit with Don Pompeo.

Cicco Palla, too, had cut back the social calls to Don Pompeo. He had been given additional work by the Deputy Mayor and must have picked over the dung of donkeys in the streets of Montelieto until late. Mariano Albarosa pressured by the shortage of able farmhands, spent the entire time working the fields. He knew he must maintain the fields profitably for his Lords and thus keep alive the privileges for his boys to share the crops on their return.

Barabba, the sacristan was the only friend remaining close to the old shoemaker. Although not as frequent as in the past, they still enjoyed their togetherness when they took occasional afternoon strolls on the outside of the town's defensive walls. While on their strolls, Don Pompeo talked to Sigismondo Barabba with sadness in his voice. More than anybody else in Montelieto he felt the awareness of what was occurring to his beloved town and became increasingly distressed.

"Look at those poor old ladies sitting in the sun by the walls," he pointed out to Barabba one afternoon. "They are delousing their heads and shirts. That, my friend, is as low as it can get!"

"I know. This morning after the early mass, Clorinda was telling Merlina she couldn't close an eye last night, for the itchings. I heard them set the time to come here for delousing. There are others, young and old, who come here to delouse on a daily basis. Merlina also told Clorinda she hadn't had much to eat for the last two or three days, except for the same diet of boiled chicory leaves," said Barabba.

"Yeah, I dread to think what is going to happen this coming winter when there will be no more chicory leaves to pick. Food supplies are so scarce that we can't obtain the assigned daily ration in two weeks' time! The pharmacist authorizes the Deputy Mayor to dispense food coupons, but the paper is not edible if the shelves in the stores are empty. Damned! They expect to win the war with this starving population? Let's walk by those two old madams," suggested Don Pompeo. "I can't stand the thought that Merlina had not had anything to eat but chicory leaves, for three days! They can delouse and kill all the lice they want, but sure as hell they cannot kill hunger," he said.

They walked where the two old madams were sitting and as they approached, the ladies stopped doing their work. They tried to cover their breasts, feeling a little embarrassment

"Do not feel we came by here to embarrass you," assured Don Pompeo. "We care not to see breasts. I just want to ask Merlina why her food coupons were not honored by the Party's store people. Had they run out of food supplies entirely?"

"No, I don't believe they had run out of food supplies entirely. They told me that the food remaining on the shelves was not to be dispensed to the holders of the coupons. That food could only be obtained for cash. Where do they think I am going to get that?" Merlina cried out.

"Damn it!" cussed Don Pompeo. Then he began to search for something inside his pocket, found two coins, and handed them to Merlina. When Clorinda looked at him with her lamentable eyes, Don Pompeo delved again into his pockets, found more coins and tossed them on the woman's lap. At that Merlina got hold of his hand and began to kiss it.

"Eh, Merlina!" Don Pompeo warned. "Be careful! We have not come here to look for sex. We came to wish you girls good luck, hoping you could obtain some scrap pasta with a slice of bread, for supper."

Don Pompeo and Barabba continued walking slowly, until they reached their preferred spot. They sat resting upon the same boulder, halfway to the end of the stroll, where they were accustomed to rest. From there they could look far and wide at the breadth of the valley below and enjoy the scenery and sunset.

"I feel somewhat troubled to look at the valley and not see the same devotion the sharecroppers had in the past for performing the chores. There are parcels of uncultivated fields dotting the valley. The poor sharecroppers all feel the shortage of strong farm hands. I have the feeling this will be a lean harvest. The wheat-threshing outfit is idled again," said Don Pompeo. "They render the wheat-threshing service on alternate days at best, and all depending on the amount of petroleum the pharmacist makes available to them. The supply of petroleum has been cut to less than fifty percent. Giovanni Del Pio must have his hands full during these days. I wonder what he is up to."

"It won't be too difficult to know what Del Pio is up to. He is the eternal workhorse. Even with his boys gone, he and Rosetta manage the farm fairly well. Of course the last two or three years, they have had the help of Peppe di Montelieto and Federico Favetta. Those two old goats of Del Pio, are turning Peppe and Federico into a couple of experienced farmers," said Barabba.

"For sure they are, and I am happy for everyone. That was a God-sent opportunity for the boys to have found work on the farms of Del Pio's clan! When the boys are in to town doing errands for Giovanni, they never fail to come to say hello, and I can tell they are happy. Just to know that some of the little *cafoni* are happy in these horrendous times is quite gratifying."

"It really is," said the sacristan. "Did you know Favetta is coming out of his impediment? He walks very steady and with lots of energy."

"Yeah! That goes to Giovanni's credit. I ought to know that much. He has ordered special footwear for Federico all along. Giovanni has great care for both of them. Every time they stop by, they are told by Giovanni to ask me whether I need anything from the farm. Look how thoughtful that old farmer is! Thanks to God I don't need Giovanni's help—yet. I still do some work for rich families," said Don Pompeo.

"You are very fortunate, Don Pompé. My wife and I struggle to make a meager living. That which Father Alfonso can spare, is all we have. In a particular way, now that Reverend Palestrina is gone and not needing help, we are having a rough time. We are grateful though to Father Alfonso. His generosity helps us to stay alive," said the sacristan.

"My dear Sigismondo, I believe we all are making bigger and bigger sacrifices. Even Father Alfonso. The situation for the *cafoni* of Montelieto is very bleak. Everyone feels the stings of shortage and hunger."

"I am fully aware of that," said Sigismondo Barabba. "Father Alfonso feels pressure from the Archdiocese every time. That demands greater retributions for the farmlands the parish gives out at sharecrops. Those demands are never met because the farming population has decreased. The young, strong sharecroppers, are fighting the war for Il Duce."

"Yes, a conflict of this magnitude will definitely destroy the lives of many throughout the world. We are experiencing that right here in Montelieto. The Commanders in Chief of the Axis nations are pushing their luck too far. Who can tell how far luck will take them before it will turn fatal?" Don Pompeo said getting up on his feet. "We ought to get back home, Sigismondo. I have chores to take care of. Also I want to open up the shop for a couple of hours before dusk. Let's go. You, too, must have chores to do. Aren't you going to help out Father Alfonso with the chores of the church?"

"I sure will. By now he should have returned from the business trip in the chief town of Frosinone."

The two wise elders began to walk back slowly toward town, chatting and enjoying the late afternoon breeze and their togetherness. As they distanced themselves from the delousing women, their bad mood improved. From time to time they stopped to take a rest, and then laughed aloud at the funny tales remembered since their childhood years. To tell funny tales even in the midst of adversity was important for those folks as a preventative for not going insane—that was the bread of soul of the *cafoni* of Montelieto.

Beneath the archway of the entrance door into town, Don Pompeo and Sigismondo stopped again. A two-wheeler dumpcart was seen coming down hill toward them quite fast. The person behind the cart pushing it, could not be seen but began sounding a trumpet attached to one side of the cart to warn pedestrians to stay out of the way.

"Malediction!" Don Pompeo said, ill-humoredly moving quickly against the wall of the nearby building in order to protect himself. "For a minute I thought nobody was pushing that dumpcart. Be careful, Sigismondo! It looks as if whoever might be pushing that is going to stop it right against our legs."

Suddenly the dumpcart made an abrupt stop, a few inches from the feet of the two elders, and an unperturbed Cicco Palla was seen emerging from behind it to appear on the scene and say: "Were you guys afraid I would run you over? That could never happen. Lately I have been extra careful. I have not run over anyone for a long time! Besides, I have never hit two people in one incident."

"We know, we know, nutty boy Cicco. You might have bruised and twisted a leg here and there, but you have never killed anybody—yet. Remember, though, that you were not hired to go terrifying the people of Montelieto! Your job is to pick up the dung in the streets. I have the impression you have spent too much of your time cleaning the dung in front of the tavern of Marianna Pipanera. Perhaps the stink of those cheap wines has inebriated you. Be careful with that dumpcart of yours, you hear, Cicco?" warned the shoemaker.

"Oh yeah! I promise you to be more careful from here on. Today has been a long, busy day, Don Pompé. I have filled several dumpcarts of manure. You can see for yourself how clean the streets are this evening."

"We have noticed that, Cicco. Today you should be praised by all the citizens of Montelieto. I am sure the Deputy Mayor and the pharmacist will also praise you."

"No, I don't believe they will, Don Pompé. Today has been a long day for them too. The pharmacist was expected back from his trip in the chief town, but has not showed up yet. This afternoon the postal van came back empty. The driver of the van said something about bombs near the railroad station. The Deputy Mayor with the postmaster, have been in the post office waiting to receive some kind of news telegram from the Prefect. Until a while ago, they have received no news of the pharmacist."

"Good Lord!" Barabba muttered. "Bombs? Let me run to see whether Father Alfonso has made it back. He, too, had traveled to Frosinone this morning to handle some business. Oh, no! Goodbye, friends."

"You see, Cicco? Sigismondo is terribly worried about Father Alfonso. He ought to be," said Don Pompeo. "Should some unaccountable thing happen to Father Alfonso, old Sigismondo and his wife run the danger of losing their only remaining protection from starving to death."

"Yes, but you can tell him not to be so terribly worried about that. If anything bad happens to Father Alfonso, I will ask the Deputy Mayor to let Sigismondo help me sweep the dung of donkeys in the streets."

"Good thinking, Cicco. You are so understanding and tenderhearted, my boy! I am not sure of Father Alfonso's feelings, but Sigismondo and I are very proud of you. In any case, we'll see what tomorrow brings. For the time being, I wish you good work and good evening."

Don Pompeo walked alone the last two blocks toward his shop talking to himself. By going back in his thoughts to the strange happenings of that afternoon, he became dejected, as though a terrible anxiety was settling in his soul. The scene of the two delousing madams and the worries of Barabba fearing not to be able to make it, stayed fixed in his mind to trouble him.

And when Cicco impassively spoke of bombs being dropped around the railroad depot, Don Pompeo imagined the worst. In that instant he saw dark shadows of pessimism cover the horizons of Montelieto. Then not really persuaded, Don Pompeo said: "Bombs around the train depot? No, I believe that is another exaggeration of Cicco. Bombs? Not here in our region," he said doubtfully.

Chapter 26

Meantime, as the reports of glorious achievements for the Axis powers were dwindling, a succession of more alarming consequences was taking place. Reports of major defeats infiltrated the news. From virtually every battlefield, the invincibility and good fortune of the Axis army had all of a sudden run its course. Back home, the new developments created widespread pessimism and anxieties. In this new scenario, people began to see the makings of a disastrous backward march to defeat.

Unproven rumors of Allied air raids upon navy yards, railroad links and other strategic points, had become reality. More alarming was the undeniable fact that younger and younger *cafoni*, not quite eighteen yet, had been issued the notification of recruitment. Those born within the first two quarters of the year were hastily sent to training bases and then immediately shipped out to reinforce the shores of the islands armed only with secondary military skills and inadequate equipment. The remaining group of youngsters were eventually recruited but sent back home on temporary leave, for lack of training facilities. Some of those new recruits wore shabby, torn uniforms and no boots, while others returned wearing military boots but still in civilian clothes.

Through hearsay and from credible sources, the news of fatalities occurring on the front lines and inside the homeland came in every day more painful and mortifying. The lives of those soldiers fighting on the Russian front and in North Africa, were put in jeopardy. Allied air bombardments upon the industrial targets, had been intensifying. The Fascist Chief of the House of Fasces of Montelieto had been caught in an air raid while attending a Party meeting in the chief town. That had pierced his pride and had mellowed his presumptuous behavior almost to a tolerable degree. He repeatedly exempted himself from future meetings, cowardly feigning poor health. His arrogance and burning enthusiasm to continue conducting rigid drills of war with the young kids, was also fading out. Still, fearing to be repudiated by his Fascist superiors, in public he continued accusing and addressing the new trainees with the same defaming appellative as in the past.

From secret military sources it was learned that the army corps at the Russian front had been encircled and overrun. The same fate impended upon the army corps in the North Africa front. With the Americans pressing from Morocco and the British from Lybia, the Axis armies had been fiercely pursued into Tunisia and rounded up in a shrinking strip of land from which their only escape was the sea. But even at the sea the Allies had placed a stranglehold, assembling a formidable fleet of ships and bombers to prevent any one and any materiel to flee to safety. By spring 1943 the Allies had achieved victory and had cleared North Africa of all vestiges of Axis power and influence. Many *cafoni* from Montelieto were taken prisoners.

The gloomy scenario of defeat hung above Fascist Rome like a hateful curse. The demeanor of Il Duce had dramatically worsened. The recurrent outbursts of anger, and long spells of listlessness, made him appear so devoid of good logic that even the most fervent supporters began to undermine his leadership and war policies.

But whatever scenario of gloom and of pessimism hung over Rome, that was of no concern for the people of Montelieto. Their number one priority was to see their kinsmen return home, safe and sound, from the front lines. Of pessimism, badly calculated policies, and failures from the capital, they had seen enough. Year in and year out, the air had permeated bad news whichever way news came. However, in spite of the gloom, the forgotten old town possessed certain characteristics that separated it from the complicated world outside. Two of those features were the lack of notoriety and remoteness of its location. If any town, or village, was to survive the furious rages of the war and the bombardments, by any measure, its name could be Montelieto.

As time went on, the old shoemaker turned more vocal against the Party and against the conduct of the Fascist pharmacist; engaging him and his henchmen, in heated verbal altercation. Between blames, suspicions and accusations, Don Pompeo challenged his rivals to cut off their legacy to the Fascist Party, and to become regular citizens. They laughed at his incitements and began to address him as a perverted partisan. That was exactly what Don Pompeo really wished to be. He wanted, in the worst way, to become an active partisan; to rally his people against the impertinent pharmacist and surrogates and get rid, once and for all, of the parasites. But that was a feat of high risk. Don Pompeo was old and getting feeble. There were no arms to be had and no capable bodies to bear them. To assemble a strong band of guerrilla, calling on ailing elders and kids, would not be the best idea at the moment.

The community of farmers-sharecroppers also, met with serious difficulties, for reaping the harvests. For the past three years, they had been troubled with lack of farm hands and all other sorts of shortages. The wheat-threshing outfit had accomplished only fifty percent of the services indispensable to the farmers. There had never been adequate supplies of petroleum for completion of the work. And everything seemed to be heading for the worse.

In the face of many obstacles and all sorts of pressures, Giovanni Del Pio, with his brother Antonio, had not been troubled as much as the others. They had pooled their resources, and with the help of the young boys from the ghetto of Montelieto, they had managed to overcome the adversities. The two brothers, for the third consecutive year of unavailability of petroleum, had reaped ample and profitable harvests. Thanks to the help of the four young men, they had sold their crops at black market, and stored the surplus safely behind the knowledge of the Fascist harvest controllers. Those stool pigeons of the pharmacist had posed but little problems for Del Pio's clan. They didn't understand the methods of using the flails to shell out the wheat, and after having been wined and dined and having had their palms greased abundantly, the harvest controllers inflated their findings so much out of proportion to make it appear to the pharmacist that even Del Pios needed food coupons.

Meantime, Peppe of Montelieto and Federico Favetta, with Giustino and Niccoló, had grown to be reliable farm hands, but were quickly nearing the age of enlistment. The likelihood of an untimely recruitment appeared certain, although they were not quite eighteen. Titus, who still attended evening classes given by Father Alfonso, had become Peppe of Montelieto's inseparable friend and companion. Every school evening, Peppe waited for Titus inside the shop of Don Pompeo, so after the class ended, they could ride the wagon together back to the farm. They also attended the Sabato Fascista drills of war still called by the pharmacist.

Don Pompeo was fond of those two boys. In his heart he entertained high hopes that some day, his beloved people of Montelieto would see better times, and that Titus would excel in school to become a role model to all. He talked to Titus at every opportunity and cautioned him to be wary of the pharmacist and his Party. Then, after having engaged the young man's attention, one evening Don Pompeo told him: "Son, ever since you attended the classes by Reverend Palestrina, I have known that you are a brave student. In these dangerous situations that we live nowadays, though, it appears extremely difficult to maintain interest in learning. The future is bleak and unpredictable, but you have to persevere. You can because you are a strong-willed Del Pio. Do not let the hindrances of the times deter you from the goals you have set in mind to achieve. Be steadfast, my son! Pursue your dreams, and someday you will succeed. You must succeed, not only for yourself, but to raise hopes in the hearts of those contemporaries of yours, who never had a chance in Montelieto. God only knows whether I'll be granted to see that day—the day when someone from our beloved town will have perfected the skills and ability to tell it all. I am old, but I still have hopes for you and for all of those," he said indicating to Titus the names on the cardboard sign hanging on the wall inside the shop. "That is my momentous hope. Highly momentous because, since the day my friends departed to go to war I have lived in unbearable loneliness."

"I understand and share that brotherly love, dear Don Pompeo. And that said, I wish to ask permission to authenticate the sign. We do not wish to leave its author unknown," said Titus.

"Yes, do that," replied the shoemaker handing the young man a piece of white chalk. Titus took the chalk and beneath the simple words scribbled on the sign by Don Pompeo that read: "FAREWELL MY BOYS, PLEASE COME BACK HOME SAFE," he wrote in large print "THE LONESOME COBBLER" and beneath that signed: Don Pompeo Gazzaladra. Then turning his attention again to the old shoemaker waited for his approval, and said: "That will clearly identify its originator."

"It surely will," answered Don Pompeo. "That's what I am, son. That's truly what I am. I am a lonesome cobbler."

Chapter 27

Don Pompeo was not a schoolmaster by any means. He was merely a proud but poor shoemaker who felt deep compassion and concern for his beloved town and its people. Those saintly virtues, above his genuine common sense, gave people who knew him the feeling that he was a great altruist. In his impassioned moments, Don Pompeo would have renounced everything he had, perhaps including his own life, if that had been enough to erase from the people of Montelieto the stigma of illiterate *cafoni* and declassed sharecroppers.

But the proud shoemaker knew the limitations. Nothing would ever change the present conditions, not even with the ultimate sacrifices. So he came to the realization that he must face the facts, continue to maintain the old lifestyle and be of help as much as he could, to the community of Montelieto.

In the mind of Don Pompeo, four years plus of global conflict would bring severe hardships to all nations involved, be they rich or poor. More severe though, he charged, the hardships would be felt by those nations whose leaders sought to rectify their national ills by promoting wars. That, he felt, was contrary to common sense and every standard of civilized society. In his discontent, he blamed and classified his beloved country on top of the list of warmongers. In the crumpled notebook inside which he had scribbled his favorite proverbs and funny anecdotes, Don Pompeo had written: "Warmongers are coward leaders who, on the shallow pretext of bettering the lives of their followers, destroy the lives of so many."

This same passage was borrowed and inserted in the eulogy given from the sacristan Barabba to Damiano, in honor of the family Grifone. Damiano had perished in the sands of Cyrenaica not too long ago and was one among the unconfirmed casualties of soldier *cafoni*, whose identity had been discovered and forwarded to Montelieto. From a sheet of paper, half scribbled by Father Alfonso and half scribbled by the sacristan himself, Barabba humbly read the eulogy in front of mourners and Fascist cortege of the pharmacist. The oft-repeated eulogy had become a routine of chosen words told and re-told from the sacristan who, by helping Father Alfonso with the services, had learned the words by heart. This time, due to the crisis of the war coming to the forefront, and for the lack of patriotism on the part of the loyal Fascists, of his own initiative Barabba bravely put emphasis on the eulogy.

So, as Barabba sensed that the pharmacist had lately been losing his fire of enthusiasm, he borrowed the proverb from Don Pompeo to say what he felt in front of everybody. First he read from Father Alfonso's notes thus: "Dear Damiano, beloved son of Montelieto. Your untimely fate has saddened your loved ones and the entire community of our doleful town profoundly. We miss you so much! In our sorrow we believe that to give the ultimate sacrifice defending

the honor and sacred soil of the motherland, is praisewor-
thy and noble."

Then after more words of praise for Damiano and further expressions of sympathy for the family, Barabba read:
"Dear fellow countryman Damiano, although your sacrifice
was total and noble, we feel it has wasted a young life for
the glory of warmongers."

Then catching the eye of the pharmacist, Barabba
(quoting Don Pompeo) said: "Warmongers are coward leaders who, on the shallow pretext to better the lives of their
followers, destroy the lives of so many." At that point the
pharmacist, struck with embarrassment, was seen heading
for the exit door without saying a word. The mourners
stayed composed until the end of the service when all
walked by the family Grifone to give the last condolences.

Meantime the struggle to meet the responsibilities of
the fields continued for the *cafoni*-sharecroppers of Montelieto. The chores on the farms followed, in a regular sequence, the development of nature and regardless of the
entanglements the high leadership had gotten those people
into. Shortage or no shortage of farmhands, the summer of
1943 had arrived. The reaping of the wheat had begun,
and it appeared that the entire population was once more
immersed in the work. Again Don Pompeo felt loneliness.

Unexpectedly Mariano Albarosa arrived in town, early
on in the morning, to do his errands. He was hoping to
purchase certain farming implements needed for the ongoing reaping, but there were no implements or tools to be
had. The blacksmith shop of Arturo was closed for lack of
strips of steel. The tin-smith and other crafts shops were
also closed for shortage of essential supplies. Before returning empty handed, Mariano Albarosa thought to stop

by the shop of Don Pompeo for a brief chat, and also to ask for the latest news.

"The news is more depressing than ever, Mariano," said Don Pompeo. "Damiano's fate has shocked his family and all those who knew him in Montelieto, immensely. We do not hear news coming from anywhere that is encouraging except that Tranquillo Fedele, who was shipwrecked fleeing Tunisia, was saved and is recuperating in some hospital. Thanks to God! The bulletin of war has not been broadcast recently on a regular basis. Even the screwball of Santamiddia seems to have slackened his efforts in calling the drills of war. He appears worried and waiting for something bad to occur at any moment. Has even ordered the barbed wires taken down from the balcony of his apartment. Perhaps he is losing trust in his Party and fears the *cafoni* might get to him if he does not put forth a reconciliatory image.

"It seems his grapes are turning sour, my dear Albarosa," said Don Pompeo continuing talking. "What is happening abroad and nationally we can learn of it only by earshot. Mail service for the public has practically stopped. Only mail of military interest arrives. Ottaviano has just delivered a bunch of new recruitment notifications yesterday. Younger and younger kids yet, are being recruited. That alone spells more trouble ahead. Peppe di Montelieto, Favetta, Giustino and Niccoló will have to leave immediately. Things are bleak for all, Mariano! Our friends in the farmland, how are they handling the pressing needs of the reaping?" Don Pompeo asked.

"We have our hands full with unattended chores. Those who had luck getting the petroleum have had a head start for the reaping. Liberato Purgatorio has been one of the first to wrap up the work. Our landlord, Signor Luigi, is already on the threshing field waiting to share the crops. He and Benito, the head mechanic, have been personally requesting petroleum from the Prefect. No luck so far. The threshing machines are on the field but stand idled at this point. It appears as if even the Del Pios will have problems if those young hired hands have been recruited," said Albarosa.

"Of that I would not be worried. Del Pios having problems? Even though they lost this current year harvest, they will come out of it fine," said Don Pompeo.

Albarosa had just left when Don Pompeo thought to replace the sticky fly-paper ribbon hanging from the ceiling. As he threw the gluey fly-paper strip, full of dead insects, into the wastebasket, he heard someone say, "Good catch this morning, huh, Don Pompé?"

"Yeah, it sure is! But I warn you to be careful because there is still another small spot big enough to catch another one. Cicco! What on earth has brought you in town, my boy, when there is so much to do on the farm?"

"Oh, we have nearly finished the reaping work but are waiting for Signor Luigi to get the petroleum needed to finish up threshing Albarosa's wheat next. While I am waiting for Signor Luigi, I came in town hoping to collect the last food coupons due to me for my work. The Deputy Mayor has not paid me since last month when he cut my hours claiming there is less dung in the streets of Montelieto. Sure—by this time of the year, all the donkeys are out in the country! But that doesn't mean I must not be compensated for my work."

"I understand," said Don Pompeo. "Looks like everyone is scraping for something. Signor Luigi is scraping to provide the petroleum for his sharecroppers, Albarosa is scraping to obtain farming implements, and City Hall dependents with even the mailman, are waiting for funds to arrive. Arrive from where? From Washington?"

"Now that I know all those people are scraping for something and waiting to be paid, I have no more hopes. I am a small potato in comparison," said Cicco, miserably.

"You could say that again!" Don Pompeo laughed.

"It is unbelievable. There are always things going bad for us in Montelieto. I wonder why this happens," Cicco Palla said with resentment.

"Stop wondering, Cicco, but get ready to listen, and hear me again telling you the reasons why bad things happen to us. Bad things happen because we are led from the braggart leadership, a leadership stubbornly inclined to warfare. A *cafone* and coward leadership, we might say, which doesn't understand how to govern. Add to that the fact that we are poor, illiterate sharecroppers, and that's what you get. We are flesh born to sacrifice. The Prefect, the pharmacist, Deputy Mayor, the Podestá and the rich ones like Signor Luigi, believe we are inferior beings, worth much less than even the donkeys in this town. I mean in their minds we are animals of burden, understand?"

"You mean Signor Luigi believes I am worth much less than his donkeys?"

"Let me explain to you, briefly, Cicco. You, me, Peluso, Albarosa, Cipollone, and all the rest, are considered to be much below the rank of beasts. We are declassed!"

"Why?" Cicco said in a defensive tone.

"Because if the donkeys that Signor Luigi and his rich colleagues bought for their sharecroppers should succumb for any reason at all, they lose valuable capital. To purchase another donkey they must dig again into their pockets. On the contrary—if a sharecropper succumbs to starvation, or is killed in a war, the rich suckers do not lose a thing. They replace the dead sharecropper with another younger sharecropper."

"Sounds like as if I am worth much less than my donkeys indeed!"

"Finally you got it my boy, finally," said Don Pompeo.

"I see what you mean, Don Pompé, but the thing which bothers me more than Signor Luigi, is to know that Damiano is gone for good."

"Sure, I understand. This time he is gone for real and Cipollone is not around to help."

"Sorry, Don Pompé. Even he is gone for real, I feel he is lucky that Reverend Palestrina gave him one of his best confessions before he was called to go to war."

"Yes, very lucky was Damiano, very lucky to have confessed his sins before he died. It tells us how prepared you must be," said Don Pompeo.

"Speaking of being prepared, I believe that doesn't apply to me. You are not referring to me, personally, are you? If you mean that before something bad happens one must confess, I shall never set foot inside the Church again. The best thing for me to do is to remain 4 F," said Cicco.

"Of course you will stay as you are. You are already past the growing age. Then even if you weren't we wish you to remain among us because our people will need you. Cicco my boy, I must tell you that every so often you really make my day!"

"Thanks, Don Pompé. I am glad to be of help."

Chapter 28

For a number of days, Elvira's voice had not been heard singing patriotic songs as she had done in the past. Perhaps the pharmacist, who wished to display a new reconciliatory image to the people of Montelieto, had prohibited Elvira to sing so loud? He also ordered that the barbed wire be removed from the balcony of his apartment. The two facts strengthened Don Pompeo's belief that the pharmacist's enthusiasm for the Party was simmering down.

Meantime the reaping of the wheat, for the sharecroppers of Montelieto, was to be completed in a few more days. Piles of sheaves of wheat were already waiting upon the threshing fields to be threshed. Signor Luigi, with the head mechanic of the threshing service outfit, felt frustrated by the alternating promises and denials of the Prefect to provide the petroleum. There was no petroleum to be obtained on a short-term basis. Although the threshing machines were already prepared to start operating, there was little hope that the work itself would start soon. Impatient farmers acted on impulse and started to beat the grains out from the husks, using the old conventional method of the flails.

The following morning after the sharecropper Albarosa had visited with Don Pompeo, a crowd of people were seen gathering beneath the window of City Hall, across from the post office. Among the crowd, there was the *Podestà*, the Deputy Mayor, two councilmen, the tax collector and the pharmacist with Father Alfonso. The postmaster was seen talking with the *Podestà* intimately, while the word spread rapidly that Il Duce had been deposed and put under arrest by the King. General Badoglio was appointed to Commander in Chief of Italy, and the news was just incredible and stunning.

The Allied invasion of insular Italy had triggered a chain of dramatic and historic events. That, without any doubt, had brought about the dissolution of a totalitarian government. When the mailman, Ottaviano, rushed to tell the shocking news to Don Pompeo, the old shoemaker was not in the least impressed.

"Should have been the other way around," said Don Pompeo. "By his do-nothing attitude and cooperation with Il Duce's aggressiveness toward war, the King has brought our motherland to its knees. Now he arrests—what? They both should be put under arrest! And for what concerns the substitute Commander in Chief, he is not the answer to our problems. He is too old, too feeble and not a figure capable of standing up to deal with this kind of pressure. These unfortunate events will drive the last nail on the coffin of destruction of our *cafoni* of Montelieto and of our beloved country," said Don Pompeo.

To predict what was going to become of Montelieto would be anybody's guess. Everybody, though, felt that the final outcome would be bleak. The Allies were said to have consolidated the beachhead operation in Sicily and had stepped up the chase of the Axis army toward Palermo and the Strait of Messina. Every hour the news from the front contradicted that of a short while back. Soldiers defected from their units and ran home. Tranquillo Fedele was the first lucky *cafone* sharecropper soldier to have made it back. He had almost recuperated from the wound suffered in the shipwreck but had never returned to his outfit. Actually, there was no longer an outfit he could return to. His regiment had been wiped out before boarding the rescue ship in Algeria. Soldiers and officers who protested the take over of their units by the former Axis partners, resisted in some measure but eventually deserted en masse.

Reverend Palestrina had arrived back in Montelieto, after days of walking from the seaport where he had been blessing the troops and the ships leaving on their assignments. However, blessings or no blessings, those ships were sunk by the Allies mercilessly. Simultaneously with the return home of Reverend Palestrina had come Peppe of Montelieto, Giustino and Federico Favetta. They reached the Del Pios' farmstead barefoot but blessedly safe after having served duty for only a short stretch.

The Reverend arrived home still wearing his robe; obviously the time for him to shed his mantle of respectability had not yet arrived. In fact, he was looked at by the Axis partners as the least suspected deserter. So Reverend stuck to his profession of churchman, helped Father Alfonso with the rituals of the parish and continued, as before, administering all the functions of his estate.

In the mind of Reverend Palestrina the war was lost. Not, of course, that he had ever believed in victory. As opposed to his rival, the Fascist pharmacist, who had dreamed of an unqualified triumph, Reverend had figured the war lost at the start. His pessimistic view of the whole situation, especially on the conduct of the leadership who harbored such ill will against the neighbors, was not based on the lack of respect for the country but based on reality. The system had been established through violence and support of the rich, but now with even more desperation and uncontrolled damage to the rich, it must be totally eradicated.

From there on, Reverend Palestrina's commitments focused not so much on analyzing the mistakes of either the past or the present that the leadership was in the habit of making, but on the welfare of the people of his preferred town. He was not a fool. He knew that the dreadful political initiatives approved in the past were bound to hurt the people of Montelieto someday.

Startling, dramatic events took place beginning by mid-summer. However, well before the Axis partners tightened their grip on the lives of the Montelieto citizens, Reverend Palestrina acted cautiously and intelligently. With Signor Luigi, his trusted sharecropper Sardone, and the Del Pio brothers, the Reverend pooled funds for purchasing petroleum at black market. The cost of it was prohibitive but they succeeded in obtaining several drums. To save the current harvest before it went to waste, was top priority and most vital for the cafoni-sharecroppers of Montelieto. The threshing of the wheat was resumed at once. Although the drums of petroleum ran dry before completing the threshing of the crops for every farmer, it was sufficient to remedy that which could have been lost. Reverend Palestrina instructed Sardone to mill all the grains he could put his hands on, empty the granary of the mansion of every kind of food supplies, and haul that to his mountain chalet.

The summer of 1943 turned out to be one of the most disastrous periods in history, for the *cafoni* of Montelieto. The Axis partners first were caught by surprise in the ousting of Il Duce, but they then began to tighten the vise of their dominance upon everything, mistrusting the newly formed government of Rome even if they had pledged full cooperation. When the King and Badoglio were believed to have made contact with the Allies, the Axis partners reacted and stepped up their efforts to liberate Il Duce and tighten further their reins. By late summer they succeeded in both objectives. But by then, the unconditional surrender of Italy to the Allies had been signed. Therefore the liberation of Il Duce brought little or no impact on the citizenry—only temporary euphoria and feeble hopes in the hearts of die-hard Fascists.

The same day on which people learned that the Italian government in exile had declared war on the Axis partners, from the hills of Montelieto, the roar of the Allied cannons could be heard from the far southeast. It was said that the Allies were attacking and crossing the river Volturno. With this new development, a journey of incredible proportions was beginning for the *cafoni* of Montelieto, who were caught between a rock and a hard place. The former Axis partners retreated to the Gustav Line and by doing so, everything came under their dominance.

Due to the cowardice of the Axis alliance, and also owing to the fact the citizens were now seen as potential enemies, plundering began. The Axis associates demanded instant servitude and discipline. They requested, confiscated and robbed them at gun-point, whatever was valuable to them including the dignity and rights the Fascists before them had left undefiled.

Meanwhile the Allies pressed relentlessly at the Gustav Line. They had stepped up their air bombardments from the Brenner Pass to the river Volturno, ever since the invasion of the Italian inland had commenced. As the air raids intensified, the farming work in Montelieto began to be proportionately disrupted. The threshing machines, mistakenly believed to be Axis tanks, had been attacked by Allied fighters and blown up. Benito, the head mechanic, two Fascist harvest controllers and three old madams had been fatally hit. Males of every age, or of any physical shape, were rounded up and assigned labor tasks for repairing the damages caused by the bombs of the Allies. The elderly, the young kids and even the handicapped were taken to work, under the bombings, throughout the lines of communications and were strictly supervised. Those who refused to comply, or who attempted to run away, were severely punished. When the pillaging intensified and the harassed farmers were robbed of their domestic animals, with the little food supplies they had remaining, guerrilla groups began to form. Clashes between civilians and soldiers occurred frequently. However, the price for that type of contention was to high for the civilians to pay. The former Axis partners would not allow the civilians to get even. They had become absolute masters and retaliated against innocent *cafoni* one hundred fold.

Reverend Palestrina and Father Alfonso, with the Fascist pharmacist, were exempt from doing labor work. So was Don Pompeo. The two churchmen were ordered to maintain unchanged the functions of the parish. The pharmacist was required to maintain open the House of Fasces and rally the bewildered die-hard Fascist to collaborate with the Axis authorities, and Don Pompeo was warned to keep the shoemaker's shop open to service the needs of the soldiers of the garrison of Montelieto before anything else. The old shoemaker had no choice. He either agreed and bent to obey the rulings issued from the new masters, or he would be held in judgment.

The remainder of the autumn turned out to be a long nightmare for all. Shortages of food, bombardments from the Allies and repression from the forces of the Axis, were reaching the critical point for the people of Montelieto. Worst among the disappointments, was to see that the Allies had been prevented from entering Latium and Ciociaria. After so many hard-fought heavy gun battles at the rivers Rapido and Garigliano, the Axis army appeared to dictate the outcome. They seemed to tell the Allies: "From here you shall not pass."

The old shoemaker was lonely and depressed. He had come to the realization that he was condemned to give his service to those he hated. He hated not so much the Axis soldiers for having taken the reins of command and for exploiting the Italian situation, but abhorred their crafty leaders for having bamboozled Il Duce and the King, to fall squarely in their traps.

Don Pompeo felt also bitter loneliness. His regular *cafoni* visitors seemed to have completely disappeared from the scene. Not that he wished them to congregate in his shop and risk being rounded up to do labor work at the front. The only visitors he saw, regularly, were soldiers who spoke another language and hanger-on Fascist collaborators who performed errands for their masters. In his loneliness the old shoemaker thought, talked, prayed and cried. He became impatient and then tolerant, angry and then resigned.

In his bursts of anger he would utter imprecations at everything and say: "Curse on our leadership. They are only efficient in leading us to the acquisition of newer and meaner masters. This malediction perhaps descended upon Montelieto, ever since its foundation. How many sorts of masters must we be slave to? First we were obligated to the Caesars, then to the barbarians, the Church, the rich with the pharmacist, and now to the Axis barbarians again? How much is enough? And if we count right, we have another kind of masters that torment us from the sky. They are called the Allies. Damned be them all!" Don Pompeo swore.

The fall progressed and ended in the same pattern: with servitude to the new masters of Montelieto, scarcity of food, massive hunger, air raids and hopelessness. People fled for the higher mountains. Those who remained behind and lacked the means of sustenance suffered unbelievable privation. Many swarmed around the Axis garrison to beg for food. It had become extremely difficult, though, for everyone to slave in order to obtain a washed-up bowl of soup. Don Pompeo, too, was in that category. He had no other means of sustenance aside from the few cents he earned from repairing shoes. Trouble was the new masters never paid up. So he, too, must have to beg for a bowl of soup. Often, for the satisfactory service performed, he was rewarded with a chunk of bread. While he chewed the hard bread inside his apartment, Don Pompeo used to comment so: "Damn, this bread tastes sour! It tastes as if it were made with top soil, yeast of petroleum and then baked in the charcoal forges of blacksmiths." Then, speaking to himself he would add: "Will the *cafoni* of this town of mine ever have the opportunity to eat white bread? No, never will we at this rate! Perhaps some day we will. But surely it will not happen until we have done with suffering all the injustices on this earth."

Reverend Palestrina was given notice, by the Axis commander of the garrison in Montelieto, to clear out of his mansion within eight hours. He was told that the clergy would not be granted privileges in those war times. After being permitted to take his personal belongings, the priest must hand the keys of his mansion over to the new self-professed owners. People were evicted from their dwellings with prepotency. Even the pharmacist was evicted from the House of Fasces, which was to be used for an ammunition dump. The Axis soldiers began to appropriate the public radio, the post office and telegraph, major public buildings and private dwellings facing strategic intersections. Helpless citizens were chased out even from humble habitations and farmsteads.

The brothers Del Pio, too, were evicted from their large farmstead with a strong warning. Axis soldiers were preparing to use the property for deploying anti-aircraft batteries. Giovanni and Antonio, though, had foreseen trouble coming and had maneuvered to haul vital food supplies, with their livestock up in the mountains, inside the barns of their properties, well in advance of the eviction. They became close neighbors of the Reverend. With the help of the young men from the ghetto of Montelieto and by relying on keen intuition, the brothers Del Pio hid and stored huge amounts of non-perishable foodstuff underground—as had done the priest with the help of sharecropper Sardone.

"This situation is becoming intolerable," commented Don Pompeo as he saw his fellow countrymen being evicted from their residences. "These evictions, regardless of who they are forced on, are offensive and detestable. They will set humans back to primitive times and below the rank of the beasts. Damn how useless we have become," said the shoemaker with a sense of incredulity. "Below the rank of domestic beasts?" he repeated. "Please, Lord, be merciful. Protect and save us from that."

Chapter 29

The eviction notice issued to Reverend Palestrina, coming from the commanding officer of the Axis garrison of Montelieto, was mandatory and irrevocable. He must leave his mansion within four hours. The notice had been worded politely but left the priest with no options to protest or negotiate. The Reverend was told that his mansion, because of its strategic location, was needed for use as command post of the Axis garrison. It was further explained to him that their plans were to restore Il Duce to his former respectability, protect him from his repudiators, and defend Italy from the self-important Allied aggressors.

Reverend Palestrina was left with no choice. Within the time allowed, helped by willing sharecroppers, he was able to salvage most of his personal belongings. Then handed the commanding officer the key and moved temporarily to a less visible farmhouse on his hilly side property, also the home of the sharecropper Sardone.

The move Reverend Palestrina was forced to make turned out to be helpful in the long run, instead of being a setback. That fitted perfectly to the schedule of actions he was preparing to take. He was also confident that his mansion, no matter in what condition, would remain there and no Axis commanding officer could claim it his.

Meanwhile the fighting for the Axis went well. Although they never reclaimed the lost ground, as they had led the civilians to believe, they held their positions at the Gustav Line, skillfully repulsing every attempt of the Allies to open up a passage to Rome. However, the give and take at the battlefront complicated further the situation of the worried *cafoni* sharecroppers of Montelieto. Consequently these men were forced to abandon their daily activities on the farms and dig bunkers instead, in order to protect themselves from the air raids of the Allies. If the farmers performed any type of farm work, they did so at night. In daylight the fighters of the Allies machine-gunned everything that moved. This caused many people to run for the hills, with their families, seeking places of safety there.

Signor Luigi, who had been one of the first supporters of Fascism, and who still believed in the magic Il Duce claimed to have up his sleeve, had also moved to one of his hillside properties run by a shepherd-sharecropper. Greedy Signor Luigi made arrangements to house the pharmacist and his family, the ailing head mechanic, the Deputy Mayor, and some other former Fascist colleagues. Nearly all the huts of the shepherds, used by Signor Luigi's dependents, became instant habitation for the former Party hard-liners. Rich Signor Luigi pledged to provide sustenance for his Axis friends until the remaining days of the conflict and victory.

Reverend Palestrina had the poor at heart and couldn't have cared less for the powerful personalities of the Fascist Party. Although he was an atheist he was liberal and a humanitarian. And also, as illogical as this may sound, he was an atheist but a strong defender of the poor.

So, just as Signor Luigi had pooled resources with his rich conservative friends on behalf of the Fascist colleagues, the Reverend also had pooled his resources. With the Del Pio brothers, Sardone and a handful of willing sharecroppers, the Reverend pledged to help out and spare from starvation as many hungry and destitute of Montelieto as he could. Del Pio's hired hands, with Titus and Sardone's boys, helped smuggle food for the hungry and helpless people of the community whenever that was possible.

Meantime the air raids and dogfights in the sky of Montelieto had become a daily occurrence. Although civilians were not the primary targets of the Allies, they were hit nonetheless. When the situation from the new, less visible habitation of Reverend Palestrina was becoming impossible to handle, he acted resolutely. First he moved Dorotea to his mountain chalet. After that he convinced Valentina to move there with her kids. Reverend did not wish to have those he cared for remaining anywhere near the Axis soldiers, or to be exposed to deadly air raids and bombing from the determined Allies. But however important and serious the need to help others might be, Reverend also had certain priorities on his agenda.

Don Pompeo, whom the priest admired and respected for his selflessness and wisdom, must be spared from further heartaches. But when Reverend suggested that the shoemaker leave and join other friends at his mountain chalet, Don Pompeo refused—as did Father Alfonso and sacristan-for-life Sigismondo Barabba. The two devoted church people told Reverend they wished to keep alive their commitments for the parish, and pray the good Lord to intervene and save all. Reverend understood. He nodded approvingly at the decision of his friends, smiled to them, and quickly departed.

After having re-settled the people for whom he cared the most inside his mountain chalet, Reverend Palestrina felt pleased and self-reliant for having assumed important responsibilities. Confident in his ability to take further actions, he became aggressive and armed himself. Reverend read in the daytime, but in the evenings traveled, brought support to the needy, and participated in guerrilla warfare. When guerrilla practices were hampered, and the group Reverend had joined was decimated in skirmishes with the Axis soldiers, he spent more time reading and meditating.

"Reading and meditating is of no help," the Reverend declared impatiently. "We need to take action! I know exactly how to solve the problems facing me."

Reverend knew so well he was the victim of his own making. He loved Valentina and their kids with all his heart, but how could the tormented priest profess that love?

Often, in his imagination, Reverend Palestrina heard the calls of Don Pompeo exhorting him to assume his fair and just responsibilities. He heard Don Pompeo say again and again: "Throw away that mantle of respectability, marry Valentina and become a good father, Reverend!"

One day, when the Reverend thought to have had enough, he invited Giovanni Del Pio and his wife, Rosetta, to the chalet. The Reverend was dressed in attire unbecoming the clergy. While chatting and sipping tea in company of his friends, Reverend Palestrina got up and, in plain view, placed several white collars and robes of the clergy inside a large box.

"Here," he said, inviting Signor Del Pio and Rosetta to look carefully. "I am tired of procrastinating and being a hypocrite. I wish to tell you that I am renouncing my oath of the priesthood and everything that symbolizes the clergy. In these times it is impossible for me to forward my formal abnegation to the church aristocracy, for lack of procedure to communicate. So, my dear neighbors, I wish to have you as witnesses for my testimony.

"My gosh!" Rosetta said. "I never knew that to reject something one needed testimonies."

"Right, you don't, but I need you for other matters," said the Reverend. Then with great sensibility he said: "My friends, I want you also to know I intend to marry Valentina as soon as possible. Perhaps this evening, if such can be arranged, and we wish to be married by you, Giovanni. You do read fairly well, don't you?" The Reverend showed Giovanni a sheet of paper upon which was written the rite of marriage.

"Yeah, but . . . "

"No 'but' here, dear," Rosetta said interrupting. "We never thought this could happen. Congratulations to both of you, Reverend."

"Please let's all remember I am no longer a Reverend, Rosetta. From here on I wish to be addressed by my first name, as the titles are often given erroneously. My name is Orazio and I shall be known as that."

"Orazio and Valentina, what a nice couple," said Rosetta. "But her kids, though—do they know?"

"Her kids? They are my kids too," said Orazio proudly.

"Incredible! Incredible!" Rosetta said looking toward her husband.

"What do you mean incredible, darling? Even the most timid at love would have fallen for the beauty of Valentina," said Giovanni sincerely.

"I am aware of that, and they have, they have fallen," she said, winking at Orazio.

While Rosetta went back to announce the news to the remaining Del Pio clan, Valentina and Dorotea were preparing for the ceremony. Giovanni, with the help of Orazio, was still poring over the words that pronounced the matrimony. The rite was to take place beneath the olive tree from where Orazio, many times in the past, had scolded the hoeing trio for having called him "Father." The same spot where he challenged them to contests of strength and stamina for hoeing. The very place where he had had a confessional built out of thickets, where he confessed the hoeing trio and where he had told them to patronize the tavern of Marianna Pipanera, get drunk, and serve penitence trying to take her to bed.

This time around, though, the former priest was outright serious. Yet the rustic location of the wedding, the emotional delivery of the rite itself, and the odd hour of the evening, exemplified the modesty of the ceremony. Nobody gave away the bride. Valentina walked alone from the chalet to the olive tree, followed by Dorotea who was limping. Orazio stood impassible beneath the tree waiting for Giovanni to begin to read.

Giovanni Del Pio had never presided at a wedding in his whole life; much less he had read the vows. He had only been instrumental in paring his cattle to mate, and that was all.

As he began reading, Giovanni perspired profusely, stumbling through the words again and again, but no one paid attention to that. Finally he read: "Now I pronounce you man and wife." Having spoken those last words Giovanni paused momentarily amid cheers and applause of the bystanders. Then turning to Orazio, he said: "You may now kiss the bride." Orazio hesitated a second or two, then pulled Valentina gently closer to him and leaning over, kissed her tenderly on the forehead.

After the wedding ceremony, no formal reception or entertainment took place. Dorotea went ahead, giving her last touch to the food table, but she was only able to serve sandwiches and cheese with prosciutto. Sardone, who had been named caretaker of the former priest's chalet, followed filling glasses with wine.

There was no instrumental music. Youngsters danced tarantellas accompanied by the humming and hand-clapping of the elders. No honeymoon followed the wedding. The happy couple spent time instead teaching their children to address the former priest as father. But all in all, the event was romantic and passionate enough to induce Rosetta Del Pio and her sister-in-law to tears.

On the way back to their plantation, Giovanni Del Pio felt proud at having been influential in presiding over the marriage of his neighbors, Orazio and Valentina. He walked spiritedly a few steps ahead of his wife and sister in law, but stopped every now and then to allow the women to catch up. Unlike the women, Giovanni had not been affected, emotionally, with the marriage ritual. He had dreaded only the embarrassment he would feel if he was unable to read the vows in front of his people. By the second stop, he turned to look at the women, waited, and as they approached he asked: "I am curious to know whether the tears you shed during the ceremony were tears of joy or of sadness."

"What do you mean sadness? The service was beautiful and romantic, and none of us could have imagined Orazio giving up the ministry for the love of Valentina," said Rosetta.

"Yes, love has no boundaries. Still I believe weddings are not functions where people ought to cry."

"I agree, although I think you should realize that we women are much more sentimental than you men. Orazio thought that marrying Valentina was the right thing to do," said Rosetta. "But never did I figure it could have happened."

"I must admit everyone was caught by surprise, including me. But, on the other hand, I know exactly how fair the Palestrinas can be."

"Fair or not, that was love written all over, my dear," sighed Rosetta.

"Yes, love for the *cafoni*! The Palestrinas deserve respect and admiration from all the *cafoni* of this town. Like his parents before him, Orazio has never ever let one *cafone* of Montelieto feel inferior in his presence, and he has been their defender even in the most distasteful situations. Now he has become related to *cafoni* through marriage, and we ought to give him our support," said Giovanni. "You see, Rosetta," he further asserted. "As the opposite of those rich rivals, who derive their strength from duplicity and malice, I believe the Palestrinas derive their strength and goodness of character from being associated with their needy dependents. However, I do not recall that one rich influential has ever succeeded in challenging their importance. In recognition of his attachment for the *cafoni*/sharecroppers, don't you think we ought to begin to address our ex-priest *cafone* as Lord Orazio instead of simply Orazio?" Giovanni suggested.

"Of course," answered Rosetta. "From here on, we all ought to address this important son of Montelieto as 'Lord Orazio,' ex-priest and father, *cafone* or not!"

"Agreed,"said Giovanni. "The Reverend Cafone—the Extravagant or Nutty Priest and . . . who knows what else? Who can really tell for sure, how many titles Lord Orazio can be identified with? And who can tell what else can stem from the declassed *cafoni* and sharecroppers ciociari?"

Chapter 30

Winter had arrived once more to Montelieto with unprecedented cold spells. Chilly winds, freezing rains and snow brought upon the troubled *cafoni*/sharecroppers additional rounds of hardships and helplessness. People began to wonder whether there would ever be an end to their sufferings, and whether nature itself had not joined hands with the furies of the war to spread among them more hunger, misery and despair.

To aggravate further the besieged population, came reports of odious brutalities perpetrated on the townspeople, from Axis guards. One proud elder, who had slaved for the Axis garrison of Monetlieto, was unable to stand the abuses and arbitrary demands of a stinging servility and sought self-destruction. The old man chose to hang himself as opposed to permitting himself to be robbed of his dignity. The more resolute among the elders, however, urged the population to have better self-control. They maintained that the example of the old man, by resorting to the sacrifice of his very life, would be destructive to the community and prove nothing to the oppressors. The time for everyone to get rid of the oppressors eventually would come. Virtually all the *cafoni* patiently followed this sound advice.

From there on, they all became more tolerant about suffering their pain in silence and, when possible, more predisposed to extend their hand to help others.

The former priest, Lord Orazio, too, had further extended his helping hand. In addition to the foodstuff he personally delivered to the hungry, he had delegated other strong-willed friends to do the same, assuming all the expenses. Jointly with his loyal dependents, Lord Orazio was able to bring vital relief to those in need. He dressed shabbily, was unshaven and displayed the image of a threadbare, raggedy shepherd—albeit a shepherd with a natural disposition for philanthropy. He became relentless in his efforts to help the poor.

Lord Orazio was crafty in disguising his appearance, but, time and again, he was apprehended by the Axis guards and forced to perform hard labor. Still, undaunted, he skillfully managed to escape every time to resume his mission of charity.

By this time, winter was ending with no sign of relief for the beleaguered community. Problems of every kind were appearing among them, in spite the good work of the former priest. Facing famine became a real and unavoidable danger. However, just when the bleak situation seemed to have reached a breaking point, beginning with the first weeks of spring, events began to change course. On the feast day of Saint Joseph, Montelieto and the near suburbs were besieged from the air. Squadrons of Allied fighters attacked; bombs fell on the outskirts of town, the communication lines, farmhouses, and the country roads and farms. Scores of horses and mules, sheltered inside barns and used as conventional Axis transportation to the front, were killed in the attack. The flesh of animals killed was like manna fallen from heaven. Long before the Axis had assessed its losses, hungry civilians had snatched every piece of flesh from beneath the debris like wild predators in the night. In the meantime, the attacks from the air continued on a daily basis. Allied fighters sneaked rapidly from behind the hills machine-gunning Axis convoys at will. Again the *cafoni* adventured forth stealing anything eatable.

Lord Orazio Palestrina's mission to help the needy was hampered. He had not been schooled in warfare strategy but, nonetheless, saw premonitory signs of disaster on the horizon. The events unfolded everyday more troublesome and unpredictable. It became apparent that soon, something—or—everything was bound to collapse. In those obscure days of intense bombardments, the former priest felt disheartened. Although he was now happily married and living comfortably in his mountain chalet, far away from any imminent danger, he nonetheless felt a bitter confinement. The mere thought of those helpless souls left behind in Montelieto troubled his mind continually. How could those impoverished elders face the future without food? Were they, perhaps, still slaving for the Axis garrison in exchange for a bowl of watery soup?

Determined to go to the rescue, Lord Orazio left the safety of his chalet one evening and, surmounting difficult obstacles headed for Montelieto. After having circumvented the checkpoints of the Axis sentinels, he cautiously crossed the Church Square to knock at the door of the shop of his shoemaker friend Don Pompeo. He knocked once more and through a narrow opening of the door he whispered: "Do not fear a thing, Don Pompé, open up, it's me."

"Reverend! By golly! What could possibly bring you in town at this odd hour of the night? Come in," said the old shoemaker shutting the door behind the Reverend.

"Never mind, Reverend, about the hour and town," answered Lord Orazio while holding his beloved friend in a tender hug. "I came here because I needed to. I wanted to tell you that I am not Reverend anymore. Don Pompeo, I am a father. A real father who has assumed responsibility for his family, same as those poor fathers you have known in Montelieto. Valentina and I are now married. She is no longer my mistress or my dressmaker. Her kids are no longer orphans. We were married some time ago by Giovanni Del Pio in a brief civil ceremony beneath the olive trees of my plantation. I wished you could have been there among my friends so you would believe I have really grown up."

"Of course I believe you have grown up. That was the honorable thing to do! What good news! I have always felt that, some day, you would become more mature, and so you have. This, my boy, calls for a happy celebration!"

"I thank you my dear Don Pompeo, but this is not the proper time to celebrate. We'll leave that for a more propitious occasion. Although I wished to announce to you that I am a father, in the truest sense of the word that is not the main reason I came to visit with you. I came to visit because as you are aware, there is not much time for procrastination. We must act! Danger is looming upon our town, every hour more alarming than the last. I came to ask you to leave with me, so together we could weather the storm, with our friends, in my mountain chalet. While you get ready, I will run by Father Alfonso to invite him and the sacristan to join us. I also wish to invite the town crier, the ragman, the two deaf sisters and as many as I can find to follow us. We will come back here and sneak away from town, through short cuts and darkness."

"Do not fret, Reverend . . . oh pardon me—Orazio! This takes a little adjustment, on our part, before we address you properly, you know? I'll thank you from the bottom of my heart for being so thoughtful in regard to us elders safety. We will not leave. Father Alfonso has promised to remain in here, bombs or no bombs, and so will the Barabbas. You know they will not abandon Father Alfonso for anything in the world. Sigismondo has made a living being a sacristan his whole life. Vittorio, the ragman, and all the rest, feel the same way. We all hang on by getting food from the soldiers of the Axis garrison, so there is no need for us to run away to the mountains. We will be fine until the Axis soldiers seek our services in exchange for a bowl of a soup. After they are gone, we will mend the problems in whichever way we can.

"Go," said Don Pompeo. "Go, my boy. You have greater responsibilities on your shoulders. The people of the mountain community need you. We don't; we are too old and do not wish to jeopardize the chances for our younger brethren. If we move we could raise suspicions. That could give motive to the soldiers to come after us and put everyone in danger. Farewell, dear Orazio. I, with the elders, will hope and pray you are safe and will return here soon to share our friendship and enjoy a new era of liberty. May the good Lord have mercy for us all. Goodbye dear Orazio."

Don Pompeo's answer stunned Lord Orazio Palestrina. The former priest proceeded to invite those of Montelieto he deemed most underprivileged and in danger, but they also refused to follow. The position of Don Pompeo reading the idea of not moving elsewhere to seek safety, appeared to have persuaded all to stay put.

"Damned!" The former priest cussed. "These people are real stubborn. The declarations of the old shoemaker, saying that the *cafoni* of Montelieto were devoid of the genes that cause embarrassment, are true. When I recall the foolishnesses of my hoeing trio, and Cicco Palla, those declarations can't be denied. I must add also that us *cafoni* are just a class apart. We are not merely devoid of the genes that can cause embarrassment, because the inhumanities we have endured have also made all *cafoni* devoid of the genes that cause fear, hunger, and despair."

On his way back to the mountains, Lord Orazio thought of the people who had decided to stay behind and felt inadequate. Although he housed scores of hard-pressed people from town, around his chalet, he wished to do more. His neighbors, the Del Pios, housed people from all walks of life. The two brothers seemed to attract refugees as if they were in the business of innkeepers. They had provided shelter for the closest kin of their farm hands, their not so well to do acquaintance, and even to southern soldier deserters who had gotten stuck north of the front lines.

"Yeah!" Lord Orazio said to himself. "The Del Pios are friendly hosts. We could call them "*cafoni* humanitarians. I do believe there is such a saintly class amongst evildoers in the world. Hell," he said with self-assurance. "If that is the case, I qualify just as much as Del Pios. Of course everyone knows I have been a nutty priest but they also ought to know that I have been, and still am, the cafone priest."

While still walking uphill, Lord Orazio thought about his beautiful wife and gave a deep sigh. Then said: "Nonsense with the aristocracy! Valentina is turning me into

cafone, a little bit more each day, and I love it. She is a
sweet and beautiful *cafona* that can enchant all those who
run across her. And even if she is not the product of ele-
gance who gives a damn? I know that in the class of grace,
candor and motherhood and—yes . . . shape, she is just unbelievable!"

Although Lord Orazio's deepest affections were focused on Valentina and their kids, he had been developing
a steadfast attachment for his place of birth, and its people,
ever since his childhood. When he was young, he thought
Don Pompeo Gazzaladra was his real uncle. By now,
though, things had completely changed. After his seminary
studies, many love affairs, priesthood and two to three
years of war duty, Lord Orazio had now matured. But because he had previously screwed up in so many ways, the
rival aristocracy, together with the Fascist leadership in
town, looked upon him as a scapegoat, and he truly wished
the old shoemaker were his uncle. He also felt more comfortable with his political ideology. The formerly all-power-
ful Duce and his Fascist Party were not hot issues anymore
and his local rival, the Fascist pharmacist was running for
his life hiding in the mountain barns with Signor Luigi.

Lord Orazio formed a series of sensible calculations in
his mind while on the way to the chalet. In his imagination
he envisioned a better future for the people of his beloved
Montelieto. On the imaginary agenda he listed a number
of priorities. First, he thought, perhaps one day, illiteracy
and unemployment could be erased. Schools and roads
could be built. Farming improvements and better appor-
tionment of their valley arable lands could be achieved in
addition to a tally of other essential projects.

One important subject that weighed even heavier on Lord Orazio's imagination was the brutal fact that through the ages the people of Montelieto had been stereotyped as illiterate sharecroppers and declassed *cafoni*. He strongly believed that all the slanderous labels of the language had been pinned on his people with one single definition—*cafoni*. But whether the term expressed in combination or separately, he believed each slander augmented the baseness and humiliation of the other.

In the mind of Lord Orazio, the stereotype was a monster of illiteracy and contempt that must be done away with in order to re-affirm the social status of Montelieto's people.

How long it would take to eradicate the disrepute, though, nobody knew. Although this uncertainty troubled Lord Orazio immensely, he never gave up the hope of rectifying the wrongs that had been done to his people and each day his convictions became stronger with the conflict spreading about Montelieto. Those hopes hinged upon the outcome of that conflict.

"Will the Allies ever come to our rescue?" Lord Orazio said on the way to his chalet. "Perhaps they will be able to defeat Fascism, destroy the system and restore in us hopes that the wrongs will be put to right. In anger, he swore aloud. "The day the monster of illiteracy is slain, the monster of sharecroppers will also die. And when both ghosts are slain, I am sure the stereotype *cafoni* will eventually be erased."

Lord Orazio, though, was also realistic. His inspiring dreams for the betterment of his fellow-countrymen entailed tremendous hard work, energy, know-how and steadfast commitments. He understood, too, that the results he wished to accomplish on behalf of his people, would contradict his very own interest. Being the biggest owner of farmlands at sharecrop in town, and wishing to give sharecroppers a new identity would certainly make no sense to big landowners of his class.

But he was an inveterate humanitarian and whatever small accomplishments he could bring about for the benefit of his people, to him made sense. So, on that note Lord Orazio said: "Damned be the fields at sharecrop! I am ready to give up that and much more, but this sluggish advance of the Allies is beginning to get on my nerves and restrict my initiative. The old despotic system has been overthrown but its forces of evil are still felt." Then prior to entering his chalet, he said to himself: "Are those fools of Allies ever going to advance to liberate Montelieto? Do they have that on their agenda? If they have, they better hurry up before a greater misfortune befalls the weary people of my cherished Montelieto."

Chapter 31

The weary and troubled *cafoni*/sharecroppers of Montelieto harbored no hopes of a safer and better future. They had never harbored any hope that the economic conditions were going to improve but, even if they had harbored anything, the critical situation they were in had wiped out every imaginable possibility of betterment. So, having been held back and made fools of, by an obstinate system of government that pursued conflicts abroad while disregarding to the economic ills of the nation, the exasperated *cafoni*/sharecroppers saw their last hopes for a better future vanish away. After the Fascist pharmacist arrived in Montelieto to head the House of Fasces, and then proceeded to apply his Party brand of discipline and doctrine, things began to change dramatically for the worse. The citizens began to experience ugly nightmares—not the kinds of nightmares which, in the past, had subjected them to the will of their rich masters landowners, but even those nightmares which subjected them to gratify an arrogant tyrant screwball and boaster of the Party in power.

However, as war hit home, that brought within itself a new order of finalities. This fact gave awareness that, from there on, their miserable situation was bound to undergo a revision. In their minds the revision meant either extinction of the *cafoni*/sharecroppers as known then (thus liberating them from unjust suffering and servility), or that could bring about the extinction of a tyrannical system once and for all. So, how could they lose?

The momentum for the finalities to take place was now at hand. The *cafoni*/sharecroppers had had enough. They had lived in disrepute for generations upon generations, and that should have been enough humiliation to occupy anybody's mind. But the reality of the stereotyped vilification of: "Flesh born to suffer," they could also accept, That's after all, what they actually were. The thought, though, that even the stereotyped denigration might undergo a change and be converted to: "Flesh born to suffer and to be sacrificed on the altar of Fascism," made them tremble. And then, as they recalled the warnings of Don Pompeo, when he would point to the picture of Il Duce over the wall of the Church Square and say to them: "That man, that man who is staring at us from that poster, one of these days will have all of us killed," at that juncture the *cafoni*/sharecroppers saw the whole world turning hostile to them.

At this point, however, despite the stereotyping the worries and warnings, events seemed to be occuring in a calculated sequence. He who had been sent to Montelieto to preach and instill in each citizen the values of Fascist, was running for his life himself. Fearing to be caught in the crossfire, the pharmacist had reneged his fidelity to the Axis associates and had fled to safety in the mountains with his peers, the Deputy Mayor and the greedy Signor Luigi.

This came as a blessing from heaven for the *cafoni/* sharecroppers. With the Fascist pharmacist's disappearance from the scene, a heavy burden was lifted from their shoulders. There would no longer be a tormentor—an overweening imbecile who called rigid drills of war for the hungry kids, while provoking their parents. The Fascist harvest controllers had also fled from the scene together with the town leadership, the tax collector and the rest of the bureaucrats. None of these would waste their time harassing the *cafoni/*sharecroppers anymore. And if all that goodness could be attributed to the determination of the Allies to bring relief, expel and eradicate from Montelieto a wicked system, everybody felt: "Let the bombs fall."

Meantime the former priest, now Lord Orazio Palestrina, spent the time with his new wife and their children, in the isolation of his chalet high on the mountain. Although his mission of benevolence had been reduced by the restrictions of an ongoing war and responsibilities of fatherhood, he nevertheless maintained the charitable work of the past to the best of his ability. Assisted by his own sharecroppers and the young hired hands of the brothers Del Pio, Lord Orazio disguised his appearance so cleverly as to manage to gain access to the town and bring assistance to those in need. The Axis guards referred to Lord Orazio as "The raggedy old man." Father Alfonso, the sacristan Barabba, the town crier Vittorio, and the two deaf sisters, referred to the raggedy benefactor conversely, as "The Saint priest."

Lord Orazio, though, had never envisioned himself to be considered priest—and much less Saint. Perhaps "raggedy," yes, but that should have occurred much later in life. Of course he had impersonated several categories of raggedy persons, but he had done so only to stick to his humanitarian principles. Should he be given a nickname at all, that should have been: "The cafone priest." Not really a *cafone* priest comparable to Father Alfonso, who was a natural for having failed to learn Latin, but comparable to someone who desired to become *cafone* by marrying a *cafona*. When in secrecy Lord Orazio reflected over his self-indulgences of the past, and the reasons why he identified with the subservient as opposed to the rich, noteworthy and powerful, his relationship with Valentina appeared foremost in his mind. She, the most desirable creature on this side of the earth, mattered the whole world for him. And if that meant to lowering his social status to that of *cafone*, so be it . . .

The firm resolve of Reverend Palestrina to reject his vows of priesthood and marry Valentina was not generally known to the citizens of Montelieto. On the outside of the group of people to whom he had offered hospitality in the premises of the olive plantation, only the brothers Del Pio people and Don Pompeo were aware of the Reverend's resolutions. Don Pompeo however, had kept the news to himself. To those elders who, like him, had remained behind in their abodes, the old shoemaker spoke of the former priest but still gave him the respectful title of "Reverend." Therefore, collectively or individually, Don Pompeo reinforced in them the belief that Reverend Palestrina was still the good-hearted—but nutty—priest of the past.

On the other hand, the clan Del Pio felt taken by surprise with the resolution of the Reverend, but not at all disturbed. They were a well-to-do family of *cafoni*, but of Christian good values who understood and who forgave human failures. They accepted the initiative taken from the

Reverend without raising criticism. In fact the brothers Del Pio and their elders before them, respected the Palestrinas indisputably. Even in the times of the past, they had avoided any conflict of interest that might have arisen with each other regarding interferences on their contiguous lands. Thus, the mutual respect had grown to high esteem. And from esteem the courtesy and support of the Del Pios proved to be of comfort and encouragement in strengthening the convictions of Lord Orazio.

Meanwhile, the missions that the former priest had carried out on behalf of the poor who were left behind, although lessened in volume for a time, had been suddenly stopped by a covert Axis maneuver. The Axis army, having executed this maneuver in the course of several nights, had amassed an enormous avalanche of machinery and soldiers at the perimeter of Montelieto. In the process, the maneuver had cut off and closed, whatever route had remained open for gaining access to, or exit from Montelieto.

Being put in difficulty and prevented from helping out his fellow-countrymen in need, Lord Orazio reshuffled his plans. His first priority was to stay close and to become more protective of his family. His next order of business was to become familiar, more than at any other time, with his neighbors; more attentive to their points of view and to discuss together, candidly and with a new mutual interest, the necessity to help each other solve the problems facing them.

Based on the surprising encroachment by the Axis army maneuver, Lord Orazio spoke to the brothers Del Pio so: "This is a bleak hour for Montelieto. The maneuver of the Axis army forewarns us of dangers. It will mark the fate of our people and of our town. Whether they have chosen our forgotten Montelieto for sanctuary on their retreat, or have chosen it to revamp from a counterattack to the Allies, is not clear. What is clear to me, however," said the former priest blasphemously, "is the damned fact that the hour has come when '(*tutti I nodi vengono al pettine*)' murder will out! All the wrongdoings of a wicked leadership, all the oppressions and hardships laden on us from an infamous system of government, must be brought to light. This is the hour when every mistake must be revealed. It is either the hour of decision, which will set the people of Montelieto back to bigger hardships and slavery, or the hour which will liberate us forever from that stereotype label of ignorant *cafoni*/sharecroppers."

At this point the two brothers looked at each other, confused by the predictions of Lord Orazio. Quickly Antonio asked: "You mean our future will be brighter? If that is true, what has the Axis army maneuver got to do with us of Montelieto being *cafoni* or not?"

As Giovanni nodded his head in agreement with his brother, Lord Orazio said: "Glad you have asked. I am no war strategist, nor a prophet, but if this operation means that the Axis army will hold on to Montelieto, that will perpetuate the evil system. If, on the other hand, they can be driven away, they must take with them the barbarism of this system, and then we will begin a new era of liberty."

"Yeah! The second option sounds much better," Antonio said.

"Of course it is better," answered Lord Orazio. "But we must be more than careful. We must remember the favorite proverb of the shoemaker Don Pompeo, who has said: 'The word liberty carries a small tag with an unbelievable high price affixed to it.' "

"Oh, yeah! We recall him saying that on several occasions," Giovanni said. "I would like to ask you though, what ought to be our rule in a situation where the Axis army relaunches a counterattack?"

"In that situation we must protect our own properties from trespassers. The resistance will produce hungry defectors and bandits of every sort. We should form teams of young watchmen to scout our lands for intruders."

"That is a smart idea," Antonio said. "Giovanni and I will commit ourselves and our resources to accomplish that. Our young farmhands, with family support, will welcome the opportunity. In cooperation with your people we will pledge our help and look forward to protect our lands, Lord Orazio, whatever it'll take."

"Very well, Antonio. That's what I wanted to hear from you. I, myself, will start the first shift to patrol our plantations in accord with one of your boys until we assign each pair the proper shift. Go now, and send me Titus. Good night, neighbors," said Lord Orazio.

Chapter 32

Titus Del Pio, an energetic young man, walked toward the chalet of Lord Orazio without having a vague clue why his teacher wished to see him. Perhaps he wanted to review the lessons of last week or assign him additional homework? Whatever the reason, Titus gladly headed toward the chalet of his neighbor before the day turned to dusk.

"I come to meet with Lord Orazio," Titus told the maid, Dorotea, who had rushed to answer the knock at the door.

"Really? Titus, you have to wait a second. First I must ask Lord Orazio whether he has time to visit with you. I will let you know right away."

"Fine, I'll be waiting," Titus said before she shut the door.

"Lord Orazio, Titus Del Pio is at the door," Dorotea said to her Lord. "He has mentioned something about meeting with you. However, I don't recall you saying anything about having an appointment with anyone this evening."

"Sorry about that, Dorotea, it just slipped my mind. Why didn't you let him in anyway?"

"Of course I wanted to, but this is not the evening you review his homework. Besides, he is carrying a shotgun at his shoulder and that frightened me."

"Frightened you? I wish you would stop acting silly, Dorotea. The Del Pios are always welcome here, guns or no guns. Even if Titus is carrying a shotgun, please would you show him inside?"

Lord Orazio chatted for some time with Titus, then fastened the cartridge-pouch around his waist and, adjusting the strap of the hunting gun on his shoulder, led the way to the outside.

"We ought to take the pathway beneath the chestnut trees. From there we'll proceed down hill on the route leading to your barns. We will go on to surprise your cowboy friends, Giustino and what's his name . . . "

"Niccoló, don't you remember him?" Titus said.

"Right, Niccoló. After that we'll visit with your uncle Giovanni's cowboys, and then we complete our beat by going to see what my sharecroppers Sardones and the Tolleranza are up to, before we return to the chalet. We must inform all those who live on the plntation about our new initiatives. I imagine your grandfather Antonio has briefed you on that."

"Yes, but not in full details."

"Well, you see, Titus, I do not want to give anybody the impression we are in some kind of danger. I believe you know we feel protected. This mountainside property we share has been made in heaven, so to speak. It is surrounded by the thick forest of oaks and chestnut trees which block the view of our habitations and barns from the roads below. The proposal to patrol our properties, with common effort, was made to your relatives from me just to put in place a precautionary measure. We do not want to become more complacent just because we enjoy the protection of nature, you know? The times we live in now are critical. That is the reason everybody must be on the alert. There is a lot at stake here, Titus. I imagine you are aware of that."

"Of course I am aware, Lord Orazio. And I also believe that by making a combined effort, our two families will be able to patrol our plantations."

"Not on an around the clock basis, Titus. It will be difficult to put together a regiment of watchmen to guard our own interests. So, our first objective must be that everybody is informed of the dangers pending. Danger could spell problems for us if we are not extra careful."

Still walking along the footpaths which separated their property boundaries from with the land of the State, the two neighbors talked about a variety of subjects having to do with Lord Orazio's plan proposed earlier in the evening. They were happy to have related essential information to their respective dependents and felt strongly convinced that these latter had received the message in a good spirit of cooperation and high sense of duty. In regard to the makeup of an around-the-clock patrol of their plantations, Lord Orazio chose to discuss that matter further but later on, with the elders Del Pio the following morning.

Before completing the circuit of their adjoining plantations, as they approached the clearing where the footway led again downward to the chalet, Lord Orazio began to focus his attention toward the frontline, as opposed to concentrating and discussing the assemblage of a patrol with Titus. That same evening he watched the front ignite to a fierce, appalling and cohesive artillery bombardment. Unlike all other failed attempts of breakthrough, the range of the artilleries of the Allies was extending dangerously close to putting under fire the entire outskirts of Montelieto.

When Lord Orazio noticed Titus staring, astonished, at the glares of the explosions, he talked to him saying: "Titus, please do not let this hellish bombardment upset you. I have a strong feeling that this latest turn of events, will determine the destiny of our days to come. It will either free us from the grip of Fascism or set us back once more to irreversible slavery. This is the last straw! But from what I can see this evening, the front has already been bent. The all-out attack of the Allies explains the gathering of the Axis troops inside our town, mountain districts and farmlands of Montelieto. I believe an eventual retreat of the Axis army to the north, is imminent."

"I am not upset, nor frightened, by this fighting, Lord Orazio. Excited perhaps, and confused, yes. The analysis you have derived is correct but must say I lack the knowledge of war strategy. The thing that confuses me most is the terrible sound of the war. I cannot imagine how anybody can escape unhurt from this horrendous tragedy."

"Your concern is realistic, Titus. But you must appreciate the fact we are quite fortunate. My family and yours are blessed to own this side of mountainous property which is not strategically suited for an army to marshal an eventual resistance from. So we could avail the protection of nature if we continue to be cautious. But you see, Titus, the war has an impact upon everyone involved in it, be they soldiers or civilians protected from nature, or not. I believe the impact will strike more forcefully upon those who are lacking adequate shelter and food. My first priority, and I am sure that of your family, when the battle commenced, was to shelter those left behind in Montelieto. However, that was not possible to do. Now is too late. To shield our families, and our acquaintances from the wrath of the war, is possible only by digging deeper. And dig deeper we must. Also I want you to note, that to eradicate a barbaric system and reinstitute a form of liberty, another form of more violent barbarism must be applied! Gentleness in overthrowing a bad system is ineffective and self-defeating. So, in order for the liberators to restore liberty, they must put in use whatever strategy insures victory. What I want you to know, Titus, is that there is danger we could be mishandled in the process of an occupation. Regardless of how good intentioned the Allies might be the war has no rationale. The danger that we will become victims of plundering, rape and destruction, is very real. That would be the lowest infamy of this era, for the *cafoni/* sharecroppers of Montelieto—that is to get screwed in the name of liberty. Damned ideologies." Lord Orazio cussed.

"That should never happen," Titus said. "When heads of States have disputes and feel imposed upon by an adversary of a different belief, they should challenge one another and leave the helpless citizens out of the quarrels."

"Yeah! That would be the thing to do, if they were not cowards. But here, I do not want to worry about the safety of any head of State. The liberators, if they ever show up, must be assured we weren't collaborators of those crooks and their evil systems. What worries me is the thought that innocents could be made to pay the price. I can't imagine my children, my wife and all the innocents paying for the mistakes of our rotten leadership. That would be abominable, disgraceful and unacceptable, Titus."

"Yes, it would be all that. My siblings, my mother, our aunts and grandmothers, being imposed upon by that type of violence? No, we can't allow that, Lord Orazio."

"Of course we will not allow that, Titus. This is exactly the reason I, with your relatives, saw the necessity to patrol our property in a joint effort. We shall see in the morning how the day will take shape. As daylight nears, I will meet with your relatives to find a solution. If we should see the situation take a turn for the worse, we will proceed in accord and will join hands if we have to, and keep the innocents out of harm's way. I hope you won't be alarmed at what I have said, Titus. Know that all of us wish you to grow to adulthood in liberty. I believe that in liberty only are we allowed to express our political opinions without fear of being locked up by the Fascist pharmacist."

Having now walked the perimeter of their contiguous plantations, Lord Orazio and Titus arrived back near the chalet, thus completing the circuit of their lands and feeling exhausted. They rested for some time, then walked to a higher vantage point above the quarry from which they were able to observe the valley below and see whether the shelling of the cannons was reaching the borders of Montelieto. Above the stone quarry, that from which the hired hands of the former priest had dug out rocks to expand his chalet, they saw the Allied cannonade closing on the center of town.

The new scenario of the war upset and infuriated Lord Orazio. Every time he was put in a situation from which it seemed impossible for him to take control, or go to the aid of his fellow-countrymen, he became even more upset. In anger he cursed at the Party and its leadership; he accused Il Duce, the Prefect and the pride-swollen Fascist pharmacist of being fomenters of destructive conflicts. In his mind and in his words, the whole Party hierarchy was a thoroughly corrupt political mediocrity. Lord Orazio also argued that in order to oust inefficient and brutal rulers, a severe form of even more brutal force must be put into operation.

"And the Allies are doing exactly that," he pointed out to Titus. "We are seeing that force being put in operation upon Montelieto this very moment, like it or not. I wonder what that poltroon of Santuccio Santamiddia is thinking of his superiors at this stage! Without a doubt in my mind, he is shrinking in size one centimeter per shelling blast. At that rate," said Lord Orazio with irony, "it won't be long before he will surely cease to exist."

"I too believe he is shrinking," said Titus. "What is difficult for me to grasp is the likelihood that our town and its people will have to pay the consequences resulting from the mistakes of bad leaders."

"Sure, I see your point, Titus. But you have to realize that brutal rulers do not go away by simply telling them they are doing wrong to their people. That type of language they do not want to understand and, therefore, they become more ruthless. They are like bad weeds that choke good crops. If you do not eradicate them properly, they will grow back much more vigorously until putting a stranglehold on the whole crop. The best way to rid of the pest is to root it out and destroy it."

Still looking in dismay at the cannonade enfolding the first houses of Montelieto, Lord Orazio and Titus walked inside the stone quarry in discouragement. Then regaining his former state of mind, Lord Orazio spoke to Titus and said: "This is the quarry from which several young men of Montelieto helped me dig out rocks to expand the chalet. Then, by orders of the supreme Duce and the Prefect, they were all sent to fight wars. Who knows where they are now? Who knows whether they are dead or alive? Of those who worked for me on a regular basis, we know that Damiano perished in the sands of Cyrenaica, same as others from the country districts. Tranquillo Fedele has been crippled for some time, and what has happened to Cosimo La-Borgia and Luigi Durezza, with the rest, nobody knows for sure. Let's hope they all will come back safe to Montelieto, including your father and uncles Del Pio."

"I appreciate your concern, Lord Orazio. My entire family hopes and prays that everyone comes back safe. The last word we received regarding the situation of my father and uncles, was that their army divisions had been taken prisoner by the British in North Africa."

"That could have been their lucky break," said Lord Orazio. "Times back I learned that part of the Army Corps they belonged to, had been taken prisoner and interned in India. I care for all, yet feel great remorse for Damiano Grifone. Perhaps you know I was fond of my hoeing trio in a special way. But more so I was of Damiano. He was the funnyman, the life of the party, so to speak, even when he struggled for carrying the burdens of his meager existence. I feel remorse because at times I led them the wrong way. Did you know they forgot that I disliked being addressed as 'Father,' but that they still insisted on calling me so? Because of their stubbornness, I called them sons of bitches! But I didn't mean to put them down. LaBorgia and Durezza didn't mind the defamation because that was exactly what they were. I could tell, though, that Damiano at times felt offended. His family was mired in poverty, but that's not the point. They were not promiscuous. So for me there was no ground to call him names. Yeah, Damiano

was a great *cafone*," said Lord Orazio with a sense of wonder. "Very smart and capable of learning anything very
quickly. Would you like to hear what funny answer he gave
me one time?"

"Sure, why not," said Titus.

"He was confessing to me beneath the olive tree, inside
the shanty made of thickets, when I gave him a little scolding for getting drunk too often and staying overnight in
the tavern of Marianna, while his old parents worried
about him. In the beginning he felt somewhat repentant
for being undisciplined, but then all of a sudden, he said:
"Father, I know you were born and schooled for restoring
the broken spirits, but I was born and schooled to drink
them."

"Wow!" marveled Titus. "I wonder where and who he
was associated with, to have learned to come out with that
wise crack!"

"Yeah, wow!" answered Lord Orazio. "Given his illiteracy, and poor choice of words, it's hard to believe. I was
very surprised myself. But then I figured out later that,
beside the tavern of Marianna, he frequented the shoe shop
of his wise friend Don Pompeo Gazzaladra regularly."

While the two neighbors were chatting, the entire pe-
riphery of Montelieto had been put under fire. Valleys and
mountains lit in one intense cannonade. As they came out
of the quarry and took another look at the town below,
Lord Orazio noticed that what had worried him early on
in the evening, was actually happening. Some of the lightning was originating in the valley, north of the exit road,
and flashing past the southeast boundaries.

"That I find hard to believe," said Lord Orazio. "The Axis army is resisting! They are shooting back at the incoming Allies." Seeing the danger of more problems ahead, he felt greatly discouraged. He told Titus they could be heading for a very long night. But in order to keep the fear to himself and not spread alarm, he explained that among many ambiguities, the fact that the center of Montelieto was not being aimed at revived new hopes. "Our town might survive this ordeal. If they are fighting for the communication routes and northward exits, our town will be spared. As of the present, there is nothing we can do. The best thing for us to do," he asserted with urgency, "is to go back to our respective farmsteads. Our families could be alarmed if we stay away for so long."

Then they walked nearby Lord Orazio's chalet, affirmed again continued cooperation between their families, wished each other good luck and went home.

That night turned out to be a very long night indeed for all those who were sheltered in the safety of the plantation. Many of Titus' relatives were awake and were gathering in the farmyard, when he arrived home. Everybody appeared to be on edge and seemed to expect the worst. Titus, too, felt spells of anxiety. So he lay upon his bed sleepless and thinking. Oftentimes Titus thought of Lord Orazio, whom he admired immensely. Whether people had addressed the former priest, Father, Reverend, the nutty priest or ladies' man, for Titus was not an issue. Titus respected the Reverend and teacher for the good skills he was endowed with, for his humanitarian instinct, and for being without prejudice. Frequently Titus had felt the impulse to follow in the path of his teacher, but time and again, he had rejected the idea. To follow on the path of a seminarian for the purpose of pursuing academic skills was appealing, but about the idea of going into the priesthood, Titus was not so sure.

The young man was maturing fast from his early teen years. If it were not for the ongoing war, decadent laws and state of anarchy, he could have been inducted in the armed forces by now. He was strong, handsome, well-schooled, and since the evacuation to the mountain farm, a very good friend of the family Palestrina. In those early times, Titus had kept his eyes on the former priest's daughter Isabella, although she was still in her early adolescence. But that didn't matter. She was precocious and exceptionally well built. Isabella was also beautiful. She combined the beauty of her mother Valentina and the good looks of her father, Lord Orazio. While Titus tossed nervously in bed half awake, often he thought of Isabella. Then as he became more aware of his strong feelings, with a clearer imagination but almost not believing himself, he uttered: "Me? Me become attracted to Isabella? The daughter of 'The nutty priest?' "

Chapter 33

The people of Montelieto had survived all kind of calamities, but had never been so close to being totally wiped out from the face of the earth.

Poverty and illiteracy, servility to rich landowners, misguidance and wars had produced a gloomy and unspeakable scenario of hardships from which there was no way out. The morning after the agreement to keep watch over their property, reached between Lord Orazio and the Del Pio brothers, unfolded to be as trouble-filled a morning ever to descend on the horizons of Montelieto. Spires of black smoke, consecutive flashes of lightning and loud blasts emanating from the cannonade, kept the community confined inside bunkers. In the minds of the people, the frightening scenario forewarned possible extinction of the town.

The brothers Del Pio sensed the same forewarnings. They felt those harrowing hours could perhaps decide the fate of their beloved town. To discuss and implement the final details about how to patrol and safeguard their respective plantations, there was no longer an immediate need. The new developments resulting from the fighting had altered the priorities. If there were to be infiltration of civilian drifters searching for food and shelter, or an infiltration of wounded Axis soldiers unable to follow on their retreat, that also would pose no imminent danger to the people of the plantation. Yet, thinking back to the agreement they had reached with Lord Orazio the previous evening, the two brothers went to meet with him anyway.

When they arrived at the chalet, he had already left. They were told that Lord Orazio was on his way to the stone quarry and that he had been greatly troubled by the intensity of the bombardment.

When the brothers del Pio arrived at the stone quarry, they found Lord Orazio intently focusing on the fighting through his field glasses. They could see, with naked eyes, that Montelieto and its suburb were under attack, cannon shellings exploding everywhere. Lord Orazio called to the Del Pios and motioned them to come near.

"Good morning, neighbors," he said. "Good to see you. But to look to our town and see it subjected to that direct pounding discourages me terribly. Knowing that our fellow-countrymen are caught in the crossfire, and us not able to bring them aid, is a great shame. We must not remain useless in the face of their misfortune and watch them perish. Giovanni, I understand that to attempt a rescue, in this situation, is difficult and dangerous. But we must try! The feat demands enormous strength, courage, alertness and common sense. Although I am aware you are capable to do what I am implying, I must ask you to remain here at the plantation, and continue provide assistence and keep order among our people in this critical hour. As soon as the situation improves I will go to the rescue. Instead of patrolling our lands I need your cooperation to let your young farmhands join me in delivering the help needed.

Please go back, forget the agreement we reached last evening, and give word to the Sardone boys, to Titus and each one of your farmhands, to come to meet me here. We will wait the opportunity to set forth toward our town as quickly as possible. Go, tell those young men I am waiting. Good luck, neighbors."

Antonio, with Giovanni, returned to the plantation as suggested, but couldn't understand the motives of their former priest Palestrina. "Was he genuinely concerned for the people caught in the bombardment? Or did he, perhaps, wish to renew his interest in guerrilla actions? If the latter is his idea of bringing aid to our countrymen that former priest of ours is crazy for sure," Antonio said to his brother with a tone of distrust

"I do not believe he is that big of a fool." Giovanni disagreed. "Perhaps he knows things we do not know. He could see the struggle reaching a critical point and, driven within from humanitarian instincts, wishes to rescue what can be rescued. Furthermore, I believe he would not put the lives of our young men in jeopardy only to appease his own ambitions. Besides, ever since he made the decision to marry Valentina he is a completely responsible individual and not the nutty priest of the past," Giovanni said self-confidently.

In the meantime, as Lord Orazio waited for the young farmhands to arrive, the madness of the war below was slowly taking on a new dimension. The gray and black smoke, hovering about the sky of Montelieto since the previous evening, seemed to be thinning out and leaving sections of the town in the clearing. The Church belfry, City Hall, the House of Fasces and surrounding buildings, although appearing damaged, could still be seen standing.

This last discovery pleased and energized Lord Orazio, re-animating his hopes and belief that the transition from tyranny to a new system of freedom and justice, would not prove destructive to the community.

However, while Lord Orazio felt carried away with great optimism, the unexpected clearing of the clouds of smoke prompted the Allied bombers to resume their deadly raids. Formations of long distance bombers stormed suddenly above Montelieto and, defiant of the Axis anti-aircraft fire, unleashed a hail of bombs on the defenseless citizens. As he saw the vicious attack on his people, Lord Orazio was stricken with intense antipathy. He became moody and hostile, unable to comprehend the logic of the Allies for trying to eradicate from the map, his beloved town. Then, saddened and heartbroken, he waited for his farmhands to arrive, and in a fit of contemptuos anger he exclaimed: "Damned will be the Allies and those who provoke wars! This last bombing of our people is the same as killing someone already dead."

The first helper to arrive at the stone quarry was Federico Favetta, the proud farmhand of Giovanni Del Pio. The young man appeared frightened and confused. He approached Lord Orazio and, panting, asked: "Lord Orazio, was that last air bombardment aimed at our town? For some time, on my way up here, I feared the bombers and loud explosions would topple this hill. Have you really seen the bombs exploding upon Montelieto?"

"Yes, I have."

"If that has happened I hope and pray Don Pompeo and all the elders are not hurt. I am worried for them, Lord Orazio."

"I know you are worried. The bombs have indeed hit our town, but the extent of damage cannot yet be evaluated. As you can see, the whole valley and town are still engulfed with fires and haze. I, too, hope that Don Pompeo, with all the elders, have escaped safely. We want to find out as soon as possible, Federico. I mean as soon as we are able to get down there. You are willing to go and help our friends, aren't you, Federico?"

"Of course I am willing to help, Lord Orazio."

Federico Favetta had not heard from his former employer, Don Pompeo, for a long time indeed. Ever since the brothers Del Pio had hired the four kids from the ghetto of Montelieto, to help out threshing the crops on their farms, Federico had been concerned for the safety of the beloved shoemaker.

During the time of the petroleum shortages Federico had grown to be a strong young man, a happy and devoted farmhand of Giovanni Del Pio, but still very much emotionally attached to his first employer and benefactor, Don Pompeo. If the conflict ever ended, Federico Favetta envisioned himself returning to Montelieto and, as before, resuming work with Don Pompeo and learning to master the skills of cobbling to perfection. His modest aspiration was that some day, he could, perhaps, own and operate a shoe shop, warrant the famous title of "Don," and be known thereafter as "Don Federico Favetta."

Thanks to Giovanni Del Pio and to Don Pompeo, young Favetta had recuperated from his childhood impediment of the foot, and was briefly recruited in the Army Forces. He was grateful to Giovanni and Antonio because, in those perilous times, they had chosen to hire the four hungry kids from the ghetto of Montelieto to help with the threshing of the crops. Most important was the opportunity afforded for him to shelter his closest of kin in the plantation of the Del Pios. Federico felt the generosity of Giovanni could only be matched by that of the Gazzaladra and the Palestrinas. His childhood dreams to own a young jackass, like few other privileged kids, were now fading away. Ever since his childhood days when he slept in the barn with the jackass owned by his father, Federico had come in contact with other sources of power beside that of his father's jackass. Horses and oxen on the farmstead of the Del Pios, airplanes in the sky and machines in the streets of Montelieto, had erased from his heart all aspirations save to be allowed to return to work for Don Pompeo and, without the interferences of a Fascist pharmacist, learn the trade of shoemaker and be happy.

The young man's dreams, however, could never have materialized in the near future; not, at least, until the precarious situation of Montelieto had been resolved. Nothing good was going to happen if the present chaos stayed uncontrolled, and the possibility still remained that the old leadership might return to power. God forbid that! The malicious leaders, lacking respect for ordinary people, could not be allowed to return as that would become the worst and most damaging curse ever to be unleashed on Montelieto.

All these questions kept hammering upon Federico Favetta's imagination while he and Lord Orazio waited for Titus, Giustino and the Sardone boys to join them at the stone quarry. The group recently arrived, came armed with their respective shotguns at shoulder and with fully loaded cartridge belts around their waists.

Titus, the youngest of the group, walked straight to Lord Orazio and said: "Good day, Lord Orazio! We are ready to take turns for standing guard over the plantation. I will volunteer to take the first shift, if you believe it can be worked out, but I leave that up to you to figure out."

"I appreciate your promptness, Titus, and admire your well-intentioned disposition, but we will not have assignments made for watching over our plantations. We have discussed the matter this morning, with your grandfather and great uncle and have concluded that the plans we agreed upon yesterday must be revised. What seemed to be a long struggle for the Allies, to fight their way out of Montelieto, does not apply anymore. This morning our town has sustained a terrible pounding. The Axis armies, in my estimation, have only one chance remaining—that is, retreat. Therefore, our mission has changed. We must depart for Montelieto without delay."

Then Lord Orazio, who until the arrival of Titus and friends had been discussing the situation with Federico, looked at the group of rugged young men and was inspired by their great sense of cooperation and loyalty.

Beginning with the air and land attacks upon Montelieto, Lord Orazio foresaw insoluble problems for the people left behind. At that point, he began to think about organizing a group of strong-willed young men to prepare a rescue mission for the imminent emergency. He took another quick look at the Sardone boys and said: "The guns you are carrying are not required for accomplishing the task we are to undertake. Evidently your father gave you permission to bear arms, for self-protection, far in advance of the facts being known to him. But we are not in need of arms at this point," said Lord Orazio, taking one more look down the valley with his field glasses. "Please leave your shotguns and ammunition in this stone quarry, and also hide these binoculars. We will not have need of either. You see, my boys, we must get to Montelieto immediately, and get inside there looking as disheveled as a bunch of beggars and ragamuffins. We do not want to raise any suspicion that we might be Axis sympathizers if we happen to come in contact with the Allies! Nor must we give the impression to Axis resisters that we are rebels seeking to even the score with them. Our mission is simply to go to the rescue of our brethren and not get entangled with the untimely moves that could hamper our efforts. Are you boys willing to go on this mission?"

"Of course we are, Lord Orazio."

"Good. I am immensely proud of you. And I wish to add that it is essential that our beleaguered people, be united for a cause. That is the first step to a solution of the problems facing us. But having said that, I am not suggesting we will accomplish this mission trouble-free. Two of the most stubborn enemies are fighting to gain advantage by holding onto Montelieto. That represents great danger for us if we enter town. But this is what we will do, even though we are not certain who will encounter first on this endeavor. Our goal is to bring aid to those caught in the crossfire and nothing else."

Then, as Lord Orazio was convinced that the group of intrepid young men was in total agreement, he said: "At the present, it appears Montelieto is in no-man's-land. But I want to remind you that it is *our* land! And furthermore, no matter whichever difficulty and unpleasantness we find ourselves into, we are committed to the well-being of our town and of our people because we know that this forgotten but well-loved town of Montelieto belongs to all of us *cafoni*, unequivocally."

Chapter 34

The fighting was still going on, but its rage was simmering down when the group of dedicated young men took off on the downhill for Montelieto. Although the roaring of the cannons and loud blasts of the shelling were still detonating some distance away the rattling of the machine guns and cracklings of rifle shots were felt more intensely and close by.

The small arms clashes raised some doubts in Lord Orazio's mind. He felt a strong premonition that the survival of Montelieto, and of its beleguered citizens, was still to be decided.

As the group proceeded further downhill, to close in on the town, the scenario of war was tangible and ominous. The air reeked of acrid, burning, explosives. Yet, proceeding forward through the perils of an invasion in progress, the former priest remained firm in his principles. He would not allow threats or snares to impede the way to achieve his objective.

Before entering the first clearing downhill, on the outskirts of town, Lord Orazio gave the order to halt, saying to his comrades: "We have managed to travel in perfect concealment and quite safely thus far. The thick brushes and tall trees were to our advantage. However, the closer we draw to Montelieto, the more we could find ourselves in a precarious situation. In that eventuality we must be adaptable. Our best strategy must be to keep covered, and to proceed ahead to the assignment as cautiously as we possibly can. For safety's sake we must split up our group and go forward in pairs disguising our appearance to intermix with the underbrush of the environment.

"Favetta and I will lead the way. Young Sardone with Giustino will follow. Lastly, Titus with the older Sardone will try on their own to reach town by flanking the banks of the creek. Each pair must see to it that our mission is carried out. I repeat, nothing must hamper our mission. Collectively or individually, we must reach town to make sure none of our brethren is caught beneath the rubble. Most importantly, we must avoid any confrontation with the quarreling giants, be they friends or foes. In my view, the two adversaries will not have compelling obligations, nor time at hand, to spend searching for civilian survivors amid the debris of caved in buildings. That is exactly where we come in. However, having said that, I am not suggesting we leave anyone behind, not even those who have caused us so much destruction and misery. We will extend our helping hand to reach out to whosoever might be in need."

So, driven by a strong impulse to go on a mission for helping those in difficulty, the former priest and Federico walked directly toward Montelieto, but smack in the midst of the impact of an invasion. They were amazed to see Axis resisters fleeing by and even more amazed to see, at close range, the infantries of the Allies in pursuit. On their first encounter with the vanguard of the Allies, Lord Orazio and Federico were quickly put under aim of the rifles. They were at first held captive but, following a quick interrogation, were released on grounds of being local civilians in search of dispersed members of their families.

Due to the fact their captivity ended in a fair and happy compromise, Lord Orazio and Federico felt more tangibly the sense of freedom conceded by the Allies. In the mind of Lord Orazio, the events unfolding from that new scenario of war, which he and his companion had stumbled against, affirmed the good feelings he had harbored for the Allies. It strengthened his belief that the Allies were not the culpable mean-spirited creatures the Fascist pharmacist had accused them of being. Nor had they come to exploit the misguided citizens. Without any doubt, the Allied mission was to replace a system of arrogance and deceit and with a new order of liberty.

But regardless how positive the first impression of the Allies might be, Lord Orazio understood that liberty commanded a high price. Liberty, as his old friend Don Pompeo would always define it, carried a small tag with a very high price. He also understood that the transformation of a tyrannical system, and subsequent transition from oppression to freedom, could not be achieved without pain.

The first evidence of the cost of freedom was attested when Lord Orazio and Federico walked through the streets of Montelieto. Piles of debris and collapsed buildings obstructed access to everywhere. They heard cries of help and despair. Young women, and very old women as well had been savagely raped. One frail girl, who had been violently assaulted, cried near the dead body of her mother. The town convent was desecrated. It had been put in ruin from rapists of the Allies. Sisters, and elders seeking refuge inside were brutally assaulted and abused. The worst letdown Lord Orazio and Federico felt, was to look upon the extensive devastation when, by entering the Church Square, they saw emptiness where tall buildings once stood. They stared, astonished to see the apartment building of Signor Luigi in shambles. It had been wrecked midway from the floor level and dumped on top of Don Pompeo's shoe shop.

"What a horrible sight!" Lord Orazio said with astonishment.

"Please, Lord, let us see if Don Pompeo is safe," implored Federico Favetta.

Giustino and young Sardone arrived suddenly on the scene, panting. They, too, were visibly horrified.

"Lord Orazio!" Sardone called. "Titus, my brother and me and Giustino, came in about an hour ago. We were stunned to see this amount of devastation. Titus, though, told us to start searching every place we figured Don Pompeo might have been hiding. My brother and Titus are still searching for him but to no avail. So far, they have not been able to find out where he might be staying."

"We have seen Father Alfonso and the sacristan, Barabba, wailing over the death of Carlotta and the deaf sister Letizia," added Giustino, cutting in. "Those two saintly women died nearby the entrance of the church. They were hit by the fragments of an exploding shell. Barabba's wife has been wounded, and Father Alfonso told us that he is worried about the ragmen Diodato and the knife sharpener Persichella. They have not been seen since the all-out bombardment."

Titus Del Pio and the older Sardone arrived where the other four were staying. They hastily approached Lord Orazio and informed him on how Father Alfonso had explained the critical situation of Montelieto.

"Father Alfonso's view concerning the elderly who stayed put in town, is bleak," said Titus. "He gave shelter inside the presbytery and wing of the sacristy, to all those who came. Many took shelter within the church, but many others refused to heed his warnings. Some took refuge in the convent with the Sisters but they, too, were assaulted. He told me Don Pompeo has not been seen since yesterday morning. But he believes Don Pompeo is with Maria Maddalena because she had not been feeling well. Father Alfonso and Barabba are aware that the building of Signor Luigi has collapsed and was dumped upon the shoe shop, but they still think Don Pompeo is by Maria Maddelena. Sadly, Lord Orazio, Sardone and I have found out that the neighborhood of Maria Maddalena's apartment is irremediably demolished. We do not know where else to look."

"We begin to look here," said Lord Orazio resolutely pointing to what had been the site of the shoe shop.

"Let's get the necessary equipment from the shop of the blacksmith Arturo, and come back here right away! Likely our beloved cobbler could be trapped beneath the debris and there is a chance he could still be alive."

Several concerned citizens from the country districts came looking for their dispersed relatives. They joined Lord Orazio's group digging through the debris and all centered their best effort between the collapsed residence of Maria Maddalena and the shoe shop of Don Pompeo. To find the beloved shoemaker seemed to be everyone's priority. But as they cleared more debris, more caved in. By evening all efforts to find anyone still alive had failed.

Lord Orazio with Titus and Federico, who had never stopped digging, were the first to discover the body of Don Pompeo. He was found crushed near his working bench face down beneath a mountain of rocks.

The violent death of Don Pompeo affected everyone. People were overwhelmed by grief. Federico leaned on the shoulder of Lord Orazio and wept unconsolably. Titus and Lord Orazio too, became distraught. Sifting through the debris, Titus uncovered a piece of cardboard. After dusting it, a legible writing still appeared on it. That cardboard had hung above the working bench of Don Pompeo ever since the days of the mobilization.

Throughout the years the writing had made public the shoemaker feelings for his people. The words written by Don Pompeo still read: "Please come back home safe, my boys!" Followed by his self-description as:

"The Lonesome Cobbler"

Don Pompeo Gazzaladra

This mournful and heartbreaking event closed a chapter of attachment between Lord Orazio, his beloved shoemaker, and the citizens of Montelieto. He knew in his heart that Don Pompeo would have given up everything for the betterment of Montelieto, and would not have hesitated to surrender his own life to erase the stigma of declassed sharecroppers and illiterate *cafoni* from his people.

That same evening the bodies of Don Pompeo and several others were brought inside the church, placed upon pews and covered with linens. Among the dozen or so bodies lined up inside the church, were the bodies of Maria Maddalena; the cleaning lady Carlotta, Merlina and Clorinda with the deaf sister Letizia. People bewailed the entire night. Others built makeshift caskets. Upon instructions of Father Alfonso, Barabba arranged for the communal funeral and eventual burial.

The following morning Father Alfonso officiated at the emotional communal funeral. Lord Orazio delivered a moving eulogy, closing with the same words often spoken by the shoemaker: "Liberty always carries a small tag with a very high price attached to it."

"What a high price indeed!" Lord Orazio said taking one last look at the casket. "What a high price liberty demands!"

After the funeral Lord Orazio felt sadness and great distress, as he wondered whether the whole episode had been worthwhile for the townspeople to undergo so much pain in order to attain freedom.

"No, I don't believe it one bit," said Lord Orazio to himself. "Not for the price of our beloved shoemaker. Or for any other *cafone* that I know," he said with certainty. "These fellow citizens of mine have nothing to be ashamed of. Their lack of education and increasing needs to earn a living have been compensated by nature in many ways. I believe that recompense is: sharp intuition and alertness to cope with adversities," said Lord Orazio.

Then he concluded that the greater shame should rest on the tyrant and the corrupt leadership, particularly upon the greedy bureaucrats, who sustained wrongdoing mainly to satiate their voracity. Be they civil, or religious, they are fake public servants that overpower, abuse and deceive the people with lies, distortion, exaggerations and simulated honesty. "We have credible examples of that here in our town. The name is known as chief Santuccio Santamiddia," said Lord Orazio.

Chapter 35

The day of the communal funerals was an extremely emotional and grief-stricken experience for Montelieto. Perhaps never since a siege had been inflicted upon the town
by a foreign force, had people experienced such a terrible
tragedy. Although on that day the sounds of war were
heard from afar, the shock and destruction of the invasion
stayed fixed in everyone's mind. They all dreaded to think
there might be more bodies in the rubble.

Throngs of refugees were now returning to Montelieto.
Each of those coming from the hillside, had a sad story to
tell. Women were raped. Families were dispersed, farmlands were destroyed, all at the hands of Allied rapists.
From the southern regions, former soldiers were also coming home. Cicco Palla had returned with his family safe
and sound. He could not comprehend the reason why his
beloved friend and defender Don Pompeo, had died. More
bodies were discovered under the rubble in town. Among
them were the knife sharpener, Davide Persichella and the
ragman Diodato Bello. A joint funeral for the two destitute
men was announced by the town crier, Vittorio Settimo, to
be held at Lord Orazio's expense. A large crowd attended
the funeral. On the way back from the burial site Cicco

Palla, too, walked with great sadness among the crowd. While many recalled to mind more fortuitous episodes of the past, which involved the two deceased countrymen, Cicco also wished to say words of praise regarding the departed dear old friends.

"I feel great sorrow for them," he said to Mariano Albarosa. "They were two good people who never bothered anyone. I miss them very much. Since I was picking up the dung of the donkeys in the streets of Montelieto, I have not seen them alive. Diodato Bello even invited me to stay over for dinner one afternoon. He told me he was cooking something special, and that his buddy Davide was coming to share dinner and bringing a bottle of red wine. Pipanera owed him that."

"Did you accept Diodato Bello's invitation?" Albarosa asked with interest.

"Hell, no!" Cicco said refuting Albarosa's question.

"But why? I can't figure out why you wouldn't say yes to such a friendly invitation," insisted Albarosa.

"Well, I didn't mean to refuse, but . . . "

"But what? You think to be better than Diodato Bello?"

"No, I don't think I'm better, I just didn't want to end up like him."

"What do you mean like him?"

"I mean dead, that's what I mean," said Cicco in his own defense. "To say the truth, Diodato was cooking something that sent out a pleasant aroma, and it almost convinced me to stay over. But in the morning I had seen him pick up the dead hen that Madam Apollonia had dumped inside the trash bin!"

"So what?" Peluso said butting in with irony. "You will never learn, Cicco! Couldn't you figure out that if Madam

Apollonia had dumped a live hen in the trash bin, Diodato and Davide had to kill and deplume it before cooking it?"

"Yeah, that's true. Damn it! I don't know why I didn't think of that," said Cicco.

Apparently the high spirits of *cafoni* from Montelieto couldn't be dimnished by the blasts of the bombs and the destruction. Their nonsense re-emerged more clownish every time those forlorn peasants got together. Perhaps by being witty, they could mitigate the pain of sharing the crops.

The casket maker Romualdo, too, had returned home and had resumed his former trade. His mother, Maria Maddalena, was no longer there to cater to him. He spent the best time in the taverns of Marianna or Caterina. For Romualdo, ironically, there was a plethora of work, as the trade of casket maker was all of a sudden profitable. But every small profit realized by Remualdo was spent to buy spirits. When people tried to purchase the casket he had displayed high on the wall of the shop, he answered politely but with an emphatic, "No way!"

"That beautiful casket belongs to me," he would promptly answer. "Someone will use it to put me into when I am found drowned in the spirits of Caterina Panzona."

People from every walk of life began to enjoy a new grade of freedom never before thought to exist. Sure, everyone in one way or another was still nursing the wounds of the invasion, but as the days went by each, more than the last, promised high hopes of betterment. The generosity of the Allied garrison played a big role for a fast recovery in many situations. They furnished the starving citizens with all sorts of food supplies and medicine at no cost, and without interfering or expecting rewards. The Allies had even

begun to compensate the damages done to civilian properties, whether they had caused them or not. They also made
amends for the rapes perpetrated on women in the heat of
the battle.

The former priest, Orazio Palestrina, had resettled his
new family in his mansion and had become more visible
and useful to his countrymen in need. By now the community knew Reverend Orazio Palestrina was no longer a
priest, and no one referred to him by the disreputable appellative of the past. To them he was respectable Lord Orazio Palestrina.

The brothers Filomeno and Gennarino Pennamoscia
had returned home, safe and sound, as had Antonio Albarosa, Giovannino Sparacelli, Cipollone and Cosimo La-
Borgia. Unfortunately, the hoeing trio of the former
Reverend Orazio Palestrina had been decimated. Of the
trio only Cosimo LaBorgia came back home unhurt. Damiano's remains had not yet been sent home from Cyrenaica,
and poor Luigi Durezza had lost one leg in Tunisia.

A new scenario of peace was opening for Montelieto
and its people. The Fascist leadership had been automati-
cally stripped of its power and of every vestige of authority.
Although the former administration had lost its control
they, nevertheless, attempted to regain it by quietly sneak-
ing inside the City Hall, pretending nothing corrupt had
ever happened and hoping to hold the grip on the reins and
again guide Montelieto.

But now the citizens were no longer obliged to accept
a tyranannical system. Under no circumstances were the
Fascist *Podestà*, the Deputy Mayor, the Fascist pharmacist
and the other arrogant cohorts of the bureaucrats, to be
allowed to exercise their professions at the expense of the

town's citizens. The old gang of cheaters had visibly shed the mantle of disdain and rudeness—but their plan of re-intruding on the affairs of the people of Montelieto could not be permitted.

On the morning, which became synonymous with the resurgence of post-war Montelieto, a group of youngsters led by Gennarino Pennamoscia, the young country boy whom the Fascist pharmacist took pleasure in abusing, forcefully invaded the City Hall.

"Out!" shouted Pennamoscia. "Out!" He shouted pulling on the arm of the Fascist *Podestà*. "And you who are hiding in the guise of lambs, go where Sparacelli tells you," he said to the pharmacist. When the infamous gang of former leaders were forced to descend the stairs down to the Church Square, Pennamoscia locked the doors of City Hall, tossed the keys to LaBorgia and told him: "Take these keys to Lord Orazio and tell him we, the people of Montelieto, wish to nominate him first citizen."

Then turning to the pompous pharmacist, he said: "We will start doing drills of wars same as those you made us do when you were bursting with pride. And the drills will include kicks like those you used to donate to me! Remember? So now march! Up and go, up and go, up and, etc.," commanded Gennarino Pennamoscia.

Two soldiers of the Allied garrison, who had come in a Jeep to deliver papers sent from their commanding officer, found the doors of the City Hall locked, but seeing people gathering in the Church Square went down to investigate. After having learned what was taking place, the two soldiers stood amusedly looking at the crowd for some time, but without interfering. Then they asked to be accompanied to the parish pastor for releasing their documents, returned, hopped back into their Jeep and left.

Meantime Gennarino continued marching his former tormentor up and down the Church Square. The frightened pharmacist limped and appeared tired. But Gennarino refused to understand. He was getting more revengeful and vindictive than ever before. By this time, the uproar involving the Fascist pharmacist was increasingly getting out of hand, and the rowdy schemers of the prank were turning more impudent and menacing. There were those who shamelessly spoke even of an upcoming lynching. However, not everyone among the bystanders enjoyed the buffoonery initiated by Gennarino Pennamoscia and his partners. The prank, although tempting at first, should never have reached the critical and dangerous point. Someone must intervene—and fast.

Among the bystanders, Federico Favetta who had happened to pass by, quickly assessed the situation and, fearing the worse, hastily ran to inform Lord Orazio. He could foresee big problems for the despicable pharmacist and wished, in fairness, to be of help.

"Madam Valentina!" Favetta said to the former priest's wife, who had answered the door. "I must see Lord Orazio immediately! Evil things are occurring in the Church Square and the people need his help and guidance."

"Sure, Federico. Go around to the gate, Lord Orazio is working in the garden. I will tell him you came to visit."

"Thanks, Madam Valentina," said Federico running toward the garden. "Lord Orazio!" he called. "This is an emergency. I must see you right this moment!"

"Come right in, Federico. What's all the rush, though? I hope it is not another of your ideas to have me accept more keys to the City Hall. That is against civilized norm."

"Oh, no, no, Lord Orazio! I have nothing to do with the keys. I came to ask your help because Gennarino Pennamoscia, Sparacelli and others who had been abused by the pharmacist are plotting to hang him. Please, hurry Lord Orazio!"

"Hang him?" Lord Orazio asked, as he headed fast toward the Church Square.

When Lord Orazio reached the Church Square, the crowd made room for him. He walked where the loudest noise was coming from, and stopped beneath the balcony of the House of Fasces. A rope attached to the railing of the balcony hung downward to the ground. Pennamoscia and Sparacelli were seen working a slipknot on it. The pharmacist stood nearby, held by two young thugs, and trembling with fear.

Lord Orazio went directly to Gennarino and seriously said: "Gennarino, son, listen to me. You must stop this nonsense of revenge, now, immediately! I understand your anger, and fully sympathize with you, but we must not let anger lead us to revenge. At times revenge seems justifiable, but it shouldn't ever be executed by good people, because that will then turn people vile, worthless, and savage, same as those who offended them. Gennarino, please leave him be."

"Of course we will," answered Gennarino. "We just wanted to let him believe he was going to hang. Never did we really intended to dirty our hands with that louse!"

"I understand but, for some time, you had Federico and me fearing the worst."

"Oh, no! Lord Orazio. We didn't mean to involve you. With the prank, we wanted to draw the attention of the community here, right in the center of Montelieto, because we have other important issues, on our agenda, that call for immediate attention. Who cares about him," said Gennarino unconcerned.

"Not many. He has already been reduced to nothingness. Still we must pardon him. We have to wish him long life so, someday, he will learn that badly delegated authority is injurious to those who have had it bestowed upon them, and unmistakably turns them to despots," said Lord Orazio.

"That means we let him go, right, Lord Orazio?"

"Yes, anytime you want to."

"We will do as told and always stand by you, Lord Orazio. Sparacelli! Untie the rope from that railing, and from the neck of that louse."

"Good boy, Gennarino. I am proud of you. Without any doubt in my mind you, and your young friends, will be the future assets to this town of ours."

Then turning his attention to his former rival, Lord Orazio said: "Santuccio Santamiddia, here we are. It took a hail of bombs to dislodge you and your kind from this peaceful town. By now you must have learned that vile actions come back to haunt the ones who commit them. They boomerang you know? They also strip humans of their dignity. So I must say I didn't wish to see you humiliated, but I still will not deny that I feel you had it coming. It is not Pennamoscia or Sparacelli's fault to embarass you. You have brought the wrath of the people upon yourself. Now for the time being I, with my *cafoni* countrymen, have no use for you and not much left to say. I believe the score is even. However, my advice to you is to leave here as quickly as you can. I mean for you to leave town, never turn back, and go somewhere to join those who share the same values as you. Montelieto, the place you have ridiculed and labeled the town of donkeys and declassed *cafoni*, will not be hospitable to you. Goodbye, and good luck, my friend Santamiddia!"

The former Fascist pharmacist listened unemotional and speechless to the reproach of Lord Orazio until it was finished. Then he was seen leaving town, silently and without turning back. The crowd paid no attention to him. They rallied instead around the former priest exultanlty and, on the signal of Cipollone, Lord Orazio was brought in, borne in triumph upon the people's arms above the City Hall. There he was nominated, by acclamation, first citizen of Montelieto.

Expelling the Fascist leadership and the Fascist pharmacist from their offices was an event forever to be remembered by the majority of people in Montelieto, a happy and auspicious day that brightened everybody's hopes for better tomorrows. In terms of grand accomplishments, the riddance of the gang of Fascist tyrants surpassed, by far, the removal of Father Ponzio from the town parish he had administered military style. The *cafoni* felt that, finally, a miracle was descending from heaven, upon their forgotten Montelieto.

To a handful of hardliner Fascists, and for those who vigorously defended the corrupt leadership, the departure of the infamous pharmacist from the town of Montelieto, set an example of high significance, proving incontrovertibly that absolute power, arrogance and disrespect for ordinary people, were not groundwork that could unite and effectively promote betterment for the masses.

Oh! If only Don Pompeo were here!

How much happier the lives of his people could be! He would be reminding them that brutal and tyrannical domination of the masses will never endure and that tyranny and oppression are only temporary. Or that they can rule only until the time when, from within or externally, a major force will rise to the defense of the oppressed.

He would also tell them that the joy of being liberated from tyranny is not something that can be weighed. If it could, he would tell his beloved fellowmen that, without any doubt, the joy would outweigh all the sacrifices suffered during the past eras. And Don Pompeo would, for sure, be telling his people: "Rise up, build on your freedom, build the schools for your children, work diligently and never let your guard down for upholding, with all the strength of your will, the precious gift of liberty."

Chapter 36

In spite of the improper naming by which Lord Orazio Palestrina had been addressed in the past, he was a man of high principles. The labels of Communist, womanizer, extravagant or nutty priest and other indelicate names, had obscured his preeminence to a degree but only in the eyes of his rivals in wealth and politics of the town of Montelieto. By the majority of his fellow countrymen, he was admired and seen as beloved first citizen. However, the fact he had been brought in triumph to succeed to the chair of first citizen, at the City Hall of Montelieto, did not comform to his principles. Even if the motives of his people were laudable, he did not wish to use that in connection with his well-to-do status and to become a role model for acquiring acceptance, popularity or importance. At that point in time, it was hoped that the transition, from a corrupt system to new equitable rules and laws, could proceed simply, without false show or pretense. The voices and will of the masses must be heard and respected. In light of this, although he had been chosen only by acclamation, Lord Orazio elected to stay put. As result, he pledged friendly, strong support, and self-determined began to take root as he worked to help his people in need.

The early post-war days were not happy times for the weary citizens of Montelieto. People were still injured and frequently dying from land mine accidents. For many, their humble abodes had been reduced to shambles and the ugliness of the rapes of their women still tortured their minds. On the plus side, however, the vanishing of the tyrant Fascist pharmacist from the scene, and having power stripped from his surrogates who had confiscated the farm products of the *cafoni*, was a relief. The *cafoni* regained peace of mind and patiently reconciled themselves to accept destiny. Better days were on the horizon of all the people of Montelieto. Everyone felt there could not be anything worse than what they had gone through—except perhaps, death. So, after their first shock of disbelief, they earnestly began to try to resume and improve on their old lifestyles.

For Lord Orazio Palestrina, too, the time to get involved had arrived. There were no alternatives and no justifications for not fulfilling his pledge and obligations. However, the task of guiding his countrymen from the quagmire of tyranny and war demanded perseverance and zeal, a challenge he welcomed. Over and above his humanitarian instincts, this former priest was pragmatic and highly motivated. He never tired being of help to his *cafoni* countrymen in difficulty, and never declined or ceased to intermingle with the lower class. His personal rejection of the ministry and subsequent marriage to the love of his life, Valentina, had given him a different but superior and positive outlook on life. That had made him a very happy and popular *cafone*.

In the mind of the charismatic and engaging Lord Orazio the new agenda he had planned for the resurgence of

Montelieto and its people from the pit of oppression, poverty and illiteracy, had a long list of priorities. To solve all the problems facing his people required total commitment and hard work. Meanwhile, the challenge Lord Orazio had foreseen, and pledged to fight with, was already upon him. However, first things dictated the priorities. So after having moved Valentina, and the kids, to the comfort of the Palestrina family mansion, Lord Orazio began to take actions.

The task Lord Orazio was anxious to undertake was one of enormous dimensions. In those early post-war days, every issue seemed to cry for first attention, and all included components of necessity and precedence. But the challenge must be put in motion, and actions must be taken regardless. Diligently, Lord Orazio began to take charge.

His first step was to re-staff City Hall with honest, trustworthy and capable citizens. The second was to rally the people of Montelieto to a common cause by inciting all to strive for achieving goals of public interest. And thirdly, under his direction, work must begin on the task of cleaning up the scattered debris around the Church Square, nearby buildings, and main streets of the town. Next in line of priority—work which everyone took delight in doing, was to strip down the House of Fasces of every vestige of Fascism, to re-paint it and organize its main hall with benches to convert it to temporary school rooms.

Being a shrewd entrepreneur, the former priest traveled in the area, seeking a breakthrough and hoping to raise funds needed for reconstruction. He traveled to bigger towns, to the chief town of the region, and to the capital itself. The figurehead in the prefecture of the chief town, a Fascist opponent of the old times, who was informally installed in that position by the Allies, shortly became a best friend. They shared the similar humanitarian ideology: Communism, (in their self-made definition and polite translation). When the funds for re-construction began flowing from America to repair the damages caused by the war, Montelieto was first among towns to get compensated. New rules and ordinances began to be reintroduced. The unemployed began to find work. Political referendums were being organized. A bright light was now shining at the end of the dark tunnel. In the pre-election days, Lord Orazio engaged in heated debates against his opponents who were seeking to govern Montelieto. Appointed only by will of the people he, too, sought the same objective but wished to be elected in a fairly and honest democratic contest.

Election Day turned out to be a day to remember—a sort of feast day for Montelieto. Each citizen was finally enabled to practice his or her civil rights and vote for the leader of their choice.

The charismatic former priest, Reverend Palestrina, was elected with an overwhelming majority, while his opponent, Signor Luigi, was crushed by an embarrassing defeat. What an event! The community rallied to the newly elected first citizen and acclaimed him with cheerful, enthusiastic shouts of: "Lord Orazio! Lord Orazio! Lord Orazio Palestrina! Palestrina!"

In spite of his new position of honor and authority, Lord Orazio continued to be the same down-to-earth son of Montelieto, as he had been in the past. Under his leadership many improvements were achieved. The physical aspect of Montelieto began to change to another dimension.

People found work, trade shops reopened, wrecked buildings were restored. Having had good success in obtaining additional funds from the regional government, Lord Orazio led the way for his people toward progress. The entire community admired and loved him. The extravagances of Lord Orazio's past were no longer in the mind of his people, and were never recalled.

Oftentimes, towards evening, Lord Orazio was exhausted. After supper, he would relax on the loggia. With Valentina, he looked at the streets below illuminated by a new system of lighting. He whispered to Valentina saying how happy he was. He kissed her, held her close to him and told her that even as exhausted as he was, he loved life. While looking at the bright sky one evening he said: "My love! I believe I have become almost as popular as Don Pompeo."

"Our dear shoemaker! He didn't deserve to die a violent, unmarked death. No doubt he was popular. He cared more for the poor kids of Montelieto than for himself," said Valentina.

"Of course he cared. That old philosopher of a cobbler would have given his life if the stereotyped labels of 'illiterate' and '*cafoni*/sharecroppers,' could have been erased from the kids of this town," said Lord Orazio.

"I am aware. But he has given his life," Valentina said with grief.

"Still," Lord Orazio continued, "there are hopes Don Pompeo's dreams will become reality."

"In what way?" Valentina wondered.

"Come here," Lord Orazio motioned to his wife. "You see that rocky parcel of land belonging to the City?"

"Yes, I see youngsters playing in the park nearby, and having fun beneath those light posts. Do you have in mind to expand or renovate that park?"

"Oh no," answered Lord Orazio. "That park, which we have built, more than meets the need for a town of this size. We have already built the soccer field, where the youngsters can practice their favorite sport and spend their energy. My idea is not to expand the playground, but to build a high school. I will never stop requesting the approval, and adequate funds from the Prefect, until the project is accomplished. The high school has been my number one goal ever since Don Pompeo suggested the project to me on behalf of the youth of Montelieto. That is the only efficient method to erase from Montelieto the stigma of being the town of donkeys and illiterate *cafoni*. Forget about the old folks, dear Valentina. They must carry the stigma to the end.

"The young, though . . . the young will have the opportunity and the privilege of acquiring an education and becoming responsible citizens, same as those of more advanced societies. I promise you, my dear, that some day in the near future, the kids of this town will be recognized and respected as Montelietesi without being unjustly stigmatized as declassed and illiterate *cafoni*."

"What a great and noble idea!" Valentina said. "That, my love, has been long overdue."

"Not for much longer will it be."

"Really?"

"Imagine what impact a high school will have on the *cafoni* of our town! I am not speaking of the seasoned *cafoni* but the young. I see the new generation changing status. They will go out in the world and be known as average citizens of of our land. That day will dawn on our youth, I promise."

"That day, my love, will be recalled by the present and all future generations."

"Of course it will be recalled. The inscription above the entrance will remind all future students of the originator of the idea of a school for the children of Montelieto."

The high school project was eventually approved, by the regional government, and authorization was given Lord Orazio to begin and supervise the construction. Where there stood fallow land a magnificent edifice was built. The completion of the school culminated with another feast day for Montelieto. Crowds of cheering citizens gathered in front of the building, waiting to know the name of their new school.

After Lord Orazio had delivered a short speech of approbation, addressed to those who had made his project possible, he called the new cobbler in town from among the crowd, and motioned him to come near. Then Orazio said: "Don Federico Favetta, please let the canvas covering the sign drop, so our friends can see."

Federico cut the ropes holding the canvas, and as it dropped to the ground, to the loud applause of a cheering crowd, the writing above the entrance door appeared clear to the view. The inscription in big, prominent, letter read:

JUNIOR HIGH SCHOOL
Don Pompeo Gazzaladra

That same evening, Lord Orazio appeared to be in a fine frame of mind as he rested upon the loggia of his mansion. When Valentina arrived to join her husband, she found him free and easy and strongly attractive as her first-time inamorato. She, too, looked attractive and at her best. The soft glow of the vespertine hours made her appear even more radiant and lovely.

While they leaned with their elbows upon the parapet of the loggia, they looked at the town below with fascination and wonderment. From the vantage point of the loggia, they could see the public park, the school and Montelieto's main streets. They also could recognize, quite clearly, people strolling by in the luster of the street lamps. Couples were seen walking along cheerfully, holding hands. To his great surprise, Lord Orazio looked at one young couple and with great excitement asked Valentina whether she, too, had noticed. He asked: "My love, isn't that our daughter Isabella walking closely and holding hands with someone?"

"Yes," Valentina answered. "That is our daughter Isabella walking in company with a boy."

"You mean she is already dating?"

"She is," Valentina said. "Sorry dear, I entirely forgot to tell you she has asked permission to go out for a short while and have a little fun."

"Well, now don't you think I am also entitled to know who is the lucky young man?"

"Of course you are entitled! Isabella is our daughter, you know? And the lucky young man is Titus Del Pio."

"T . . . T . . . T-Titus Del Pio?" Lord Orazio was barely able to mumble with amazement."

"Yes, Titus Del Pio. That tells you how efficient a teacher you have been to the boy."

"Really? I am? If that is the argument I must say to you that, under no circumstance, have I been teaching Titus to go dating Isabella—the daughter of the former priest."

"My dear former priest, like it or not, Isabella is growing up. And she also is beautiful and the daughter of a father whom I love very much."

"Yeah but . . . but don't you believe Titus is a little bit older than Isabella?"

"Of course he is older, but they still make a very handsome couple," said Valentina indulgently. "Titus' disparity in age to Isabella is the equal of yours to mine. Now don't you believe we handled the age question extremely well?"

"Damn right we did," swore Lord Orazio. "I would say we handled it perfectly."

"Fine. Now I want to tell you, that even when you are a little excited I can't stop loving you," said Valentina.

"I love you too," said Lord Orazio drawing Valentina to him in a tender hug. "I love you lots more than the day we first met. You recall that day, darling?"

"Yeah, I do recall—but actually it was night. However, that doesn't matter much. I too love you more than the day we first met. We made many people believe I came to your family mansion exclusively to take measurements for sewing your shirts."

"Nonsense, that trickery was only believed by Dorotea," laughed Lord Orazio. "Don Pompeo, though, knew I was not growing so rapidly as to need measuring that often."

"Right, not on an every other day basis. While speaking of measurements though, I must say that we could use the first one to sew your shirts now," said Valentina.

"Who needs shirts now? I only need you. When you are near me, I want to feel that sweet warmth of your beauty with shirts or no shirts. That makes me go insane with love," said Lord Orazio, placing his chin above Valentina's blonde hair.

They both cherished that warm closeness as if they were two young teenagers in love. After a while, from that very position over the loggia, Lord Orazio looked up at the sky full of gleaming stars and asked Valentina: "Do you think I deserve all this goodness, my love? Namely: You, Isabella, Gianpaolo, and the admiration of our people? Do you really believe I am worth that much?"

"Of course you are! You are a true philanthropist with a great, soft heart. And you are always putting the public's best interests first. That is one reason the citizens of Montelieto admire you. I also believe someone greater is looking over you and me, from above."

"Yeah! That could be our dear beloved *cafone* friend, Don Pompeo," said Lord Orazio playfully. Then looking once more into the beauty of the night sky, at the flashing of a falling star that shone over the loggia, he exclaimed: "What a great sight from this angle, my love! I must admire it in spite of its remoteness. Damn how magnificent and beautiful is our sky this evening!"

Then the former reverend, overcome by amazement, said: "I am still an unbeliever, my love, but this evening I must admit I am convinced that some kind of supernatural power is thriving up there!"